*Siobhán
Riordan*

Girltalk

ALL THE THINGS YOUR
SISTER NEVER TOLD YOU

Carol Weston has been writing for teens
ever since she was a teen. Her articles
have appeared in many American
publications including *Young Miss,
Seventeen, Glamour, Bride's,
Cosmopolitan, Redbook, McCall's,
Woman's Day, New Woman, House &
Garden* and *The New York Times. Girltalk*
is her first book. Carol received her B.A.
in French and Spanish Comparative
Literature from Yale University in 1978
and her M.A. in Spanish from
Middlebury in 1979. Carol is also the
author of *How To Honeymoon* and is now
working on a sequel to *Girltalk* based on
letters from teenagers. She and her
husband, Robert Ackerman, and their
cat Chanda live in the Upper West Side
of New York City.

GW00362887

Girltalk

ALL THE THINGS YOUR SISTER NEVER TOLD YOU

Carol Weston

Edited by Lorna Read and Jill Eckersley

A Pan Original

Pan Books London and Sydney

First published 1985 by Harper & Row, USA
This revised edition first published in Great Britain 1987 by
Pan Books Ltd, Cavaye Place, London SW10 9PG
9 8 7 6 5 4 3 2 1
ISBN 0 330 29669 8

Printed and bound in Great Britain by
Richard Clay Ltd, Bungay, Suffolk

Grateful acknowledgment is made for permission to reprint
adaptations of:

'How Well Do You Know Your Best Friend?', 'Icebreakers',
'Are You and He a Good Match?' and 'Are You Too Nice?'
reprinted with permission from *Young Miss* magazine.
Copyright©1983, a division of Gruner & Jahr, USA
Publishing.

'9 Sticky Dating Situations and How to Handle Them' and '28
Dating Ideas Guaranteed to Steal His Heart' taken with
permission from *Young Miss* magazine. Copyright©1984.

Dedicated to the memory of my father,
William Weston

Contents

Siobhán Riordan

3. LOVE: FALLING IN, FALLING OUT

4. SEX: WHAT YOU SHOULD KNOW BEFORE SAYING YES

5. FAMILY: CAN'T LIVE WITH 'EM, CAN'T LIVE WITHOUT 'EM

6. SCHOOL AND MONEY: YOUR FUTURE STARTS HERE

7. DRINKS, DRUGS, ETC: AND I PROMISE NOT TO LECTURE

8. A QUARTET OF QUIZZES: GETTING TO KNOW YOU

Acknowledgements

I want to be brief, but I'm feeling awfully grateful. So here's a bouquet of thanks to:

Sarah Ackerman, for being my friend, surrogate younger sister, and inspiration for this book. She read the entire rough draft and scribbled wonderfully helpful 'goods' and 'yuks' all over it.

Rob Ackerman, my husband, for being a first-rate (if ruthless) editor, for his excellent suggestions, and for being so supportive and loving.

Irv Levey, my editor at Harper & Row, for his encouragement, for coming up with the original idea with me, and for taking a gamble on an article writer.

Treld Bicknell, my editor at Pan, who gave *Girltalk* life outside the United States and who, with Lorna Read, Jill Eckersley and Marion Lloyd, worked so hard to adapt it for the United Kingdom.

Marybeth Weston, my mother and role model, for reading my first draft, red pencil in hand.

Jane Wilson of JCA Literary Agency in New York and Vivienne Schuster of John Farquharson Ltd in London for being such warm and terrific agents.

Ragdale Foundation, a writers' colony in Illinois, for my five productive and peaceful stays there.

Dr Irving Distelheim, who looked over my sections on acne and sexually transmitted diseases with dermatological expertise.

Dr Stephanie Bird, who filled me in on the nitty gritty of abortions with gynaecological savvy.

Dr John FitzGibbon Jr, who reviewed the *Drinks, Drugs, Etc* chapter and never tired of answering questions.

Dawn Raffel, John Carlo Mariani, Mark Weston, Eric and Cynthia Weston, and everyone else who contributed time, thoughts and enthusiasm.

The libraries I holed up in.

Young Miss magazine for permitting us to reprint and adapt six articles I wrote for them.

Last but not least, my teenage cat Chanda. She sat on my lap as I wrote, purring as my word processor hummed. Because Chanda hates to be disturbed, and because purring and humming are happy sounds, I kept on plugging.

CW

Hello

I'm impressed with you already. I don't always read introductions. I hope you'll also read the *Body* chapter, which tells
how to have a clearer skin and prettier hair, explains menstruation, body talk, and what guys worry about, and gives the latest
information about bulimia, anorexia, and sensible dieting. The
chapter on *Friendship* will interest you if you adore your best
friend but sometimes feel smothered, or if you ever wish you
could ease into a different group. The *Love* chapter can help if
you wonder how to flirt without sounding like a jerk, how to
break up without breaking down, or what to do if you've told a
guy you're busy all this Saturday and next, but he doggedly
invites you out for the following three.

Turn to *Sex* to learn what you should know before saying *yes*,
myths and facts about V.D. (venereal disease), and how to get
and use contraceptives. Flip to *Family* if it's hard to believe your
parents were both teenagers for seven years each, if it's difficult
to get used to a step-sister or -brother, or if you feel your family
could benefit from professional counselling. *Education* offers
ways to deal with touchy teachers, improve your marks, and get
into college or university – if that's where you're heading.

Are you wondering about summer jobs and careers? The
Money chapter is full of lucrative ideas and can help you plot your
future, write your c.v., and shine in an interview. Want to know
the real story about tobacco, dope, cocaine, or alcohol? Read
Drink, Drugs, Etc. Take the *Quartet of Quizzes* to find out how
jealous you are, how well you know your best friend, how
compatible you and your boyfriend are, and whether you are *too*
nice.

Girltalk: All the Things Your Sister Never Told You lends a hand
in your leap from confusion to confidence. Read it from cover to
cover, or skip around, pausing whenever you're curious. It's
your personal encyclopedia.

Even if you do have an older sister, I'll bet you have a few
questions you'd feel funny asking her. This book is loaded with
answers. It's full of the stuff I wanted to know when I was
growing up and the stuff it took me years to figure out.

Although shaping your life isn't easy, growing up shouldn't
have to hurt too much. There's no such thing as a true grown-up
anyway, just as there's no such thing as a typical teenager.

What's great about being your age is that you have it in you to
become whomever you want – and you're becoming yourself.

CW

1. Body

Looking and Feeling Your Best

Too fat, too flat, too tall, too small – hardly any of us is one hundred per cent happy with our appearance. It's especially hard for you now. Your body may be growing in all directions, blemishes may freckle your face, hair may be sprouting here and there, your period may be a mystery. What is going on inside you anyway? Are you stuck with your features and figure?

Beauty does make a difference in first impressions. But so do friendliness, sense of humour, intelligence, thoughtfulness. And who said you had to be 'flawless' to be pretty? With a little effort, anybody can look attractive.

Since you and your body are together for a long, long time, you need to learn to take care of it. This chapter will show you how to make the most of your attributes and how to be your most healthy and radiant.

Do Guys Worry About Their Bodies?

Before we launch into a discourse about breasts, periods, diets, cosmetics, and other female concerns, you might be wondering if boys ever worry about their bodies. Answer: they certainly do.

Sure, a few wink in the mirror each morning and think they're God's Gift to Manhood – and Womankind. But most wrestle with some puberty-related anxiety.

Guys wonder whether they're tall enough, whether their biceps bulge enough, whether their chest and facial hair will ever grow. They wish their voices would get deeper and stop croaking. They wish they weren't hungry all the time. They're tired of having pimples and being clumsy and lanky. They wish they were more handsome and that their hands wouldn't sweat when they ask you to slow dance. A few may even fret about someday turning bald and beer-bellied.

Guys worry even more in communal after-sports showers, and public or school lavatories, because they imagine someone might be checking out their private parts. Someone probably is. Guys want to be 'well hung', though penis size isn't that important in a sexual relationship. Some boys even worry that their organ is crooked!

Here's another male concern. Most guys in their mid-teens begin to have wet dreams. They wake up to find they've ejaculated during the night, and they wonder if that's normal. Yes. It's also normal for guys to get erections at odd times – when they wake up, or in maths lessons, or when they're minding their own business on the bus to school.

Many guys feel uneasy about their sexuality. Are they over-sexed if they masturbate a lot, or under-sexed if they don't? If they have an orgasm quickly when they masturbate, does that mean they'll be premature ejaculators in years to come? If they haven't started dating, or if they've played sex games with other guys or admire their male P.E. teacher does that mean they're gay? If they have an X-rated fantasy involving an 'old lady' teacher, does that mean they're perverted? No, no, no, and no. Guys grow at different sexual speeds and need not be alarmed by early tame or wild imaginings or experiences.

In one important way, girls have an advantage over guys in the Worry Department. Most guys don't discuss their growing pains with their friends or families, whereas, luckily for us, most girls do. It's not uncommon for a girl to complain, 'Mum, I wish my breasts were bigger.' But rare is the guy who would say, 'Dad, I wish my penis were bigger.' It's a shame guys aren't more open and honest with each other and it's their loss. They have as many questions, troubles, and fears of inadequacy as girls, but fewer outlets. Guys tease and taunt each other, yet usually worry alone. They don't even have many magazines or books to consult. But you do. So keep reading!

Everything You Ever Wanted To Know About Breasts

Back to us girls.

If you're like me, you sometimes get fed up with your figure.

Why can't it just settle into a shapely 36-24-36? Why can't your breasts be medium instead of mountains or molehills?

It's frustrating that your body's timetable answers to hormones and heredity rather than to your own wishful thinking. If you haven't started developing yet, you may be feeling short-changed. If you've been developing for years, you may worry you'll wind up with watermelons. Either way, you might envy the average girls who strut around the changing room parading their bra-and-panty sets.

I envied them. I was in a mad rush to grow up. I couldn't wait to get my breasts and get rid of the braces on my teeth, to start getting periods and stop getting pimples. At fourteen, I was a restless, late-blooming flatso. I dressed behind curtains and cringed at breast jokes.

Why are you a sailor's delight? Because you have a sunken chest! What do members of the Itty Bitty Titty Committee wear instead of bras? Band-aids! Pretend you're a boy for a minute. Ahh . . . doesn't that take a load off your chest? Quips circulated about ironing boards, bee stings, pancakes, and fried eggs, as well as bouncing boobs and knockout knockers. Poor Denise, girls said, was so flat she could wear her bra inside out. And people teased Erica that she'd knock down passers-by if she turned without warning.

At first hardly anybody was happy. My friend Alice was as distressed about being buxom as I was about being flat. She sported baggy shirts to hide her dramatic décolletage.

It was Alice who told me of the Best Breast Test. 'To find out if you need a bra, place a pencil underneath one of your boobs and see if it stays up,' she explained. I ducked into the bathroom. . . and my pencil clattered to the floor. Alice handed me two of her outgrown junior bras anyway – 'booby' prizes, since she'd graduated to larger sizes.

Status was at stake when classmates discussed bra size. The ideal seemed to be As in school and Bs in bust. I never made the grade! Later, when the subject switched to boys, books, babysitting, I'd sometimes still be thinking bosoms, boobs, breasts. Would mine ever grow?

I wish I could have realized that I would make it safely to womanhood. I wish I could have foreseen that although I'd never rival Dolly Parton, I'd end up perfectly content with my own measurements, just as Alice now feels good about her curves.

Yes, *Playboy*'s pages do tend towards the well-endowed, and not long ago some breast-oriented fellow paid over £700 at a London auction for a 36-D bra worn by Marilyn Monroe. But small-breasted women have admirers too. What's more, sagging is not a problem for us, and while it's hard to look voluptuous, it's sometimes easy to look slim.

Most girls' breasts start swelling when they're between the ages of ten and fifteen – usually twelve or thirteen. Some girls grow the 'right' amount just when their friends are developing. But many are ahead of or behind the pack and feel self-conscious or impatient. It's nice to know you're not the only one who has anxiously compared your chest with the next girl's. It's even nicer to know that ultimately almost everybody ends up with the bust that goes best with her figure and learns to accept and enjoy her own shape.

The catch is that if you feel like a freak in the meantime, that's the image you project. Who wants to hang out with a girl who is totally preoccupied with her bust? It's not true that guys favour girls who are 'well-stacked'. Guys like girls who feel good about themselves.

Although many girls are concerned about being concave or convex, I hope you can appreciate your own curves. Bodies look their most attractive when they are firm and in shape, whether they resemble hourglasses, pears, or beanpoles. The days of girdles, bustles, corsets and 'falsies' are behind us. Now big is beautiful and flat is fine and medium is marvellous. So throw back your shoulders when you walk. Take off your T-shirt when you swim. Don't be like me who agonized too long over nothing – if you'll pardon the pun.

You may have seen articles and ads about plastic surgery, and wondered if it would be possible to improve the size and shape of your own breasts. Let me warn you that cosmetic surgery is extremely costly, somewhat risky, and it doesn't always work. That said, if your breasts are so mammoth or minuscule that they are causing you severe physical or psychological problems, you can always consult your GP and he or she may recommend National Health Service treatment. Usually though, serious breast reconstruction surgery is for older women; cosmetic surgery is available to people who have had a mastectomy due to cancer, or who have been involved in some kind of disfiguring accident.

For instance, if you fall off a speeding motorbike and damage your face, doctors would try to repair your features as well as possible. But your GP is not likely to be very sympathetic if you just want to swap your mini breasts for new maxi ones. Instead, he or she may tell you not to despair, that you still have some growing to do and that, besides, you should try to make peace with your body and shape. If you are embarrassed because you feel your bust is too big, remember that an awful lot of your skinnier sisters probably envy you something rotten!

One thing every girl should get into the habit of doing as early as possible is examining her breasts once a month. Breast cancer among girls and young women is exceedingly rare and ten out of eleven women will never develop breast cancer, but even so you should familiarize yourself with your breasts so that you will notice any changes. Even lumps, and some discharge from the nipple, may be normal. But consult your doctor, particularly if you notice changes in your breasts after the age of seventeen, or if your mother has ever had breast cancer. Check your breasts each month after your period has finished; the examination only takes a few minutes but it *is* worth it. It's a matter of life and breasts.

Here's how:

1 In the bath or shower (since wet skin is slippery), keep your fingers flat and move them all over your breasts, checking for lumps, knots, or thickening.

2 Lie down in bed or on the floor. Put your right hand behind your head, and with your left hand, check your right breast. Move your fingers in circles around your nipple, including the area around your armpit. Repeat with opposite hand and breast.

3 Sit up and, with arms overhead, inspect your breasts in front of a mirror to check for changes. Squeeze each nipple gently to check for discharge.

Since you are probably still developing, your breasts are supposed to be changing – and that's quite natural. So don't be alarmed. I'm just recommending that you do the monthly three-step breast-checking routine and become acquainted with the contours of your breasts, so that if any change ever does occur, you'll know right away.

A free leaflet containing lots of information about your breasts is available from The Women's National Cancer Control Campaign (WNCCC), see page 281. Simply write to them enclosing an SAE (a stamped, self-addressed envelope).

In case you've wondered whether the miracle creams and exercisers you see advertised which claim to increase your bust size actually work, the answer is no. Breasts are made up of fat and glandular tissue, but not muscle. So exercising with a chest expander won't enlarge your breasts, though it may tone up your chest muscles so that your breasts *look* firmer.

Creams and massage can temporarily stimulate and increase the blood supply in the area of your breasts, as in sexual arousal, but that swelling doesn't last.

The best breast advice of all is to grin and bear them – whether yours are big, small, or slightly asymmetrical. Anyone who loves you will love you for *you*, regardless of your breast size or shape.

Is Your Period A Question Mark?

Can you imagine how scary it would be to start menstruating if you didn't know anything about it? Suddenly you'd be bleeding! Down there! I'd have been petrified if I hadn't known that the menarche (first period) is as much a part of puberty as developing breasts. Even if you've had your periods for years, you may not understand it completely or know what to do about cramps or tampons.

My first encounter with the paraphernalia of periods came when I was about six. My brother and I found white cylindrical cardboard tubes in the bathroom wastebasket, left there by our mother. We slipped them on our fingers and played puppets. Little did we know they were Tampax applicators!

Years later, when I was ten, my friend Alice (the one who was practically born with a bra on) was staying the night and we compared what we knew about menstruation, which wasn't much. We made a pact to tell each other when it happened, and sure enough Alice started her period that year.

Most girls start when they are twelve or thirteen, but more

than one in ten start when at primary school. Starting anywhere from nine to sixteen is not uncommon, and when you start depends not just on age but also on weight, percentage of body fat, and dietary habits. A girl's first period usually occurs after her breasts have begun to develop and her pubic hair has begun to appear.

My body was in no hurry. When I finally got my period, I was fifteen and a half and had been going out with a guy for six months. The first time is rarely a dramatic flood for anybody; usually it's just a little red on the toilet paper you're using, or a few drops of blood on your panties, with little warning before-hand. (Wash stains out with cold, not hot, water.) When I started, I felt relieved, and my friends seemed to think it was cause to celebrate. My mother said, 'Congratulations, welcome to womanhood.'

This is the gist of what menstruation is all about. Once you start menstruating, you are capable of having a baby, and every month your body gets geared up for possible motherhood. A tiny egg (you're born with thousands) matures in one of your ovaries, is released and sent down a fallopian tube, and even-tually reaches the uterus. Meanwhile, your uterus, or womb, has been preparing for the egg's arrival, and its lining is now thick and velvety. If the arriving egg is fertilized by a sperm, your uterus is ready to protect and nourish it. The fertilized egg, or ovum, will grow in your uterus and, in about nine months, you'll have a baby. If your egg hasn't been fertilized (you haven't had sex or you've been careful about contraception), then you're not pregnant. Your uterus has no use for the thick, spongy lining it has been building up. Much of the lining is therefore cast off, and that, along with some blood, body fluids, and the disinte-grated egg, comprises the six or so tablespoons of reddish brown menstrual flow that flushes out through your vagina for three to six days each month. Once you start menstruating and your cycle becomes regular, you'll have periods (except during pregnancy) until they stop at menopause, which usually occurs when you're between forty-five and fifty-five.

Are your periods already regular? Mine didn't become regular for over a year. Even if yours are, you may sometimes miss a month or several months. As long as you know you're not preg-nant, some irregularity shouldn't worry you. Nerves, plane rides, poor nutrition, weight gain or loss, even a cold can throw off your cycle. Mysteriously, sisters' or roommates' menstrual cycles sometimes become synchronized when they live together, so their periods may be off schedule as this first happens. And one-third to one-half of very athletic women often skip periods, although they are still fertile. (I know a marathon runner who hadn't menstruated in years, but when she and her husband decided to have a family, she had no problem getting pregnant.) If you are extremely thin and are skipping periods, try to gain weight and they may begin again. If you're worried about your monthly cycle – it's very irregular or painful – keep track of when you get your periods and talk to a doctor.

Do you know when you're about to get your period? I usually mark a small x on my calendar on the first day of each period so I'll know approximately when to expect it the next month. Most girls' cycles are about twenty-eight days, but they range from twenty-two to thirty-four days. Some girls may worry that their period is late, but if they'd kept track they'd realize that they simply have a long cycle.

Sometimes I'll be super-sensitive or weepy or tensed up, and the next day, bingo – I'll get my period. I don't usually suffer from headaches, backaches, cramps, cold sores, or nosebleeds as a few of my friends do, but I'm prone to a spot or two, I feel heavy, and once in a while my breasts get so tender it hurts just to walk down the stairs! That's nature's way of warning me that my period is on its way. Other times I'll have no symptoms at all, or my symptoms will come a full week or ten days before my period.

It's smart to be aware of your own premenstrual symptoms so you'll carry a tampon or towel in your bag (a good idea anyway), wear panties at night if you think you'll start (not your new white ones), and try not to scream at some innocent person just because you are short-tempered. (Studies show there are more family arguments, traffic accidents, crimes, and even suicides among women who are in their premenstrual week than among other women.)

If you ever miss school or parties because your periods are so bad, do consult your doctor. If premenstrual tension (PMT) is a real problem for you, there is a pamphlet, price £1, called *Advice for Younger Women*, written by Dr Alan Stewart and his wife, Maryon. Contact the PMT Advisory Service, *see page 280.*

Or check your local bookshops for *Curing PMT The Drug-free*

Way, by Moira Carpenter. It's published by Century-Arrow, costs £2.95 and is very informative.

Advice on PMT is also available from the Basingstoke Clinic, *see page 279*. Just write to them mentioning your problem and enclosing an SAE.

Women who are on the Pill rarely suffer premenstrual discomfort and are as regular as clocks, but the Pill has some disadvantages – more on that in the *Sex* chapter.

What should you do when you have your period? Everything you'd do otherwise! Swim, play tennis, dance, go out. Shower each day, eat healthily, get lots of sleep and exercise. If you have intercourse, use contraception, because menstruation is no guarantee that you won't get pregnant.

Using too much salt is never good for you, and it's particularly smart to avoid it now, since it makes you retain fluids and look puffy. You're losing iron, so eat meat, eggs, raisins, whole grain bread. Liver is also wonderful for you if you can stand it – I can't! The calcium level in your blood is down, so drink plenty of milk. Your blood sugar is down, so eat small healthy snacks (not sweets) to keep it up. Now is an especially good time to take daily vitamins. Alcohol, by the way, affects you more than usual at this time, so beware.

Constipation can be a problem around your period. If it is for you, exercise and eat bran, vegetables, salads, apples, prunes, and other fruits; drink plenty of water, juice, or even coffee. (Have you tried reading on the loo?) Regular bowel movements are crucial to overall health and extra important now to avoid cramping.

Which should you wear, tampons or towels? Do you realize how great it is to have a choice? Before 1921, women wore a cloth napkin they washed and reused. Next came bulky napkins attached with belts. Nowadays it's so easy!

Most sanitary towels have an adhesive side that sticks to the inside of your panties. You can choose thin or thick towels – also called napkins, pads, panty-liners – depending on your flow. If you're not having your period but are scared you might spot or start in the middle of a class or film, wear a towel as a safety precaution. (Some spotting may be normal, particularly if you use the IUD or the Pill or if you've gained or lost weight. Otherwise, see your doctor. Some white or yellow discharge is also normal, but if yours is thick and lumpy, or unusual for you, see your doctor.)

What about tampons? I find them more convenient than towels for the first day or two because they're smaller, less messy, more comfortable, and there's no odour. They're a must when you go swimming. Some tampons come with tube applicators (such as Tampax), and others you push in with your finger (such as Lil-lets).

Manufacturers also make deodorant tampons, but some women are allergic to them. There is no smell anyway until your menstrual flow meets the air, and by then you're throwing the used tampon away – in the waste bin wrapped in lots of paper, or in the toilet, if you are positive the plumbing is excellent. In some places they can block up the loo!

Most tampons come with directions for first-time users. If you haven't tried them, buy small tampons (regular or mini size) and give it a go when you next have your period. Relax, read the guidelines, aim the tampon towards the small of your back, and push it in just far enough so it's comfortable. You may go through several before you pop one in right, but inserting tampons is like whistling – once you get the hang of it, you'll never forget how.

The only possible reason you might not be able to use a tampon is that most girls have a thin layer of skin, called the hymen, that partially covers the opening of the vagina. But rarely does the hymen seal the opening completely, so just as there's room for your menstrual flow to come out, there's room for your tampon to go in. (In case you've heard otherwise, you're a virgin if you haven't had intercourse, whether your hymen is or isn't intact.)

When your flow is light or medium, use a regular tampon. When your flow is heavy, usually on days two and three, use a super tampon. (Heavier girls sometimes have heavier flows.) Still worried? You can always wear a tampon with a towel as a back-up. Change your tampons at least every four to six hours.

In high school, my friends and I used to be afraid we'd stain our white pants or skirts. If you're careful, you need not worry. Maybe I've been lucky, but I've never yet sprung a serious leak.

We also worried that tampons would get lost in our bodies. That can't happen because your cervix, which is the gateway to your uterus, is too small for a tampon to slip through. If it did somehow slip up your vaginal canal, you'd just wash your fingers and tug it out. But that possibility is highly unlikely. And it can't slip down because your vaginal muscles hold it up.

A few years ago, you may have heard about a rare illness called Toxic Shock Syndrome, which is a sudden high fever of over 102°F, accompanied by vomiting, diarrhoea, a sunburn-like rash on the palms of the hands and the soles of the feet and a drastic drop in blood pressure. It is a sometimes fatal disease which occurs most frequently among menstruating young women. If you ever have the above symptoms, contact your doctor, and if you are wearing a tampon, yank it out! Now that I've got you in a total panic, I must tell you that Toxic Shock Syndrome is incredibly rare – only a few thousand cases (and far fewer deaths) in the whole world. The particular type of tampons associated with the disease are not available in Britain anyway. To avoid any kind of infection, do change your tampons regularly – never leave the same one in all day – and avoid using tampons with a built-in deodorant as you might be allergic to them.

You need to find a tampon which is the right absorbency for you, because if you use one which is more absorbent than you actually need, it could cause dryness and irritation of the vagina. The best thing is to start with a mini or regular size, and only if you find that it cannot cope with your menstrual flow, try a super.

As soon as you begin shopping for tampons, you'll notice that there are two distinct types, the long ones, like Tampax, and the shorter, more compact ones such as Lil-lets. Try both, and find which is more comfortable for you. Ask your mum, your mates and your older sister, if you have one, about which sanitary protection they use, and why. A good way of trying out different types and brands is by keeping an eye open for sample offers in magazines.

Dr White's run a special service for anyone with any questions about sex, their body, or periods. They also have a useful leaflet on the subject of becoming a woman, called *Body Talk*. To obtain a copy, or to get info and answers, write to Sister Marion at The Advisory Service, *see page 281.*

By the way, do you ever feel embarrassed when you buy tampons or towels? You shouldn't. Half the population buys or has bought or will buy them. Besides, you don't quake when the guy at the counter sees your toothpaste, soap, deodorant or cologne, do you? Tampons or towels are just one more way of keeping clean and confident. So no blushing in the chemist's!

On the other hand, while you should never feel ashamed of menstruation, you don't need to get the megaphone every time your period comes. Menstruation has been a taboo subject in the past, and I'm not encouraging you to be hush-hush about it, but don't go to the other extreme, either.

(For what it's worth, I feel the same way about getting up to go to the toilet. You can say, 'Excuse me, I'll be right back,' or 'I must have a pee.' I prefer discretion. But then I'm the type who runs the tap water when I'm in the loo and others are within earshot.)

The Right Height

Just as you can't control how big your breasts will be or when your period will come, you can't control your height. You're stuck with it, so the sooner you accept it, the better.

My short story is that I was the runt of the litter. My brothers are both over a foot taller than I. Even my mother is an imposing 5 foot 7 inches, but, as she explained, 'You take after Grandmother.' And Grandma was a shrimp.

In school, I was always at the end when the teacher lined us up by height. Instead of seeing eye-to-eye with people, I saw eye-to-neck.

I finally put my size in perspective and stopped fretting. I also stretched a few inches skyward and am now a towering five foot two, eyes of blue. (The average height of British women is 5'3½''.) For me, the bright side of being petite was that I went out with lots of guys, tall and small. I still receive terrific hand-me-downs (actually hand-me-ups) from my teenage sister-in-law. And I'm the last one to get wet when it rains!

Are you tall? 'Giraffe' girls may be frustrated now but are lucky in the long run. (Aren't you tired of waiting for the long run?) Tall women look elegant in clothes that make shorties look frumpy. At work, they look authoritative. Another plus? Tall women can eat more than their short sisters. Be grateful, too, that you can reach the top shelf, and can see the film no matter who plonks down in front of you.

If you are afraid you'll soon be ducking under doorways, take heart. You may have reached the end of your growth spurt. A girl's growth spurt starts about the same time as her period and usually lasts one or two years. That's when you're shooting up up up, and past the boys. It takes them a couple of years, but most catch up.

If you ever feel you're all arms and legs, fear not. That's normal, and your body will sort itself out sooner than you think.

Whatever your height and proportions, stand straight and learn to wear clothes and shoes that suit you. If you're short, don't wear high heels constantly though, because they aren't good for your feet or back. Shop assistants, friends, magazines and mums can help you figure out which styles work best for you. Singer Toyah Willcox got to the top though she's only 4'11'', and Princess Diana soared to the heights of royal fame at an elegant 5'10''. Both look fantastic; you can too. There are special-ist shops and store departments for both the tall and the tiny.

Winning The Weight War

Do you eat to live or live to eat? Most people do both, and even if you would briefly consider trading in your brother for a pep-peroni pizza, that doesn't necessarily mean there's cause for concern.

However, weight control *is* a problem for too many of us. No one wants to be roly-poly fat or starvation skinny. Yet it can be difficult to eat healthy balanced meals and maintain a comfort-able in-between weight. Are you so calorie-conscious that weight is controlling you rather than the other way around? Are you dieting desperately or feeling guilty every time you eat even though friends swear you're a toothpick? Or are you chubby but unwilling to recognize it, or chunky just to spite your gymnast mother or health-nut father?

The media may be partly to blame. Food commercials say eat! eat! eat! but the actress munching the cake is skinny! skinny! skinny! Fashion magazines also brim with mixed messages. On one page: the latest fad diet of grapefruit and alfalfa sprouts. On the next: new recipes for strawberry cheesecake and gooey cho-colate mousse.

What do you do? Your boyfriend gawks over svelte models in underwear ads, but if you're together at a fancy restaurant, he doesn't want you to order just a salad. Your mother says you could stand to lose a few pounds, then prepares steak and kidney pud, your favourite, because she loves you.

In my house, it was my father who stuffed turkeys, fried bacon, stirred gravies, rolled dumplings, flipped pancakes, whipped cream, grated chocolate. I cleaned my plate with gusto.

Somehow I managed to get away with it and be a bit of a stick – until I was in my last year of school. That's when I went to France to live with a French family. France! Home of tempting breads, pastries, cheeses, and *haute cuisine*! Suffice it to say I over-indulged. And my metabolism caught up with me.

I scarcely realized I was gaining weight because I thought of myself as the skinny-bones I'd always been. Yet when I returned to my home in Armonk, New York, everyone seemed more interested in the dozen pounds I'd put on than in my newly acquired fluency in French or my impressions of the Louvre. Most frustrating was that I'd gone from underweight to over-weight without ever having appreciated the time when I might have been 'just right'.

I cut back on my munching, bought a calorie counter, and stayed seated at dinner while my brothers hopped up for seconds and thirds. Most of the weight fell off pretty fast. Since then, however, I've had to watch myself, exercise, and not gobble chocolate biscuits with abandon.

Just last week, a friend seemed surprised when I declined her offer of a milkshake. 'C'mon,' she said, 'you don't have to worry about your weight.' Wrong! The only reason I occasionally look as though I don't have to worry about my weight is that I *do* worry about it.

The trick is to be sensible. You don't want to be a blimpo-saurus, a Renoir model, a Miss Piggy lookalike – but you also don't want to be neurotic about every half-inch of flesh on your body. I prefer to be two pounds over my ideal weight than to be obsessive and frantic about calories.

Even if you do lose a pound per thigh and trim two off your behind, you still won't be tall and blonde (like Princess Diana) if you're short and brunette (like me). And your life won't change just because you get rid of your spare tyre. It *might* change because, after losing weight, you may start to feel more cheerful, self-assured, outgoing. People respond to a gain in confidence as much as they do to a loss in weight.

Work to become fit instead of fat now, because you are setting your eating patterns (good habits now mean good health later), and because, as the saying goes, if you don't watch your figure, no one else will.

The following section on weighty worries offers fifty-five dieting tips. I hope you don't spend your life jumping on and off the diet merry-go-round. Nor should you be on a perpetual diet, because your body will simply make do on less food by slowing your metabolism.

Confidence is cumulative. So accept yourself or change. How much you weigh is up to you, but keep nutrition in mind if you diet. It's especially vital now while you're still growing.

Don't Window-Shop At The Bakery
And Fifty-Four Other Dieting Dos And Don'ts

Dieting is not hard if you alone have decided you are ready to lose weight. The secret is to eat less. The average teenage girl burns up about 2,200 calories each day. You'll lose weight if you consume fewer. A pound of body weight equals 3,500 calories. Adults generally need about 15 calories per pound per day. For instance, since I weigh about 110 pounds, I need about 1,650 calories.

You should exercise to improve muscle tone, but an hour on the sports field burns about 200 calories and does not entitle you to wolf down a thick slice of chocolate cake. An hour's jog burns about 600 calories – a lot, but still less than the calories in that dessert. Why not pass on the cake? Or just have a taste of a friend's.

The idea is to eat like a bird instead of a horse. Dieting isn't fun, but when your tight pants feel loose and your flabby belly is firm, you'll be glad you slimmed down. So if you are overweight (and only if you are overweight), summon your willpower and win by losing.

1 **Don't** eat if you're not hungry.

2 **Do** eat slowly, putting your fork down between bites and talking during the meal. A table is not a trough.

3 **Don't** take big portions. Take small portions. Think slivers, not slabs.

4 **Do** stop before you're full, because it takes about twenty minutes for your belly to figure out what your mouth has been up to.

5 **Don't** take big bites. Take small bites.

6 **Do** brace yourself when you're going to eat at someone's home. Don't arrive famished. Decline politely on seconds.

7 **Don't** eat absent-mindedly. Enjoy what you're consuming, or don't bother. (The first two Jaffa Cakes are scrumptious. Can you really taste the sixth?)

8 **Do** exercise at least two hours a week, and remember that muscle weighs more than flab – and looks better. Swimming, jogging, gymnastics, dancing, skipping and cycling are great for all-over trimming. Think appearance and inches, not just pounds.

9 **Don't** waste calories on fizzy drinks. Drink calorie-free herbal teas or nutritious juices, such as tomato or grapefruit.

10 **Do** keep peeled carrots, celery sticks, tomatoes, green grapes, radishes, and other vegetables and fruits ready for snacking or for taking on a trip.

11 **Don't** buy fattening foods, and ask the family shopper to skip the sweets counter. It's easier to resist the stuff when it's not around. Never go shopping on an empty stomach.

12 **Do** consider meeting instead of eating. Write to Weight Watchers *page 281*, or phone them for details of local groups.

13 **Don't** take diet pills or any slimming aids without a

doctor's go-ahead. Some are dangerous; others make you irritable; others make you lose water, not fat.

14 **Do** eat well-balanced meals daily that include foods from the four major food groups: grains and cereals; fruits and vegetables; meat, poultry, and fish; and dairy products. Avoid sugary things, and realize once and for all that crash diets are unhealthy.

15 **Don't** weigh yourself every day, because your scales won't immediately register last night's bag of peanuts. Weigh yourself at the same time every few days. Don't expect to lose more than one or two pounds a week.

16 **Do** be patient if you're dieting wisely but losing slowly, or if you've reached a plateau. Some people have faster metabolisms than others, and the very plump usually lose faster than the slightly pudgy. Keep dieting and you'll keep losing.

17 **Don't** get discouraged if people don't notice your weight loss right away. You don't notice every two pounds others gain and lose.

18 **Do** take a walk or call a friend or write a letter when you get a food craving.

19 **Don't** load your wholemeal bread with butter and jam, or your baked potato with butter, or your pasta with a rich cream sauce.

20 **Do** eat breakfast. Your body will thank you more for breakfast than it will for an extra seven minutes' sleep. Instead of skipping any meals, eat small meals. (According to some studies, if you consume 1,500 calories divided into six small meals, you'll lose weight faster than if you consume the same calories in just three meals. Check calorie charts to learn which foods are most fattening.)

21 **Don't** talk about your diet all the time. You'll bore everybody silly.

22 **Do** keep busy, and food will become less important.

23 **Don't** blow the rest of your diet day just because you munched a Marathon at lunch.

24 **Do** order fish, chicken salad, or something light when eating out.

25 **Don't** have one potato crisp. It's easier to have none.

26 **Do** remember that calories count even when it's your birthday, even when you're on a date, even when you have a test that day, and even when you're scraping out the mixing bowl!

27 **Don't** mistake the new womanly roundness of your breasts, bottom and thighs for unsightly flab.

28 **Do** use a small plate if your dietetic dinner looks pitiful on a big one.

29 **Don't** start a diet right before exams or your period or when other concerns are making you tense.

30 **Do** cut down on salt because it makes you retain excess water. Avoid things like salted snacks and crisps. Season your food with pepper and spices. (Canned vegetables come salted; so eat them fresh.)

31 **Don't** gorge yourself on Sunday in preparation for the diet you might start on Monday.

32 **Do** drink lots of water between meals. Drinking will make you less hungry. Keep iced Perrier or bottled spring water in the fridge and the teapot ready for a cuppa. Sip juice or clear soup before dinner.

33 **Don't** fill your plate at a salad bar until you've checked out all the offerings.

34 **Do** consider taping a picture of you-at-your-tubbiest *or* sleekest on your fridge. (I know a man who wired his fridge with a gadget that asks, when the door is opened, 'Are you really hungry, Fatso?')

35 **Don't** leave a knife on the cake plate. It makes it too easy to slice off a wedge when you were really just passing by.

36 **Do** brush your teeth when you want to put something in your mouth. The just-brushed feeling will cut down on your desire to munch.

37 **Don't** fry when you can boil, steam, grill or bake.

38 **Do** buy tuna packed in water instead of oil; canned fruit in its juice, not in syrup; skimmed milk, not whole milk; thin-sliced bread, not regular bread; white meat (e.g. chicken, fish), not red meat (e.g. burgers, steak). Today's supermarkets are health-conscious, with wholemeal and low-fat products.

39 **Don't** guide yourself by weight charts, because your bone structure may not be average. Ask your doctor or school nurse what he or she thinks you should weigh.

40 **Do** consider writing down everything you eat during one week. That can help you figure out when extra calories slip into your diet. It also curbs eating when you report cheating.

41 **Don't** snack without asking, 'Is this worth the calories?'

42 **Do** pick up a five-pound bag of potatoes after you lose your first five: that's how much weight you no longer lug around. Mirrors and scales don't lie, but it takes time to adjust your self-image.

43 **Don't** become a vegetarian unless you research exactly what you'd need to eat each day to get enough protein.

44 **Do** learn how to use chopsticks. They'll slow you down when you eat Chinese food, and at other meals too.

45 **Don't** let your menu get boring. Experiment with herbs, and try new vegetables such as Chinese leaf and mange-tout peas, and seafood such as mussels and squid. Learn to adore salad, but go easy on dressings.

46 **Do** resist. Mere minutes of fudge joy equal flab that could take days of dieting to lose.

47 **Don't** sit through TV food commercials – change the channel.

48 **Do** consider making rigid rules for yourself. It may be easier to know you won't allow yourself to snack after 9 p.m. than to have to test your willpower every evening.

49 **Don't** window-shop at the bakery.

50 **Do** use a fork if you must taste the ice-cream. You'll be aware of each bite.

51 **Don't** underestimate the pleasure of holding back. When you say no to seconds you'll feel strong and virtuous.

52 **Do** think of getting through one day at a time rather than freaking out over the prospect of surviving three weeks without chips.

53 **Don't** drink diet sodas or use sugar substitutes. They don't re-educate your palate. Instead, get used to less sweet food slowly. A recent report said that Britons should cut their sugar consumption by half. So try having just one teaspoon of sugar, then a half, then a few grains, then finally none (hooray!)

54 **Don't** keep dieting when you've reached your ideal weight. You may want to lose a few extra pounds since you may gain a few back. But quit when it's quitting time, and then work on maintaining your new weight level. Don't congratulate yourself with Fig Rolls. Treat yourself to a pair of jeans – in your new smaller size.

Losing Too Much: Eating Disorders

If preoccupation with food interferes with your life, if you see yourself as plump even though others swear you're underweight, or if you truly believe that if you were thin, you'd be happy, you may be prone to an eating disorder. Eating disorders are diets gone wrong, diets that are self-destructive instead of self-improving. Anorexia and bulimia have become increasingly common. One teenage friend of mine said that eating disorders have practically become a fad.

Anorexics starve themselves and bulimics stuff themselves compulsively, and some abuse laxatives or make themselves throw up. Many are so pleased to be looking slim that they overlook the permanent damage they may be doing to their bodies. If you are anorexic or bulimic, or exhibit symptoms of both disorders, you are not alone. But you also probably can't cure yourself alone. Start taking vitamins and try to go three days without feasting or fasting. If you can't, consult your GP or write to Anorexic Aid *see page 279*, enclosing a large SAE plus four first-class stamps, or you can phone them on Wednesday or Thursday mornings.

Anorexia Nervosa

Pam is in her late teens. She is a perfectionist. She is as emaciated and bony as a prisoner of war or a famine victim, but she insists that her belly sticks out and she wants to lose a little more weight.

Her friendships have changed. Her family is concerned. They think she looks skeletal and urge her to eat more. But that just makes her defiant, so she hardly touches the food on her plate. Pam thinks about food a lot, and she cooks for others. But while food fascinates her, eating repels her. So she feeds her dinner to the dog, or hides it, or throws it out when no one is looking. When someone *is* watching, she may eat, but may later take a laxative or make herself sick. Occasionally her willpower falters and she binges, but afterwards she vomits or fasts with added determination.

Losing weight makes Pam feel in control. Her parents have always demanded a lot of her, and she expects a lot of herself. She found it was easier to diet than to get good marks at school, or master the piano. After Pam shed the five pounds she wanted to lose, she kept dieting and exercising rigidly. She is plugged into the idea of putting as little as possible into her body. It gives her a sense of power, even of superiority, to know she can live almost without food, that she can resist what others find irresistible.

From 120 pounds, she's down to below ninety. She's lost some hair as well as weight. Some of her skin is scaly. She feels cold and bundles herself up in layers of clothes. She has problems sleeping and suffers from constipation and sudden muscle cramps. When her periods stopped (amenorrhoea), Pam wondered if her whole system was shutting down. But she hadn't felt too comfortable about menstruation anyway or the prospect of dating and future pregnancy. What finally scared Pam was that she went from feeling super-energetic to feeling debilitated. And when her sister came home from college, she took one look at Pam and started to cry.

Pam has a classic, all-too-common case of anorexia nervosa. If she doesn't get help soon, she could die or suffer lifelong problems. There *is* such a thing as being too thin.

Anorexia nervosa has been described as a psychosomatic and psychosocial illness in which irrational fear of being overweight leads to compulsive dieting. It can affect anybody, but statistics show that ninety to ninety-five per cent of sufferers are women, especially young women. Some women diet successfully or lose weight in an illness, then continue dieting until they've lost as much as twenty-five per cent of their original body weight. As many as one in 200 women may be anorexic, and six per cent of those with serious cases die. They starve to death or die of infections or heart failure. Others wait too long before they seek help; although they recover, they've done irreparable damage to their bodies due to drastic chemical imbalances and malnutrition.

Anorexia contributed to the untimely death in 1983 of singer Karen Carpenter, who died of heart failure when she was thirty-two. Princess Diana's sister, Lady Sarah, also suffered from anorexia, as did Lena Zavaroni.

If you think that a friend or family member may be an anorexia or bulimia sufferer, do contact Anorexic Aid on their behalf, and pass on the information.

Treatment may include short-term individual therapy, hospitalization, family therapy, or behaviour modification therapy. It will entail gaining back some weight, learning to eat a balanced diet, and readjusting emotionally to overcome the phobia of weight gain and begin to deal with underlying troubles. You can recover. Your periods will return. You'll look healthier and feel stronger and more confident. You will get to a point at which wilful starvation no longer appeals to you.

Bulimia

Jessica is not underweight. Her friends don't even realize she has a problem. But Jessica knows she's a compulsive eater, and she feels disgusted and guilty. At times, that guilt sends her back to the kitchen, where she eats a packet of biscuits, a bag of sweets, half a pie, or a tub of ice-cream. She scarcely pauses between bites because she doesn't want to acknowledge what she's doing. After a pig-out, Jessica goes straight to the bathroom and vomits.

At first, she thought throwing up was a great way to get to eat her favourite foods without gaining weight. That was back when she had to use her finger to make herself vomit. Unfortunately, her unhealthy whim led to frequent self-induced vomiting, and now when she bends over, the food comes up on its own. Her mouth hurts and sometimes bleeds, and lately Jessica has been depressed by her yo-yo feast-or-famine eating patterns. Her fixation with food has got in the way of her social life. It has also diverted her attention from her other real problems.

Jessica spends a lot of time in the kitchen and bathroom. She binges about a dozen times a week. Sometimes she gorges on spaghetti, pizza and bread instead of sweets. Sometimes she gets rid of it by using a laxative, or a diuretic instead of vomiting. But her weight doesn't fluctuate much – which frustrates her all the more.

Her parents think she simply has a healthy appetite. No one suspects that Jessica has a problem, because she covers her tracks. She hides her food. When she wants ice-cream, she doesn't just have a choc-ice, she has two – and then a couple of King Cones washed down with three Strawberry Mivvies.

Her obsession is becoming expensive. Once she stole £10 from her father's wallet for food. That made her feel terrible, and *that* made her binge extra. She wishes she could stop, but sometimes she panics and is afraid she has forgotten how to eat normally.

Jessica suffers from bulimia. If she continues to binge and purge, she may cause permanent damage to her body.

Bulimia (literally, 'ox hunger') is common among young women and more prevalent than anorexia. Some anorexics 'recover' only to become bulimic, which means they haven't really faced the conflicts behind their eating disorder. Also, just as some anorexics may avoid facing their sexuality by regressing to an almost prepuberty state physically, some bulimics mask their curves in fat.

A bulimic's habits are harmful. By vomiting right after eating, the bulimic throws up not only calories but water and digestive fluids as well. This can cause dehydration and a serious imbalance of body chemicals. The stomach acids that come up the oesophagus and pour into the mouth can cause bleeding, gum disease, and tooth decay. Fasting leads to malnutrition and kidney problems and may stunt growth. Abuse of laxatives and enemas can make the bulimic prone to constipation and bowel lesions. In severe cases, the bulimic's eyes may be bloodshot and the hands and feet may be numb. Often the bulimic feels out of control, isolated, and depressed.

If, like Jessica, you are bingeing and purging and are always eating because of emotional rather than physical cues, you need help. Talk to your family or doctor or contact Anorexic Aid. You can learn to modify your eating behaviour, to take reponsibility for your body, to express tensions in more constructive ways, and to be nicer to yourself. You will get better and, with determination, you will stay well. But the longer you are bulimic, the harder it is to recover.

Excited About Exercise

Don't think exercise. Think making friends, feeling stonger, losing weight, and living longer.

I hate the idea of exercise. But I love to cycle, swim, hike, dance, and play Frisbee. My friend Judy and I used to jog almost every day in summer when we were neighbours. It was a great way to keep in shape and have a chat. Jogging is perfect, too, for getting to know guys. I used to feel far too shy to ask a guy out on Friday night, but I didn't think twice about inviting

Tim or Neil or Robert to go jogging.

Too many British teenagers give up any form of exercise once they leave school. Don't be amongst them. Hockey and netball might not have been your thing, but go swimming or join a tennis club or a keep fit or dance class. A super social life might result!

This year I joined an aerobics group. In three weeks, I had thinner thighs, a firmer bottom, and several new acquaintances.

If you're a solitude fan, exercise can provide a time to be alone. Bliss can be a solo bike ride. If you're alone but want distraction, do sit-ups in front of the television, or dancercise to the radio.

Will exercise make you voraciously hungry? On the contrary. Exercise actually suppresses appetite. If you exercise just before a meal, you'll get a double benefit. You'll eat less, and you'll burn calories faster, because your circulation speeds up. Plus, if you've just worked out, it's easy to feel health-minded and forgo the sundae. My favourite times to exercise are before dinner (when I'm getting hungry and tempted to snack) or first thing in the morning (so I start my day awake).

You may be getting enough exercise in the gym, but why not go out for a sport or enlist a friend with whom to run or play tennis regularly? A minimum of twenty minutes of aerobic exercise three times a week is a must for health and well-being.

Walk whenever possible. Why bother with the bus when you're only going half a mile? Same with lifts. Don't press the button – climb the stairs!

If you want to take up jogging, be sure to start slowly and walk when winded. Other precautions?

- Get a good pair of running shoes.
- Warm up and finish by stretching.
- Jog flat-footed or roll from heel to toe – don't run on tiptoe.
- Jog on grass, not concrete.
- Don't jog right after eating.
- Don't jog near traffic or at dusk.
- Breathe through your nose, not your mouth, especially in a polluted city.
- When you come up behind somebody, say 'Excuse me', or 'Good morning' so the person doesn't think he or she is about to be mugged.

One thing I like about exercise is it makes me feel I've earned my daily shower. When I step into it all hot and sweaty, I feel extra-clean and fresh when I step out.

I even jogged on my wedding day, with Judy, my matron of honour. My mother, aghast, was afraid we'd fall and have to hobble down the aisle. Instead, jogging made us both feel less nervous. And our cheeks looked naturally rosy.

Anybody out there think exercise is unfeminine? Once upon a time, it may have been considered unladylike for a woman to be athletic, or have a vicious backhand. Today, staying fit is sexy. Ask Jane Fonda and Victoria Principal.

Too tired to exercise? Nonsense! A twenty-minute walk invigorates you more than a twenty-minute nap. Regular exercise gives you energy rather than sapping it. And yes, you can and should exercise during your period.

Tennis, running, ballet, swimming, yoga – they're all marvellous, but you can also burn calories and tone muscles by doing a private belly dance as you brush your teeth. Or by walking briskly instead of shuffling your feet. Or by scissoring your legs as you talk on the phone. Or by pressing your feet down while studying as though you alone are preventing the floor from rising.

Here ends my Physical Fitness Pep Talk. Start exercising, if you don't already. It'll lift your spirits, improve your complexion, firm flab, relieve stress, strengthen your heart, speed your circulation, and leave you full of vim and vigour.

Body Sweat, Body Smells

A couple of years ago, you hardly perspired, let alone had body odour. Now some of your glands are working hard to keep you cool, and that may mean underarm wetness. Some say, 'Horses sweat, men perspire, and women glow,' but while *glowing* sounds pleasant, *smelling* is another story.

Fight back! Shower or bathe daily. If necessary, use antiperspirant (to stop the wetness) or deodorant (to stop the odour) or a combination product. I prefer roll-ons, since pressure sprays pollute the atmosphere. Change brands periodically, since each product loses some effectiveness once your body gets used to it.

Try to wear cotton or well-ventilated clothes, certainly cotton undies.

While we're talking body odours, is wind ever a problem? If so, avoid notorious foods such as beans, cabbage, radishes, and spicy foods; don't have too many fizzy drinks or apple juice, and don't chew gum endlessly. And eat s-l-o-w-l-y.

Want to smell like lemons, flowers, or exotic essences? If your skin is sensitive, don't take bubble baths or bath essences, because some can cause vaginal or urinary irritations. Instead, wear cologne. To sample testers, spray a little on your forearm, wait a few moments, and sniff. Your nose gets confused after three or four fragrances, so it may take a week to decide which to buy. Don't go too sweet or heavy, and remember that a little goes a long way. The effect should be subtle as a whisper.

Clearing the Way For Smooth Skin

Do you have a peaches-and-cream complexion? Do you even know anybody who does? Often when you want to look your best, your skin may look its worst. (*Teen* is truly a four-letter word!) More than ninety-five per cent of the population runs into some acne trouble at some time. Many girls find their hormones are going haywire and pimples are popping up on their faces with the dependability of dandelions on a spring lawn.

The good news? Proper care can improve your complexion, medicated make-up can hide your blemishes, girls' skin troubles are generally not as bad as boys', and your flare-ups are only temporary. Soon your angry skin will calm down – and you can start worrying about wrinkles!

If scrupulous hygiene, bags of fresh air and a healthy diet don't seem to be working, and if the special medicated creams and lotions available at the chemists don't improve that spot one jot, then see your doctor and he may refer you to a dermatologist – a doctor who specializes in skin disorders.

Like Adrian Mole's, my teenage diary is loaded with skin worries, such as: '*My face is a pimple patch but not as bad as usual.*'

After a year or two of private battles, I went to see a dermatologist.

'Help,' said I.

This is what he said:

---

1 Don't eat chocolate, nuts, sharp cheeses, or shellfish. Don't drink coffee or colas. (Other dermatologists claim chocolate is OK and point out that different people's skin reacts to different foods, and that it is worth finding out what in particular makes you break out.)

2 Hands off! Don't rest your chin or forehead in your palms. Don't pick at blemishes or squeeze blackheads – you can end up squeezing them in instead of out.

3 Drink plenty of water and juices; get a little sunshine; get lots of exercise and sleep.

4 Wash your face gently but religiously twice a day, and wash your back and chest well when showering.

Then he wrote out a prescription for antibiotics and recommended a cleansing soap. I followed his orders, and my complexion improved.

New antibiotics and effective soaps are constantly being developed. Benzoyl peroxide and retinoic acid (vitamin A acid) help reduce the plugs in pores. And many dermatologists prescribe antibiotics such as tetracycline and erythromycin for oral or topical use. Of course, pregnant women should not take most drugs, and whenever a doctor prescribes a treatment, it is essential to follow directions precisely.

Should you curb your diet as my specialist suggested? Maybe. Some experts say diet has nothing to do with pimples. You know your skin best, so you be the expert. If you eat a Mars bar, does your face erupt like a Martian volcano? Why not run an experiment? Eat a forbidden food one day and see if you break out the next. Or eat healthily for a few days and see if your skin looks extra pretty. Try this after your period so you don't throw off the results. You may end up devising your own off-limits list to include foods that make your skin react most. (Chips, Pizza?)

But pimples do not live by food alone. No matter what you eat, you may be a craterface for a while. Acne outside is a sign that you're maturing inside. You may break out around your 'time of the month', or when you are stressed or scared or excited – or for no reason at all. Acne is not affected by one's sex life. And acne is not a losing battle, because you win in the end.

Meanwhile, don't forget to wash (not scrub) your face. Many pimples despise soap and water and will pack up and flee if you wash regularly. Your best zit-zapping plan of attack is to wash with soap and warm water morning and night, and rinse well with cool water before patting dry with a clean towel. Keep your hair clean, because greasy hair means greasy skin. (A shower a day helps keep the dermatologist away.) Never apply make-up before washing your face.

If your skin is soap-sensitive, try a medicated brand or any other mild soap. If your skin is dry, use a gentle creamy soap and a moisturizer. You can also spray your face with a plant mister before moisturizing. The mist will make your skin as happy as it makes your asparagus fern! If your room is overheated, you can buy a vaporizer or put a pan of water on the radiator for added moisture. Prone to chapped skin? Smear body lotion on your elbows, knees, hands, and feet.

OK. Let's say you've been eating bran, wheat germ, and other wholesome foods; you're washing well; you're exercising; you don't *use* make-up let alone sleep with it on; you swab your skin with a good product at bedtime – yet you still wake up every once in a while with a pimple the size of a tepee at the end of your nose.

What should you do? Wear an Elastoplast to school? Say to friends, 'Can you believe this horrendous zit? I'm so ugly! My face looks like a relief map of the Andes!' Stay home and watch *East Enders*? No! Your best bet is to dab on a little medicated makeup and forget about it. In senior school, my handsome older brother Mark once told me he didn't mind when his date had a blemish or two because it made him less self-conscious about his own slight acne.

Hang in there. Your face will soon clear up, and I doubt there will be a single tell-tale scar.

Speaking of complexion complexes, consider for a minute that golden tan we all crave. True or false: you want a TV star's tan and you don't care if you look like a prune in thirty years.

If you answered *true*, I'm with you. Baking in the sun is a sensuous luxury, and a deep tan under a white dress is striking. But when you are forty-four pushing fifty and your skin is dry, leathery, and lined, and you've already had a cancerous cyst removed, you'll probably wish you could step into a time machine and throttle your former self.

What's more you *can* tan without burning or inviting skin cancer. Here are a dozen tips.

1 Always bring a T-shirt or long-sleeved blouse with you to the beach or pool. Buy a pretty hat to protect your pretty face.

2 Start tanning gradually. If you lie out for a full hour on day one, you won't look stunning by nightfall, you'll look like a lobster in pain. And if you're indoors up North all year and suddenly go for a week's holiday in the tropics, your skin will not appreciate the surprise.

3 Douse yourself with a sunscreen lotion when you bathe. If you pour on the baby oil, you'll burn to a crisp. Start with a product that has a high sun protection factor, such as 15, then later use a lower SPF, such as 8. If this numbers business, and the sheer variety of products, are confusing to you, ask the chemist for help.

4 Don't trust those clouds. Around seventy to eighty per cent of the sun's ultraviolet rays shine through them.

5 Don't scorch at midday. The sun is strongest – and most harmful – from 10 until 2.

6 Know thyself. If you're fair-skinned, you may burn easily.

7 Always reapply your protective oil or cream after you have been swimming.

8 Stay away from sun lamps. Why wither your skin without getting the fun of the sun?

9 Take extra precautions when on holiday abroad. The Mediterranean sun is a lot stronger than ours.

10 Take extra care if you're skiing, because snow reflects the sun's rays.

11 Know that birth control pills and certain antibiotics can make your skin more susceptible to burning or blotching.

12 Use a moisturizer after sunbathing, so your skin will stay smoother longer. For best benefits, apply after you wash or bathe, while your skin is still moist. Remember, British girls' skins are the envy of the world. The damp, cool climate means that Britons seldom end up with wrinkled, leathery complexions or skin cancer, like women in hotter countries.

A Nose Is A Nose, And What About Ears?

You've tackled your skin troubles. What about the rest of your face? If you can't stand your nose and ears and think cosmetic surgery might be the answer, think again. As I said in the section on breasts, it's painful, risky and horribly expensive. Besides, a new nose won't guarantee that you'll be elected Miss UK or Carnival Queen. Plus, by replacing your distinguished feature with an ordinary one, you're losing part of your individuality. Barbra Streisand might never have made it if she had an everyday nose. Who nose?

So think twice, then twice more. Is your life really being ruined by your hook nose or big ears? Or is it your attitude that needs fixing? If you change your hairstyle, don flashy earrings, make up your eyes, apply lipstick and smile – won't that do the job?

Ear piercing is a less dramatic kind of cosmetic surgery that you may want to consider carefully.

If you want to pierce your ears, first be sure you can. Do you bleed more than most people? Are you unusually prone to allergies and infections? Do you have skin that scars easily? (I do.) If you answered no, no, no, then you can get your ears pierced.

But don't have a friend do it. Go to a doctor or qualified jeweller. It's not expensive and it doesn't hurt much. Then keep your gold sleepers in for about four to six weeks before wearing other metals or wires. And at first you'll need to swab your ears regularly with the lotion you'll be given to minimize the risk of infection. If your ears become red or swollen, consult your doctor.

Eye Deal

Do you need glasses? Fifty-six per cent of men and sixty-seven per cent of women wear glasses or contact lenses at least some of the time. Seeing your best is part of looking your best. Don't squint or let your marks slide or say a mere 'hi' in the hall because you can't identify the friendly hunk approaching you.

In college, I went to the theatre with my friend Gilbert and, feeling coy, tried on his glasses. What a shock! I could see the actors' expressions rather than just fuzzy features. I hadn't realized what I was missing. An optician confirmed that I needed glasses for plays, films and driving. So I got framed! Now I love seeing leaves on the trees, feathers on the birds, windows on the skyscrapers, faces in the crowds.

Do you get headaches after you read? Is your vision blurry? Do you have trouble making out road signs, small print, subtitles, or words on the blackboard? Get your eyes checked annually. If you need glasses or contact lenses, don't wait around.

Glasses come in all sorts of attractive shapes, colours, tints, and styles. Some people look better with them on than off. I know a graduate student who owns half a dozen frames and wears them to match her outfits and moods.

Contact lenses often cost more than glasses, require more care, and take some adjusting to. The payoff is that lenses don't change your appearance and do offer better peripheral and straight-ahead vision. Your optician can help you decide if you want soft, hard, or extended-wear contacts, with tinted or clear lenses.

Hard lenses come in two types, the original 'hard', which is a thin, inflexible disc which fits over the coloured part of your eye, and the new 'gas permeable', which allows more oxygen to reach the eye, and which some wearers find more comfortable.

Soft lenses are floppy, sometimes so thin that they resemble tiny circles of cellophane, and also come in two kinds: the ones you take out at night, and the 'extended wear' lenses, which can remain in the eye continually for several months, but which are a lot more expensive than the other types of lenses.

Caring for contact lenses is easy once you get into the habit. At first, you'll find yourself constantly referring to the instructions, but changing the solution and doing the weekly super-clean soon becomes second nature. Any good optician should be able to give you leaflets about lenses, or ask about them next time you go for an eye check-up.

A Mouthful About Mouths

My first dentist was a horrible man with a nervous tic. He used to make me kiss him on the cheek each visit and he was stingy with the anaesthetic. 'Raise your hand if it hurts,' he'd say, then ignore me as I waved wildly. His motto was probably : Drill, fill and bill.

We changed dentists. My new one is friendly, painless and capable. He doesn't hand me stereo headphones when he works, but, well, you can't have everything. My only complaint is that sometimes he asks, 'How have you been, Carol?' then pops a water-sucking gizmo under my tongue so all I can mumble is, 'Fffahn, jjus ffahn.'

This dentist always gives me sunny sermons about oral hygiene. Brush and floss. Morning, noon and night. Carry floss and a toothbrush in your bag for use after lunch – the brush should have soft bristles and be replaced often. 'At least rinse your mouth,' he pleads, 'and avoid sticky sweets and sugar-coated gum.' 'Coffee, tea and cigarettes stain your teeth,' he warns, 'and cola rots them.' I go to him every year, but none of his advice impresses me as much as the block-letter sign that hangs in his office: IGNORE YOUR TEETH AND THEY'LL GO AWAY. Thirty per cent of Britons aged over sixteen have no natural teeth. Isn't that awful?

Run your tongue over your teeth right now. Do they feel coated and grimy or slick and clean?

Does the tap water in your town contain fluoride? Fluoride

helps strengthen teeth. That's why a fluoride toothpaste is the best cavity-fighter. Do your gums bleed every time you brush? You don't want to develop periodontal (gum) disease, so floss religiously.

Do you ever have halitosis? To prevent bad breath, use a mouthwash and brush your teeth and even your tongue and the roof of your mouth gently with toothpaste. If you're going out, don't eat onions or garlic bread. Carry mints with you. Your breath is still bad? You may have indigestion, an infection, or tooth decay, so see your dentist.

A college friend and I thought up a tactful way to inform each other when we had stale breath. We'd say 'B²' (for bad breath), which certainly beats 'Your breath stinks!'

If you have braces on your teeth, remember you're not the only one, and your teeth will soon look fabulous. Meanwhile, steer clear of lipstick if you don't want to accent your mouth. But don't stop smiling.

Your wisdom teeth probably won't appear for several years. If you're lucky, they won't appear at all or they'll grow in straight. If not, welcome to the club. You may have to get them removed.

After your teens, you'll be less cavity prone. But the teeth you have should last a lifetime (that's seventy-four years for most women), so take care of them.

Hair Care

I hope you're happy with your hair. I'm pretty happy with mine. I wore it long in secondary school and I've had it short ever since. Mine is the wash-and-wear variety, but I understand the angst of those with less manageable hair. My college roommate got up hours before class to wash, dry and straighten her hair. And my mother stayed up late at night to wash, dry and curl hers.

Shall I tell you three stupid things I did with my hair when it was long? First and worst, I hunted in it for split ends – a waste of time and a good way to go cross-eyed. (Getting my mop chopped broke that habit in a hurry.) Second, I sprayed a bleach product in it when I was ten. Months later, when the brown roots grew in, my half-and-half hair looked cheap and unattractive. Third, I didn't know about brushing tangles out *before* shampooing or about using a conditioner, so I often emerged from the shower with a head full of sailor's knots. End of confessions.

How about you? Are you shampooing as frequently as you need to? Meryl Streep said that to be beautiful, 'You hold in your stomach a lot, and you just wash your hair a lot.' Shampoo short hair every day if necessary; shampoo long hair less often so you don't damage it.

Choose a suitable shampoo for dry, oily, regular, or damaged hair or for a dandruff problem. Then switch brands occasionally, because your hair may get used to a product and not come as clean the twentieth time as it did the first.

Why do the directions suggest you lather and rinse, then repeat the whole process? Because that way you'll use up the shampoo in a flash and quickly shell out another £1.25. Unless you let your hair get so greasy you could fry an egg in it (heaven forbid), one sudsing should suffice. Work up a lather in your hand before you apply it to your hair. If your hair is long or particularly dirty, go ahead and use a dab of shampoo for round two. Massage your scalp with fingertips, not nails. And be sure to get out all – all – the shampoo. Until your hair squeaks, don't hop out of the shower.

If you have dry, brittle, or damaged hair, you may want to use a conditioner. Combing your hair with a wide-tooth comb or brushing it with a straight brush with soft bristles and rounded tips will help, too, because that activates oil glands. Let your hair air-dry whenever possible.

When your hair is wet, don't brush it. Comb it with a wide-tooth comb. Keep combs and brushes clean by washing them with shampoo. Some hairs will fall out whenever you comb or brush. Don't worry unless you're losing lots of hair in chunks.

The following are foolproof ways to destroy your lovely locks:

- Braid strands so tightly they snap off at the hairline.
- Tug off curlers violently so hairs break.
- Blow-dry hair with high heat and no attachments between curls and red-hot wires.
- Get your hair permed or chemically straightened too often.
- Eat too much junk food.

I once asked a man who cuts hair, 'Do you think women look best in long or short hair?'

His answer: 'They look best in hair that is well styled and well kept up.'

But who can you trust with a pair of scissors? At hairdressing schools you can often get a cut and style for nothing, local salons may charge up to £10, and fancy city ones could cost £20 or more.

What's important is to look around until you find a stylist you like. If you admire a friend's cut, ask who did it and make an appointment. Once you're in the chair, trust the pro or speak your mind. Don't let anyone hack away a foot of hair while you save your tears for Mum. If you're happy with the job, remember the stylist's name and become a regular customer.

Don't hide behind your hair. Long hair needs to be trimmed every few months. Short hair, every six to eight weeks. Hair grows fastest in summer. Sounds expensive? Sometimes you can save money by shampooing at home or skipping the blow-dry. Call ahead and ask. Or have a competent friend do the job.

What about body hair?

About two years before your first period, your pubic hair probably started growing straight and fine at first, then coarser and darker. About six months before your first period, your underarm hair may have begun to appear. You may even have a few tiny hairs around your nipples.

Lots of young women don't get rid of the hair on their legs and underarms. If the hair doesn't bother you, don't bother it.

If you *do* want silky legs and smooth underarms in summer or all year long, you may want to start shaving. Once you begin, your hair won't grow back quite as fine as it was, so you may have to continue shaving.

Shaving is easy. Use a cream or soap and try not to nick yourself. I like disposable razors. If you're shaving in the tub, be sure to clean it afterwards so you won't leave a ring for the next person.

You could try an electric razor. (Not with wet legs or the experience would be shocking!)

Waxing is another alternative. You can buy a do-it-yourself product, or go to a salon, where it hurts less and costs more. The effect of waxing is long-lasting, and the technique is popular in Europe.

Using a depilatory cream such as Immac on your legs seems slow and messy to me, but that's another option.

Do you have a moustache? I do. Not a handlebar, but a noticeable nuisance nonetheless. Every so often, I have to cream the fine hairs off with depilatory cream. If you use one, make sure it's suitable for facial hair. It doesn't leave stubble or stimulate growth, and it beats five o'clock shadow!

Some women prefer bleach. I don't think much of white moustaches. You could wax it off (ouch) or, if the problem is serious, you might consider electrolysis. It's not cheap, but it is permanent because it destroys hair roots. Your doctor can recommend a practitioner. Don't expect overnight wonders. I know someone who has had electrolysis for four years now.

Ditto all the above for any other unwanted body hair: on your chin, belly button, thighs. If your eyebrows are very bushy, or if you have an almost-eyebrow between your eyes, you may want to tweeze or cream away those hairs. I knew a girl who looked as though she had one long eyebrow instead of two short ones. I didn't know her well enough to say so, but she would have looked prettier if she'd tweezed or dissolved the middle brow. I hope some close and gentle friend eventually made the suggestion, and I hope the girl was mature enough to say, not 'Mind your own business,' but 'Thanks for letting me know'.

Nice Nails

Modesty is fine, but it's crazy not to recognize and enjoy your good qualities – particularly if you're going to feel awful about one puny pimple or one unwanted hair.

That said, I hope you won't slam your book shut if I tell you straight out that I have nice nails. I didn't always, but I do now and I show them off by painting them vivid colours from cherry blossom to spiced apple.

The thing is, I bit my nails to the quick at school. The class creep once walked past me in the hall, jammed his hand upside down in his mouth, and pretended to gnaw – a cruel imitation of yours truly.

He made his point. Not only were my nails ugly, but the

nibbling habit itself was ugly.

I tried to quit. I tried bad-tasting polish. I tried wearing gloves during scary movies. I tried nail hardener. I taped my mouth shut while doing homework. I wore Elastoplasts on my stubs at night. But I didn't stop for good until my husband proposed to me.

Rob presented me with an antique diamond ring that had belonged to his grandmother. I couldn't wear such a beautiful ring on such an unsightly hand, so I dredged up all my willpower and kicked the habit.

If you're a biter, you don't have to get engaged to break the habit. When you're truly ready to quit, you'll quit.

Check your nails. Maybe you've never bitten, but are they looking their best? Are they ragged or uneven or dirty? Are they so long they look like claws? People *do* notice.

Use an emery board and file your nails in one direction only. If you want to polish them, start with a clear base coat. That strengthens them and keeps them from turning yellow if you use coloured polish. Let each coat dry thoroughly before applying the next coat. And make sure the polish on all ten nails stays on. No bare spots! (I often carry the bottle of polish I'm wearing tightly sealed in a plastic bag in my handbag.) Remove all old polish before applying a new colour, even if that means giving yourself a manicure every few days.

I don't think expensive polishes stay on any better than cheap ones. All polishes last longer if kept in the refrigerator.

If colourful nails don't appeal to you, skip the glass bottles and cotton-wool balls. I think polish is fun; you may think it's frivolous or only for special occasions.

Cosmetics and Clothes

A girl in my senior school, Vivian, always stood tall, wore chic, pulled-together clothes, did her make-up just right, and carried herself confidently. She assumed she was beautiful, and no one questioned her.

Looking through my old school photos, I see that she was pretty, but no prettier than Judy or Jen. Yet because Vivian made a point of looking her best, she glowed with self-assurance. She didn't come across as vain or affected. She came across as striking.

Attitude and self-esteem really are half the battle. Remember the song from *West Side Story*? 'I feel pretty, oh so pretty . . . ' Maria had the right idea. If you think pretty instead of mousy, others start thinking of you as pretty instead of mousy.

Positive thinking alone can't turn an ordinary girl into a Miss Perfect. But if you like yourself and play up your best features with make-up and clothes, everyone will think of you as beautiful. As Helena Rubenstein said, 'There are no ugly women, only lazy ones.'

Make-up is a remarkable option. Just consider the before/after faces you've seen in magazines, or how cosmetics made Julie Andrews look like a man in *Victor/Victoria* and Dustin Hoffman look like a woman in *Tootsie*. I didn't wear any make-up in my early teens and I rarely do now when I'm at home writing. But I love putting it on when I go out. A little brown eyeshadow, dark mascara, eyeliner, blush, lipstick – and abracadabra, I look and feel more glamorous! Face-painting is fast, creative, and, for me, one of the pleasures of being female.

Inexpensive make-up often works as well as the expensive stuff. Experiment, and throw make-up out when it gets runny or flaky or old. Don't borrow a friend's make-up. If your eyes or skin get irritated, try hypoallergenic varieties, such as Almay. Also beware of free make-up offers stores – the beautician will encourage you to spend thirty quid on supplies afterwards.

With make-up, less is more attractive, and the soft and subtle look prettiest, especially on young girls and especially during the day. You want people to think 'You look pretty', not 'You do your make-up well'. Study magazines and friends. And don't wear so much that you feel plain and frumpy without it. If you don't wear any, that's fine. Lots of boys prefer the natural look.

What about clothes? Do you have a passion for fashion? I can't afford to update my wardrobe every season, and I couldn't get away with gold lamé trousers anyway. (Where would I wear them?) But I like keeping an eye on mannequins, models and friends. I try to create new looks by playing up accessories – a shiny belt, round red earrings, a bracelet. Since I love flat, comfortable espadrilles I've bought them – at about a fiver a pair – in a rainbow of colours.

Keep your clothes clean and in good repair. Give things to charities each year and put summer clothes away in winter, and winter clothes away in summer.

Figure out what colours and styles are in vogue and look best on you, then try new combinations. Some clothes make me look dumpy, while others make me look slender. Dark colours flatter me, but pretty pastels wash me out. Accent your best figure feature with bright colours and play down your worst with dull ones. Trade clothes with friends; give and accept hand-me-downs. As you get to know yourself, you'll create your own style.

You project your personality and interests through clothes. Are you arty, punky, sporty? Show it! If you're a romantic, you may favour ruffles, tapestry and lace. If you're athletic, you may prefer tracksuits and casual clothes. Modern fashion says anything goes if it suits you. If you're shy, you'll feel awkward in a pink leather jacket and matching Mohican!

Looking like everybody else is fine, and safe, but why not learn to express yourself? With flair! With the right attitude, make-up and wardrobe, you can sparkle, and your individual fashion look needn't cost a lot, either. Even some famous pop stars shop at Oxfam and second-hand shops. If you visit the haberdashery departments of big stores, you'll often find remnants marked down. And if you're nifty with a needle, you can be the envy of mates who pay full price for items you stitch up for a song.

Even Beautiful Girls Get The Blues

Yes, there have been times when I'd have swapped my features for the face of a cover girl and my body for an actress's show-stopping curves. But those of us who haven't won any beauty contests should remember that those who have don't necessarily lead happier lives.

One of my old school pals is a model now, yet although black-haired green-eyed Danielle always looks terrific, she doesn't always feel terrific. She's not deluged by dates. (Are guys scared of her? Are her standards impossible? Do guys assume she's spoken for?) When they do call, Danielle wonders if they really care about her or if they're after sex or just want to show her off like a trophy.

Meanwhile she's already worrying about what she'll do in five years when her face-based career could come to a thudding halt.

Danielle has few girlfriends with whom to discuss her insecurities. 'When I meet a girl, I feel I have to bend over backwards being nice or she'll think I'm conceited.'

Her confession shamed me into realizing that when I meet a knockout beauty, I'm not always my most amiable. Part of me feels threatened and almost wants to believe that although she's stunning, she's also shallow, boring, or quick-tempered.

You may be more magnanimous. You may have no trouble immediately liking a girl who is gorgeous, brilliant, talented, rich, happy, and seemingly picture-perfect. If so, you deserve a *Saint* before your name. Most of us want to glimpse a filling in that dazzling smile. We want our goddesses to be human.

Another pitfall of being beautiful is that beauties are often judged by ridiculously high standards. Have you ever seen a famous film star in a magazine and instead of thinking, 'She looks exquisite,' thought, 'She's looked better' or 'She's not *that* amazing'? It must be tough knowing the pressure is on to look breathtaking day in and day out.

I'm not saying we should feel sorry for gorgeous women or assume *lovely* means *lonely*. But it's good to look at the flip side of beauty. Plus we Miss Averages try harder, and that usually means developing our personality and intelligence — traits that never fade.

Sleep Tight

Are you sleeping too little or too much? If I sleep less than six hours, I'm grumpy. More than ten, I'm groggy. Sleep is essential to keep your resistance up. But if you're sleeping away half the day or napping constantly, you may be using sleep as an escape mechanism. Insomnia, too, is often a sign that something is troubling you and needs to be talked out.

For most people, nodding off is not a problem. When it is? Skip the coffee, cola, tea, or chocolate at night because they contain caffeine, a stimulant. A cup of milk or camomile tea accompanied by a warm bath or not-for-school book is a more soothing choice for the wide awake. Don't take sleeping pills; they're addictive. And try to think of occasional insomnia as an opportunity: to do schoolwork, write in a diary, or read a short story.

When you're ready for bed, take off socks and underwear and put on a comfortable nightdress or pyjamas. Lie on your back on a firm mattress, ideally without a pillow or with a fairly flat pillow. In that position, your spine is aligned, none of your organs or limbs is squashed, and you won't wake up with a crick in your neck or your cheek all puckered with wrinkles from the sheets. Now breathe rhythmically from the bottom of your lungs through your nose. Imagine yourself floating. Tell your muscles to relax, one by one. Drift. Zzzzz. . . .

Glandular Fever: A Teenage Disease

In my first year at college, my motto was: Work hard, play hard. For two months, I got up at 7:30, went full steam until dinner, studied until 9:30, partied until 1:30. Late to bed and early to rise proved unhealthy and unwise and was the start of my demise!

To put it more succinctly: I got glandular fever.

It was a cold November, I was run-down, I hadn't been wearing my hat or gloves, and I'd been ignoring a sore throat. The lymph glands in my neck began to swell, and I remember watching somebody jog (my sport!) and thinking, 'How can he have so much energy?' I went for a blood test, and my fear was confirmed.

My case of infectious mononucleosis, the medical name for glandular fever, was diagnosed early, but there are no magic-cure pills. 'Get plenty of rest and sleep and eat a balanced diet,' was all the doctors could recommend. 'Avoid contact sports, because if you rupture your spleen, you're in big trouble.'

I took it very easy for a week and felt better fast. But some cases knock people out for months.

Glandular fever is still a mysterious viral illness. Anybody can contract it, but teenagers and people in their early twenties are most susceptible. Although it's been called the kissing disease, you can get it without kissing, and it's not as contagious as you might suspect. It's more contagious in the incubation stage (before it's diagnosed) than afterwards.

If you've had glandular fever once, you are unlikely to get it again. Let's hope you don't get it at all.

Whenever you have bizarre symptoms, take them seriously. It's easy to make a doctor's appointment. Don't let anyone call you a hypochondriac when *you're* the one who is hurting. Maybe the doctor will say 'It's nothing, false alarm', but then your mind will be at ease. Or maybe all you have is a common cold and need to be reminded to rest, drink plenty of fluids, gargle with salt water, and take medication. Or maybe your stomach or head hurts due to stress and not physical factors. Fine. Psychosomatic bellyaches still ache, so it's important to know you may need not an antacid, but to start untying the knots.

I try to take as few pills as possible. When I do take them, I follow directions carefully. Don't just swallow a pill. Down it with plenty of water.

In the *Sex* chapter, I'll tell you all about sexually transmitted diseases. Illnesses not commonly associated with sex or teenagers aren't covered in this book. If you don't have diabetes, epilepsy, anaemia, asthma, or any other disease, count your blessings. If you do, follow your doctor's advice and take extra good care of yourself. You, too, have many blessings to count.

Disabilities

Just as we often take our youth and health for granted we often take our 'normal' bodies and minds for granted.

Millions of people aren't so fortunate. Some have slight dyslexia, a treatable reading disability. Others have severe cerebral palsy. Others are paraplegic. Others are deaf or blind. Others . . . well, the list could go on and on.

I'm not suggesting we thank our lucky stars each day for our twenty fingers and toes and our ability to wiggle them – although that's not a bad idea. I am saying we should remember to treat disabled people with respect, not with condescending courtesy, unwelcome pity, cruel teasing, or grudging avoidance. Too many people act as though disabilities were contagious and all disabled persons were also retarded or unfeeling.

As Ted Kennedy, Jr, who lost his right leg to cancer, eloquently put it, 'Disabled people are not unable people. . .we are people first and disabled second.'

If someone is deaf and can lip read, don't shout. Face the person, speak slowly, and enunciate well. If someone is blind and hesitating at an intersection, don't grab the person's arm. Offer help without insisting. If you're baby-sitting for a little girl and she points and says, 'Why is that boy in a wheelchair?' don't scold the child. It's natural for her to be curious. Tell her it's impolite to point, but give her an answer. 'Maybe because of an accident or an illness or because he was born with weak legs. He uses the wheelchair to get around.' If you yank the child away and make her feel uncomfortable, you're reinforcing the idea that disabled people should be shunned.

Have you ever been with a friend who has parked in a space reserved for the handicapped, then got out limping and giggling? To someone else, the convenience of the space is not a laughing matter. I'm for finding another parking place and being glad you're able to walk the extra yards.

If you are or have recently become disabled, it's bound to be very hard at times to accept your limitations and society's prejudices. I hope you'll ultimately concentrate on what you *can* do and not get bogged down in what you can't. Whatever your handicap, social services and the various national charity organizations are there to advise and assist you. PHAB (Physically Handicapped and Able-bodied) run all kinds of courses and activities which handicapped and able-bodied people can join in together. PHAB, The Spastics Society, the National Deaf Children's Society and the Royal National Institute for the Blind *see pages 280–281* will all offer good, constructive advice about work and social life.

To quote Ted Kennedy Jr again, 'It is not that people are handicapped. It's that they're physically and mentally challenged.'

Speaking Of Body Language

Ever notice the ads that show before/after shots of women who have supposedly lost weight, increased their bust size or got rid of pimples and varicose veins? In the before pose, they're slouching and frowning. In the after photo, they're standing tall and smiling. No wonder they look better! That's what body language is all about.

If you look around you in a crowded railway station, you can make some fairly accurate guesses about people by 'reading' their bodies. You can't know how they feel about a nuclear freeze, but you may be able to tell how they feel about each other.

Imagine that on one bench you see a man and a woman with two feet of space and two briefcases between them. They're reading with their legs crossed in opposite directions. Are they friends, business partners, relatives, strangers?

If you guessed strangers, you're probably right.

How about the couple on the next bench? They're talking, smiling, looking into each other's eyes. He brushes her hair with his fingers; she gives his arm a squeeze.

Chances are they started dating recently. If they'd just met, they'd be less forward; if they were married, they'd indulge in less PDA (public display of affection).

The twist is that if you can figure out facts about people just by tuning in to how they sit, stand, touch, or move, they can do the same about you.

Body language can speak louder than words. A wink can start a romance and a hug can stop a quarrel.

My mother always nagged me to – ready? – stand up straight, pull back my shoulders, tuck my behind in, not wrinkle my forehead, not swing my arms too much as I walked, look people squarely in the eye, and shake hands firmly without fracturing fingers. My response was usually an exasperated polysyllabic 'Oh, Muh,uh,uhmmm!' but now I'm grateful. Because I learned to look confident, people started treating me as though I were confident, and I began to feel confident.

Do you have teachers who move and gesture while they lecture? You probably pay more attention to them than to the ones who sit behind the desk, arms folded, shoulders drooping. Teachers can tell if you're fascinated or bored by whether you're leaning forward attentively or slumping and drawing on your shoe. So sit up – your marks may go up, too.

Caution: you can't always read strangers correctly, because body language varies somewhat from person to person and culture to culture. For example, some people look down to show respect rather than maintaining eye contact. And Continental teenagers do more hugging and cheek-kissing than we do.

Or consider the limp handshake. I used to teach English to a charming Japanese woman who had just moved to America. Yoko bowed beautifully but shook hands about as energetically as an old Labrador. One day we worked on it. Now Yoko can shake as well as a politician – and I can bow!

No matter where you are, you probably want your body to show that you are warm, open, and amiable. Unless you insist on being centre stage and gesticulating wildly, or on clinging to dark corners and standing tense and immobile, you probably aren't closing out anybody. If you think your body doesn't register as friendly, relax and smile so others feel welcome. You'll start meeting new people and making new friends. Speaking of which, let's move on to the *Friendship* chapter, shall we?

2. Friendship

You Don't Like Everybody; Why Should Everybody Like You?

The phrase 'just friends' makes little sense to me: friendship should never be trivialized.

It takes time and effort to make new friends and keep old ones. It's not easy to overcome shyness, listen to someone else's troubles, phone or write when you're busy, get together with the girls when you'd rather spend time with a guy. But it's worth it. I don't collect coins, stamps, or china cats, but I guess I collect people. Friends are one of the staples of my life.

Friends congratulate and console, heighten pleasure and ease pain. Judy sent a bouquet of flowers when my publishers offered me the chance to write this book. And I was matron of honour at her joyful wedding. Jen drove for miles to be with me after my father died. And we talked for days after she broke up with a man she loved.

You can get by without being popular; you can live without a boyfriend; you can survive without one particular best friend. But if you have no friends, you're missing out. After all, a friend who likes you teaches you to like yourself. Friends exchange the gift of self-confidence. This chapter is about making lasting friendships with girls and guys and, most vital, making friends with yourself.

Girlfriends Last Longer Than Boyfriends

I'm not knocking romance or saying that you can't be friends with an ex-boyfriend, or marry your first love. But chances are that, in ten years' time, you'll still be in touch with some of your current girlfriends, whereas the guys in your life now will be in someone else's life by then.

In secondary school, I spent thousands of hours with a terrific green-eyed curly-haired boyfriend. Today we exchange Christmas cards every few years. I also spent endless afternoons with Judy and Jen. Today, though we live in different cities, they are still my close friends.

Same thing happened in college. I dated Chris, Walter, Steve, Bruce, Ray – lots of guys, lots of fun. But most of the college boyfriends I keep up with are the ones I never kissed. Meanwhile, the girls I knew in classes, dormitories, and dining rooms are still my friends. When Helen, Ellen, Amy, Sonia, and I got together at a class reunion recently, we had a great time.

Don't turn down dates. But be aware that your summer loves may not last until autumn, whereas the friendships you make with other girls now may last a lifetime.

Ten Ways To Make Friends

You'd like to make friends and widen your social circle? Don't just stand there – smile, laugh, talk, listen, ask, whisper, admire! As Ralph Waldo Emerson said, 'The only way to have a friend is to be one.'

---

1 **Work out whom you want to be friends with and why.** If you want to be friends with Melanie because she's popular or Sandy because she's pretty, it will probably be more difficult and less rewarding than if you want to be friends with Sue because you both love to write, or Barbara because you're both into hiking. Your future friends are the people with whom you share interests.

You can also learn by observing the people you want to know better. Why do you wish Lois were your friend? If it's because she is always 'up' or funny or considerate, then cultivate those traits in yourself.

2 **Get involved with spare-time activities.** If you're interested in sports, join the local tennis club or sports centre. If you're interested in politics, join the student council and meet the politicians. Stars in your eyes? Try out for the school play. If you don't make it, don't stay home. Help with sets or lights or props or programmes.

By being active and on the go, you keep meeting people, and you stay busy and interesting. Besides, someone who is enthusiastic about lots of projects usually makes better company than someone whose main spare-time activity is sitting around. So don't spread yourself too thin, but don't sit there like a blob of mayonnaise.

3 **Introduce yourself and remember names.** Don't wait for someone to make formal introductions or for a person to decide he or she would like to meet you. March right up and say hello. When I say, 'Hi, I'm Carol,' to a girl I've never met, she doesn't give me a funny look. She says hi back.

I wasn't born with a skill for remembering names. But I've learned to be good at it. It's easy. When someone introduces herself, listen to her name and repeat it: 'Glad to meet you, Janice.' A few sentences later, use her name again: 'Janice, where are you from?' Make a point of catching the name the first time, and you won't forget it so quickly.

Some people try to remember names by associating them with the person. Jim is slim, Toby is tubby. Whether you remember names by paying attention in the first place or by using an elaborate mnemonic device, it's a knack you should acquire a.s.a.p.

What if you say 'Hi, Tim,' in the canteen and Tim doesn't remember your name? He may feel embarrassed as he mumbles an unadorned 'hi'. But he may also rush to ask his friends who that friendly girl is.

4 **Master the art of conversation.** Don't you hate it when you're in the middle of telling a story and someone

interrupts? You're describing your date with Roger to see the *Casablanca/Play It Again, Sam* double bill. 'No sooner did the lady behind the counter hand me my popcorn,' you say, 'than I slipped and spilled it! Roger turned around and – ' Then some loudmouth butts in, '*Play It Again, Sam?* I saw that! Woody Allen is fantastic! I was just reading this interview. . . '

You'll make friends faster if you let people finish their sentences and thoughts. Let them talk, and listen to what they're saying. If someone says she just got back from holiday, don't immediately chime in, 'So did I.' Ask, 'How was it?' 'Where'd you go?' If she says she went pony-trekking in the Welsh mountains, don't say 'Huh'. Encourage her to tell you about it by nodding, looking her in the eye, asking questions requiring more than a yes/no answer, saying 'Really?' and peppering her paragraph with 'That's amazing,' and 'How incredible'. What if that same loudmouth Woody Allen fan interrupts her story? Wait till the interrupter has finished, then invite her to pick up where she left off by saying, 'So what *did* you do when the horse bolted?'

People like to talk about themselves, and a good listener is always appreciated. Besides, you learn more by listening than by talking.

That doesn't mean you should act as if you'd been struck dumb. But just as unpunctuated sentences don't thrill your English teacher, non-stop chitchat won't win you instant pals. If you're sparing no details ('Last Friday, or maybe it was Thursday, I'm not sure, anyway, Robin and I went to that seaside place, you know the one with the pier that's really long, anyway, so he goes, "I like this place," so I go, "It is pretty," and he goes, "Yeah," and we looked at the clouds – there was this one that looked exactly like a scoop of vanilla ice-cream. . . '), you're boring somebody. Beware, too, of talking too much about yourself. (Have you heard the joke that defines an egotist as someone who is me-deep in conversation?)

The ideal conversation should be divided into half listening, half talking. If you tend to be too quiet, force yourself to speak up more in class and at meals. You don't have to expound on the politics of Latin America, but say something. Promise yourself that every day you will hold a brief conversation with at least one girl, guy, teacher, someone at the bus stop, or someone you hardly know. A little shyness can be endearing, but if you're *too* timid, some will misinterpret your shyness as snobbery. Worse, you aren't meeting people. Yet you have nothing to hide. You have as much to offer as the bolder kids – who sometimes feel anxious, too.

5 **Develop charm**. Is charm something you're born with? Not necessarily. If your father is a Lord somebody-or-other and your mother is a French film star, the odds are in your favour. But anyone can learn to be irresistibly charming, to both guys and girls.

Charm is empathy with style. It's making sure no one feels left out. It's telling your friend's parents that their home looks like it belongs in *Ideal Homes* (if it is well decorated) or saying that you've never tasted such fabulous apple pie (if it is truly delicious). It's offering a hand when needed. It's being supportive instead of sarcastic. It's answering, 'Are these jeans too tight?' with 'I think your other pair is more flattering,' rather than 'God, you've put on weight!' It's helping someone get his foot out of his mouth instead of laughing at his *faux pas*. It's apologizing when it was your fault. And when it wasn't, it's saying, 'I don't think I explained this very well,' instead of, 'I can't believe you messed it up!' It's giving a guy the benefit of the doubt. It's making a girl feel good by tuning in, drawing her out, and showing with and without words that you are enjoying her company. It's listening to the end of a story when you realize no one else is. It's laughing at someone's joke even when it wasn't funny.

As you first practise charm, you may feel phoney or manipulative or as though you're trying too hard. But soon it should feel more natural and become more genuine.

People like people who like them. So if you find someone you like, and you project that fondness or respect, you have a head start on turning a stranger into a friend.

6 **Give and get compliments graciously.** Flattery may not get you everywhere, but it won't hurt in your quest for friends. When you admire something, say so. Everybody loves a sincere compliment, so learn to praise generously. 'What a great necklace!' 'Your handwriting is so neat.' 'Our netball team would be nothing without you.' 'You drive really well.' 'You have the sunniest smile.' Hardly anyone would greet a warm compliment with a cold shoulder.

If you want yours to have extra impact, pay tribute to something that usually goes unnoticed. If you ran into Paul Newman buying a cheese sandwich at the ABC bakery, you wouldn't make an impression with 'You have the bluest eyes'. Same principle with classmates. Yet you'd be surprised at how delighted the local cross-country champion would be if you told him he has a beautiful voice. (Don't be insincere. False flattery will endear you to nobody.)

You're not a compliment butcher, are you? Some people mean well but their compliments come out back-handed, so instead of sowing the seeds of friendship, they're paving the path of animosity. I once made the mistake of telling a girl, 'You've lost a ton of weight!' instead of simply 'You look wonderful.' My slim would-be friend looked more grim than grateful.

Other gems to avoid: 'Your complexion looks clear today.' 'Your hair looks so shiny – you must have washed it.' 'This is really tasty; you didn't cook it yourself, did you?'

And when the tables turn? Do you accept compliments gracefully? If a guy says, 'I like your shirt,' do you immediately say, 'I like yours, too'? Do you gasp,

'You're kidding, I've had it for centuries'? Do you explain, 'I picked it up for 50p at a jumble sale in the Scout hall'? The best way to accept a compliment is to smile and say, 'Thank you.' If you like, you can add, 'It's nice of you to say so.'

Beware of fishing for compliments – you might come up with a boot!

7 **Don't rush it.** Friendship at first sight? Could be shaky. You'll hit it off with some people instantly, and you'll click with others fairly fast, but friendships, like plants, take time to grow. Some friendships that are quickly made quickly fade.

If you try to hurry a friendship, you may come off as pushy or too heavy and intense. If you ask dozens of questions, you may seem nosy instead of friendly. Don't be too modest, but if you blow your own trumpet too loudly or launch into your life story too soon, you'll sound like you're in a job interview instead of a social situation.

I remember having lunch in college with a friend named John. The subject was mountains, and he was telling our table about how he'd climbed Mount Kilimanjaro. I was so impressed I nearly fell off my chair. Not only had John scaled such heights, but he had never mentioned it before. If John had described the same feat when we'd first met, I would have been impressed, yes, but I might also have thought, 'What a show-off' or 'What a name-dropper' or 'I bet he couldn't wait to get that in.'

So take your time making friends.

8 **Be willing to risk rejection**. Just as you don't like everybody, everybody won't like you. Some people just aren't going to be as amicable as others. Their loss.

In the meantime, be known for your niceness. If you hide in a shell, you won't meet anybody, let alone cultivate friendships. Open up, be visible, take a chance. State your real views, not what you think will make you accepted. Then if Brenda acts snooty, you wouldn't want to be her mate anyway. (Who wants snooty friends?) If she's nice, it was worth the risk.

Is everybody gossiping about you behind your back? Probably not. When you get right down to it, it's egotistical to think your personality is a hot topic of debate. And what if the lunch table *does* discuss you the second you get up to leave? Relax. If you're a warm, caring person, you have no reason to worry. What they're saying may be all good. As Oscar Wilde put it, 'There is only one thing worse in the world than being talked about and that is not being talked about.'

9 **Arm yourself with zest and zeal.** Charlie Brown is a lovable loser, but most of us gravitate to winners. When I ask an acquaintance, 'How are you?' and she grunts about backaches, allergies, and fights with her sister, it doesn't make me want to join her for a bike ride. Snarls and complaints won't help you make friends.

If you are depressed, share it with your family and close friends, but try not to take it out on people you scarcely know. I remember one guy in school who never smiled. I'd say, 'How's it going?' and he'd shrug and sigh. I'm not proud to admit it, but I never did make the effort to find out what was bugging him.

You don't want to come across as little Suzy Sunshine. But if you act happy and confident for two days and say an audible, positive 'hello' to lots of new faces, you may be amazed to find they'll cheerfully greet you back. Next thing you know, you'll be *feeling* happier, and the smiles will come on their own.

10 **Give parties.** One way I made friends after moving to a new town was to give parties. When word is out that you're throwing a party, near-strangers start falling all over themselves to become your pre-party bosom buddies. Of course you see through them. But at least you are all taking the time to get to know each other.

What kind of party should you give, invitation only or open house? Find out what your parents will allow.

How about an American-style slumber party with eight or ten girls? It's fun to tell ghost stories and raid the refrigerator. If everyone brings her own sleeping bag, it shouldn't be too much trouble. Or invite the guys to a pot-luck dinner or brunch. These don't require much preparation. Tell one guest to bring the bread, another to bring dessert, another to bring hors d'oeuvres, and so on. You can provide the main course (inexpensive spaghetti? bake-ahead quiches?), and everyone can join in the washing-up.

Other ideas include barbecues, picnics and get-togethers that wind up at the cinema, swimming pool, skating rink or sports centre. How about playing charades, or Trivial Pursuit? Theme parties are fun, too. That's when you're supposed to wear only black and white, or all come as someone out of *Crossroads* or *Dallas*, or all dress as tramps or vicars. If you have friends who like to bake, you could give a cake and biscuit party where everyone brings a different kind that they've made, samples some of everyone else's, then takes home a small assortment. If you and your friends have clothes you are tired of, you can give a clothes-swapping party – why not?

Don't wait for someone else to give a party and then hope that Steve, Maggie and Tony show up and talk to you. Draw up the invitation list yourself.

The Pursuit of Popularity

For a long time, all I wanted was to be popular. No such luck. The Rothman twins and their trendy circle did me the favour of talking to me, but I was never important to them. Wanting to get in with them and not succeeding was lousy for my ego, but thank heavens Judy talked some sense into my head.

'What's so great about the Rothman twins?' she wanted to know.

'They're popular,' seemed like a pretty feeble answer, but I gave it to her anyway.

'The masses look up to them. Big deal! They may be perfectly wonderful, but they've never been wonderful to you. With all the nice people out there, I can't believe you're hung up on them. Will it damage your reputation if you are seen with less popular people? Will it injure your image? I swear, Carol, sometimes your values make me ill.'

At this point, I'd usually want to tell her to shut up. But Judy was a genuine friend who knew me thoroughly and liked me anyway. And she had a point. Since the most popular crowd wasn't spending time worrying about me, it was pretty crazy for me to spend time worrying about them.

If you are popular, congratulations. If not, relish your close friends and try not to care about the others. It may help to realize that popularity has a flip side. Sure it must be fun to be a trend-setting centre of attention. But some popular girls actually feel cramped by their clique of admiring cronies.

Melissa, a college friend, told me about the disadvantages of being popular. She said she felt terrible when she was elected class prefect because she knew her opponent cared more about school issues. 'And there were sides of me the girls never knew. Since they liked me because I was funny, I felt I always had to be "on". If I was depressed, I couldn't cry. Sometimes it was as if I didn't have any friends.' Melissa sighed. 'I'd be lying if I said I didn't enjoy feeling liked and important. But it made the transition to college hard. No one here knew they were supposed to treat me as someone special. I was just another student – except that I was full of myself.'

Your Friends Don't All Have To Like Each Other

One advantage of not belonging to a clique or the clique is that you can have many diverse friends to suit your multi-faceted personality. It used to bother me that Judy and Jen didn't like one another as much as I liked each of them. But they had friends whom I didn't take to, either. And why not?

It also struck me as odd that during the school holidays, I'd write such varied letters to my friends. Gossip about tasty guys to Nancy. Pontification about the meaning of life to Norma. Was I being phony? Was I being the person each wanted me to be rather than the person I was? No; I had chosen several friends for my several selves. Different people bring out different sides of us.

So if your friends Mary and Emily are incompatible, see them separately. It doesn't matter if Lynn doesn't understand what you see in Julie. If she criticizes you for making plans with Julie, examine her motives. Critical people are often insecure. Is she jealous or worried you'll stop being as close to her? Reassure her that you value her friendship as much as ever. Maybe Lynn's concern is that Julie may be a bad influence – she sleeps around, or takes drugs. Decide for yourself whether she's right or not, and whether to heed her warning.

When friends of yours meet any of your other good friends, increase the chances of their taking to each other by making introductions that open up topics of conversation between them. Say, 'Mary, I'd like you to meet Liz – she's a nature lover, too.' P.S. Don't be so worried about whether everyone else is having a good time that you're not having a good time yourself. If your friends see that you're tense, they'll feel strained, too.

Can A Guy Be A Friend?

Sure. It may be hard to be friends with an ex-boyfriend, yet it's easy to have other guys as friends. Your friendships with Eddie at work, Pete next door, or your friend's brother Stephen are probably fun in their own right, and they also help you feel comfortable with guys in general and give you inside insights into the male psyche.

My friend Gilbert and I went to films, plays, meals and parties together. We didn't flirt; we talked. We didn't worry about the impression we were making or if our hair was sticking up; we were at ease with each other. I could discuss some subjects more easily with him than with girls, and I felt safer going to some places with him than with girls. I'm now married and Gilbert is engaged, but we're friends for good.

Some of the best romances start as platonic friendships, but if you suddenly find you're smitten by a boy who has always been just a friend, proceed with caution. Why? Because if the fling doesn't work out, it's hard to go back to being friends again afterwards. (R.J. and I got along great until I had to go and kiss him. After that, we felt awkward and the friendship – maybe not as solid as I had imagined? – fizzled out). If a guy you think of as a friend has a one-way crush on you, try to drop gentle hints about your other romantic interests and don't make a big deal of his changing feelings. His crush may pass. His friendship can endure. If he doesn't take the hint and continues to be more flirtatious than friendly, you may have to spell it out – but do it as kindly as you can.

You may sometimes feel jealous of your male friend's girl-friends, and he may envy your dates. Make time for each other. Your mutual friendship can outlast your separate romances.

Fights And Friends

Even the best of friends argue. That's fine. It's better to express resentment openly than to let hostility build up. But it's also better to lose an argument than to lose a friend. And no matter how solid a relationship is, it's still fragile if it's not handled with care.

If you fail an exam or miss out on a job you've been inter-viewed for, you may feel very angry. Don't take it out on your chums, thinking they'll love you no matter what. Don't say, 'I hate the way you flirt with every bloke who comes by' if what you mean is 'I'm so angry I failed my exam'. Instead, share your frustration. Too many people blow up at friends and family when their rage stems from an entirely different source.

What if you are genuinely peeved at a friend? What if Jill made plans with you and cancelled at the last minute, and it's not the first time she's let you down?

You could proclaim, 'You take me for granted.' But Jill might say, 'I do not.' You could insist, 'You always stand me up or come two hours late.' But Jill might counter, 'I've never once been two hours late.' She'll be right, you'll be wrong; she'll have learned nothing, you'll be madder than ever.

A smarter approach would be to address the issue as specifically, tactfully, and rationally as possible. Don't weaken your case with a generality and don't lose your case with an overstatement. Say, 'Jill, next time we do something, I'd appreciate it if you turned up – on time. It hurts me that I seem to take our plans more seriously than you do.'

Keep your voice down, talk slowly, say 'I . . . ' instead of 'You . . . ' (that sounds less accusatory) and mix positive with negative. Instead of lashing out at her, say, 'Your friendship means a lot to me; that's why I feel hurt when you seem not to care. It's also why I was glad two weeks ago when you got to my place for tea on time.'

At the end of an argument, give each other a hug. If you can't – because you're still fuming – then keep thrashing things out.

Whenever you're unleashing anger, less is more. A boyfriend and I once agreed to meet outside the door of a concert hall, but I ran into a pal and went ahead inside as he parked the car. It turned out that by the time he'd found a parking space and looked for me, the concert had begun and he couldn't get in. When I met him later, I sheepishly asked, 'Are you mad?' He could have blasted me non-stop for twenty minutes. Instead he simply said, 'No. Disappointed.' I felt one inch high.

Are you and your friend disagreeing about which movie to see? Compromise. See her choice this week, yours next week. Are you becoming competitive? Talk it out; strive to outdo yourselves, not each other. Are you on opposite sides politically? Don't shout, 'I can't believe you think that!' Say, 'I feel differently.' You don't have to agree on everything; you're friends, not clones.

Do you give in too easily? Some girls back down and beg forgiveness when they have done nothing wrong. Don't be belligerent, but don't apologize for breathing or sob at the first sign of a confrontation. Assert yourself!

Before *you* start a fight, have your facts straight. Before you explode, 'Why didn't you invite me to your birthday party?' be sure your invitation isn't in the post.

Eleanor Roosevelt said, 'Nobody can make you feel inferior without your consent.' When someone insults or teases you, don't fight or cry or raise your voice – that's his or her intent.

Ignore the comment or ask, 'Why do you need to put others down to bolster yourself?' It's usually best to fight fire with water. Later you can decide whether his or her 'Your breath could kill a herd of hippos' was pure maliciousness or whether you should invest in a mouthwash.

What about when you're the one who's in the wrong? Did you spread a secret when you should have kept your trap shut? It's too late to clean up that mess, but don't make matters worse by starting a cold war. Have it out. Your friend has a right to be upset. Listen and accept the blame. You could protest, 'I didn't know it was such a deep dark secret.' But should you have known? Rather than be self-righteous, admit your mistake and apologize sincerely. (By the way, while you'll win an audience if you gossip, you'll win respect if you don't. And secret-keepers get a bonus: you wouldn't believe all the juicy gossip I hear since friends know I'm close-lipped.)

In college, some friends and I once talked and played music until five one morning. The next day the girl on the other side of the thin walls told me she'd slept terribly. She was about to launch into a tirade about how rude and selfish we'd been, but I disarmed her (saving her lungs, my ears, and our rapport) by pleading guilty. 'It was rude and selfish of us. I apologize, and it won't happen again.' I made sure it didn't.

Friendship means sometimes having to say you're sorry.

Staying Friends

Can you remain close when your friend moves or goes to college? Absolutely. Samuel Butler said, 'Friendship is like money, easier made than kept.' Yet with a little effort, friendship *can* be forever. My family moved when I was eleven, so I could no longer sleep at Debbie's once a week, but I managed to keep up with her, and we still see each other often. When I left new schoolfriends to study in France, I made *amis* abroad but stayed in touch with mates at home. In college, I made more friends, again without losing important old ones.

Obviously I've let go of lots of peripheral pals over the years. And lots have let go of me. (Some people want to leave their past behind.) But it's not that hard to stay friends for keeps if you want to.

How do you stay close? You show that you continue to care. You may someday run into a long-lost friend and simply pick up where you left off. But usually you'll want to keep up the communication while you're apart – and not just on birthdays.

Write letters. It's not a chore; it's fun. Scribble a note when you have a free moment, or after a date when you're too keyed up to go to sleep. Tell your friend what you've been up to and how you've been feeling. Send photos and news of mutual pals. Keeping up a correspondence often strengthens friendships. Some people can express on paper what they repress in person. For instance, it can be easier to write 'Sue, I miss you' than to say it. Plus, petty aggravations don't get in the way of long-distance friendships. So send a card every so often. It takes less time, money, and energy than you'd ordinarily be spending on each other. Writing may also help you sort out your feelings about the way things are going. Don't be super-rigid about who owes whom a letter. It won't hurt you to send an extra missive, but it could hurt your friendship if you both keep silent just because you've lost track of whose turn it is.

I have a few postcard pals. Writing a postcard takes three minutes and costs next to nothing. You don't have to fuss with an envelope, and you can pack in piles of news. Why not make a pact with a faraway friend to exchange frequent postcards? Liven up the deal by agreeing to send the craziest, prettiest or silliest ones you can find, or stick to a favourite theme, like dogs, or sunsets.

Another alternative is to send a cassette tape. That takes longer and works only if you both have a tape recorder. But hearing your friend's voice is the heart-warming pay-off.

Maybe you can visit each other at weekends or during the holidays. Expect some changes – and late-night catching up.

And how about the telephone? You could call each other at set times, say every other Saturday morning or the first of every month. The danger is the bill. Call at night, at weekends, or during other not-too-expensive times, and keep it brief.

Telephone Tactics

How true is the stereotype? Do teenage girls and telephones really stick together like Superglue? When I remember how Judy and I tied up the line for hours (we lived right next door to each other) and how Jen used to call me where I was baby-sitting and sometimes the Matthews wouldn't have left yet and Dr Matthews would answer and Jen, the chicken, would hang up – well, I still blush to think of it.

You may be spending over a thousand hours on the telephone during the next few years alone. So follow these telephone tips. And use the phone book.

1 After you dial, let the phone ring at least eight times. The person may be in the bathroom or on another line. (Don't you hate it when you bash your shin on the coffee table while lungeing for the phone – only to hear the dialling tone?)

2 Say, 'Hello, may I please speak to Peggy?' or 'Hello, Mrs Williams. This is Carol Weston. May I speak with Peggy, please?' It's more polite than 'Is Peggy there?'

3 Don't play guessing games. Introduce yourself immediately. Unless your name is unusual, give your last name, too. I know lots of Johns, and it is embarrassing when I'm not sure which one I'm talking to from the start. Even when I phone my aunt, I'll say my full name because she probably isn't expecting to hear from me and she may know other Carols. If I'm talking to an editor, I may even identify myself beyond my name. 'Hello. This is Carol Weston. I sent you the article on werewolves . . . ?'

4 If the person you called sounds rushed, ask, 'Did I catch you in the middle of something?' or 'Do you have a minute?'

5 In your lowest, least shrill voice, chat. Pretty voices are
   more pleasant than dull or squeaky ones. You're concerned with the way you look and smell; give equal time
   to the way you sound.

6 If you're talking on the phone, talk on the phone. Don't
   watch TV or grill sausages at the same time. I hate it
   when someone phones me, then bangs around in the
   kitchen. I want to believe the person called to converse,
   not to make a chore go faster. At least I'd like the caller to
   be candid about it – then I can grab my nail polish or do
   my dishes. (And don't eat or chew gum on the phone,
   either. It sounds terrible on the other end.)

7 After you've talked, don't say, 'I gotta go now.' Say,
   'Well, it's been nice talking to you; I'll see you on
   Monday' or 'I'd better let you go but thanks for helping
   me with my homework.' (If the caller won't get off the
   line, say, 'Well, Shirley, thanks for calling' or 'I won't
   keep you' or 'I'm glad you phoned, and I look forward to
   seeing you at Laura's.')

8 When you first answer a call, make your *hello* sound
   cheerful even if you're feeling foul. If it's not for you,
   take the caller's number and message, and *write it down*.
   That way your family won't mind taking messages for
   you. (You *do* have pen and pad by the phone, don't
   you?)

9 Does your friend's family have an answering machine?
   Don't crack up or hang up. Just say, 'This is Katie Evans
   on 444-4444. I'd like Deborah to return my call when she
   has a chance.'

10 Don't let an unknown caller know when you're alone.
   Say, 'My father can't come to the phone right now; may I
   take a message?'

11 What time to make a phone call? Never at mealtimes, or
   too late at night, which usually means not after ten.
   And, if you're ever calling a friend in another country,

remember to consider the time difference. (Consider the cost, too. International calls are expensive!)

12 Don't be caught out telling a lie. In this era of technology, if you say, 'I called all weekend,' to a person with an answering machine, your honesty will be distinctly suspect.

13 If you ever get repeated obscene or nuisance phone calls, tell your parents if possible. If not, report it to the operator, who will then intercept your calls in the hope of putting the crank off. British Telecom have a leaflet telling you what to do about crazy callers. It's available from your Area Manager.

Being A Good Guest

I remember when my friend Debbie's mother invited me for dinner. 'We're having liver,' she said. I told you how I feel about liver in Chapter 1, and there was no way I was going to subject myself to such a meal. But did I have the guts or know-how to decline graciously? I did not.

Within earshot of Debbie's family, I called home and said, 'Dad, the Kirks invited me to dinner, can I stay?'

'Certainly,' said my father.

'Oh c'mon, just for dinner,' I wheedled.

'I said you could,' my father replied, slightly bewildered.

'Pleeeease, Dad? . . . Well OK then, could you pick me right up?' Fortunately my father figured out my ploy and within minutes was in front of Debbie's, tooting his horn. But there are easier ways to wriggle out of a dinner invitation.

A simple 'I can't tonight, Mrs Kirk, but thank you, I appreciate the invitation and I'd love to stay some other time' would have done nicely. Parents love that kind of courtesy.

Whether you are accepting or declining an invitation, always say thank you. And if you have spent the weekend at a friend's house, write a quick note afterwards to her parents. The longer you put off writing the thank-you note, the better the letter must be.

Do you want to be a good guest? Here's how:

1 If you'll be spending a few days with a family, bring a gift: a box of chocolates, pretty soaps, a plant, a book, or something you've made yourself, perhaps. If visiting from the country, you could bring some local honey, home-grown fruit or veg, or flowers; if you hail from the city, bring goodies from a French bakery, or an Italian deli. Local specialities like Devonshire or Cornish cream, or shortbread, are another idea. If you're good with a camera, you might take some pictures during your stay and send them copies afterwards.

2 Don't be painfully shy with your friend's parents. Try to start a conversation by complimenting your hostess on the food, or something in her home such as a picture or an ornament: 'What beautiful flowers! Are they lilies?'

3 Offer to help wash and dry the dishes.

4 Make your bed and be as neat as possible in the bathroom.

5 Mind your manners (napkin in your lap, don't start eating until the hostess does, use the outside fork first, break your bread and butter it piece by piece, don't slurp your hot soup or tea . . .)

6 If you sense that your friend or her family might want a moment alone, quietly read a book or magazine. Don't expect to be entertained every second.

7 If your friend's family is taking you out to dinner, don't order until they do. You'd be embarrassed if you asked for shrimp cocktail if they were planning to go for just main courses.

8 Leave when you planned to or you'll wear out your welcome. As Jane Austen wrote in *Emma*, 'It was a delightful visit . . . perfect in being much too short.'

When Friendships Change

What if you don't fit into your old gang anymore? Maybe you got in with them when you felt insecure, but now you realize they aren't your type. Maybe all they care about is Saturday night bottle parties and you think drinking is stupid. Whatever the reason, you want out. What do you do?

If it's your group's smoking, drinking, exclusivity, or wildness that makes you uncomfortable, you could say so. Without being judgemental, say that you feel rotten after you stay up all night or you don't see the joy in getting high all the time. (You may discover that the others aren't that enthusiastic either.)

The best way to start moving away from a gang is to be extra attentive to girls outside it. You won't change your social circle overnight. And I hope you won't start being mean to your friends, or trying to turn people against them. But, if you ring up new friends and spend time with other girls, new friendships will follow.

When special friendships change, it can ache as much as or more than breaking up with a guy. It'll hurt if your tomboy friend suddenly turns into a young lady, or if the girl next door gets a boyfriend and discards you like scrap paper. You used to be able to share every thought. Now you each worry that the other is taking everything wrong. Try to be patient, accepting, and open about the adjustments you're making. True friendship can survive the awkward times.

I remember a heart-to-heart my friend Jen and I once had. We'd both been quietly feeling smothered. Somehow the responsibility of being best friends at thirteen had got to us. We each needed time for other people. After several uncomfortable weeks, we talked about our problems. Imagine our relief when we discovered we'd both been upset about the same thing! Jen and I decided to be 'bestest' friends instead of 'best' friends. That left us feeling less possessive and obligated to each other, yet just as caring. Once we stopped feeling as though we *had* to spend every waking moment together, we had more fun when we *chose* to see each other.

I also remember a run-in with Judy. As I confessed to my diary, *'I feel like I don't have a best friend. Judy's changed. I'm sick of her telling me my faults. Her frankness is beginning to nauseate me.'* Suffice it to say I'm awfully glad we made up, and Judy's candour is still one of the traits I most like in her. So don't let ordinary squabbles and moodiness damage extraordinary friendships.

Of course, just as you'll continually add friends to your life, you'll also let others go. It's natural to outgrow some pals or find you are growing in different directions. You'll want to stick by a friend who is going through a hard time (parents' divorce, problems at school), but what if there is no legitimate explanation for a friend's change or selfishness? Or what if you and a friend just don't click any more? You could try clearing the air. You might say you've noticed things have cooled off between you but you'd like to work at staying close. Or you could decide to drift away with as few hard feelings as possible. (Always try to have more than one close friend; you can't expect one person to answer all your emotional needs.)

Grudges and hate are a waste of energy. I resented a friend-turned-bitch for almost six months until I realized that while I was practically developing an ulcer, this hot-and-cold girl was dating, partying, and not giving me a second thought.

Don't bother hating people because they don't accept you, or because they threaten you, or because you see in them some characteristic you don't like in yourself. Channel your feelings elsewhere; focus on your friends, not your enemies.

Ten Ways To Lose Friends

Friendships can be forever but, too often, they fall apart along the way. If you want to keep your friendships in good repair, don't sabotage them. Heed this what-*not*-to-do list:

1 Agree wholeheartedly when your friend says, 'I acted like such an idiot' or 'My party was a total failure.'

2 Neglect your friend whenever a guy comes into the

room. Drop her whenever a guy comes into your life.

3 Stay on and on, leaving only when you're pushed out the door. Then, as soon as you get home, phone to talk.

4 Use your friend for her homework, hand-me-down clothes or social status.

5 Become a bore: constantly whine and complain, blab endlessly about your diet or boyfriend, or turn anything anyone says into a springboard for you to talk about yourself.

6 Become dependent and get jealous every time your friend talks to anyone else.

7 Be so envious of your friend's marks at school, her clothes, looks, athletic abilities, relationships with boys, or whatever, that you no longer enjoy her company or what *you* have.

8 Demand that your friend tell you everything. Promise not to tell. Then spill the secrets.

9 Criticize and say 'you should' a lot; try to change your friends and run their lives.

10 Notice when you need your friends but not when they need you. (For instance, call when you're upset but be impatient with their tears.)

Be Your Own Friend

If you like yourself, others will like you, too. Even if the popular girls *don't* know you're alive, and Jimmy Harvey *doesn't* ask you to dance, you are still a good, worthwhile person with lots to offer. Believe in yourself!

Concentrate on your good points (yes, you do have some!). If you're speaking up in science class and a little voice inside you whispers that you sound like a twit, tell it to shove it. Listen instead to the voice that's whispering, 'Hey, you know your stuff.' This is hard to pull off when you don't know a mollusc from a molecule. Try to be as bright, caring and warm hearted as you can, then give yourself the approval you deserve.

Some insecurity is normal. At times, I'll catch a glimpse of myself in the mirror and think, 'Carol, you are the fattest thing that ever waddled.' At other times, I'll think I'm so adorable I'll want to pinch my cheeks. So why not concentrate on pluses instead of minuses? I could sink into total despair if I thought about all the guys who didn't ask me out, all the articles I wrote that didn't sell, or all the skills (like singing or sewing) I haven't learned. Or I can bask for a moment recalling good times I have had, articles I have had published, skills I have acquired. I'm for basking; how about you?

When you consider your personality, give yourself credit for being energetic instead of clobbering yourself for being short-tempered. (Then work on lengthening your fuse.) When you look at your past, emphasize sunny-side-up periods; don't brood on scrambled ones. If you insist on recalling what a nerd you were last year, think about how you've grown since then. And how tough times help you appreciate happy ones.

Do you constantly put yourself down? Stop. Don't discredit yourself by saying, 'I'm a bitch; I can't help it,' or 'I'm jinxed; it's my fault the rain spoiled the picnic.' When an unlucky thing happens, think 'What a drag!' not 'I'm unlucky.' Be less hard on yourself. Measure yourself by reasonable – not impossible – standards.

Pretend you're a contortionist: give yourself a pat on the back instead of a boot up the backside!

When you're in the absolute pits (and we all fall in occasionally), don't moan endlessly to your friends. Do something active you can be proud of and start pulling yourself out. Do a five-star job on your schoolwork or the letters you're typing. Or astound your parents by cleaning the kitchen. Or go on a longer-than-usual bike ride. Or listen to upbeat music, see an absorbing movie, read a fun magazine, take a hot bath. Write in a diary. Start a scrapbook or look one over. Volunteer to help someone who needs you – doing something nice for someone else can lift your spirits, too. Tackling a project that isn't fun in itself (tidying your room, doing homework, doing some charity work) can also make you feel better. Do something you know you do well, or try something you've never tried. When you've been knocked down by life, try and come back fighting.

Believe me, I get the blues too, and I can go off the deep end with the best of them. I'm not saying you should ignore anger or sorrow or let them build up inside you. But after you express negative feelings, sit down, close your eyes, breathe deeply, and think 'calm'. Then do something to get back in gear.

You could stay depressed for ages, but what's the point? Why not strive to keep things in perspective? Why shoo happiness away? Whatever is upsetting you will probably pass. Things could probably be worse, but aren't.

One technique that has helped me is to keep a list for a few days of what I've done – not what I *have* to do. Tuesday might say nothing more than: 'exercised, showered, dressed, read paper, looked up and read three articles on drunk driving, had a sandwich, wrote two pages, sent a postcard to Aunt Lisa, bought typing paper, cooked and ate dinner with Rob, called John and Linda, read a great short story.' For me, that's a fairly typical fine day. Yet when I'm down, that can feel like an I-didn't-get-anything-done day. Keeping a list helps me see straight.

Don't let yourself wallow too long. If you do call a friend, don't just unload your woes. Listen to her insights and advice. If you can't shake a long-term depression alone or with the help of friends and family, try getting some outside help.

Before you seek professional help though, think about this: in some ways *wholeness* is as important as happiness. Feeling down helps you grow up and become sensitive, wise, and empathetic. Feeling low is part of being human. And you can't always expect smooth sailing – especially if you're making waves.

If you're comfortable with yourself, you'll feel lonely less often. Everyone is alone from time to time (even on Saturday nights), but try to think of those hours as precious solitude, not painful loneliness. Depend on yourself. Learn to entertain yourself, whether by reading, cooking, bowling, exercising, gardening, thinking, or whatever.

As Abraham Lincoln put it, 'Most folks are about as happy as they make up their minds to be.' I won't quibble with honest Abe. Happiness doesn't just happen. You have to invite it over and welcome it in. Be true to yourself and do things that please you and things that please others. Even happiness can be a habit. Even depression can be habit-forming. You may have to work at being happy and you can't be happy all the time, but self-contentedness (which is how Aristotle defined happiness) is within your grasp. So seize the day! (Bonus: happy people tend to be healthy people.)

Since I'm ranting and raving about how you should like yourself, I'd better add: don't go overboard. If you become conceited or smug or self-satisfied, you'll drive your near and dear ones away. A little modesty, please. There's room for improvement in everybody – in you, in me, even in the girls you envy and the guys you adore.

Speaking of guys (always one of my favourite pastimes), let's talk about that elusive stuff called love.

3. Love

Falling In, Falling Out

Love is wonderful. And love is a mess.

Love is soppy smiles; giddy phone calls; deep talks on long walks; singing in a snowstorm; squashing into the same section of a revolving door; identifying with every lyric on the radio – and feeling excruciatingly alive. Love is also dashed expectations; quarrelling because you care; missing him the moment he says goodbye; aching when he flirts with someone else; longing for another letter; losing sleep over night-time daydreams – and feeling blissfully deranged.

Love? I'm still trying to figure it out myself. It's the most complex emotion going. Heady, heartbreaking, poignant, breathtaking. And *I love you* means different things to different people at different times.

So while I can offer facts about menstruation and diet problems, and while I can provide rights and wrongs about applying for a job or to college, I can't claim to have a hold on love. Love knows no facts, few rights, few wrongs. Love is full of contradictions.

Nonetheless, here's a chapter full of tips. How to let guys know you're interested, how to keep dates fun, how to let love last, and how to survive a break-up.

Just keep in mind that love is something you have to learn the hard way – which, lucky you, also happens to be the fun way.

Getting Started

The first love letter I ever received was when I was eight, in Mrs Gemunder's class. A blond boy named Billy passed a scribbled scrap of paper from the third row on the left, where he sat, to the

84

second row on the right, where I sat. It read, 'Do you like me? –
Yes – No.'

This was exciting. I immediately ticked Yes. But I wasn't going
to make myself vulnerable for nothing. No fool I; in my brand
new joined-up writing, I added, 'Do you like me?' I handed the
note to my neighbour and watched as it passed from person to
person to person to Billy. Billy read it. He looked up. He met my
gaze. He smiled.

Ah, things were so simple then.

By the time I was in secondary school, they were complicated.
Why? Partly because I was love-hungry, desperate to be going
out with somebody. It scarcely mattered whom: I was in love
with love. Here are some typical lines from my diary:

> **Tuesday:** *I don't think Jake likes me. But Nick (yuk!) told a kid he'd ask me
> to dance every dance at school. I'll say no!*
> **Thursday:** *In dance class, Jake danced with me. He likes me!! I decided to
> change my future all-girls party to a mixed party.*
> **Wednesday:** *Jake doesn't like me. I bet he likes Danielle.*
> **Thursday:** *Jake doesn't like me because I like him.*
> **Friday:** *I'm not going to say hi or anything.*
> **Thursday:** *I've given up on Jake. He doesn't like me. I like Evan a little.*
> **Saturday:** *The dance was okay. Jake didn't dance with me and Nick did
> only once.*
> **Wednesday:** *I got thrown in the lake by some senior boys. Fun!*
> **Friday:** *My party was a success, but no boy likes me.*
> **Monday:** *In Music, I wrote a note to Jen about boys and Mr Parsons took it
> and said he'd read it aloud if I didn't behave. I behaved.*
> **Friday:** *I don't know which boy to like.*
> **Saturday:** *Dave is so cute and strong. So is Hugh. So is Walter.*
> **Friday:** *The last dance of term wasn't that good because no good boys like
> me.*
> **Sunday:** *I am so in love with everybody.*
> **Thursday:** *I went rowing with Walter.*
> **Tuesday:** *Hugh Dalton may have seen a CW / HD on my French book.
> God!*
> **Wednesday:** *I love jam doughnuts.*

Fortunately, I didn't permanently give up boys for doughnuts.
By the time I was fourteen, I had a new curly-haired crush.
According to my diary:

> *Jen and Judy prodded me and I mustered up all my courage and asked
> him, 'Are you going to the concert tonight?'*

> *'Why?'*
> *'Oh, I don't know.'*
> *'Are you?'*
> *'I was planning to . . .'*
> *'I'll be there.'*
> *Then at 6:45, It happened. He called me. He looked up my number and used his index finger seven times for me!*

Guess what? After that fateful concert, he and I ended up going out for three shining years.

So don't despair. There will be dry spells in your love life, times when you think, 'It's not fair, even rubbish gets taken out!' Fill those boyfriendless days with friends, family, work, sports, books and yourself. And remember that it's OK not to always have a boyfriend. It certainly beats settling for a creep.

Be patient. There's enough love to go around. If you keep sending out signals, someone is bound to come your way.

What signals? Keep reading!

Sending Out Signals

You can't force a guy to like you. But you can stack the odds in your favour. How do you let the would-be Love of Your Life know you're interested without seeming too forward?

Easy. Sort of. Remember the *Body* and *Friendship* chapters? Wash your hair, watch your weight; dress to look your head-to-toe best. Be on the go; work on listening skills; project confidence even when your stomach is doing somersaults.

Well, all that advice applies whether you're looking for girl-friends or a boyfriend. Try not to be self-conscious. You can chat away to girls, so don't go all silent with fellas. Don't avert your eyes in the hall or stare at your shoelaces at the youth club. Even if he turns your knees to mush, try to be your attractive, easy-going, approachable self. (*Approachable:* that means not always being locked inside a group of eight girls.) You can even flirt a little.

Flirt? Yes. Flirting without being a flirt is an art. If you flirt with every guy in sight, girls will resent you and guys won't take you seriously. But if you never flirt, the guy you're crazy about may consider you one of the crowd forever.

- You don't like the word? Call it something else. Flirting is simply an informal way to let him know you enjoy his company, without your going out on a limb. It doesn't mean batting your lashes, giggling every time he breathes, or cooing, 'Your after-shave smells diivvviiiine.' And you don't have to wink or whisper. Just try a smiling, straightforward 'Hello.' Or pay him a sincere compliment. Ask questions and show interest in his thoughts and plans.

I used to worry that my mind would go blank when I was in the library and about to run into my curly-haired heart-throb. So I actually kept a hidden list of things to tell him. (He wasn't always able to play Mr Cool as we talked, either. Once two of his friends flew a paper plane at him that read, 'How's your love life?')

Some girls like to drop hints to mutual friends to test the promise of romance. Third-party inquiries can work or can back-fire, so use discretion. Unless you're pretty sure he likes you back, I wouldn't make your crush public, even though many girls choose to. It's also not always a great idea to ask a boy point-blank if he likes you. If you put him on the spot, and he says, 'No,' you'll wish you hadn't been so curious. And if you tell him flat out that you like him, it may make things awkward unless feelings are mutual.

Send out non-verbal signals, too. Look at the guy, look away, smile ever so slightly. Pull your chair closer to his. Touch his arm gently as you make a point. Whatever. It should feel relaxed and in the spirit of fun. It should communicate: 'I'm friendly; I like you'; not 'I'm lonely; I need you.'

Tune in to what his eyes and body are saying. But don't jump to happy conclusions just because he's maintaining eye contact. However, if he's making small talk, encourage him. Guys get acute anxiety attacks, too, and many are reluctant to make the first move because they're scared of the big R. (Rejection!) If he says something tentative, like, 'I'll see you at the match,' say something positive, like, 'I hope so'. If you both adore the same group and he says, 'We should go to one of their concerts,' say 'I'd love to.' (But don't pant, 'Yes! Yes! Anytime! I'm always free.')

What if his eyes are lighting up, yet he's not issuing any invites or almost-invites? Are you bold enough to ask him out, or almost ask him out? If so, try something like, 'Isn't it great that a pizza place has opened on the High Street?' He'll put it together that if he invites you for pizza, you won't turn him down. Of course, if he's a victim of the 'once bitten twice shy' syndrome, you'll have to be extra patient. Maybe you could suggest studying together or ask him to join you and a group of friends at a bowling alley or skating rink.

I know a woman who flirted with a guy who flirted back, but made no plans. Finally she got up her nerve and oh-so-casually mentioned, 'I'm having a party tomorrow night if you'd like to drop by.' He said he would. And she? She ran home and frantically organized a get-together with all her friends. Know what? The couple are now happily married!

Warning: keep your flirting low-key and ambiguous. If you're coming on like a steamroller, he may run for cover.

A date once told me, 'Hey, I don't want to get married,' to which I retorted, 'I didn't propose.' But perhaps I had been sending out I-sure-would-like-to-go-out-with-you-all-the-time signals instead of I'm-having-fun signals.

It's happened to me the other way around, too. Gordon wasn't eager, he was over-eager, and that sent me packing. According to my diary: *'I really like Gordon, but at sentences like, "You're good for me" and "Do you realize you single-handedly got me out of a depression?" I withdraw. I'm also uncomfortable when he stares into my eyes, which he does a lot.'*

So show him you're interested, but don't go overboard. Once in a while, especially if he's so-gorgeous-you-could-just-die, you may have to tell yourself, 'Down, girl, down!'

On Your Marks, Get Set – Relax!

Will the real you please stand up? If the guy you worship from afar doesn't respond to the real you, he'd make you a lousy boyfriend and there's no point in longing for him. But if you are yourself – your real self – and he's smitten, what could be better? You can relax, say what's on your mind, and relish his fondness for the true you, shortcomings and all.

It may turn out *you're* the one who is not as interested as you once were. It's easier to fall for a stranger on whom you can project storybook qualities than for a human being with good and bad traits. If you find your heart-throb doesn't have the fantasy personality you'd conjured for him and that you're on different wavelengths, OK. That's an important discovery.

If he's talking about football and you hate football, you could pretend to be enthralled as he explains a strategy. But at best, you'd be dooming yourself to boring afternoons watching games on the box or on the field. Moulding yourself into the girl you think he wants will leave you stifled. Plus if Mr Football finds out he's gone over the top about a non-existent sports fan, he won't be too pleased, either.

Developing some of your sweetheart's interests is a compliment. Pretending you already share them is not. Be yourself, not the girl he wants you to be (or the girl you *think* he wants you to be – see, it gets complicated!) He's bound to find you out sooner or later, anyway, so better self than sorry.

Icebreakers: Twenty-Two Ways To Launch A Conversation

Flirt? Relax? Maybe you think you can't even strike up a conversation with a guy, let alone pull your chair closer and be your nice normal self. Boys are people too, and you might be forgetting that lots of them are as intimidated and tongue-tied as you. Most would welcome it if you took the first step. The shy guy in your choir group, the hunk jogging alone at the school track, the genius in your computer club – they may all have noticed you but not known what to say. So for Pete's sake (and Scott's and Jack's and your own), speak up!

Here are twenty-two conversation-starters. Don't memorize them, because they're not slick pick-up lines. They're just natural ways to get a discussion rolling. Ready?

---

1 What did you make of question number 12? (He's behind you in maths, looking over his homework.)

---

2. What good films have you seen lately? (You're side by side in a ticket queue at the cinema.)

3. Did you see who scored that goal? (He's in front of you at the football match.)

4. Why can't they ever serve anything decent here? (You're waiting for the lousy burgers the canteen has the gall to call lunch.)

5. What was London/Manchester/Scotland like? (He's new in town.)

6. What an adorable dog! (Or terrific boots or lovely sweater or great motorbike.)

7. Do you have change for a pound? (While he's checking, keep talking.)

8. Do you know where there's a bookshop near here? (Maybe you can walk towards it together.)

9. Hi. (He's bound to say 'Hi' back.)

10. Have you been here before? (You're at a local landmark, a skating rink, a sports centre.)

11. So where are you from? (A tried-and-trusted standby to be used on trains, buses, in queues, at parties, the seaside, concerts, fairs – you name it.)

12. How far do you usually jog? (You've caught up to him and now maybe you'll do a mile or two together.)

13. What time is it? (When he answers, compliment him on his watch or say, 'Phew! I thought it was later,' and say why you're relieved.)

14. May I share your history book? (Don't forget yours on purpose, but if you left it in your desk, don't miss an opportunity!)

15. I know you from somewhere – were you ever in the Rangers/at Ferndene Primary School/at the Meadows Estate Youth Club?

16. Been here long? (You're in a long queue, or you're at a

station or bus stop.)

17 Have you ever studied Civics before? (You've both just received your course schedule for the next term.)

18 I can't believe it's raining again! (Cliché? Maybe. But discussing the weather gets conversations off the ground.)

19 Where did you learn to type so fast? (Or draw so well, take photographs, read palms, fix bikes, dance, act, or play the guitar.)

20 Doesn't this remind you of a scene from *Dallas*? (Or any other television show, film, or book).

21 You're Amy's brother, aren't you? (As if you had the slightest doubt – but that's his cue to ask who you are).

22 Did you read about the new cinema complex they're building?/McDonalds they're opening? (Or about any other school, local or national news item).

Think up your own questions, too, because breaking the ice is step one to melting his heart.

Is Cupid Stupid? Or Does He Just Have Poor Aim?

You aren't breaking the ice and sending ask-me-out-ask-me-out-ask-me-out signals to the wrong guy, are you? Try not to fall for your sister's boyfriend, your art teacher, or the married postman. Are you desperately in love with a famous film star or musician? No problem, so long as you don't care too much whether he cares back. Have you lost your heart to the town heart-throb every other girl is head-over-heels over? Fine – you may be the one he chooses. But brace yourself for the likelihood (alas) that he won't single you out. What if you've been flirting for months – or worse, years – with the same guy and are convinced you could rock happily together as grandparents, yet he still scarcely knows you exist? You're inviting the blues.

Some girls subconsciously pick out-of-reach boys to drool over. Deep down, they don't feel ready for the possibility of sex, commitment, or connecting with someone who might argue with them or fall short of their impossible standards. It's safer to love from afar, and if unrequited passion doesn't daunt them, no harm done.

However, if *you* are ready for the real thing, why not shift your love energies? Give up gracefully on the movie idol. Focus on the sensitive and available, though less widely acclaimed, guys. Look again at the boy next door; stop writing off the foreign exchange student whose eye may be on you.

Maybe you think you can't help it. You want an honest-to-goodness relationship, but you've fallen for the Class Hunk who happens also to be your best friend's boyfriend. He's forbidden, but he's the only one who fuels your fantasies.

You know what? I hate to be the bearer of bad news, but you'd be wise to take a deep breath, yank out Cupid's arrow, and find a more suitable object for your affections. Don't pine away, love-sick. Sometimes Cupid misses his mark.

My pragmatic advice may seem unromantic, but it'll probably make you happier in the long run. It's hard to avoid crazy crushes. It's hard to control desires and turn off dreamy thoughts. But you can do it. A crush is like a small flame. You can fan it into a forest fire or, if it's hopeless or off-limits, you can snuff it out.

If your love-life, real or imagined, tends to be painful, look for a pattern. Are the guys you go for all the kind your mum hopes you'll marry? Good – if you like them as much as Mum does. Are they nice even though Mum wouldn't take to them? OK. But if you're always aiming too high or too low, or if the guys are all handsome but shallow and oblivious to you, or if one after another is abusive, mean, taken, gay, faraway, unattainable, or your basic Mr Wrong, try to be kinder to yourself. Try to end the destructive pattern. Don't keep thinking you'll be the one to reform a guy's character.

You're also not doing yourself any favours if the instant you get a guy, you tire of him and try to make another conquest. Or if you and your boyfriend are close and going strong, yet you flirt suggestively with every other guy who is attracted to you.

The point isn't just to have a boyfriend. The point is to have a warm, wonderful relationship with a boyfriend. You deserve that, don't you?

Saying No Nicely

All right, so there you are, relaxing, laughing, asking questions and hoping that you're charming Rob. But no. You're charming Cecil. And Cecil asks you out. (Nerds tend to have impeccable taste.)

What do you do?

If he says, 'You wouldn't like to go with me to the school debating society would you?' and indeed you wouldn't, say no. Say it nicely, but say it fast. 'I'm sorry, thanks for asking,' is sufficient. If you say, 'I'm busy that day,' then Cecil may ask you out another day, and it would be cruel to show up at the debating society with someone else. So don't tell a lie you'll be caught in. If Cecil is from another district and doesn't know your friends, you could say, 'Thanks, but my boyfriend wouldn't like that!' That's a white lie, but it spares his ego. If he gives you the creeps, don't give him any encouragement; don't say, 'Oh, I would have loved to – maybe another time?'

What if Cecil is persistent? What if he asks you out five Saturdays in a row, and every time you say you're busy, he asks about the following week? What if he invites you to the Christmas party and it's only September?

Most guys can take a hint, but some need you to spell out the deflating truth or they won't get it. If you must break the news to Cecil that he's not your type, be gentle. Say something like, 'You're a nice guy and I'm flattered by your invitations, but I want us to be just friends, OK?' You could even tell him that you admire his brains or personality but that he's just not right for you. Use tact, but make sure he gets the picture because you don't want to give him false hopes.

What if – miracle of miracles – your Ideal Boyfriend calls and asks you out for Friday, but you've made plans you can't break? Don't give him the 'I'm sorry, thanks for calling' line or he may interpret it as a polite brush-off. Be effusive. Say, 'I'd love to see that film with you but I can't miss my grandmother's eightieth birthday dinner. Could we go on another day?'

Perceptive guys learn to tell the difference between a don't-call-back no and a please-call-back no.

But why should they be the only ones to put their egos on the line? Even if you're too scared to ask him to a school play, you can still phone and ask about algebra homework. If he wonders whether you're more interested in him than in the homework – so much the better.

Twenty-Eight Dating Ideas Guaranteed to Steal His Heart

The good news is that sometimes, just sometimes, Mr Wonderful asks you out, you're free, you accept, you start seeing each other, and suddenly you're going steady.

By now, you've danced together at the disco, shared popcorn at the local Odeon, played video games, jogged side by side, munched pizza, wandered the shopping arcade, even beaten each other at miniature golf. Running out of rendezvous? No! The fun has just begun.

When your guy says, 'What do you want to do?' don't shrug your shoulders and say, 'I dunno.' That's not being pleasantly agreeable – that's boring! Whether you live in the town or in the country, have spending money or are broke, there are plenty of plans to make. (P.S. Many of these would be fun to do with girls, too.)

---

1 Greet the dinosaurs at a natural history museum, or check out other museums. You may find exhibits of classic cars, jukeboxes, waxworks, cartoon art, costumes, or Roman pottery.

2 Check the local papers to find out if a nearby farm offers a pick-your-own-fruit deal.

3 Explore an arts centre, then attend a concert, film or lecture there.

4 Put on albums and aprons and bake bread. Give him some to take home.

5 Listen in on an interesting case at the local court, then discuss how you would vote if you were jury members.

6 Pack croissants and jam in a basket and head east to a hilltop to witness the sunrise. Or meet just before sunset with a picnic, Frisbee, poetry book or sketch pad.

7 Go to the races and watch cars, horses, sailing boats or runners speed to the finishing line.

8 Who cares if you're unco-ordinated? Sign up for a free introductory dance class. Or go roller-skating or ice-skating – try holding hands without losing balance.

9 Browse at an antique shop or jumble sale. Pick out off-beat gifts for each other – you don't have to buy them.

10 Take karate or cookery lessons.

11 Visit a pet shop and fall for the kittens, puppies, turtles, and guppies.

12 Check newspapers and store bulletin boards to find out about concerts, country fairs, auctions, outdoor art shows, church bazaars, boat shows.

13 Plant an outdoor garden or a windowsill of potted herbs.

14 Have tea and crumpets at a fancy hotel restaurant.

15 Play tourist in the big city nearest you. Take a sight-seeing bus tour, join a group visiting a cathedral or historic house, or go on a boat trip up the river. Or walk, walk, walk.

16 It's windy? Go fly a kite!

17 Raining? Stroll under one big umbrella, then head inside to play Monopoly, rummy, or Scrabble.

18 Go to a zoo and pause at the aviary, snake pit, and

monkey house. Or go to an aquarium and watch the sharks get fed.

19 Rent a bicycle built for two and head to the hidden waterfall only you know how to find.

20 Go to the theatre, even if it's the local amateur dramatic society – or, better still, join!

21 Many health clubs offer free classes to prospective members. Work up a sweat together!

22 Attend a professional football, rugby, hockey, basketball, tennis, or other sports game.

23 Is there a river or stream near you? Rent a canoe or rowing boat, take along poles and bait, and go fishing.

24 Take advantage of a local business that offers free tours: from newspaper plant or television station to biscuit factory, paper mill, or stock exchange.

25 Feed the ducks and geese at a pond. Feed the sparrows and pigeons at a park.

26 Is it true that greasy spoon cafés offer great food? Find out! Order different dinners and split them between you. Or start the day right by meeting for breakfast.

27 Take a walk at a botanical garden, conservatory, or arboretum and see how many trees and plants you can identify.

28 You live near a planetarium? Study the exhibit on constellations, and that night, grab a blanket and star-gaze.

Should You Date Older and Younger Guys?

Sure, why not? The guy I went out with at school was a year older than I, and I'm a bit older than my husband. My father was fourteen years older than my mum, and the age gap didn't keep them from having a solid marriage.

If you go out with a guy who is your age, give or take two years, great. Younger boys aren't all immature and older men aren't all lecherous. However (I bet you knew a *however* was coming), if your sweetheart is years younger or is in his mid-twenties or thirties, that does give me pause.

Let's say he's years younger. That may make you feel safer than you would if you were going out with someone your own age. Fine. But be sure you also feel secure with boys your own age who may challenge you more. If you think your ego needs a boost, make a list of your best qualities and commit them to memory.

Is your boyfriend not a boy but a man? Going out with an older man may give you status and prestige. The price? Growing up fast, ready or not. You'll be a woman for the rest of your life, but you're a teenager for only a few precious years. A man may not be content to snuggle and kiss for hours (one of the finest features of young love) and may apply sexual pressure. He may also be bored by your tales of failing a test or having a row with your brother, yet you're entitled to share such stories.

One schoolfriend told me later that in the long run, she felt going out with Rick, who was in his late twenties, was not a good idea. She couldn't take him to any school activities, or out with her friends. And she got so used to adult company that at college, she found the students childish and felt alienated. Plus as she got older, she stopped idealizing Rick, and that new attitude didn't always thrill him.

Although you may be proud to have won the attentions of an older guy, ask yourself why he isn't dating women his own age. Sure, it's because you're so terrific, but even *you* may be still more terrific when you have ten more years of maturity and experience behind you.

Some men love the intensity and enthusiasm of young girls – girls who supposedly aren't jaded and haven't 'seen it all'. But you want to be loved for yourself, not your sweet-young-thing innocence. Is your older man intimidated by marriageable career women? Does he revel in the hero worship you may be giving him? Are *you* using *him* because he has money, a car, sophistication? Your caring may be genuine, but it can't hurt to question his motives and your own.

Pretty soon, age gaps will hardly matter. Twenty-two? Twenty-eight? Thirty-three? Three adults. But the same gaps among twelve-, eighteen-, and twenty-three-year-olds can mean you're living in different worlds.

Should You Date Someone from a Different Ethnic, Racial or Religious Background?

I went out with a wonderful Spaniard for nearly four years. The idea of a Madrid marriage did occur to Juan and me. But I wondered if it would be hard to teach our future kids Spanish and English. And would Spain's happy-go-lucky *mañana mañana* style drive me up the wall? Would I end up finding Spanish chivalry sexist? Would I get homesick for America? Would I be able to write well in English in Spain? (Hemingway did, but he was Hemingway!) Most important: Would our love truly be enough to make up for my leaving my family, friends and country an ocean away?

Maybe. Maybe not. Juan and I broke up for other reasons – but that's another story. The point here is that keeping a relationship in top form isn't easy under any circumstances (witness the divorce rate), and marrying someone of a different nationality, race, religion, or background can make harmony even harder.

Yet who's talking about marriage? As for dating (and friendship), yes, go out with whomever you want. Broaden your horizons. Gain insights from other people's perspectives. Expose yourself to other values and customs. I'm very grateful for the years with my 'Don Juan'.

If your romance turns serious (or if your parents make life miserable), *then* ask yourself serious questions. Couples who cross boundaries of religion, race or colour usually do encounter extra friction and conflicts. Ask yourself whether you have substantial doubts about the rocky ride ahead. (Everyone has some doubts.)

Also, be sure you love your guy for his personal qualities and not to prove to yourself and the world that you are open-minded or colour-blind or tolerant or big-hearted, (e.g. don't date someone of a different skin-colour or social background *just* to be rebellious).

My parents got married when conventions were rather stricter than they are now. Mum is Texan and Dad was Russian-born and it worked for them. But love doesn't always conquer all.

Ask your heart and head what is right for you.

Nine Awkward Dating Situations and How to Handle Them

No one would play the dating game if it weren't fun, but sometimes even the best evenings go awry.

Of course, some girls get all worked up over nothing. If they need to go to the loo during the interval, they ignore nature's call, twist their legs, wriggle, suffer through Act II, and finally bolt from their date's car without so much as a goodnight kiss. That's silly. Instead, they could simply have said, 'Excuse me, I'm going to the Ladies, I'll be right back.' A guy won't be put off – he'll probably say 'Good idea,' and head for the Gents.

Then there are the girls who are too flustered to eat in front of guys. They fear the guy will think they're little piglets or will laugh if they spill gravy on their sleeves. Question: Are you appalled that boys eat to stay alive? Question: Would you crack up uncontrollably if a boy smeared ketchup on his cuff?

When you're dealing with guys, it sometimes helps to ask yourself what you'd do if you were with your best friend. If you had to go to the loo or were sloppy with the soy sauce, you'd take it in your stride. So listen, if your bag of Maltesers flips upside down at the cinema and they all go rolling down the aisle, don't let it destroy the rest of the evening.

Here are nine sticky predicaments, complete with ways out.

---

1 You came to the disco with a guy who likes you a lot but whom you consider only a friend. While he's chatting with someone else, the guy you've quietly adored for months appears, strikes up a conversation, and asks you if you'd like to dance. What do you do?
- Flirt, talk, tell him you'd love to dance with him, but that

you really shouldn't because you came with your mate Matthew. If you're friendly, he won't be discouraged. Who knows? His interest may even double: you're not only attractive and popular, but you're considerate, too. Feeling bold? Suggest you meet there next week.

2 Watching fireworks on Guy Fawkes night was fun, but now you feel as if you're battling with an octopus. You don't want to put him off entirely, but you don't want to go any further yet, either. And struggling to hold down his roaming hands has taken the fun out of kissing. What do you do?

• You could fiddle with your handbag, straighten your hair, ask about his childhood, announce that you're starving – but why not speak your mind? Tell him straight out that you like him and look forward to getting to know him better, but that you don't enjoy feeling so pushed. If he's a decent person who cares about you, he'll adjust his pace to yours. If he continues the passion play, ask to be taken home and don't go out with him again. His loss.

3 You've had a crush on him for weeks and this is your first date, a double with a pair of his friends. After the film, you all get in your guy's car, which is parked on a side road. Suddenly the couple in the back seat grow quiet and the windows start steaming up. Your date drapes his arm over your shoulders. You're torn: you feel attracted to him, but also self-conscious and rushed. What do you do?

• Realize that he, too, may be ill at ease. Perhaps he's feeling pressured by his back-seat buddies. Suggest taking a walk or going for a bite to eat nearby. That way you can get to know each other better before deciding to cuddle up.

4 All week you've been psyched up for your blind date. Your aunt gave you such a build-up about her colleague's son, you were expecting a cross between Adonis and your favourite rock star. But when the doorbell rings, you find yourself shaking the sweaty hand of a seventeen-

stone boy with bifocals and braces on his teeth. 'Ready to go dancing?' he lisps, and your heart sinks to your toes. What do you do?

- Make the best of it. Stay open-minded, and the evening will be more fun. You're learning more about guys in general. Besides, he might be charming or witty or introduce you to a boy more your type. If you're friendly without leading him on, you'll feel good about yourself. Later, thank him and shake his clammy hand before he has a chance to try to kiss you. If he's already lungeing forward, turn your head so his lips land on your cheek. (P.S. Tomorrow you can rant at your aunt.)

5 He obviously likes you because he's asked you out every weekend for a month. But each date ends the same way: you talk until midnight, then he leaves without even a goodnight kiss. The anticipation is driving you crazy! You've considered making the first move, but you're shy and fear that if you're the aggressor, it might threaten him. Still, you can't go on meeting like this! What do you do?

- If you think he likes you only as a friend, try to appreciate the friendship for what it is. But if you're pretty sure he's just too timid to take action, subtly let him know you'd welcome his advances. Sit close to him, or if you're walking, brush against him gently. Leave your hand near his. Linger before getting out of the car or at the doorway. Look into his eyes. You could even let your gaze wander briefly to his lips. Or give him a peck on the cheek.

6 He's being so quiet you could scream. It's a twenty-minute drive back to your home, and you know you can't single-handedly keep the conversation going that long. Usually he's talkative, but tonight it's Monosyllable City. What do you do?

- Is he silent because he's angry or upset? Ask him what's on his mind. Say, 'You seem a little quiet. Is anything getting you down?' He might want to open up and tell you.

  If you think he's just feeling shy, realize that he probably appreciates your breezy efforts to keep the conversation rolling. Try asking 'why' and 'how' questions. What *would* you really like to know about him? Remember, too, that you don't have to talk all the time. Is silence golden? Well, silver at least, and it is natural. The expression 'a companionable silence' means just that.

7 Your parents don't like the guy you're going out with, and he senses it. The one time you invited him to dinner, the tension was thicker and heavier than your mum's home-made stew. Now, at a concert, he suddenly asks 'Your parents don't like me, do they?' What do you do?

• Let him know your parents criticize *all* your friends because they feel protective. (Then ask yourself if your polite explanation is true, or if there are legitimate reasons behind their coolness.) It's also possible that your folks wish you'd spend more time with them or worry that you're neglecting your work, and they are unfairly using your guy as a scapegoat for other concerns.

   To help everyone get along, remind your parents of your boyfriend's strengths and accomplishments. And tell him about their interests. If he can get your dad talking about mystery novels and your mum talking about music, they may establish a rapport after all.

   Before you meet *his* parents, make sure he smooths the way for you. It's better to ask his mother, 'Do you enjoy being an estate agent?' than to have to start from square one with the awkward 'Do you work?' First parental meetings usually go best when they are brief and informal.

8 You're having dinner together at an Italian restaurant. You've just taken a bite of Bolognaise when your old boyfriend – and his entire family – stroll in and plonk themselves down at the next table. Suddenly you can hardly keep track of what your guy is saying. What do you do?

• You could shovel down your spaghetti and make a run for it. Instead, just explain the situation, excuse yourself, and say a quick and gracious hello to your old love and his family. Get it over with. Your date shouldn't object. Greeting your ex shows you're mature enough to remain on speaking terms with someone who once meant a lot to you.

And if you're *not* on speaking terms? Explain your uneasiness, and say you're going to shift your chair so you won't be facing that table: you want to concentrate on the him-and-now. If you still feel awkward, later you could suggest having ice-cream cones elsewhere for dessert – your treat.

9 A guy you really like takes you to a boring party on the other side of town. After a few hours you want to leave. He doesn't. You feel stuck because you came in his car, you don't know anyone else who could drive you home, and you don't want him to think you're a wimp for wanting to go already. What do you do?

• Since you like him, it might be worthwhile to stick it out a little longer. Summon your second wind and introduce yourself to two strangers; or start a new discussion with your guy about sports, family, movies, pets, school, current events. Yet your needs are important, too, so whether you have an official curfew or not, don't be shy about reminding Mr Rowdy that it's getting late. (You might even whisper that you'd hoped you two would have a moment alone before saying goodbye.)

If he wants to stay another hour and you want to leave now, agree to exit in thirty minutes. If thirty minutes comes and goes and he still refuses to budge – or if he's not willing to compromise in the first place – consider telling him that you're going to find a safe way to leave. Phone your dad or a minicab. You're going out to enjoy yourselves, and you don't have to put up with a bad situation any more than he would.

Eleven Surefire Ways to
Ruin a Romance

(No, silly, I don't recommend them.)

1 Be a policewoman. Now that he's your possession, don't let any female thieves near him.
- Wrong! Just because you want him doesn't mean everyone else does. Your heart-throb might be another girl's Cecil, and vice versa. Besides, if you play the tough cop, your fella might just act like a criminal – and make a run for it! Stop worrying. Relationships that are trusting and sturdy can withstand a few external distractions.

2 Play hard-to-get and other games.
- If you've been doing all the giving, calling and caring, you may want to lean back to see if he'll lean forward. I won't argue. But if you get in the habit of trying to arouse jealousy, play mind games, or jump to conclusions about each other, conflicting messages will shoot back and forth, and your romance may become a jumble instead of a joy. If you really care about each other, you both need to know where you stand.

3 Talk about commitment on the first date.
- Bad idea. Don't worry so much about tomorrow that you hardly enjoy today. Neither of you should swear eternal loyalty to each other, anyway. Love is not a trap. If you start making him feel bad for not spending every second with you, you may end up with even more time on your hands. Remember: pushy people push people away. If you love someone, it's wiser to let him go. If he comes back, he's yours. If he doesn't, he never was.

4 Worry about his ex.
- She's his *ex*, remember? You're his *now*. Everybody is entitled to a past. Work on making this current romance

as mutually satisfying as possible.

5 Be dependent: now that you've paired off, you don't need anyone or anything else.

● Boring! A guy and girl can't be everything to each other. Don't let your love life become your whole life. Don't let it eclipse your other friends and activities. Besides, if you spend time apart, you'll have more to talk about when you're together. You'll also be less broken up if you two ever break up. Going out with someone should add to your self-esteem, yet a girl who always depends on a guy may wind up feeling like a half-person.

6 Take him for granted.

● Some girls forget that relationships, like potted flowers, need to be taken care of. Other girls take their guys for granted because they figure, 'If he likes me, there must be something wrong with him.' No matter how long you've been seeing a guy, if you still care, let him know.

7 Open old wounds.

● Suppose he did go out once with the local flirt while you were away. You've rehashed the episode nineteen times since then and he's begged your forgiveness. Now what? Let it go. Get on with the present. Going over and over past bruises just prolongs the hurt.

8 Love him only when he's feeling cheerful and strong.

● That's not nice. You may be most drawn to him when he's up and confident, but he needs you most when he's down and out. Don't be a fair-weather girlfriend.

9 Get hung up on three little words.

● If one of you whispers, 'I love you,' and the other isn't ready to echo the phrase, it doesn't have to be a problem. Some people are afraid of the words but not the feeling. Others drink two beers, get randy, and say, 'I love you,' when they mean, 'I want you'. It's good to try to recognize the differences between 'in love', 'in like' and 'in lust'. However, as my poetic mother put it, it's not always necessary to 'label it love or libel it lust'.

When my senior school boyfriend and I were first going out, I wasn't ready to put my feelings for him into words. I told my diary: *'We concluded that we have very strong affectionate feelings for each other. He calls it love. I call it nothing.'* (By the way, I finally came around!)

If you declare love before your relationship has had a chance to develop naturally, your guy may panic or question the depth of your emotion. If you both profess love prematurely, then break up a month later, you may both feel more confused and distraught than if you hadn't given a name to your feelings.

10 Analyse the relationship to death.

- If you spend most of your time together monitoring the progress of your relationship rather than enjoying it, you'll sour it. Sometimes one evening of fun can do more to recharge a romance than three of heavy discussion.

11 Harbour unrealistic expectations.

- You're infatuated. Lo and behold, just as the music, films and magazines promised, it's heaven – for about two weeks. Then he criticizes your best friend. And you accuse him of being a snob. It turns out your Superman has a Clark Kent flip side, and his Wonder Woman is touchy. Should you stop seeing each other?

No! Once you get past all the moonlight and roses stuff, you find the nitty-gritty of two imperfect individuals trying to deal with each other.

So don't set yourself up for disappointment. Don't put your guy on a pedestal, and be appalled when he falls off. Don't imagine you'll change him. No one is perfect. If you want your fella to be thoughtful, funny, clever, athletic, and so gorgeous-looking that everyone does a double take, you're asking too much. (Do *you* match up to those standards?) And if you're asking too much, you're like the wide-eyed child who blows up a balloon until it gets bigger and bigger and bigger – and pops.

I'm not saying you should settle for just any old boy-friend. You should expect to go out with someone who treats you considerately. But your love won't stay super-intense every day. And it's OK for Prince Charming to muddy his white horse once in a while.

I could go on, but the point is: once you get a romance flying high, don't force it into a crash landing!

Breaking Up Without Breaking Down

Breaking up? Maybe you and your boyfriend can turn things around. Love is moody and goes through growing pains. Have several heart-to-hearts before you accept heartbreak and heart-ache.

Maybe, sigh, your waxing love has waned for good, and no one is to blame. Or you both realize that as much as you care, you just aren't each other's soulmate or future spouse. Not every-body you go out with is someone you'll hope to go out with forever. Which means you'll probably survive more than one break-up in your life.

Break-ups are hell. At college, I remember looking out of my third-storey window on to the courtyard below and seeing the guy who'd just suggested we 'cool things' flirting merrily with another girl. Later, breaking up with Juan hurt terribly because I simultaneously lost boyfriend and best friend. Plus we both still harboured left-over love.

My senior school boyfriend and I? We broke up more than once. You've heard of false starts at races, right? Well, we had a few false ends. From my diary when I was sixteen:

I guess I was having my doubts. Apparently he was, too. He said he wanted to talk. He said the world is too big not to see other people. He was afraid of getting so serious.

'Face it, our lives and friends are completely different.'

'But it hasn't mattered.'
'But it has.'
He asked if I wanted to give breaking up a try.
'No, but I don't want you to feel obligated.' By now, I was crying.
'You really do care, don't you?' We kissed. 'I love you; maybe I love you too much.'
We said goodbye.
He stood in front of his car for a while, looking down and at me. Then he left. I sat on the grass in front of our house. Ten minutes later, I heard his rumbling Saab coming back!
He said, 'I was driving away and I said to myself, "You stupid ass — what did you do that for?" '
I smiled. 'We gave it a try.'

Should we have broken up then and there? Maybe. False ends are usually indicative of problems, and we eventually did part ways. Of course, reconciliation can be fun. (*'I'm falling in love all over again. Like when we first met. . .'*) But dragging out pain is a drag.

Can *your* relationship be saved? Is it worth saving? Deep inside, you and your guy probably know when it's goodbye time. When the relationship is more exhausting than exciting. When costs outweigh pleasures.

If you ever break up with a guy because he is violent or alcoholic, don't feel guilty. In many ways, you're doing him a favour, because he may then have to confront his problems. Don't ever give a guy an ultimatum ('I'll break up with you if you don't . . .') unless you are prepared to follow through.

How do you go about breaking up? Gingerly. The process can be likened to removing a plaster. You can do it gradually, pulling each fine hair as you go. (Oooooouuuuuch!) Or you can yank it off. (OUCH!!!) It hurts either way. Falling out of love is harder than falling in.

As painful as breaking up is, however, remember that the end of one thing is the beginning of something else. And breaking up is better than hanging on to a threadbare, one-sided, or mismatched relationship.

Sometimes these insights come fast, sometimes not. Do tell yourself: if your love was meant to last, it would have. And that freedom has its frills: you've been missing out on the fun of flirting, playing the field, and spending time with your pals and yourself.

Among the other fish out there are sharks and minnows, but also lots of good catches. What initially charmed your ex will charm your next. Or who knows? What *irked* your ex may charm your next.

If you've been given your walking papers, remember the bad times. After a break-up, we have a tendency to recall long talks and long kisses and to forget fights and not-so-good bits. His smoking irritated you? He was tightfisted? Great. Write down all the reasons behind your break-up and remember them as you grieve.

But do grieve. Tears help you heal, and you can't expect to be over him instantly. In fact, the hurt you feel now is a tribute to your love and your ability to love.

Break-ups don't always come complete with explanations, and that can add to the confusion. If you and your guy can be gentle and honest with each other about why the end has come, it may help your mutual growth and recovery. But too often, it doesn't work that way, and you're both left to puzzle it out on your own. Sometimes you get the Big E so suddenly you feel as though you were watching a film and somehow missed the last scene.

Stay busy! You could feel sorry for yourself for weeks, but you have better things to do. Dress up and see your friends. (Remember – the ones you didn't neglect just because love entered your life?) Don't cycle past places where you used to meet. Don't listen to Your Song. Put away his photograph. Jog. Get your hair cut. Buy a blouse. Take up a new hobby. Read a novel. Write to your grandma. Cuddle your cat. It's OK to stay in bed for one whole day if you want – but then get up and at 'em.

At first, you'll see flashbacks and mull over your last conversations, but fill your time so you don't sink into too much self-pity, guilt, rage, or remorse. (A little is natural.) Try not to suffer from withdrawal for too long.

If you meet someone else right away, he'll lift your spirits. Yet it's best not to race into romance on the rebound (or to get involved with a guy who's doing that). Give yourself time alone first. Patch up your broken heart before you give it away again. It's only fair to both of you. Sometimes relationships overlap, but that makes healing harder.

Can you two remain friends? Some former couples pull it off and if you can swing it, bully for you! You may find, when the hurt has healed a little, that you can see each other as friends, without suffering, but it may take a while to get to that point.

I do recommend trying to end things in a peaceful, dignified way. Don't threaten, beg, bitch, or scream at him. Don't slag off last week's Mr Wonderful to your mates. Don't hope he'll see the light and come crawling back. (Or if *you* instigated the break-up, don't try to get back together if you know you'll just be ending things further down the road.) You'll retain more self-respect if you can thank your guy for the good times, wish him the best, and move on.

(Then again, if he was a two-timing, double-crossing, total jerk about the whole thing and you want to blast him, I won't stop you. A violent break-up may help you deal with your anger. Or wait until you're alone, then punch pillows or tell him off in front of your mirror.)

Above all, don't conclude that love isn't worth it. Your broken relationship was not a waste of time. You enjoyed it and learned from it. Even if you got burned, weren't the sparks and toasty glow great while they lasted?

After you begin to feel stronger, get back into the ring. Not that there's anything wrong with going a long time without a boyfriend. But do check out the menu: Martin, Jeff, Brian, David, Terry, Ken, Joe. . . . Variety is spicy. And trial and error isn't such a bad way to go.

Lasting Love

Some romances take nosedives, others wind down and die natural deaths, and a few last a lifetime.

Tonight over dinner, a woman told me about her school reunion. She described a bunch of adults milling around a gym wearing name tags attached to photos of their former selves. 'I saw three old boyfriends,' she said. 'Dull! Dull! Dull! Neither Jay nor Karl nor Danny appealed to me. I'm lucky I made it to Jeremy.'

I tell you this because back in school, she never imagined that being dumped by Jay, Karl and Danny would be something she'd be thankful for one day. Yet love isn't always supposed to be forever.

Holiday romances are especially notorious for being picture-perfect. . .and short-lived. Why do so many summer loves fade with the autumn leaves? Because, as soon as you're back on home ground, the guy who thrilled you in Torquay or Torremolinos may seem like a stranger. Even if you live near one another, now that you're back at work or school, you both have less free time. Plus, the intense infatuation stage may be just about over by September, anyway. If you really want to try to keep the romance going, by all means do. Phone, write letters, plan meetings. A fling *can* last a lifetime. But if you realize that you may have to let each other go some day, you may feel less devastated if that day comes.

People change and drift in different directions. And great boyfriends don't always make great husbands or fathers, anyway. Be aware, too, that to a certain degree, you may now be bewitched by love in general and not by Charlie in particular. Do you mostly adore Charlie or do you mostly adore adoring and being adored?

There's no way to control how long a relationship lasts. For now, if you want your current love to continue, try to be friends first and foremost. Give each other room to grow. Keep your cards on the table. Keep your sense of humour about you. If the magnetism lasts, and you remain compatible as you mature – if you grow up without growing apart – your love just may endure.

Getting married while you're a teenager, however, is usually short-sighted. Teenage girls often visualize the rosy side of marriage (being together all the time, your own home and double bed) and forget about the added responsibilities of playing house (laundry, vacuuming, cheque-book balancing). If you have super-high expectations of what a marriage is, look around at the married couples you know – your parents, relatives, neighbours, friends' parents. That's marriage: for better and for worse. Marriage can be marvellous, but it doesn't make other troubles go away. And marrying to escape problems often just causes more problems.

The younger a couple marries, the higher the chances of divorce. Four times as many teenage marriages break up than later marriages. And many teenage spouses have less education and less money than couples who postponed marriage.

How can you know now whom you'll want to eat breakfast with when you're fifty-nine? Take your time before choosing a life partner! And why jump from life-with-parents to life-with-husband anyway, without first testing the waters alone or with roommates your age?

My sister-in-law Lisa and her husband Andy were teenage sweethearts who then played the field for several years. When they finally got engaged, they did so with open eyes. They'll never have to wonder what other loves could offer.

Another friend called off her wedding at the last minute. I admired her guts. As she put it, 'Better to be mortified this month than miserable for years.'

Before you marry anybody, soon or someday, make sure you thoroughly (thoroughly!) discuss your attitudes about money, children, sex, housework, education, religion, where to live, personal goals, and just about everything else under the moon. You're not both going to live with one of your parents, are you? (Their roof, their rules.)

Should you live together some day? It's up to you. If you do, may I suggest a one- or two-year limit to the arrangement? When time's up, marry or set each other free.

True love *can* last. But if your fifth-form romance fizzles, don't languish forever. Another romance will blossom. And fade. Do you want to get married someday? A love that can stand the test of time will come along. Mature love grows and will wait until you're ready for the security and sacrifices that come with saying *I do*.

Love Notes

Love at First Sight or When the Chemistry Is Right:

I could tell you Rob and I fell in love at first sight because an instant zing did flash between us. But then love at first sight only holds up if it survives a second glance, a third stare, and a fourth cross-examination. Intrigue at first sight? That I'll accept. Falling in love is lovely, but so is stepping in, and it's OK if you and your guy didn't feel immediate thunder.

He Said He'd Phone You and He Didn't:

Guys do that. They say, 'I'll ring you', at the end of a date even when they won't. It's not to string you along. It's their way of being polite. Like when we say, 'Thanks, I had a good time,' even though the evening turned out so awful and it would have been better to have stayed home, polished shoes, and changed the cat litter. Of course, your guy might be shy. Or he might call in a few weeks. Don't glue yourself to the phone. If you can't stand the waiting game, call *him*. And remember that if he didn't call because he didn't like you, you wouldn't want to go out with him anyway.

There's No Such Thing As a Free Dinner:

If he wants to pay, I won't argue. Just don't order the most or least expensive entrée on the menu. But why not offer to share expenses or invite him out once in a while? Say, 'My treat.' (That's more graceful than 'Let me pay.') Don't let a fella spend a lot of money on you if you suspect he'll feel you owe him fifteen quid's worth of gropes and heavy breathing. Some guys spend money on girls during a date, then think they're entitled to squeeze it out of them afterwards. If you invite *him* to the theatre or a concert, let him know ahead of time that you plan to treat him (or that it's OK to split expenses).

Even if You Find Mr Right, Things Will Go Wrong:

Not such bad news, really. Keeps you on your toes.

Chivalry Is Alive and Kicking:

Feminism is great, but I also like it when a man holds a door open for me, and I make a point of holding doors open for men – and women. If a guy helps you on with your coat, don't lecture him on women's rights. If he opens the car door for you, don't get on a soapbox; get in, lean over, and unlock his door for him. I'm all for male gallantry and female courtesy.

Love and Looks:

If you run into your heart-throb when you're wearing your
tracksuit, don't cringe. Smile. He looks great in *his* tracksuit,
doesn't he? On the other hand, do always try to look presentable.
And if you know you'll be seeing him, make an extra effort to
look decent. Love makes girls blossom, but then many take their
guys for granted and go to seed. Beware: love is blind, but not for
long!

Guys Get Nervous, Too:

Once my brother, Eric, had an 8 p.m. date with a neighbour. He
came into my room at 7:55 to ask, 'Do you think I should be a little
early, right on time, or a little late?' I said I didn't think it
mattered. But that exchange mattered to me – it taught me to
relax, because guys get nervous, too.

There Is Such a Thing As Being Too Honest:

Yes, you should keep the lines of communication open, speak
your mind, and not lie. But no, you don't have to tell your
boyfriend how far you went with each of your former fellas.
Don't unburden yourself by lumping the burden on him. You
also don't need to share every little thought that pops into your
head, or tell him how you hate your fat thighs. *You* decide where
to draw the honesty line. Love is sometimes saying what you
think the other person wants to hear instead of the truth, and
sometimes saying the truth instead of what you think the other
person wants to hear.

Whoever Said a Girl Can't Give a Guy a Flower?

Not me.

Long-Distance Love:

I've been there. It can work. But exchanging eloquent love letters that skim above daily strife makes it easy for you both to romanticize the relationship. When you're actually about to see each other again, allow for an awkward period of getting reacquainted.

Going Out with More Than One Guy at One Time:

I've been there, too, and it's not as much fun as you'd imagine. It takes a lot of psychic energy to care a lot about two guys – and I for one never have been a fan of roller-coaster rides. If you think you and your guys can handle a triangle, OK. But if you two-time on the quiet, you may get caught, and you'll probably feel guilty. What about just casually dating more than one guy? Sure, why not?

Life Can Be Exhilarating Even When You're Not in Love:

Absolutely!

Kissing, Etc.

Kissing comes naturally. The best way to approach it is not to worry about who does what to whom. Just take off your glasses and be soft, sensual and creative! If you think your boyfriend is more experienced than you, don't panic. First of all, he too, may be a novice. And second, you may be a fast learner. (Practice makes perfect!) Besides, he'd probably prefer to be your kissing instructor than have you be an expert who has picked up pointers from every member of the rugby team.

Kissing expresses caring. Don't feel compelled to break any kissing-without-breathing records or to jam your tongue into the guy's mouth if you don't want to. But if he explores your mouth with his tongue, try to enjoy the feeling rather than tensing up. And if your tongue is the more adventurous, that's OK, too. Beware of beard burn, which is when his five o'clock shadow scrapes your chin. And (uh oh, here comes a stupid joke) don't ever say to a vampire, 'Wanna neck?'

My school boyfriend and I sometimes argued about necking in public. He took offence because I didn't like it. Once he even asked, 'What are you going to do on your wedding day in front of all those people?' But I stuck to my guns and we did our smooching in private.

Decide how you feel about the *whos*, *hows*, *wheres* and *whens* of kissing. Kissing and cuddling go a long way. The happiest marriages are among couples who haven't forgotten how to express this kind of spontaneous, caring affection.

What about sex? Don't rush into it. From television and films, you may have gathered that some adults rush through the preliminaries. Yet instant sex is often sound and fury signifying nothing, to steal a metaphor from Shakespeare! And many adults miss the kissing, hugging, back-rubbing and hand-holding.

How did *you* first find out about intercourse? Did a more experienced schoolmate tell your whole table one day at lunch? Did you stumble on a raunchy book when baby-sitting, or in your parents' room? Did your mother sit you down to discuss The Facts of Life?

Now that the secret's out. . .

4. Sex

What You Should Know Before Saying Yes

If you're not yet having sex – three cheers. If you are, I hope that you don't have sex for the wrong reasons: your friend is involved in an X-rated romance; or your sister has gone all the way; or your boyfriend is putting on the pressure; or you think you gain points if you score.

Sex should someday become a pleasurable, meaningful, guilt-free part of your life. But sex before you're ready or sex with the wrong guy is no fun. So proceed with caution. There are good reasons why you should wait.

This chapter is for those who are already sexually active and for those who intend to be virgins until their wedding night. It gives the lowdown on contraception, pregnancy, abortion, self-stimulation, sexually transmitted disease, homosexuality, rape, incest, and other topics you may wonder about.

To Do It or Not To Do It: That Is The Question

Once upon a time, unless you were married, you didn't want anybody to think you'd gone all the way. Now lots of teenagers don't want anyone to think they haven't. Years ago, girls couldn't say yes. Now many can't say no. Back then, some dreaded the thought of being sweet-sixteen-and-never-been-kissed. Now some fear they'll be sweet-sixteen-and-never-been-____.

Let's just say too many girls are forgetting that virginity is not something to get rid of or feel ashamed of. Too many are feeling rushed into sex before they are ready.

If you are a virgin, you may be asking yourself if you are ready. Yes? No? Maybe so? It's a tricky question because it brings up many other questions.

- Are you responsible enough to use birth control every single time?
- Are you really mature enough to have a baby or an abortion if the birth control fails?
- Do you feel free to say no?
- Are you certain he won't give you a venereal disease?
- If having sex goes against your parents' values, can you handle doing something they (or you) consider wrong?
- Do you love the guy, and does he love you?
- Have you been going out for a long time? (Two months is not a long time.)
- Are you close friends and not just partners in passion?
- Will you feel good about the decision the next day?
- Have you weighed the pros and cons?
- Will it mean as much to him as it will to you?
- Do you truly desire him physically? (Most girls don't feel intense sexual desire in their early teens.)

I'd want to answer all yeses on that miniquiz before considering saying yes to any guy. Sex at any age before you're ready is a bad idea. Better to let sex be something to look forward to. The suspense and wanting and anticipation make the eventual act more special.

If you can wait, wait. If you have doubts or think you would have regrets, wait. If you think being easy is the way to get or keep a boyfriend, wait. If you think you might lose any self-esteem if you say yes, wait. If you think your decision is based on wanting to rebel or wanting to conform, wait. If you can wait, wait.

What if your boyfriend is pressurizing you? You're both in love and have been petting for months, and he says he's frustrated out of his mind? What if *he's* ready but you're not?

First of all, heartless though this may sound, nobody ever died of frustration. It doesn't do a guy any harm to have an erection and then not come (have an orgasm). That happens to him when he sees a sexy movie or thinks about Page 3 girls. (I was sixteen when I wrote in my diary, *'Judy and I were discussing erections. Can boys calm down or do they have to let it out? Eric* [my brother] *enlightened me that they could calm down.'*) Secondly, lots of guys would prefer the frustration of not making love to the frustration of not kissing, so it's unfair for them to make you feel so guilty. Thirdly, if you have sex for his sake, you're short-changing yourself; you should be making love *with* him – not *to* him or *for* him. Sex goes both ways. It's not one person letting the other do things or one owing the other something. Fourthly, many fellas feel they have to ask, to prove how masculine they are. Your boyfriend may be no more experienced than you and may even be relieved when you say no. Fifthly (for serious relationships only), the two of you may want to talk about petting to orgasm or finding a way to relieve the frustration without risking penetration and pregnancy.

Lines? Some guys use a variation of the ancient, 'You would if you loved me.' You can reply, 'You wouldn't insist if you loved me.' A guy who doesn't care enough to be patient and respect your point of view doesn't care enough. Or he might argue, 'Everyone else is.' Fine. Why isn't he with everyone else? Or he might try the old, 'We might die tomorrow.' True. But we probably won't. And the only way to stay sane is to have hope and confidence about the future: your own and the world's.

Having intercourse means literally and figuratively opening yourself up to someone else. That's a Big Deal. Even if you're not a virgin, it's still a Big Deal – it's always a Big Deal (and now with AIDS a growing risk, it is an even Bigger Deal!) If you went all the way once with Ryan, you don't have to do it again with him or anyone else until you know you're ready.

Are you concerned about what you think your friends think? Believe it or not, virgins in your school are probably the silent majority. Recent statistics say that one in eight under sixteens have had sex. That means that seven out of eight are still virgins. According to a survey in *Woman* magazine in 1984, almost a third are still virgins at nineteen.

Once you've said yes to someone, it is harder to say no the next time. It also becomes harder to sort out how you feel about the guy. And if you and he do break up, the split may become more painful. Also consider this: some couples aren't as sexually compatible as others. What if sex isn't so great with you and Neil? Will your relationship deteriorate?

Girls who do have sex should be discreet. To kiss and tell is all very well, but it's wiser to kiss and shut up. I'm amazed at how much I knew in school about people I shouldn't have known anything about. My diary is peppered with tidbits (names changed) such as: *'Lance Harmon and Polly Shoor screwed when she was superdrunk,'* and, *'Mike is very upset with Diane for telling how far they went. He found it "intimate and personal". Diane did, too, but she told Jen who told Carol who told Judy who told Steve who is best friends with Mike and mentioned it to him.'*

So if you aren't going to keep your legs crossed, at least keep your mouth shut! Then, if gossips gossip, ignore them. 'Tease'? 'Slut'? 'Prude'? Labels are idiotic. Try not to use them or listen to them. Some nice girls do and some nice girls don't.

True Confessions: My First Time

Your first time is important. You remember it forever. Not that the second time or the third are run of the mill or that sex should ever be less than memorable. But there's only one first time, and the moment stays with you, for better and for worse. Are you expecting instant ecstasy? Don't. Many guys and girls find the first attempt is awkward and clumsy, no matter how meaningful and poignant.

I hope your first time is with a steady, caring partner. That's how it is for most women. Others give away their virginity to someone who hardly appreciates the gift: the old everyone-else-is-doing-it-so-I-might-as-well-get-it-over-with approach.

My first time was also my boyfriend's first time. We were in love and we'd waited and postponed and planned and were responsible enough not to insist on spontaneity. Nor did we want to be high or drunk; we wanted to be *there*. So we discussed it, got birth control, and finally tried to do it. And tried and tried. I was tense and scared and, as I confessed afterwards to my diary, *'It took an hour of true struggling.'* Then the condom broke and so did the mood as I rushed to the phone to call the family planning clinic. (The phone call was eventually followed by a test, but I was lucky and wasn't pregnant.)

To be honest, making love that first time was neither painful nor particularly enjoyable. I didn't bleed (many women do) and I didn't come (most women don't).

In my diary, I reported the lack of blood and commented, *'Maybe my hymen isn't even broken,'* and, *'Maybe I'm still a technical virgin.'* Right, and maybe the Pope is really a Moonie. Perhaps my wonderings were part ignorance, part wistful thinking. It isn't easy to say goodbye to girlhood.

It's Easy To Get Pregnant; It's Easy Not To

You can skip every other section in this book if you want, but read these next few pages. Maybe not this year, maybe not next year, but before you get involved in a sexual relationship. I've never made love without contraception. When my husband and I decide to try to have children, I'll put away the protection. But not until then.

It doesn't shock me that so many teenagers are having intercourse. But I am appalled that so many are doing so without birth control.

If you are sexually active, I won't stand in front of you waving a chastity belt. But if I could, I might show up waving a diaphragm. Sex without contraception is like skydiving without a parachute.

These are the widely published but hard-to-believe recent statistics:

- More than 100,000 teenagers in the United Kingdom became pregnant in 1983, of which 37,400 had abortions.
- One in fifty under-sixteens gets pregnant.
- The present generation of fifteen-year-olds has a one in ten chance of having an abortion before the age of twenty.

- Twenty-five per cent of abortions are to teenagers.
- Almost *one third* of teenagers in a recent survey in *19* magazine said they 'sometimes' or 'mostly' took chances and didn't use birth control.
- A survey in *Woman* found that *half* of women didn't take precautions the first time they made love!

If teenagers were better informed, these statistics could change. But too many parents and daughters get flustered when the topic of sex comes up. Too many schools don't teach sex education or teach it poorly or teach it at the wrong time. Too many young people don't know the facts and spread misinformation. And too many sexy songs and steamy movies make everybody randy but offer no clues about how to keep from getting pregnant. (Does James Bond ever ask the girl in his arms if she's protected?)

It's your responsibility to protect yourself. We can get huffy about that. Why *hasn't* a contraceptive pill been invented for guys? Why don't males play a bigger role in birth control? Meantime, though, we're the ones with wombs, so *we* need to know how to avoid unwanted pregnancy.

Some girls (and this kills me) hesitate to get contraceptives because that's consciously admitting that they're having sex and they're not ready to face the fact. They think, 'Since I'm not using birth control, I'm not really having sex.' Listen, if you're not ready to be responsible about intercourse, you're not ready for it. Which is fine. What's not fine is to deny what you're doing and wind up as another pregnancy statistic. Don't ignore the cause-and-effect nature of sex and pregnancy. If you're adult enough to have sex, be adult enough to protect yourself.

Other girls feel contraceptives take the romance and spontaneity out of lovemaking. Pregnancy and babies don't do much for romance and spontaneity, either. The idea of reckless sex is all very nice during those minutes of heavy breathing. But it's not worth the weeks of worry as you pray for your period. It's only common sense to be prepared.

Still other girls don't use contraceptives because they are afraid their parents would find out. First of all, pregnancy is a more frightening prospect than upset parents and harder to hide than a packet of pills.

Secondly, if your mother did find your pills, who knows? She may be more relieved than outraged.

Some girls have sex without contraception because they think they want a baby. They imagine sweet smiles and booties and aren't aware that babies get screaming hungry at 4 a.m. and usually aren't toilet-trained for two or three years. Babies require work, attention, and money. If you think a baby will bind you happily ever after to a guy, you haven't met any of the thousands of single mothers whose former boyfriends deny paternity and refuse to pay any maintenance. Too many babies are born out of wedlock and into social security.

It's dangerous to be naive. I know lots of intelligent girls and women who were unhappily surprised by pregnancy. One had a baby daughter, gave her up for adoption, and still thinks and wonders about her. Several had abortions and felt sad for months afterwards. Two got married, and if you ask me (I know you didn't, but I'll tell you anyway), I don't think either marriage will last. In couple number one, the husband feels trapped and resentful. And couple number two's baby boy was born severely handicapped, and so far it seems neither groom nor bride is mature enough to cope with the responsibility.

Sure, some unexpected pregnancies lead to happy endings, but lots don't. Besides, you can have babies in your 20s and 30s, so there's really no hurry. As a matter of fact, pregnancy is riskier for teenage mothers and their babies than it is for more mature women and their babies.

Once you realize that using contraceptives makes sense, you need to determine which kind is best for you. The following section can help you decide. You may be interested to learn that, of the 61,000 or so sexually active young women who attended Brook clinics in 1984, some of whom were married, approximately:

82 per cent chose the Pill
7 per cent chose a condom
5 per cent chose an IUD
5 per cent chose a diaphragm
1 per cent chose other methods

Because of the risk of AIDS condoms are steadily gaining in popularity. Unfortunately, however, many girls don't use any contraception and those who do don't always use it carefully enough to ensure maximum protection.

Please promise yourself that until you are ready to be a mother, you will make the effort to use contraception correctly and responsibly every single time you make love.

The Age Of Consent

You probably know that there are extra problems for anyone under sixteen who is having, or thinking of having, sex. That's because as the law stands, it's illegal for a man to have sex with a girl who is under sixteen – the so-called age of consent.

That doesn't mean that once you are sixteen, anything goes. There is no 'right age' for sex. But if you're under sixteen and someone is trying to persuade you to have sex, you know the law is on your side. He could be prosecuted, and you can tell him so.

Of course that doesn't help if you happen to be a fourteen- or fifteen-year-old involved in a loving, caring relationship. Maybe you want to make love, or you already have, but you don't know how to go about getting birth control. A doctor who prescribes the Pill for you is, technically, helping you and your boyfriend to commit an offence. You may have heard of Mrs Victoria Gillick, who tried to ensure that doctors prescribing contraception to under-sixteens had to tell the girls' parents. There have been so many legal rulings recently that everyone – doctors, counsellors and, most of all, teenagers – is pretty confused! What should you do?

- If you can wait till you're at least sixteen, I hope you will. Surveys show that older teenagers tend to enjoy their first experience more anyway.
- If you can confide in your mum, dad, aunt or older sister, or a sympathetic teacher or Youth Club leader, ask their advice.
- Call your nearest Brook Advisory Centre, *see page 279*. They will give you all the help they can whatever your age and without telling your parents.

- Rather than taking no precautions at all, at least insist that your boyfriend use a condom, which is available from chemists without a prescription, or free from clinics (more on condoms in a minute).

One thing you *shouldn't* do is go right ahead and trust to luck, or rumours about 'safe' sex. You *can* get pregnant the first time. You can get pregnant even before your periods start. You can get pregnant if you have sex standing up, or even if you cough or pee straight after. Coke douches and Clingfilm are not reliable contraceptives. Don't take risks. The stakes are too high.

Birth Control Methods

The Pill

The Pill, a combination of synthetic hormones similar to progesterone and oestrogen, works by suppressing ovulation. With no ripe-and-ready egg present, a woman can't become pregnant. Used properly, it's almost one hundred per cent effective. No mess, no fuss.

The Pill has some real advantages if taken without fail at about the same time each day. The doctor will usually prescribe a twenty-one-pill packet (take one each day for three weeks, then on the Pill, you can make love with complete spontaneity and skip the week of your period before starting again). Once on the Pill, you are without fear of pregnancy. (Borrowing one of your friend's Pills, however, does no good at all – for you or her.) The doctor who prescribes for you will explain exactly how to take your particular Pill. If you're not sure, or you don't understand, ask questions. Do listen to the doctor about exactly when you should take your first Pill (normally the first day of your period) and how soon you will be protected. Ask if there is an information sheet which you can take with you to remind you.

Some say the Pill may be linked to increased risk of blood clots or heart problems. But most experts now agree that the new low-dosage Pill poses no serious health hazards for young women. Many say its benefits far outweigh its risks: not only is the Pill safer than childbirth, but it may protect against ovarian cancer in young women. Nor is the Pill a risky new discovery – it has been around since 1960.

Who should think twice before going on the Pill? Girls who are quite underweight or who do not yet have well-established periods, girls who smoke, girls with certain medical problems (such as high blood pressure), and girls who are forgetful and might miss a day. (If you miss a Pill or two, use a back-up method.) But for most sexually active girls, the Pill may be an ideal method of birth control.

Does it make you gain weight? When I was briefly on the Pill, I didn't get puffy. Nor did the Pill cause me nausea, spotting, depression, or headaches. But some girls do suffer these side effects. Pluses? The Pill makes your periods regular, shorter, and less painful. If you suffer severe period pains, you may want to ask a doctor to consider prescribing the Pill for you.

I must admit I'm not comfortable with the fact that the Pill alters you internally. But then I'm not big on pill-taking in general. Unless you are engaging in regular, frequent sex, I don't think it's worth it to fool with your body chemistry.

Are you on the Pill and not having sex? That's silly. Are you having sex because you're on the Pill? That's nuts.

The Mini-pill

This kind of Pill contains the sex hormone progesterone only and can be taken by women for whom the 'combined' Pill isn't suitable (e.g. older women and smokers). It works by altering the lining of the womb and thickening the cervical mucus so that the sperm can't penetrate. It's not quite as effective as the 'combined' Pill. You have to take it at exactly the same time every day, so you need a terrific memory! So far, it seems to have fewer health risks than the 'combined' Pill, though it can make your periods irregular.

Condoms

Condoms, also called sheaths or rubbers, are an easy, accessible and safe method of birth control and are 85 – 98 per cent effective. You can buy them without a prescription at any chemists, and they are free from the FPA and Brook clinics. The usual brand in Britain is Durex.

Just before intercourse, the boy unrolls the condom on to his erect penis. If penetration isn't easy, use prelubricated condoms – don't use Vaseline or petroleum jelly for lubrication, as this can weaken the rubber. For extra protection, buy condoms that have a reservoir tip in which semen can collect, or buy those which are coated with a spermicide for added security. After intercourse, your partner should withdraw right away and hold on to the rim of the condom so it doesn't slip off. Use a new condom every time and never use one which is more than two years old.

Condoms protect you from pregnancy because sperm are trapped in the thin rubber sheath. There are virtually no side effects associated with them and they have the great advantage of offering protection against cervical cancer and sexually transmitted diseases. Some guys complain that condoms diminish their pleasure, but worrying about pregnancy and disease while making love cuts down a couple's pleasure, too.

Diaphragm with Jelly or Cream

Have you ever seen a diaphragm or cap? Picture a flexible beige mini-Frisbee with a rubber ring around the edge and you've got the idea. A doctor measures you to determine what size you need before prescribing the diaphragm. He or she should check you again yearly to make sure the size is right, and more often if you gain or lose more than ten pounds, have a baby or an abortion. The diaphragm is not effective if it doesn't fit properly or if it has a hole or tear in it. So replace it at least every two years and make a habit of holding it up to bright light to check for a rip or filling it with water to check for a leak. (Heard the one about the dumb lady who kept her diaphragm near the bed – nailed to the bedpost?)

Diaphragms are not much more complicated to put in or take

out than tampons, and a doctor or nurse will show you how.
Once it's inside, you shouldn't be able to feel it.

Anywhere from six hours to six seconds before intercourse,
you should prepare the diaphragm by squeezing at least a tea-
spoonful of spermicidal jelly or cream into the bowl of the dome
and around the rim. Before inserting the diaphragm, pee and
wash your hands. After intercourse, leave it in for at least six
hours but never over twenty-four. If you make love again during
this time, insert more jelly or cream without removing the diaphragm. Later, after removing the diaphragm, wash it gently
with warm water, dry it, and store it away from heat in its
container.

The diaphragm prevents pregnancy because the rubber
barrier in front of your cervix physically blocks the speeding
sperm, and the jelly or cream chemically kills them. It is 85 – 97
per cent effective, but because some girls and women occasionally put it in incorrectly, forget to use it, run out of jelly, or lose or
gain weight but don't get remeasured for size, the effectiveness
statistic is lower.

The diaphragm has become more popular recently. It's convenient if you want to have sex during your period because it
catches the menstrual flow. I'd especially recommend it if you
only have sex once in a while and don't want full-time birth
control for part-time sex.

IUD

IUDs (short for intrauterine device, also known as the coil), are
easy and effective, but are not recommended for young women.
They're better for women who have already had kids and cannot
use other methods of birth control. The reason?

Side effects. Some users get heavy periods and cramping. All
users risk perforation of the uterus, ectopic pregnancy (pregnancy which occurs outside the womb, usually in a fallopian
tube), spontaneous abortion, and increased chances of pelvic
inflammatory infection, which could lead to sterility. Users are
also more susceptible to sexually transmitted diseases.

Natural Family Planning (or Rhythm Method)

I bet the guy who sings, 'I got rhythm, I got music, I got my girl, who could ask for anything more?' ends up with more: a houseful of babies! While it's wise to know how the rhythm method works so you know when you are most and least fertile, it's risky to rely on rhythm as a means of birth control because your cycle changes. It takes a lot of motivation and personal teaching to use the rhythm method and is best practised by more mature couples. If used properly, it is 85 – 93 per cent effective – but *only* if used properly! 'What do you call couples who use rhythm?' asks an old joke. 'Parents.'

You should know that you are most fertile at about the mid-point of your menstrual cycle (about two weeks after your period starts) and are least likely to get pregnant during and right before menstruation. Got that? In other words, assuming you have a regular twenty-eight-day cycle (and for most women, that's a false assumption), if your period begins on January 1, you will ovulate sometime around January 14. One of your ovaries will release a single egg into one of your fallopian tubes, and that egg will travel towards your uterus. Your egg can be fertilized any time during the next two days, and sperm can live inside you for up to four days. So if sperm meets and fertilizes egg anytime that week – hey presto, you're pregnant. The rhythm system therefore says: no sex before, during, or after ovulation. So you would abstain (or use other contraception) at least from January 11 until January 17 in that hypothetical cycle.

Many conscientious women do more than mark their calendars. They check for variations in their cervical mucus and body temperature and note conditions (stress, travel, sickness) that could cause an irregularity in their cycle. Such precautions make rhythm a little more effective.

The problem with rhythm for girls who don't have regular cycles is that they can't predict when they are ovulating. If you have a period the first week in January and not again until the second week in March, it's hard to know when you were most fertile. Other girls may be absent-minded and have trouble remembering which days are safest.

Still others might feel passionate on a 'dangerous' day and not have the self-restraint to say no.

Rhythm is safe and is sanctioned by the Roman Catholic

Church. Although I do *not* advise it as your sole method of birth control, I do recommend that you learn when you are most fertile. Why? So that now you never ever take a chance during those times, and later, when you may want to start a family, you'll know when you'll be most likely to conceive. Remember that rhythm or no rhythm, you can get pregnant any time – even during your period.

Withdrawal

Don't count on it. It takes a whole lot of will power for a guy to pull out the very second his pleasure is most intense. Even if he means to withdraw before ejaculating, he might slip up, and that means millions of sperm racing in search of your egg. A drag if pregnancy is not your intention. Besides, I know I couldn't relax if I were depending on someone else's self-control to keep me from getting pregnant.

Even if your partner does withdraw in time, it may still be too late. A few drops of clear, lubricating, sperm-filled liquid may be secreted even before he ejaculates, and all it takes is one sperm (and one egg) to make a baby. Men may produce as many as 80 million sperm daily.

Morning-after Pill

If you have been raped or have taken a mid-cycle risk and are scared of being pregnant, or are in some other emergency situation, you might consider getting a morning-after pill. You can visit your GP or clinic straight away and be given two pills which must be taken twelve hours apart, and which alter your hormone balance to prevent pregnancy. These pills can cause some side effects. They are not ordinary contraceptive pills – so don't just take an extra dose of yours, or anybody else's. If you want to take the morning-after pill there's no point in dithering, though; for it to work, it must be taken within seventy-two hours of having sex. After that, it may be too late.

Sterilization

No way! This is only to be contemplated by older women who
have completed their families.

The Sponge

Unfortunately, not very effective. Other drawbacks? Some users
complain that the sponge expands too much inside them and
becomes difficult to remove. Others say that it seems to fall apart
inside them. Still others say it makes them very dry and irritated.

New Methods

Researchers are always coming up with new ideas. Implants, for
instance, are tiny rods implanted in your arm which release a
gradual, steady dose of contraceptive into your body and are
effective for one to five years. Intra-vaginal rings fit in the vagina
and release hormones which are effective for three months in
preventing pregnancy. These other methods may be available in
the near future and your clinic or GP will be able to give you
further information.

Abortion

Wrong. Abortion is not a method of birth control; it's a too-late
last resort. Read on.

What If You Are Pregnant?

I hope you're dipping into this section out of idle curiosity. I
hope you're a virgin or have used birth control whenever you
have made love.

But you may be reading this because you're pregnant.

Pregnant. It may not seem fair. Perhaps you've only had inter-course one measly time in your whole life. Or maybe you and your boyfriend were always careful about contraception – except once. Or maybe you mistakenly believed a myth like you can't get pregnant the first time or you can't get pregnant if you don't come.

So you missed a period, were feeling tired and occasionally nauseated, had to pee often, and noticed your breasts and belly beginning to swell. Did you wait around to see if your next period would come? No.

You bought a home pregnancy testing kit from the chemist. Or, two weeks after your period was due, you went to the doctor, clinic or chemist with a sample of urine (passed first thing in the morning). You waited for the result and. . .you're pregnant. Now what? For a time, you can't believe it. You deny it. You cry a lot. Then you talk to the counsellors at the Brook Advisory Centre (there are Brook Centres, in Birmingham, Bristol, Coventry, Edinburgh, Merseyside and London – *see page 279*, the Family Planning Association (check your phone book for your nearest branch), or the British Pregnancy Advisory Service – *see page 279*. You consider telling your boyfriend and maybe even your parents (they may be angry or hurt, but the chances are they'll stand by you.) Telling a friend may be a comfort, but if your friend tells a friend, your news could become public.

Start considering your options, each with pros and cons. Find out as much as possible, and decide what's right for you. Your boyfriend may beg you to keep the baby. Your girlfriend may advise you to have the baby, then give it up for adoption. Your parents may urge you to get an abortion. Easy for all of them to say. What do *you* want to do?

Think about yourself first – before boyfriend or baby, friends or family. You're the one who has to make the decision and live with it.

Keeping the Baby

Before you decide you want to have and keep the baby, think about what you're getting into. Having a baby is not like having a doll or baby-sitting for two hours, then leaving with money jingling in your pocket. A baby is a huge responsibility. I hope to have a family someday, but at twenty-seven I'm still not ready for that responsibility. Are you sure you are?

Thousands of teenagers each year decide to have and keep their babies. Some end up feeling trapped, resentful and cheated of their childhood. Would you find it frustrating to wear maternity clothes while slim friends wear sexy dresses? To be stuck inside changing nappies while friends are down at the disco? To have to leave school or college, or abandon your job, and try to live on social security while friends are making career plans? Maybe you want to finish *being* a kid before having a kid. Maybe you aren't ready to be tied down. You probably will be able to offer a baby more in the future. Being a mother with no money, no husband and no prospects is very hard. Four out of ten low-income mums who are confined to the house with young children suffer from depression.

Be realistic. Can you afford a baby? Are you mature enough to handle having a baby now? Healthy enough for labour and motherhood? Willing to give the baby all the attention it demands? Will you get married or raise the child alone? Picture your situation a year from now; five years from now. Will the baby's father or your parents be able to help you during all this?

Some girls decide to have and keep their babies and it is a wise, happy choice. The baby's father is proud and supportive and can earn a living for the couple and the toddler. Or the teenage girl's parents care for mother and baby and the teenager is able to continue her education and career plans. Obviously if you are an older teenager and you and your boyfriend are already engaged, your chances of feeling good about keeping the baby are better than if you are fifteen and the baby's father doesn't want anything to do with you. But many couples who marry because a baby's on the way end up miserable. Don't forget that most teenage marriages end in divorce – and that's counting teenagers who aren't parents.

If you do decide to have the baby, see a doctor now and start getting antenatal care and taking antenatal classes. If you think you might have a sexually transmitted disease, go to a doctor for tests and possible treatment or your baby could be born blind, deaf, or otherwise defective. To make sure your baby is born as healthy as possible, eat nutritiously (cut out junk food!) and don't drink, smoke, or take drugs while pregnant. Drinking is linked to birth defects; smoking to small, weak babies and premature births. The incidence of premature and underweight infants and infant mortality is higher among teenage mothers than mothers in their twenties.

If you decide to have your baby – if your baby is a wanted baby – do all you can to start its life right.

Getting an Abortion

Many teenagers with unwanted pregnancies end up having an abortion. It's not an easy decision and, afterwards, some feel guilty and sad and wistful. But many also feel a deep sense of relief, especially if the pregnancy was the result of rape or incest or loveless sex or if the girl knew in advance (perhaps through amniocentesis or an ultrasound scan) that the baby would be abnormal or unhealthy.

An early abortion (one that is performed during the first twelve weeks of pregnancy) is safer, cheaper, and simpler than a later abortion. In most cases, you cannot have an abortion during the last three months of pregnancy. (So make up your mind. Don't let time make the what-to-do-if-you're-pregnant decision for you.) Having one abortion by a competent gynaecologist won't damage your reproductive organs, but having several abortions, particularly late abortions, may make it hard for you to carry a future pregnancy to term. The longer you wait, the more complicated and expensive the abortion.

Abortion has been legal in the UK since 1967 but how easily and quickly you get one on the NHS depends on where you live and on your doctor's attitude. If you are pregnant and you want an abortion, then you are much luckier than girls of twenty years ago in your position. Back then many drank bottles of gin, had scalding-hot baths, threw themselves down the stairs, took various pills rumoured to cause a miscarriage, or visited highly dangerous and horribly expensive back-street abortionists in the hope of ending their pregnancies. Many ended their lives instead. Fortunately, today you can, at the discretion of your GP, obtain a free abortion on the NHS or pay for one privately at a registered clinic.

Your GP is your first port of call. But you may feel you can't approach him or her, for some reason. And some GPs are against abortion. If yours is not sympathetic, or if you'd rather not consult him or her, contact the BPAS (British Pregnancy Advisory Service), a non-profit-making charity that provides the most reasonably priced abortions in the country (See page 279).

Facts About Abortion

Legally you can get an abortion right up to your twenty-eighth week of pregnancy, but in practical terms this means twenty-four weeks to allow for any confusion over dates. In fact, very few abortions are carried out as late as that.

Methods of terminating a pregnancy vary according to the patient's wishes, medical reasons and how many months pregnant she is. It is possible to have a day-care abortion, but most patients stay in the clinic overnight, where qualified staff can keep an eye on them and make sure no problems arise.

If you are under twelve weeks pregnant, the suction method is generally used. Between twelve and sixteen weeks, it may be either suction or a D & C. A D & C (Dilation and Curettage) involves scraping out the womb, but some doctors are reluctant to stretch the cervix in a very young woman. If you are more than sixteen weeks pregnant, the method would probably be induction under general anaesthetic.

In 1986, the BPAS charged £3 for a pregnancy test, £24 for counselling (including the pregnancy test if required), £112 for vaginal surgery, £220 for a D & C up to nineteen weeks, and £252 for an abortion after that time which involves more complicated surgery and a longer stay in hospital. But do phone and check on the current prices.

If you wish your abortion to be kept a secret, the BPAS service (and indeed most services) is totally confidential. But, if you are under sixteen, parental consent for an abortion is advisable. Let's hope that you'll be one of the wise, careful, lucky girls and that it really will never happen to you.

Giving Up Your Baby

Maybe you're too far along in your pregnancy to have a safe abortion. Or maybe abortion is against your principles. So you're going through with your pregnancy. You're seeing a doctor and taking good care of yourself because you want to deliver a healthy baby.

But you've decided not to keep it. About a thousand women each year choose the adoption option. They realize they are too young or too alone to be the kind of mother they'd like to be.

If you are considering adoption, some may ask, 'How can you give away your baby?' but you have to ask yourself, 'How can I keep it?' Some may think you should pay for your 'mistake', but the emotional cost of delivery and adoption are certainly price enough. Others may think you're cold-hearted. I think it is big-hearted to offer your baby to a couple that desperately wants a child, has been waiting for one, and is ready and able to give yours the future it deserves. There are far more couples who want to adopt than available babies to be adopted.

Quite a few organizations can give you advice and counselling if you are thinking about adoption. BAAF (British Agencies for Adoption and Fostering – *see page 279*) produce helpful books and leaflets on the subject and can put you in touch with adoption agencies in your area. The Brook Advisory Centres, Family Planning Association and the social worker at the hospital you are attending for antenatal care can also answer questions and help you make your important decision.

What happens if you decide on adoption? After your baby is born and you leave the hospital, he or she goes straight to a temporary foster mother, or to the adoptive parents. This isn't the end of matters; you still have a certain amount of time in which to change your mind, the limit normally being about four and a half months. After six weeks you sign a formal document giving your agreement, but the court does not grant the final adoption order until your child has lived with its adoptive parents for at least three months.

You may wish to keep your child's birth and adoption a secret. Since the Children Act of 1975, adopted children have had the right to see their original birth certificate at the age of eighteen (seventeen in Scotland). This doesn't mean that your child will automatically try to trace you. Many grown children don't want to meet their natural parents. And, besides, it can be difficult trying to locate the parent since few people live in the same place for eighteen years. However, if you wish there could be some contact between you and your baby once he or she is grown up, some adoption societies will allow you to write a letter to be passed on to your child, should he or she ever enquire about you.

Deciding what's best for your baby is very difficult. If you do choose to get your child adopted, don't torture yourself with guilt and don't feel you didn't love your baby enough to keep it. It takes a lot of selfless courage to give your child up and you are doing it because you believe that, this way, your baby will have a better future.

Once you have made the choice on abortion, adoption, or keeping and raising your baby, commit yourself to that decision. I wish you luck and I beg you to use birth control in the future. Be careful, not careless. If you think I'm being hard on you, let me add that plenty of older and married women also get pregnant without intending to.

Here's hoping you can make the most of your own life before you start someone else's.

Do-It-Yourself Orgasms

I have nothing against masturbation, but I hate the word. It sounds so serious. So clinical. About as sexy as the word *genitalia*. Plus *masturbation* conjures up some of the left-over hogwash that people used to preach: how boys who play with themselves go blind and girls who touch themselves go crazy.

More teenage boys than teenage girls masturbate regularly, but the girl who has discovered that stimulating her clitoris or clitoral area can bring pleasure and relieve tension is far from rare. I'm writing this not so you'll jump into bed with yourself once you get to the last paragraph. I write so that if you sometimes engage in what has been wrongly labelled self-abuse, you'll know there is nothing shameful or even unusual about it. So put away the guilt.

Some 'sexperts' even argue in favour of self-stimulation and say it is a healthy way for a young woman to get acquainted with her body. She can show her body how to climax, feel confident about her ability to have an orgasm, and later, when making love with a guy, find it easier to come or be better able to show him how to help her come. That's better than feeling frustrated or worrying that you're frigid or thinking you're the only one who has never felt that rhythmic throbbing and doesn't know what the fuss is about. Masturbation also makes more sense than having sex when you're in lust but not love.

Some girls worry that they are 'spoiling themselves' – they fear they'll never come 'the normal way' with a guy once their body has grown used to manual stimulation. Yet only a minority of women regularly reach orgasm during intercourse without additional stimulation of the clitoris. Some macho lovers may feel that if the friction going on between his penis and your vagina isn't enough to make you come, it's your fault. More mature and understanding men may be eager to help you climax by touching your sensitive clitoris before, during, or after intercourse.

Some girls find their own private orgasms may be more intense than orgasms with a lover. No crime in that. Sex with a caring partner is still more gratifying than sex by yourself. So unless you feel you are becoming dependent on or obsessed by masturbation, there is no cause for concern. Besides, solo sex can't make you pregnant or give you a disease.

I don't mean to be making a sales pitch for masturbation. But if you've already discovered that you can give yourself an orgasm alone – you don't have to apologize. Because it's not so terrible to love thyself.

Are You Gay?

You may sometimes wonder if you're gay. Don't assume you are homosexual if you once had a lesbian encounter. Or if you are a teenage tomboy. Or if you had a crush on a woman. Or if you are a vehement feminist. Or if you had an erotic dream about a female friend. We are surrounded by magazines and films brimming with super sexy women; it'd be nearly impossible not to notice their appeal, but that doesn't mean we're gay or bisexual.

Of course being lesbian is not sick or perverted. Life may be hard for gays sometimes, because some cruel, insecure people make fun of women and men whose sexual choices differ from their own.

No one knows for sure why some people are homosexual. It may not be a choice but given, an orientation determined by genetic, hormonal, and/or environmental factors. Homosexuality is common and if you are gay, you are not alone.

Yet why label yourself or announce that you are gay unless you are really sure and have excellent reasons for making your private life public? If you are gay or think you might be and are having trouble with your feelings about it, talk to a counsellor or look in the phone book to see if there is a Gay Switchboard in your area. London Friend Women's Line, *see page 280*, may be able to refer you to local help.

Sexually Transmitted Diseases

I don't want to give you the impression that sex is scary and will leave you either pregnant or diseased. Sex is wonderful. But it's most wonderful when it's worry-free. And it's most worry-free when you're informed, careful, and responsible.

We'll zip through this section as fast as possible. I'm not keen on thinking about pus, pain, itches, and sores any more than you are. But what you don't know can hurt you. And it's better to have the facts than to have VD.

VD stands for *venereal disease* and can be very dangerous. Lately the term *STDs* has also been used to mean *sexually transmitted diseases.*

Anybody can get STDs; they are contracted by having sexual relations with an infected person. Common? Yes. Over 60,000 people get STDs in Britain every year. Over 50,000 cases of gonorrhoea are reported in the UK every year, more than half in people under twenty-four. Unfortunately, because the symptoms in women are often internal and hard to detect, many don't even know they are carrying the disease until it has done its damage. You can catch a disease, get cured, and get it again. And you can have more than one type at one time.

STDs are particularly serious in pregnant women, because certain diseases can be passed on to the baby, who may be born blind, retarded, or otherwise abnormal, or who may die soon after birth. With proper medical care, the threat to the newborn can usually be eliminated.

If you have several sex partners (who have several sex partners who have . . .) or if you have a classic tell-tale symptom (sore, swelling, unusual discharge, or pain or persistent itch in the genital area), see a doctor or go to a Special Clinic (listed in the phone book under VD or STD). Don't try to diagnose your own symptoms or postpone an appointment, because although the symptoms may disappear, the disease won't; it may continue causing trouble inside you.

I do not tell you untrue horror stories. Masturbation will not make you blind or crazy or sterile. But STDs can. If they are left untreated, some types can kill you. They do not go away by themselves.

If you have a sexually transmitted disease, the person who gave it to you should be notified – the clinic will tell you how this can be done. That way he, too, can receive treatment and stop spreading the disease. (This is one case in which you *should* kiss and tell.)

Modern drugs (praise be to Sir Alexander Fleming, the discoverer of penicillin!) can cure many cases painlessly. Finish any prescription as directed, and be sure your partner is also being treated. Then go for a follow-up check-up. Even for herpes, which doesn't yet have a sure cure, there are medicines that relieve discomfort.

How can you avoid getting STDs? Be sensible and selective about whom you share your body with. Don't fool around with someone who fools around with lots of girls or guys. When you have sex with someone, you're not just having it with him, but with his previous lovers as well. Check to see if your partner's genital area seems clean and healthy, or ask the guy if he has any infectious condition. (You're too embarrassed to ask? What are you doing naked with him!?) If you're not sure of his sexual past make sure he uses a condom – that reduces the chance of spreading disease. Contraceptive foams and creams also kill some germs. Some experts say it's a good idea to urinate as soon after sex as possible (to flush out any germs) and to wash your hands and genital area with soap and water before and after contact.

Obviously, if you are a virgin or have one steady, faithful, uninfected boyfriend, you don't have VD and need not feel paranoid.

The following are among the major STDs.

Herpes

Q: What's the difference between love and herpes?
A: Herpes lasts forever.

Alas, there's nothing funny about herpes. Herpes is common in the most well-brought-up, well-educated circles.

Oral herpes is mild. It may appear as a mere cold sore or fever blister in the mouth. Genital herpes is more serious, and in women is characterized by recurrent sores around the genital area. Sufferers may experience itching or burning, pain, fever, and an outbreak of genital blisters that dry up and go away in a few weeks but may reappear at unpredictable intervals, often at times of stress and especially during the first year of infection.

You can get genital herpes by having sex with someone who has open herpes sores. Your sores could appear two to fourteen days after exposure. When the herpes victim's symptoms are dormant, his or her condition is much less contagious, but it is still a good idea to reduce the risk of spreading the disease by using a condom.

Even the not-so-terrible oral herpes can become genital herpes through oral sex. In plain English, if a woman with blisters in her mouth has oral sex with a man, the next week he could discover blisters on his penis. Guys with cold sores can also inadvertently give their girlfriends genital herpes. Similarly, if you touch a mouth or genital herpes lesion and then rub your eyes or tinker with your contact lens without first washing your hands, the virus could move to your eyes (ocular herpes) and if left un-treated, can cause blindness.

If you have genital herpes, keep your genital area clean and dry. Wash with plain soap and water. Consider using a hand-held dryer to dry off. Wear loose-fitting clothes. And forgive yourself.

Many herpes victims feel angry, depressed, guilty, frustrated,

and isolated. Imagine sleeping with one person who wasn't
considerate or ethical enough to warn you of his active herpes
outbreak, then finding you have an incurable disease and feeling
like a sexual leper. But there is life after herpes. The stigma has
lessened. There are new antiviral drug treatments. And soon
there may be a cure or a vaccine.

For more information, contact the Herpes Association, *see
page 280*.

AIDS

Acquired Immune Deficiency Syndrome (AIDS) is a still incurable and usually fatal disease. Most of its victims have been
homosexual or bisexual men, intravenous drug abusers and
their partners. In the past some people have even developed
AIDS following blood transfusions, though all blood used in
Britain is now screened for AIDS. Women can get AIDS, too, and
their babies can be born with it. AIDS victims' immune systems
stop fighting and protecting them against certain infections.
Victims may feel profoundly tired, get sick often, lose a lot of
weight, develop a cough, fever or lesions – and then become
unable to ward off disease. Up to five years can pass between
contracting the virus and coming down with the disorder. AIDS
is usually spread when someone has oral, anal or genital sex with
an infected person, or when someone who injects drugs shares a
contaminated needle. You can't get AIDS by donating blood.
AIDS may not seem to be a threat in your social/sexual circle, but
knowledge is essential, and everybody will breathe easier when
its mysteries have been unravelled. Meanwhile, say 'NO' to sex
if your would-be partner is bisexual, a drug abuser or has been
promiscuous. If you don't say no, insist that he wears a condom.

Gonorrhoea

The 'clap', as it is commonly called, is subtle but serious. Infected
women may notice a pus-like vaginal discharge, painful urin-
ation, and vaginal soreness. But most women have no symptoms
whatsoever, which is why it is vital to have a check-up if you

sleep with someone you're not sure about. Throat and rectal gonorrhoea are other variations on the theme. If it is left untreated, gonorrhea can lead to arthritis, heart trouble, inflammation of the reproductive organs, and sometimes sterility. Pelvic inflammatory disease (PID) is the most common complication of gonorrhoea. Symptoms may include abdominal pain, increased menstrual cramps, and lower back pain. PID can result in scar tissue forming inside the fallopian tubes and blocking passage of the egg into the uterus – in other words, sterility. Antibiotics usually work in treating gonorrhoea and PID.

Chlamydia

Chlamydia is easy to treat – but hard to detect. Up to 80 per cent of infected women have no symptoms. If you have genital burning or itching, unusual vaginal discharge, between period bleeding, or any other worrisome symptoms, you may want to ask your doctor to test for chlamydia. The disease is common, dangerous and does not go away by itself. Many women have gonorrhoea and chlamydia at the same time – but, unlike gonorrhoea, chlamydia cannot be treated with penicillin.

Syphilis

Syphilis symptoms may include a genital or oral chancre (lesion or sore) followed by a rash anywhere on the body and loss of hair in patches. Then symptoms go away. Syphilis is not very common, but if left untreated, continues to do devastating damage to the victim's brain, blood vessels, and heart – damage that may not show up until years, even decades, later.

Genital Warts

Genital or venereal warts are caused by a virus. They usually develop one to six months after intercourse with an infected person. Soft pink or red warts may be flat or look like tiny cauliflowers and appear in the folds of a woman's labia. There may be a link between genital warts and cervical cancer. Women who have had genital warts should have regular smear tests, as should all sexually active women. The warts are highly contagious and can usually be removed in two or three treatments.

Vaginitis or Thrush

Almost all women get some type of vaginitis at least once, and it isn't always contracted from sex. Vaginitis is not very serious but does require treatment with pills, suppositories, and/or creams. Symptoms? Severe vaginal itching or burning and an increase and change in vaginal discharge. You may be more prone to vaginitis if you douche or use deodorant sprays or bubble baths (these can irritate your vulva and kill friendly bacteria). Or if you wear tight pants, or panties or pantyhose with a nylon rather than a cotton crotch (nylon keeps in heat and moisture, allowing organisms to grow). Or if you're taking oral antibiotics and/or birth control pills (they may create vaginal conditions favourable to a yeast or other infection). Or if you have sex with someone who is infected or have sex without enough lubrication. Be sure to wash your vulva with mild soap daily. And always wipe from front to back after a bowel movement.

Cystitis

Almost all women get cystitis at least once. It is a bladder infection, not a venereal disease, but it is associated with sex. If you feel as if you have to pee constantly yet it burns like Hades when you try, and nothing comes out, or your urine is bloody, you may have cystitis. It's been dubbed 'the honeymoon disease' because one cause may be a suddenly active, vigorous sex life. See your doctor, but in the meantime, go easy on the sex, soak in a warm tub with no oil or bath foam added, and drink plenty (gallons!) of water and liquids, especially lemon barley water. Steer clear of alcohol, coffee or tea, which may irritate your bladder even more. You may also want to see your GP for medication because, while the symptoms may disappear in two days, the infection may last for two weeks.

Scabies

A scientist named Bonomo discovered the itch mite in 1687, and scabies continue to plague children, teenagers, and adults. You can get scabies from having sex, holding hands, or simply sharing a towel with an infected person. Tiny mites mate on the skin, and then the female mite burrows into the skin and lays eggs. They may appear on hands, armpits, breasts, genital or rectal areas or elsewhere. Scabies can be treated quickly with medicated lotions.

Crabs

Crabs are little parasitic lice that nestle in pubic hair and itch like the devil. They look like moving freckles. They are not a venereal disease but are a sexually transmissible nuisance. Ask for advice from your doctor, clinic or even the chemist, as you can buy over-the-counter lotions. Make sure you wash and dry all your clothes and linens (on the hot setting) before declaring victory over the little beasties.

Nasty things can happen to everybody, so beware. Let's hope you don't get any STDs. Ever.

Rape

I am lucky. I have not been raped. But I will share an experience with you that frightened me. Here's what I wrote on 9 February in the diary I kept when I was fourteen:

> . . . Now for the unbelievable thing of the day. I was working on my maths assignment after school in an empty classroom when that stupid janitor walked in. As usual he made remarks about his girl-chasing youth, and he asked whether I played around with the boys, adding, 'Sure you do, sure

you do' and 'You're not afraid of me, are you?' (I hate him so much.)
Anyway, once or twice he's touched me around the bra area. That could be
unintentional but I doubt it, especially after today. Today I was sitting at
the desk wearing a dress. He said, 'You must get cold going around in bare
legs,' then rubbed my leg high above my knee and added, 'Oh yes, you're
wearing stockings. Are your pantyhose tight?' (What a queer!) I mumbled,
'I guess so.' Then that guy I hate took his hand away. I yanked down my
dress lower and he asked, 'Why are you pulling your dress down?' Think-
ing it was none of his business, I just shrugged. Next he put his hand above
my knee again and started working his way up. Suddenly he remarked,
surprised, 'Oh you have panties on underneath.' Not realizing his fingers
were up so high, I desperately held down my dress. He said, 'What are you
worried about?' At this point I was giving him really dirty looks and
holding down my dress with all my might!! He said, 'What are you afraid
of? C'mon, let me have another peek.' (I can't stand him. Who does he
think he is?) Finally he must have given up and he went back to vacuum-
ing. Now get this. He then said, 'I know what you're hiding – your little
brown moustache. That's it, isn't it? Do you comb it every night? Sure you
do. Well, yes or no?' I said no. He added, 'Well you put your hand on it.' I
shot a really mean look at him and went back to my maths. He said, 'You
know I'm doing you a favour letting you in here.' I retorted, 'OK. So I
won't come here.' He said, 'You can come. You're not afraid of me.' I
ignored him and finished my geometry. God!!

I didn't tell a soul back then. Now I wish I had. For all I know, that
old man may have harassed – or molested or abused – some
younger or more impressionable girl. How could I have been so
naive as to think there could have been anything unintentional
about his pawing my flat chest? Why did I just sit there? Because
he was a grown-up? Because I thought adults were always right?
Was I so trusting I didn't realize I didn't have to take that from
anybody? So intimidated by and respectful of my elders that I
didn't know I could talk back and take off?

That disturbed individual scared me without scarring me. But
many women have been less fortunate. Nobody knows how
common such incidents are, because many victims don't report
them. But one survey suggests that one in six London women
has been sexually abused or raped at some time.

Women are more vulnerable than men. We don't need to be
paranoid, but we do need to be cautious. And informed.

Did you believe any of the following myths?

Myth No. 1: *Only girls get raped.*

Truth: While the majority of rape victims are young women, anyone can be raped. Rape is a crime of violence, not passion. Rapists look for easy targets, not sexy figures. Teenage girls, old women, even boys get raped.

Myth No. 2: *Most rapists are strangers.*

Truth: The majority of reported rapists are 'friends', acquaintances, or relatives, and many 'date rapes' go unreported. If a guy you're dating forces you to have sex against your will, that's rape. If your neighbour or cousin or friend's brother or the telephone repairman or the father of the kids you baby-sit for makes you have sex when you did not freely give consent, that's rape. Many of the offenders are married; many of the crimes were planned.

Myth No. 3: *The victim was asking for it.*

Truth: Nobody asks for rape. Rape is sometimes random, but if the victim happens to be wearing a bikini top or 'provocative' skirt, she is no more to blame than is an elderly nun or a retarded teenage girl wearing an overcoat. The rapist is to blame.

Myth No. 4: *Most rapes happen in dark alleys.*

Truth: Most rapes and assaults happen at home – in the victim's home or at the place where she is baby-sitting or visiting. 'Date rapes' or 'acquaintance rapes' often occur on the rapist's home ground, often on weekend nights.

How can you reduce your risk of being attacked? Take a self-defence course or learn judo or karate. I know a 110-pound schoolgirl who floored a 180-pound mugger. It certainly took him by surprise. And for safety's sake:

- If you are at home or in a car, make sure the doors and windows are locked.
- If it's night-time, don't walk alone, especially in rough neighbourhoods.
- If you are out alone, walk briskly and with confidence. Don't project fear.

- If you are lost, don't ask a strange man for directions and don't give your home address.
- If you feel suspicious of a man behind you, cross the street or walk in the middle of the street. Don't slow down or go towards bushes, alleyways or dimly lit areas.
- If you're feeling scared and see a respectable-looking woman, walk next to her. (A man once saw me enter a cinema alone, then went in and sat behind me. I spotted another lone woman a few rows back, sidled up, asked if I could join her – and she and I have been friends ever since.)
- If the phone rings, and you're alone, don't let a stranger know. (Why not lift the receiver, shout, 'I'll get it', to the walls around you, then say hello?)
- If you're alone on a bus, tube, or train, sit near the driver or conductor, and don't prepare to get off until the last moment. No one needs to know ahead of time which stop is yours.
- If a scruffy-looking guy is alone in a lift, don't get in. If a dubious character gets in and you're alone inside, coolly get off at the next floor.
- If you're out at night, no need to carry your entire pay packet, cheque book, credit cards (if you have them), etc. Leave non-essentials at home. And carry your doorkeys separately in your pocket just in case your bag is snatched.
- Hitch-hiking is never a wise thing to do. If you really must hitch, don't do it alone or at night when many drivers have been drinking.
- If you're in a car with a guy, check the door handle so you'll know how to get out fast, if necessary. If the guy giving you a lift home gets too friendly, don't announce your intention of leaving, just get out at the next traffic light he stops at. And always be choosy about whom you accept a lift home with from a party or disco, anyway!
- If you are nearing your home or car, have your key ready.
- If you and a guy are going to park the car for a necking

session, avoid stopping in secluded back roads or lovers' lane set-ups where he or a less trustworthy man could take advantage of you. (My parents encouraged us to park outside our house. Safe and sensible, though my brother, Eric, sometimes teased me when he heard the car pull up at 11:30 but didn't hear me walk in until 12:00.)

Since we're imagining the worst (I trust you're not reading this alone at night in a creaky house), let's imagine the worst of the worst. You're jumped on by a rapist. What do you do?

Unfortunately, there's no simple answer. It depends on you and the situation. Some advise women to be passive, especially if the rapist has a gun or knife. Others say to try to repel him: vomit, drool, pee, tell him you have your period or herpes or AIDS. Many say to be assertive: scream, yell *rape* or *fire* or *help* or *police*, struggle, carry a whistle at all times and blow it like mad. Others say to fight back if you know what you're doing: bite, scratch, knee his shin or groin, gouge his eyes, punch his stomach, bend back his little finger, beat his face with your keys or the heel of your shoe, yank at his testicles when he least expects it. (When you think about it, he may be in a pretty vulnerable position himself.) Some say to go limp: turn into a heavy, immobile weight. Others say to use psychology: ask him sympathetically about his life or tell him your father was just killed in a car crash. Shock him; catch him off guard: outsmart him.

I have a friend who was assaulted by a teenage boy when she was a teenager. Eleanore was so furious she yelled, 'Oh go home and behave yourself!' He left!

What would *you* do if you were approached? Think about it now.

I don't think I'd have the guts or know-how to poke a rapist's eyes out, but if I had my wits about me and thought I stood half a chance – a big *if*, to be sure – I'd scream bloody murder and run like a sprinter.

You knew this was coming. We're about to imagine the worst of the worst of the worst. You've been raped. Now what?

Lie. Promise the rapist you won't tell anybody. Then go straight to the nearest police station or hospital or call a Rape Crisis Centre. Call even before you bathe, clean up, or change, because the authorities usually need physical evidence if you prosecute. The majority of rapes go unreported, but if you press charges and land the creep in jail (not always easy), you'll feel good about your revenge and good knowing you probably protected someone else. (Most rapists rape again.) Many Rape Crisis Centres provide a counsellor or support team who will accompany you to the hospital or police station and help you begin to deal with your rage, humiliation, guilt and disgust.

A married friend of mine was raped. She didn't get pregnant, beaten, or pick up a sexual disease, but she was so turned off by men and sex afterwards that for a long time she was unable to enjoy making love with her husband. Finally she joined a therapy group that helped her sort out her feelings and retrieve her self-esteem and sense of control. She is now slowly learning to trust again and to blame just that one man – not all men and not herself – for her misfortune. She is learning to stop demeaning herself for not having resisted and to start congratulating herself for having survived.

Incest

Incest isn't sexy, and if there were a chapter in this book devoted solely to abuse or crisis, I would have included this and the rape section under that heading.

Sexual contact between relatives or close family members is taboo and illegal but not as rare as we would like to believe. Since so many cases go unreported, it's difficult to guess how common incest is, but a survey in *Woman* magazine suggested that one in ten women in Britain have been involved in incest. Alice Walker's prize-winning novel *The Color Purple* gives a heart-rending glimpse of the fear and anguish that usually accompany incest.

Offenders come from every class and walk of life. They may be violent alcoholics or conservative churchgoers, but the fact is that three-quarters of sexual assaults by adults on children are committed by somebody the child knows. Often, the victims are children who don't question their elders and don't realize at first how exploitative and out of the ordinary their situation is. They may mistakenly believe that Father knows best.

'If you don't do as I say,' a father or stepfather may threaten, 'I'll beat you.' 'If you don't let me do this now, I'll do something worse next time.' 'If you tell anybody, I'll kill you.' 'I'm your father – I should be your first man.'

The girl may be afraid to say 'no'. She may be afraid that if she tells her mother, her mother won't believe her. Or will blame her. Or will break up the family, then hate her for it. Or the girl may worry that if she does *not* tell, the experience may happen again – to her or to her little sister.

I've heard accounts from a boy who was sexually approached by his mother and from a girl who was sexually attacked by her grandfather. Those who quip, 'Incest is best', haven't experienced its terror and guilt.

If you are a victim of incest, you are not alone and you are not at fault. You are the same good person you were before the troubled adult made use of your body. The offender is messed up, not you. But you may want to seek help before your pain, anger, and humiliation can turn to scars that make it hard for you to respect and love other men. Tell a trusted adult who will believe you: a family member, teacher, doctor, group leader, school counsellor, minister, or rabbi.

You can also get help from people who have been through the same problem, and from trained professionals, by calling one of the Incest Crisis lines or the BBC's Childline (*see page 279 and 280* for telephone numbers) or any young people's counselling service, local social services, or the NSPCC. Your father won't be immediately hauled off to jail, nor will you be thrown into a foster home. In most cases, you and your family can begin to get the therapy you all may need. And you can learn how not to let the difficulties of your past ruin your future, and how not to let someone else's problem become your own.

A final word: The most common form of incest happens between brothers and sisters and usually has a less devastating effect on future mental health. Lots of us have played some form of 'doctor' with our brothers when we were little children. If you played a more advanced or older version with your brother, and now you don't think about it or worry about it, OK. But if past 'play' still upsets you or gets in the way of new relationships, talk to a counsellor and start feeling better.

5. Family

Can't Live With 'Em, Can't Live Without 'Em

So much for sex. If your mum and dad hadn't had it, you wouldn't be here. But they had more than sex. They had a family.

Some say the ideal family provides roots and wings. The catch? Most families aren't ideal.

Novelist Leo Tolstoy wrote, 'Happy families are all alike; every unhappy family is unhappy in its own way.' The reasons behind some families' unhappiness are, indeed, diverse and complex. You may have problems with parents or parents with problems. Or you may get along fine with your parent or parents but wish you could say the same about your brothers and sisters or step-parents.

If yours is an open, affectionate, supportive family, you are lucky. I bet you like yourself and I hope you are appreciative. If your family always bickers, yells, ignores, or hurts each other, these pages can give you clues about how to end destructive patterns. It's worth working towards more communication and caring, possibly even through counselling. You can't just break up with your family as you can with a boyfriend, so strive to improve things on the home front. Love takes work.

This chapter is for every daughter who is growing up, up, and away.

Problems With Parents

Why aren't you all getting along as well as you used to? That's a hard one. If it's not the case in your family, terrific. If it is, fluff up a pillow, sit back, and let's try to figure out what went wrong.

Surprise. Nothing went wrong. It's absolutely normal for parents and teenagers to go through some rough times. Why? Because when you were a child, you probably obeyed your parents without question, and now you question everything. You may have thought they were infallible, and now you know they make mistakes.

Consider your parents' point of view. Not so long ago, you idolized them and depended on their approval ('Mum, Dad, watch this, watch this, watch this!'). Now you eat and sleep at home but would just as soon be with your friends. Once, you reached for your mother's hand when crossing the street, and now, when she occasionally reaches for yours – right in public – you could just die of embarrassment. Yet your parents, like you, need to feel needed and loved. They want to get along with you as much as you want to get along with them. And they have to put up with you as much as you have to put up with them.

You think it's easy for your mother? She's noticing a wrinkle here, a grey hair there – and you wake up more attractive every day. She may feel her life is becoming routine, whereas yours is (or is about to be) brimming with kisses and compliments, new people and places. Of course she's proud and happy for you, but she may also feel a tinge of envy – and hate herself for it. Even if she works outside the home (as many mothers do), it may be tough for her to see you as a person who won't need much mothering any more.

And your father? Do you think it's easy for him to see his darling daughter's eyes light up with every mention of Tom, Rick, or Larry? He remembers his wild teenage times and may hate to think of his little girl getting tangled up with men. If he's going through his own mid-life crisis ('Have I accomplished what I set out to do? Is there more to life than this?'), he may be too preoccupied to sympathize or help with your adolescent identity crisis ('Who am I? What do I want to become?').

So everybody's got a different perspective, and you're all clashing madly. You may quarrel because your parents are too protective, permissive, indifferent, nosy, demanding, critical of your friends, or embarrassing. Or maybe they're bogged down in problems of their own.

One in seven British families is headed by a single parent and one and a half million British children are in one-parent families.

Although I refer to *parents* in the plural, the following suggestions apply to single parents, too.

If Your Parents Are Over-protective. . .

They probably mean well. They probably want to know where you're going and with whom and when you'll be back ('Not later than 10:30!') because they love you and worry about you. Even so, it's hard if you have the strictest parents and earliest curfew around. How do you get your parents to stop treating you like a baby? Not, I repeat, not, by throwing a tantrum, stomping to your room, slamming the door, and blasting them out with your music. If you want them to start treating you like an adult, act like an adult. If you want more privileges, take on more responsibilities. To get your folks off your back, you may have to show that you can manage on your own – whether by getting up in the morning or getting a job or doing your chores – without needing to be nagged.

What if you'd like a later curfew? Don't whine, 'Everybody else gets to stay out until midnight'. Instead, wait for a relaxed moment and ask your parents if you could have a trial compromise curfew this weekend. Try to sound rational, not emotional, as you ask if they'll let you stay out until 11:15. Say you want to learn to become gradually more independent so you'll be able to handle it when you eventually leave home. Then make an effort to be more responsible. You might volunteer to do another chore around the house – vacuuming the living room? mopping the kitchen floor? – in exchange for more freedom.

(If you're thinking, 'Another chore! Whose side are you on anyway?' let me point out that a carefree childhood can be misleading. The 'lucky' girls who don't have to help at home often freak out when they're on their own or married because they hadn't realized how many tasks need doing. I agree, however, that it is unfair if your parents distribute chores in a sexist way. You *can* mow the lawn and your brother *can* wash dishes.)

If your parents don't agree to the later curfew, tell them they're almost asking you to be disobedient or resentful. Or simply ask again next week, perhaps upping the check-in time by only fifteen minutes.

If they agree to give the 11:15 curfew a try, *get home on time*. If you walk in at 11:25, you've blown it. If you won't make it in until 11:20, phone ahead. If you arrive at 11:05, you may have won their trust and earned a new improved curfew.

As far as parents wanting to know where you're going, forgive me again, but I think that's fairly reasonable. No, they shouldn't give you the third degree and, no, you don't have to fill them in on every detail. But parents tell each other where they're off to and until when. It shows they care and it's important in an emergency. From my diary when I was thirteen: *'Mum, Dad, and Mark got home after 1:00 a.m. and didn't call — worrying me and Eric to death.'* See? If they're going to be late, they should phone, too.

How come you don't want to tell them where you're going, anyway? Because they'd disapprove? If you are experimenting with drink or drugs at your boyfriend's while his parents are away, maybe you can see why your parents worry.

One more thought: sometimes life is easier when you have cut-and-dried rules. In the days when nice girls wouldn't think of getting plastered or having premarital sex, they didn't really have to deal with those pressures. The answer was no, and that was that. Now, since many young women can make up their own minds about such matters, it can be a struggle to decide what to do. My point? That it sometimes helps to know what's off limits and what isn't. It's a relief to have rules – not unfair, inconsistent rules, but not no rules.

If Your Parents Are Too Permissive. . .

Maybe you feel your parents would let you do anything, and that they don't, as Rhett told Scarlett, give a damn. Frankly, they probably do.

Your parents may believe that, since you'll have to learn to be self-sufficient eventually, better now, under their roof, than later by yourself. Or maybe they worry that if they say, 'No TV before dinner,' or 'No dates on weeknights,' you won't like them as much. As with over-protective parents, it may be that they are raising you the best way they know how and with your well-being in mind.

My parents were fairly permissive. They made me absolutely promise I'd never ride a motorcycle, but otherwise I had a lot of leeway. Mum and Dad's easy-going attitude made me feel trusted, not neglected.

How about *you*? If your parents' lack of rules makes you uncomfortable and you'd like more reassurance that they care, tell them. Shock them with: 'Believe it or not, I wish I had a curfew,' or, 'Give me some guidelines.'

Many teenagers nowadays wish their parents would provide more rules. If your parents just won't, or can't, then give yourself rules. You will make your bed every day. You will start your homework before dinner. You will be tucked in by eleven. Eventually you live by your own rules, so it doesn't hurt to start disciplining yourself early.

If Your Parents Seem Indifferent. . .

What if your parents not only haven't set rules but never ask about your life, friends, schoolwork? They're so busy with their jobs and friends, they don't seem to have time for you. What if you just don't seem to communicate? That hurts. Of course they may be patting themselves on the back for not being nosy, nagging, interfering parents. If so, you need to let them know you'd like to have more talks. They may be flattered, but unsure as to how to bridge the gap. Sometimes a man who has spent his whole adult life getting ahead in business may not know how to be a sensitive father. You may not be able to convert him and may have to accept him as he is, flaws and all. Or reject him. Or in a few years, closeness may be easier, as you see them as human beings, not just as parents.

It *is* worth trying to get through to a stony parent. Are you trying? If your dad asks, 'Where have you been?' and you say, 'Nowhere' that's not setting the groundwork for friendship. Rather than being upset that your parents aren't attentive the second you come home from school or the minute they walk in from work, plan a time for a visit. Say to one or both, 'How about if we play Trivial Pursuit or cards and talk tonight after we all get our work done?' Or, 'Let's go for a walk after dinner.' If one parent is running an errand, go along. If both are relaxing in front of the television, join them for a while. Or leave a note on their bed: 'I don't say it often, but I love you.'

Try to draw your parents out. Try: 'How was work today?' When your parent grunts, 'Fine,' say, 'No, tell me about it. I hardly even know what you do.' If your folks are in a good mood at dinner, ask about how they met, about their first date, first kiss, honeymoon. You could get some surprises!

Don't forget the little ways to show you care. Compliment the person who made dinner. Praise your mum or dad for trying to give up smoking or lose weight. Ask your dad if his cold is going away. My father used to stock the refrigerator with mushrooms (I adore mushrooms) when he knew I was coming home from college for the vacation. It was a small detail, but it made me feel loved. By the way, if you do something loving, then afterwards wait for applause, toasts, and thank-you notes, it doesn't count as much.

No getting around it, some parents really don't or won't or can't care. You can bend over backwards to please or displease them, and it doesn't make an impression. Maybe you can forgive them some day for being so unemotional. In the meantime, work to please yourself and reach out to other friends, adults, and family members for role models and for the love you deserve.

If Your Parents Give You No Privacy . . .

A lot of teenagers feel that their parents invade their privacy. If your parents ransack your drawers, rummage through your handbag, enter your room without knocking (or without waiting for you to say, 'come in'), read your mail and diaries, listen in on your phone calls, throw out your old clothes or magazines, or borrow your belongings without consulting you first, you can legitimately be angry.

Have you given them reason to be suspicious? If parents find out that their daughter smokes or drinks or has sex, they may – again, for Daughter's own good – try to keep track of what she's up to.

Try to get your parents to trust you more by being more open about your whereabouts. Satisfy their curiosity by telling them a little about your friends, activities, and schoolwork.

They are wrong if they think they have a right to know everything you do, but you are wrong if you think your life is none of their business.

In person or in a note, gently ask them to try to respect your privacy and your need to keep some things to yourself. Don't shout 'Leave me alone!' Explain that you aren't doing anything bad and that you love and need them but that you have your own separate life.

If they won't stop snooping, you could consider hiding or locking up your personal things, or leaving them with a trusted friend. What a shame. But take heart. Pretty soon you *will* be on your own.

If your Parents Expect Too Much. . .

Some parents' expectations are so high that nothing you do is enough. Because I was a good student, my parents got used to good reports. At first, I wanted Mum and Dad to make a big deal of my marks every term, yet they seemed to take them for granted. Finally I told them how I felt. They said they were proud even when they didn't show it. More important, I began working to please myself, not them.

If your parents expect the world, they may mean well. They may even want you to accomplish what they meant to but didn't. If they encourage you (as my parents usually did), they are being helpful. But if their plans for you are too lofty, they may be setting everybody up for disappointment.

You may have to sit them down and explain that you *are* trying hard in school. Or that mastering the flute is their dream, not yours — you'd rather concentrate on photography. Or that it's not reasonable for them to expect you to do all the cooking and cleaning and still lead your own life.

Some parents may never be satisfied. Try to accept this as their shortcoming and recognize your strengths even if they don't. This isn't easy, but you can do it.

Other parents may have difficulty giving praise because they're feeling jealous or inferior. If this is the case, you could subtly remind your parents how grateful you are for their help and encouragement along the way.

Still others are convinced their child is God no matter how much of a mess their little darling makes of things. That way they get to award themselves the Best Parent Prize every year. Parents should praise their children, but they shouldn't go overboard. If you start believing you're picture-perfect, you'll be in for it later when you have to face up to your failings.

Finally, some parents – the kind I hope you have – have high hopes for you and encourage you, without undue pressure, to reach for the sky, yet want for you what you want for yourself and will love you unconditionally.

(P.S. That's a lot to ask. And don't forget, you can't expect your parents to be Supermum and Superdad any more than they can rightfully expect you to be Superdaughter.)

If Your Parents Don't Like Your Friends or Boyfriend. . .

When I was ten, one of my friends said, 'I hate you!' to her mother, and her mother told her to stop playing with me. Me! Mild-mannered level-headed polite little me! She had decided I was a bad influence on her innocent child. I'm biased, of course, but I think she was mistaken. Sometimes parents' judgments are wrong.

But sometimes they are right. Come to think of it, I was an unpredictable ten-year-old. That very week I'd nicked five coloured drawing pins from the police department headquarters during a Girl Scout trip!

Anyway, just as you don't like all of your parents' friends, they won't like all of yours. But do introduce everybody so they can give each other a chance. And make sure you aren't picking friends to please or spite your parents.

If they like some of your friends but dislike one in particular or don't like your boyfriend, obviously you aren't going to dump that person heartlessly. But ask yourself – and them – why they disapprove. Maybe your father would have trouble watching Daddy's little girl waltz off with *any* young man. Maybe your mother is jealous of your closeness with girls your age. If so, their opinions of your friends may not be valid. Why not meet your mates outside, at school, and at their homes more often than at yours?

Perhaps your parents have reason to believe that Greg is dishonest, is taking advantage of you, or drives too fast; or that Paula has a bad reputation, is ill-mannered, or is involved with drugs. Have you been swearing more than usual or acting in a surly, listless or sullen way? Have you lost interest in your work? It's possible your parents criticize your friend (I know you're tired of hearing this, but picture yourself in their position) for your own good.

My parents never warmed up to my brother's friend Zeke. One evening we three kids gave a big summer party, and Mum and Dad were nice enough to stay upstairs and out of the way. Dad did, however, peer out their bedroom window from time to time to check on things. That's when he saw Zeke, slightly drunk, tossing lighted matches into the forsythia. Dad came down yelling, and I couldn't blame him.

Your parents may be particularly touchy about your boyfriend because they may be afraid you're going to get pregnant or run off and marry him. Tell them you're responsible and having fun, not making life commitments. If they haven't met your boyfriend, have them meet informally. They may decide he's not such a bad guy, after all.

Some parents are going to like your friends so much that they may not know when to leave you to yourselves. If your parents try too hard to befriend your friends, handle the situation with care, because they may be feeling a little middle-aged or lonely. Meet your friends elsewhere. Or have a short chat with your parents at your home, then explain that you are all going to your room to talk. You're entitled to.

If Your Parents Embarrass You . . .

I have a friend who is embarrassed by her parents because her parents are poor. They also happen to be one of the warmest, most giving, most down-to-earth couples I know.

Other friends get embarrassed because their parents are rich. You compliment the grand piano in the hall or the painting on the wall, and the friend starts apologizing.

Try to appreciate whatever it is your parents have to offer and stop cringing just because your foreign-born mother makes occasional grammatical mistakes or your father goes to the shops in shorts and knee-high socks and always smokes a pipe. Others may see them as endearing characters.

If you are embarrassed because your parents have drinking problems or bad reputations, the problem is stickier, but remember that you are a separate individual. If someone mocks you, you can admit, 'My mother's behaviour upsets me, too, but it also upsets me when people judge me because of her.' Or you can tell a teacher, 'I feel terrible that my father called to complain about my exam results. I'm really sorry.'

Can you speak directly to your parents about how they humiliate you in front of their friends or yours? Maybe. You can't say, 'Mum, get rid of your accent.' But you can say, 'Mum, I know you meant well telling Tina to stand up straighter, but I don't think it's your place to comment on her posture.' You can say, 'Dad, please don't compliment me in front of friends. It was sweet of you, but I felt ridiculous when you wolf-whistled in front of John.' Or tell your parents, 'Please stop asking me to play the violin for your friends. I feel like a complete idiot when I have to perform.' If your parents love to tease, you can't change them, but you can warn your friends they may be in for some ribbing.

Decide for yourself if a showdown is worth it. My father sometimes made me speak a few lines of French when we had dinner guests. I usually obliged because although I got a little embarrassed by it, he got a big kick out of it.

I also had to develop a sense of humour about Dad's quips on my budding figure. From my diary, age fifteen: '*I was going to the dance and Mum said to Dad, "Doesn't Carol look nice?" Dad put in his usual, "Yes, but what are those bumps on her chest?"*' Thank heavens he kept such cracks in the family.

In most cases, the soundest advice is to be open, caring, and honest, and to try to talk as adult to adult, not child to parent. Tackle problems as they arise. You and your parents are separate individuals. Agreement isn't always possible. But harmony is worth working towards.

Parents With Problems

When you're a child, you don't think of your parents as having any problems. Now you're older, you know better.

Family strife may come from parental problems that have almost nothing to do with you. If your parents fight or get divorced, it is probably because of problems between them: changing values, loss of trust or respect, money troubles, infidelity. Or your family may be in turmoil because of alcoholism, illness, or unemployment. You may get caught in the middle and you may ache because of their problems, but their problems are not your fault. And just as your parents aren't failures if you're not happy, you aren't a failure if they aren't happy.

If Your Parents Fight a Lot . . .

My parents had a happy marriage, complete with occasional arguments. When I was fourteen, I wrote in my diary: *'It hurts and upsets me when Dad uses a harsh manner with Mum because I know twenty years ago they were newlyweds.'* Yet now I realize it's impossible to feel and show intense love every minute after years with someone. And in a way, arguing shows that they still care about each other.

When you go out with a guy, you're trying to have fun for a limited period of time – two hours after school on Wednesday, four hours on Saturday night. When you're married, you're trying to have fun and take care of each other and make a living and pay taxes and keep a tidy home and get food on the table and maybe raise a family for an unlimited period of time. It's a bigger challenge. Your parents may be very much in love yet sometimes feel the need to let off steam. A little airing of tension is healthy and productive. It may not be pleasant or even fair, but it is tolerable and normal.

And if they quarrel constantly? It's hard on you, but it's not *because* of you (or your brothers and sisters). Childless couples squabble, too. Even if your parents do blame you or use you as a scapegoat (I hope they don't), how well they get along is up to them, not you. Their happiness is their responsibility, just as yours is yours. If you worry that they'll split up as soon as you leave the nest, you need to realize that you can't live at home forever to serve as buffer zone or keeper of the peace.

What can you do if they're always blowing up at each other? Not much. Accept their troubles as their troubles and try not to take sides or become the confidante of either one. Go on living your life, because you can't make their problems dissolve.

You *can* attempt to make things easier on them. Try to be less demanding during their rocky times. Clean up after yourself around the house, be extra kind, offer to make dinner for the younger members of the family so your parents can go out alone. If things are getting out of control, you could (easier said than done) suggest they talk to a marriage guidance counsellor, adding, 'I love you both and I hope you can work out your differences'. This may help. Or it may not.

Keep things in perspective. You and your brothers and sisters probably fight even though you love each other. Some well-matched parents fight a lot. Some fight for a few months, then go back to being their quiet, resilient selves. And – I hate to say it – some hold hands all the time, then end up in a divorce court. Just because your parents raise their voices is no reason for you to jump to conclusions. Even if your parents are separated, they may get back together, though it's best not to count on it.

If Your Parents Get Divorced . . .

Ouch. This is official. Since one in three or four marriages ends in divorce, it's also common, and you're not alone. But it's painful. And it may force you to grow up before you're ready. Your parents may start leaning on you. You may be alone more than you like. Money may become scarcer, responsibilities more plentiful. You may move. Or have to deal with step-parents. Or be separated from a sister or brother. You may wish things would go back to normal.

They won't. And even if you'd been an absolute angel every second your parents were together, it's almost guaranteed they'd still be apart now. So if you're feeling guilty, stop it. If you're hoping they'll get back together, try to stop that, too. Get your-self to remember, if only for a few minutes, some of their worst fights.

Accepting hard times is part of maturing. It rains on every-body's life once in a while, and then the sun comes out again. In the meantime, your umbrella is to try to get on with your world – friends, school, work, sports. You need a lot right now. Don't cry alone. Talk about how you feel to your parents. Or talk to a teacher, relative, young people's advisory service, or friend (maybe one whose parents are divorced).

If one parent starts telling you things you don't want to hear, be understanding (your parent is hurt) but gently say, 'Mum, I don't want to hear about how stingy Dad is or how rotten your sex life was,' or 'Dad, please don't tell me about Mum's affair; I can't do anything about it and it just upsets me – I'm sorry'. It's not fair for you to have to play parent to your parent. (On the other hand, if your parents put on a false brave act, tell them it's OK to share their sadness with you.)

It's tricky if one parent tries to use you to find out what the other is up to. You might say you are having a hard enough time adjusting and you don't want to be a go-between. Say, 'Ask *him* if he's seeing anyone else, not me.' It's also awkward if your parents try to win you over with gifts. Don't let your loyalties be bought. And don't let one parent make you tell tales on or stop seeing the other.

It might be a good idea to try to be part of any discussions about custody and access rights. Keep at least a spare toothbrush at the house where you may spend weekends or holidays. Better still, make one bedroom drawer and one bathroom shelf offi-cially yours. This will make both you and the parent you're living with feel more secure.

Some kids are relieved when their parents divorce. The war is over, and the parents may end up more content, alone or re-married. Some kids have more independence than ever and some enjoy a new sense of closeness to both parents. One friend told me she thinks of her family not as a broken home but as two happy homes.

Other kids are devastated. They'd accepted their parents' marriage as a permanent fixture and now their family is one more statistic. Is your parents' marriage over? Coming to terms with that sad truth gets easier with time and distraction. But you can't deal with it until you believe it. Be patient with yourself. Allow yourself time to feel angry and depressed.

It takes a long while to get from one part of your life to another. Remember that the end of one chapter marks the start of the next. Take your time grieving for the way your family was, then turn the page. Things won't be the same, but they may come out better than you expected. And by simply surviving this terrible time, you'll probably emerge a stronger, deeper, more compassionate person. (If, instead, you let yourself become glum, cynical, or an object of pity, you aren't doing yourself any favours.)

Although your parents don't love each other in the same way anymore, they probably each love you as much as – or more than – ever. If one of your parents does suddenly drop out of the picture, it's going to hurt like hell. Parents are irreplaceable. But new people always come into your life too, and divorced or widowed people remarry. You'll be loved because you are lovable.

If Your Parents Drink Too Much . . .

The *Drinks, Drugs, Etc.* chapter talks about alcohol. But if your parents (not you) have the problem, they (not you) are going to have to recognize it and deal with it. If your parents have one or two drinks after work every day, that doesn't point to alcohol dependency. But if that one drink changes their character, or if they can't control the drinking or become mean, moody, maudlin, or just plain pass out, then your parents may be alcoholics and you are indeed in a difficult situation. You may feel disgusted, ashamed, angry, resentful, disappointed. Keep in mind that alcoholism is a disease – partly acquired, partly inherited. And you can't get your parents to change until they admit that they have a problem and are ready to work on it. I know one boy who poured his mother's entire liquor supply down the drain, but the mother replenished it that week.

What can you do? Stay out of the way when your parents are drunk, and don't provoke them. Contact Alateen (see page 279), who run local groups where you can talk to other teenagers whose parents are alcoholics. Many of the approximately three quarters of a million problem drinkers in Britain are parents with children who, like you, are caught in a love/hate situation. Al-Anon (see page 279) is for entire families of alcoholics. You could also talk to an adult you trust. And you could suggest (results not guaranteed) that your parents attend an Alcoholics Anonymous meeting (see page 279 and find out details of local groups), or that they get in touch with ACCEPT (see page 279). Be encouraging, not critical. If your parents have come to grips with the problem, they may be ready to get help. But if you keep making excuses for them, covering their tracks, or letting them be abusive, they are getting away with being irresponsible and may not feel motivated to change. (You may want to escape the whole scene yourself at times, but don't do it by taking up drinking yourself.)

If Your Parent Is Ill . . .

The idea of losing a parent worries most teenagers terribly. But, for the moment, let's not assume ill means dying, OK? Many of my friends' parents have survived heart attacks and cancer and complicated operations. In each case, the scare brought the family closer.

If your parent is ill, it's hard on everybody. How you did in the tennis match doesn't seem to matter to anyone any more – maybe not even to you. Your whole family is frightened, tearful, and tiptoeing around. There may be money problems. You may have to take on more responsibilities than you can handle.

Talk about your worries with each other and show your love to the ailing parent with words, hugs, cards. You all need each other a lot right now. Be thoughtful and helpful. If the strains are too much, talk to a relative, a friend, or an adult outside the family.

If Your Parent Loses His or Her Job . . .

Be supportive. Your parent's self-esteem may be suffering, and your understanding, love, and respect will be appreciated. The parent may be moody or withdrawn or may sleep or drink more than usual. Cut back your own spending and try to make extra cash baby-sitting or at other work. Maybe you could even buy some groceries. Even if your admiration for your mum or dad is stronger when your parent is on top of things, your parent needs your love now. Take advantage of the parent's extra time by doing things together: walking, cooking, going to the zoo, playing games. Every family crisis provides an opportunity for new family closeness.

If Your Parents Both Work . . .

Ha! Just checking to see if you were paying attention! If your parents both work, that's not – or doesn't have to be – a problem. Coming home to an empty house may be a jolt if Mum or Dad had always been a house spouse and you'd got used to snacks and conversation after school. You may miss that time of closeness, but there are advantages of having two working parents, besides the obvious economic ones. Since both my parents worked, I learned independence early and didn't struggle with the career-versus-marriage question because I knew that women, like men, can have kids *and* careers. Some sacrifices have to be made, but both parents can be breadwinners and breadbakers.

If your working parents like their jobs, that can be a plus, too. If they lead stimulating lives of their own, they might be less likely to invade your privacy; be over-protective or abusive; or become dependent on alcohol, drugs, food, soap operas, or you.

If Your Parents Are Abusive . . .

If you frequently get hit or threatened, it probably doesn't help to know that lots of other teenagers are also beaten, neglected or abused by their parents, or to know that parents who punish their children like this are sick and in the wrong. If you are a victim of abuse, you need help. Your parent needs help. Your sisters and brothers need protection. You should report your parent to someone in authority, for all your sakes.

It's one thing if your parent lost control once and slapped you harder than he or she meant to. That's not praiseworthy, but it may, if followed by apologies and explanations, be forgivable. But if your parent uses you as a punching bag, *you* could grow up with physical and emotional scars even though your *parent* is the one at fault.

If you've been brutally smacked around more than once, consider contacting the NSPCC, the social services, youth counselling services, the National Women's Aid Federation, or the National Children's Home Family Network, who deal with any family problem, including abuse. See page 280 for telephone numbers.

Emotional abuse may not leave you visibly black and blue, but it's horrible to be picked on all the time. If the nicest thing your parents ever say to you is, 'Get lost,' or, 'Our lives were easier before you came along,' it becomes difficult for you to believe in yourself. Your family needs professional help and if they won't go to see someone with you, you should go alone. Making the initial call is hard. Talking to a therapist or social worker is not so hard – it's a relief and a release.

If you cannot stay in your home, there are places to go, besides your friends' or neighbours' homes. If you're over sixteen, don't rush into marriage to escape your home circumstances or you may find yourself in another trap. And don't run away without knowing where you're running to. Too many runaways end up desperate and poor and deceived; many become prostitutes or pushers or strippers. That doesn't have to happen! There are half-way houses and shelters for battered teenagers and wives. If you are under eighteen, you have a right to shelter, protection, education and support.

If you are driven to run away, and I sincerely hope you won't be, the Mothers' Union runs a 'Message Home' service. You don't have to tell them where you are, but they will let your family know you're all right. The numbers to call are on page 280.

In most cases, if you have terrible problems with parents or parents with terrible problems or a bit of both, you'd be wise to get some expert help before things get any worse. There's no longer any stigma attached to getting outside help. It's a lot smarter than staying in a no-win situation. So keep reading!

You're Crazy If You Need
Counselling and Don't Seek It

Counselling is not only for the weak or the crazy. It's for the person who is smart enough to realize she could be happier and strong enough to realize a trained professional could help her find that happiness.

Let me be clear. You don't trot off to the doctor's each time your tummy hurts, and I'm not saying you should run to get your head shrunk (or expanded) each time you're upset.

From my diary when I was sixteen:

> *Life is like a rerun. There's no one to talk to and I don't want to be alone. I'm sick of pressure, even peer pressure. I'm sick of being told to pick up Eric here and there. I'm sick of Fran and I haven't even seen her yet. I'm sick of my driving teacher flirting with Danielle. I'm sick of my bosses at the pharmacy thinking I'm high-strung. I'm sick of my messy room – I never clean it. I'm sick of getting no sleep – it's 1:11 a.m. now. I'm sick of not improving at piano – I hardly practise . . .*

That's not jolly, but it's OK. It's the kind of mood that feels awful, yet mostly disappears by morning. Part of being a teenager – and a person – is getting into life's ups and downs, smiles and frowns. (Now you know why I'm not a poet.)

But some problems, ruts, and moods are too big to handle alone. If you're anorexic or alcoholic or suicidal, you probably can't recover without outside support. If you've been abused, talking to a counsellor may speed the healing. If your parents are divorced or your sister has died, an objective listener can help you cope with your sorrow. If the idea of kissing petrifies you, a counsellor can help you be more comfortable with your sexuality. If you've been shoplifting or binge buying, a counsellor can help you control your urges. If you've been generally down, a therapist can help you get back up. Sometimes you feel trapped when you're not. Your doctor can find out if your depression is due to a chemical imbalance and, if so, can prescribe not talking but medication and possibly a diet.

It may be that your whole family could benefit from counselling. For instance, if your home life is unbearable. Or if your father is the heavy, your mother never even disciplines the dog, and it's screwing you up. Or if it's next to impossible to adjust to your step-parent or half-brothers. Or if your home is full of misdirected anger. You all yell at each other when you're actually mad at friends, teacher, bosses. You could put up with family friction and assume – accurately, perhaps – that you'll all get along in a few years' time. But why deny yourselves the possibility of getting along now?

Not that counselling guarantees instant family or personal happiness. You have to work towards that. But it is a step in the right direction. And if you're carrying around a lot of excess emotional baggage, sooner or later you'll want to unpack.

How do you find a good counsellor? Contact the National Association of Youth Counselling and Advisory Services (*see page 280*) enclosing an SAE. You won't be found out or 'exposed'. The referral can be confidential, and your sessions can be your secret.

If you belong to a church or synagogue, counselling may be available through them. Ask.

Your family doctor may be able to refer you to a psychiatrist, if you need one.

Short-term therapy may be all you need. Going for counselling doesn't have to mean years on the couch.

You may decide you don't feel comfortable with a particular counsellor. Fine. Find someone else. Or try group therapy. Or perhaps an anonymous phone call to a hot line for your particular problem can provide comfort, insights, and reassurance.

The point is, if you need help, it's out there. If you've lost your appetite or can't sleep or work because of troubles, don't come apart at the seams. If some people envy your popularity or money or brains, but you can't see past the 8,600 logical reasons you have for feeling miserable, seek help. It's no disgrace. What is unfair to yourself and your loved ones is to be chronically depressed for months on end, with or without good reason, yet to do nothing about it except cry and complain.

Teenage Suicide

Grim statistics: there has been a twenty per cent increase in suicide in under twenty-fives over the last decade. It's thought that suicide is now the number two cause of death in this age group, after road accidents. In 1984, 309 young men and 54 young women killed themselves, but it's not known how many teenagers have attempted suicide and failed.

Suicide is often a cry for help; victims are hoping to be found and rescued.

Listen, kiddo, there are always reasons to feel despondent, just as there are always reasons to feel happy. You may have considered suicide briefly at some moment. You may have thought, 'That'll show 'em,' then realized it would show you, too. If you have ever contemplated suicide, please please please tell your doctor or make a call to the Samaritans, who have 181 centres and 21,000 volunteer 'befrienders' in Britain. They are listed in all phone books and in local papers, and you don't have to be on the point of suicide before you call.

Do you have a friend or family member who is talking about suicide? Who is more than a little accident-prone? Who isn't eating or sleeping? Who is suddenly giving away valued possessions or withdrawing from favourite activities? Don't brush it off. You owe it to him or her and to your own peace of mind to alert a responsible adult. If a friend mentions that he or she has considered suicide, take him or her seriously. It isn't true that those who talk about it never do it.

I'm not going to tell you, 'It's your party and you can die if you want to'. Because I don't think you really want to end your life. I think you want to *change* your life. And there's a big difference.

Brothers and Sisters

I have a friend whose big brother swore that if she cupped her hands around a bumble bee and held them together, the bee would become tame. She spent months hunting bumble bees, finally caught one, clamped her hands round it, and – well, you can guess what happened. (Hint: she wasn't pleased.)

Brothers and sisters. When I was growing up, I had no sisters, but brother, did I have brothers! Just two older ones, actually: Mark and Eric. Yet it felt like a houseful.

We three sometimes got along, sometimes squabbled, and sometimes played tricks on each other. It's all in my diary.

I was about to go to bed when I found out Eric had set my alarm for 2:00 a.m.! . . . .Mark and I tried hard to convince Eric he was balding. . . . Eric told me my faults for about half an hour including that he'd rather have been an only child. . . . Eric was mad at me so he slammed the car door shut. But its window shattered and that made him even madder because he'll have to pay. . . . I drove to Jen's but Eric cycled over and quietly drove the car away. When I was ready to drive home, I thought the car was stolen and I got hysterical. . . . Judy, Eric, and I visited Mark at Brown University. The visit was fun except that besides giving Mark and his roommate Charlie a dozen cupcakes, we were a pain. For example, Mark had a huge test and we gave him no time to study. We twisted Charlie's pipe cleaners into little animals. We insulted their sloppy room. We made them find extra beds. We put a peeled banana in Mark's bed and he thought it was something else. I parked illegally and the car got towed and Mark had to pay to retrieve it, etc. etc.

Somehow we've all forgiven each other, and we're very compatible now (well, not aalllwaaays but most of the time).

Becoming lifelong friends with your brothers and sisters isn't easy. But you're stuck with them forever. And the bond between you may be all the deeper for the mischief you shared. The expression 'Blood is thicker than water' is one way of putting it, yet it's true you can count on family even when friends let you down. Besides, who else knows you and your parents inside out and remembers the day your kitten got stuck in the filing cabinet and how Grandma always brought Extra-strong mints when she visited?

I know, I know. I'm making it sound ever so rosy, but some of you are stuck between a snobby bossy know-it-all big sister and a bratty kid brother who gets away with murder. Or you've got a one hundred per cent perfect, can-do-no-wrong sis, and only you know that behind the charming façade, she's a number-one pain. Brothers and sisters are for keeps? That may be the last thing you want to be reminded of.

Hold it right there. For a start, are you even half as nice to your sisters and brothers as you are to friends and strangers? If not, that's one reason they aren't always nice back. It's wonderful that family members feel comfortable together. You can take your shoes and make-up off. But if you're so familiar that you don't bother being kind, civil, or interested in each other's doings, then no wonder communication breaks down.

Example. If your brother says, 'Nice haircut,' and you got your hair cut *last* week, you could say with a sneer, 'How observant of you', or you could say, 'Thanks.'

It's hard to get along with someone who hogs not only bathroom and television, but parents' attention as well. Here are some tips on handling siblings' feelings and making your own feelings known.

- *If you're jealous of your brother*, tell him. You may find he envies or admires qualities in you, or that deep down he's sometimes insecure, too.

- *If you think your parents favour your sister*, don't hope they'll pick up on your inferiority complex – speak out. If your parents are lavishing time on your sister because she's got mumps or is getting married, be patient. Their attention doesn't mean they love her more than you. It may mean they think she needs them more right now. (Direct from my diary: *'I feel like crying. Dinner was awful and the conversation was Eric's college choices again. What originality!'*)

- *If they label you two The Clever One and The Pretty One*, either of you could tell them Clever is beginning to feel ugly and Pretty is starting to feel stupid.

- *If your parents favour you*, you could bask in the glory, but be generous. Say things to them like, 'Isn't Lynn a marvellous actress?' or 'Can you believe how good Lisa is at science?' When your parents have favourites (their mistake), you and your siblings may become competitive and jealous (your loss).

- *If your brother acts like he knows everything*, tell him you're glad he's there when you need help, but you wish he wouldn't volunteer advice when you don't ask for it. Tell him you want to make up your own mind, not conform to or rebel against his ideas. He may be in a let-me-prove-how-mature-I-am phase. Things get easier once you're both secure and independent.

- *If you have always idolized your sister and then find out she's an ordinary human being after all*, that's called growing up. It's OK.

- *If your sister is Ms Amazing*, stop competing and focus on what's amazing about you. Think of your family as a team: the 'better' each member, the 'better' the team.

- *If you and your sister are rivals in school or sport*, decide what area *you* like best and work on excelling in different subjects or sports (unless you both absolutely love the same things). Learning to co-operate and compromise with siblings is often how you first learn to deal with strangers.

- *If your kid brother always wants to tag along*, spend a little time with him, but explain that you want to go out alone with your friends. If you occasionally offer him your undivided attention and let him say hello to your friends, he may be more willing to respect your time out.

- *If your sister steals your boyfriends*, tell her she's hurting you. And that you're glad she approves of your taste, but even if she 'wins' Dave, she's losing more than she's gaining. She may be sacrificing sisterly love for a fleeting romance.

- *If you want to get to know a brother better*, start a conversation and listen. Instead of doing chores separately, do them together and talk. Go for a bike ride and ask his advice or tell him what you like best about him. Knock on his door and confide in him: you have a crush on Bob, or Mum has been nagging you and it's driving you nuts. Ask what worries him most. Stop making fun of each other.

- *If you like your brother's friend and think the feeling might be mutual*, maybe, just maybe, he can arrange a casual double date to the skating rink or swimming pool. (Eric did it for me!)

- *If you and your sister share a room*, try to set a few rules about neatness and privacy and try not to let petty things get to you. Tell each other (calmly) what you like and dislike about the arrangement. And get a curtain or room divider if the going is tough.

- *If your sister goes away on holiday or to college*, phone and write; it may strengthen your bond.

- *If your sister is a nerd*, don't tease her about what a nerd she is or she'll become even nerdier and hate you, too. Praise her for what she does well and boost her confidence.
- *If your brother is getting married and you're worried you won't be as close to him*, expect to feel a little jealous and left out at first (I did when Eric married Cynthia), but give your brother credit for knowing a great person when he finds one. You may gain a sister, not lose a brother.
- *If your brother discourages you from taking on challenges*, prove him wrong by excelling at them.
- *If your sister's recent eating or drinking habits worry you*, say, 'It may be none of my business, but I care and it concerns me that you're getting so thin (or drunk). Is something bothering you?' Don't expect her to thank you and reform immediately, but continue to show love, and she will appreciate it. If you're very worried, you could tip your parents off. (I don't mean telling tales if your sister has a half of lager. I mean getting help if you think she's losing control of her life.)

That's enough *ifs* for now, don't you think? It's hard to generalize, because each family, brother, sister, and situation is different. It depends on many things, like how old you are and your relationship and family size and age gap and birth order.

Birth order. Have you heard the popular birth order theories? Some experts believe that where you fit in your family may determine where you fit in the world. They contend:

- The first-born, since he or she deals with adults right off and teaches younger members of the family, is often bright and verbal and achievement oriented, but may be stubborn or a worrier.
- The middle child, since he or she is a practised diplomat and referee (who, alas, may occasionally feel overlooked by Mum and Dad) is likeable and socially adept.

- The youngest child, since he or she may get heaps of attention, might grow up confident, secure, sociable – and a little spoiled.

Of course, your individuality is far more important than family position. Besides, if you're the only daughter in a family of five (like my friend Judy, a middle child), you're going to get more attention than an average middle child. And if you were born long after the others (like my sister-in-law Sally), you may sometimes feel like an only child.

What does it feel like to be an only child? It depends. My sister-in-law Cynthia says it felt just fine. 'When I went to other people's houses, I thought, "Nice place to visit, but I wouldn't want to live here – too chaotic!" ' The pros of being an only child are that you may get undivided attention and feel very loved, you never have to share a room or get punched by a bully of a brother, and you learn early to be independent and, perhaps, imaginative and a good reader. The cons are that you may get more parental attention and solitude than you'd like, you won't get the inside info on what makes boys tick, and you may feel less comfortable in a group of kids. If you are an only child, work on making close friendships. And if your parents will let you, think about getting a pet. A pet can be an important family member. (I've had the same sweet Siamese for fourteen years!)

My husband's mother is a twin. She experienced the advantages of always having a playmate and best friend and the disadvantages of rarely getting Mum and Dad all to herself. If you're a twin, you two might consider attending different schools and dressing differently. The connection you share will probably never fade, but it's crucial to develop separate identities.

If you are adopted, you may feel curious about your natural mother and father, and wonder if you have any natural sisters and brothers. Once you are over eighteen, you now have a legal right to see your original birth certificate. If you are sure you want to do this, write to the Registrar General at the address on page 280, and ask for an application form. You must also have counselling from a social worker who will discuss the possible consequences of investigating your background.

Many adopted children are happy just to know the name of their natural mother. It's up to you whether or not you try to make contact. There is a self-help organization for everyone involved in the adoption triangle – you, your adoptive parents, and your natural parents. It's called NORCAP, and you should write to them at the address on page 280 enclosing an SAE for more details.

If you are adopted, I hope you know that families who share their home and love are as close as families who share genes. And I hope you feel special knowing how much your parents wanted you.

Step-families: Step by Step

Just about everything I said about parents and brothers and sisters goes for step-parents and step-brothers and -sisters, too, but getting used to new family members is a whole new kettle of fish.

If you're a step-child, you're keeping company with 980,000 other British under-18s who live in step-families. If you suddenly become a step-child, perhaps you can make friends with someone else who has gone through the adjustments you now face. You may find it helpful to contact Stepfamily, an organization set up specially for people in step-families. Their address is on page 281, and they run a helpline service as well as a newsletter and leaflets for all members of step-families.

Some teenagers accept a parent's death or divorce and welcome new family members. *You* may wish your step-parent or step-parents would make a grand exit, or that a good fairy would appear and whisk you away. (It worked for Cinderella.)

If you were happier before the stepmother, stepfather, or live-in lover came along, keep these thoughts in mind.

- You may take a dislike to your step-parent because you miss your natural parent. You may even feel like a traitor for liking the 'replacement'. But play fair. Treating the newcomer like a substitute teacher or blaming the step-parent for family upheaval makes life harder for everybody. Befriending the step-parent doesn't diminish your love for your absent parent.

- You may feel fed up and left out. A lot of parental attention that went to you now goes to someone else. Ask your parent to go for a walk or shopping or jogging or museum visiting or to do *something* alone with you. Make a date of it. Make a weekly date of it. Then don't bitch about The Invader; talk about positive things.

- Try to be happy for your happy parent. Just as you need friends your own age, your parent – though he or she probably loves you to bits – may have felt lonely at times and wished for adult company. If you are happy for your parent and sad for yourself, it's OK to say so.

- Be relieved: with someone else to care for Mum or Dad, you won't feel depended on. You will feel freer to go out with pals or leave home.

- Think of the step-parent as a plus, not a minus. Arrange time alone together. Don't expect instant love. Let rapport or friendship develop. Who knows? If your step-parent has natural kids elsewhere, he or she may feel the same odd sense of betrayal and disloyalty you do about investing in a new relationship while missing a former one. Ask yourself if you'd still think she was a shrew, or he was a thug, if she or he had been introduced as a friend's parent.

- Try not to let your feelings towards your step-parent depend on whether he or she is generous or permissive. If you're expected to follow a whole new set of rules, try to obey, or have a family talk about compromises and trade-offs.

- Allow time for change. Instant harmony won't happen. It may take a year or two to settle in as a family, more if you see each other only at weekends or school holidays.

- Don't forget that your step-parent is making adjust-ments, too. Consider this: your step-parent fell for your parent yet married a package deal. Fine. No reason for any guilt. But it's not all hearts-and-flowers from that end, either. If you want to get closer, one way to begin is, 'I've been sort of stubborn, but I'm ready for us to get along.' Stilted? Maybe. Effective? Probably. Or try, 'It must be weird having an instant family.' (If the step-parent grunts and grumbles, 'It isn't what I bargained for,' then my sympathy is with you.)

- If you've really tried and just can't get along – sigh – learning to deal with the step-parent will teach you toler-ance and social skills. Watching the step-parent's inter-actions with your family will give you insights on how other families operate. If the situation is beastly, you might be able to move in with your other natural parent or with a relative or friend.

- Step-brothers and -sisters add more confusions, rival-ries, dimensions, love and good times to the pot. You're not obliged to love them, but it's worth working towards (1) truce, (2) friendship, and (3) family feeling. Some step-siblings get along better than natural sisters and brothers. If you're the newcomer and you think your new step-sister feels threatened, say, 'We both know you're your mother's one and only, but I appreciate her trying to make me feel at home.' If you're the one who will have to share your home, phone or write before the marriage and say 'Welcome to the family.' Realize that your parent, too, may be going out of the way to show the newcomer goodwill.

Take it one step at a time. Share your feelings. As John Lennon sang, 'Give peace a chance.'

Relatives in the Parlour and
Skeletons in the Cupboard

It's easy to take relatives for granted. It's easy to think of your parents' folks as old fogies and not as the ones who cradled your mum, taught your dad to drive, baked birthday cakes, walked down the aisle on their wedding day, and watched with excitement as your mother, pregnant with you, got bigger and bigger.

Your relatives shared memories before you were born, and they've been through crises and quarrels like the ones you're going through now. Sure it's important to dress up, be polite, and show them respect, but why not really get to know them? You probably won't like all of them, and not all of them will find time for you, but you may find you adore many of your relatives and vice versa.

If you have a complete set of doting grandparents, you are very lucky. Let them know you love them. If one of your parents' parents died before your birth, ask about him or her. Your parent may welcome the chance to tell you stories.

Get to know your older relatives while you have the chance. Get them to tell you their stories first-hand. What was their childhood like? What were their hardest and happiest times? What were *their* parents like? What are they most proud of? How did they meet? What was your dad like at primary school? What was your mother like as a teenager?

You may treasure the advice older relatives give you. When I was sixteen, I wrote in my diary, *'Grandad told me to "spar with the boys" but not to fall in love, but Grandma said I'd be in and out of love many times before marriage.'* (Grandma was right.) If you have a tape recorder, you may want to tape relatives' stories.

Or have them write stories down. The best present I ever gave my father was a journal of blank pages in which I asked lots of questions. Some of the questions were light, such as 'What are your favourite forms of exercise?' (Dad wrote, 'Jogging to refrigerator, fetching the mail, signing cheques.') Others were more serious, such as 'What was it like meeting Mum?' (Dad wrote, '. . . From about the third date, we were bonded for good.') Now that I don't have my father, I can't tell you how glad I am to have some of his thoughts written in his own hand.

Years ago, when families didn't scatter so much, grandparents often lived with the family. In some places, they still do. When I stayed on a French farm, grandparents Mémé and Pépé lived with us, as did great-uncle TonTon. It caused some tensions, sure, but mostly it was nice for the teenagers to learn from the elders' wisdom and skills, and for the elders to enjoy the teenagers' energy and enthusiasm.

Don't be embarrassed by your relatives. You are you, and they are they, and besides, nearly everybody's family has at least one eccentric but sweet uncle who saves paper bags and wears wide, garish ties and socks that slip down because the elastic has worn out.

Do you have any problem relatives? If you look deep inside almost any family – including all relatives and in-laws – and open the cupboard door, skeletons will come toppling out. Never mind the adulterous half-brother or the bisexual aunt. I'm talking about real loonies. In my extended family, a cousin shot her husband and then herself, only she died and he lived and . . . well, I don't mean to one-up you on family sagas but to let you know that if your step-grandfather drinks and your second cousin is in jail, *you* need not feel ashamed.

If you feel you got short-changed in the Relative Department – you hardly have any, or the ones you have are indifferent or uninteresting – take heart. I bet certain teachers, parents of friends, and friends of parents will become like loving relatives to you.

When Loved Ones Die

When someone you love dies, it feels like the worst thing in the world. I wish I could tell you that you get over the loss in a hurry, but you don't. I will say that after you have mourned, you may end up stronger (if you've survived this, you can survive anything), you may have a better perspective on your setbacks (you won't pout and say 'This was the lousiest day of my life' after merely failing an exam), you may become more sensitive (since you've 'been there', you can empathize with other people's sorrows), and the rest of your family may grow closer than ever.

Of course, you'd probably prefer to be less strong, less wise, less sensitive, and less close to your family than to have to deal with death. Yet Death doesn't ask. And if you're lucky enough to be long-lived, you probably will have to deal with the death of loved ones somewhere down the line.

Thinking about death may help us appreciate our finite lives and may remind us to show our love to those who make our lives richer.

My father died in his sleep when he was sixty-eight, a few years ago. I still cry about it once in a while and I still sometimes say, 'my parents', when I mean 'my mother'. But I have finally got to the point where I can smile when I remember Scrabble games and driving lessons and cooking side by side. Or when I remember that among his things was a leather glasses case I'd made for him at school when I was eleven. Or when I recall that whenever he left after visiting me at college, I waited the hour and a quarter it took for him to drive home, then phoned, and he always picked up the receiver and said without hesitation, 'Yes, Snippo, I got back safely.'

It took a long time, but I can finally feel thankful that I had such a caring father rather than feeling heartsick that I had him for only twenty-five years. I can feel thankful that the bond we shared is sealed and safe. And that you lose your father only once.

But it still hurts. Remember that journal I told you I gave him? One of my questions was a fill-in-the-blank. I wrote, 'I'd think it was pretty neat if Carol – .' Dad answered, 'published a book.' Well, here's the book, but I can't give Dad an autographed copy.

Mourning is the pits. Dad was my biggest fan, and when he died, I felt stranded. My mother and brothers and I comforted each other, but we were all in pretty bad shape. Suddenly a huge hole was in our lives, and we kept falling in because we didn't know how to step around it. I also felt guilty about sobbing to Mum; she had just lost her husband, yet I was asking her for solace.

Seven weeks after Dad's death, I was still a mess: unable to work, unable to play. Dad's life was over and mine was at a standstill. A friend suggested I 'talk to someone', meaning that I see a counsellor. The words stung, because I'd always 'had my head screwed on right' – as Dad had often put it. But I knew my friend was right.

What I didn't know was whom to call. (I didn't have one of these handy books around.) Baffled, I started leafing through the phone book under P for psychology, T for therapy, and at last, M for mental health.

I was shaking as I dialled the first number. The receptionist said someone could return my call after the weekend. The weekend? I couldn't wait that long. I dialled another number, got no reply. I dialled a third number.

'My father died and . . . ' my voice cracked, '. . . I'm having a hard time dealing with it.' The woman on the other end said, 'Do you want to come in and talk about it?' Did I ever!

I got on my bicycle, rode to the Evanston Hospital Crisis Intervention Centre, met Mickey Jordan, and blubbered to her for a solid hour. I showed her Dad's picture, described the funeral, told her about the other people in my world. During the next few months, we met seven more times. The sessions with Mickey were invaluable. She helped me accept what I couldn't change and untie some knots that were in the way of my getting on with my life. She helped me work out how to step around the abyss of my father's death. She helped me regain my lost confidence and realize that although my father is dead, he will always be alive inside me.

If someone you love dies, you may not need or want to seek professional counselling. You may find enough strength in your family, your friends, your religion, your memories, yourself. You may be able to stick to your routines and get through one day at a time. Try to pamper yourself. And don't go by any *shoulds*: 'You should have been nicer'; 'you should feel better by now'; 'you should cry more'; 'you shouldn't be enjoying a silly television show'. It may take months or several years for you to absorb the shock and believe that the loved one is gone forever. There may not be a turning point in your recovery, but there will be a turning time. Almost everybody who has grieved is left with some sense of guilt, some feeling of being robbed, and some unanswered questions. But eventually, you will accept that your life goes on and you will risk loving other people.

What can you do or say if your friend has lost a brother, sister, parent, friend, or relative? Do *not* avoid the friend because you don't know how to act. Your friend needs you now. Say you are sorry. And be there to listen. You don't have to bring up the subject, but don't change it if your friend brings it up. If your friend's mother dies, she can't talk *to* her mother, so she may want to talk *about* her. Listen.

If her mother had been sick for years, it's not your place to say, 'Her death was a blessing in disguise', or 'Cheer up', or 'Be brave', or 'You never really got on with her anyway', or 'Don't question God's wisdom,' or 'Maybe your father will remarry someone nice.' I also never liked it when people said, 'I know how you feel', because I always felt 'You do not'. But those people meant well, and the grieving need to be tolerant, too.

Just listen to your friend and agree that it must hurt an awful lot. Listen even if she wants to share a detail that seems horrible (how skinny her mother looked in the hospital, what it was like throwing away her old clothes). Even if your friend seems snappy or neurotic, she probably appreciates your being attentive. Be tolerant of her moods because she may be up and down for a while. If your friend loses a family member, she may be saddest months after the death when the loss really hits her. And she may never be her very same old self again.

When I was in my mid-teens, my mother learned of the death of a friend and cried and carried on for hours. I tiptoed about and stayed out of her way. Later Mum said she wished I'd gone into her room and given her a hug. Now I wouldn't need to be told.

Do you want to write a note to someone faraway who has been through a loss? (I appreciated every single letter I received.) Your card doesn't have to be long. In fact, instead of expressing your sympathy, then going on to say how you've been doing, it's nicer to keep to the point, then follow up later with chattier letters. Often the bereaved are deluged with letters when they are still feeling numb, and then nobody writes when the pain settles in.

If you chickened out of acknowledging someone's loss months ago, do it now. Some of my friends worried about writing a belated sympathy card because they were afraid they'd 'remind' me of Dad's death. Believe me, one mourns without reminders. And even when friends' cards made me cry, the tears were welcome and healing.

What do you write? 'I was so sorry to hear about your mother's death. I know how much you loved her and how much she loved you. My thoughts are with you.' Something like that, but in your own words. It doesn't have to be even that long. If you like, say something wonderful about the person or include a telling anecdote. 'I'll always remember how your father took me to Casualty when I cut my chin and my parents were at work. I was so scared, and your dad just kept making jokes and asking me about my teachers and boyfriends. He was a wonderful, funny, generous man.'

Whether someone you love dies or someone you know suffers a loss, remember that brighter days are ahead. Time doesn't heal but it helps.

6. School and Money

Your Future Starts Here

Just the other year you were in primary school singing *All Things Bright and Beautiful*. You looked up to the eleven-year-olds and pretended you had lots of homework because it made you feel grown-up.

Now you have lots of homework. Does it make you feel grown-up? No. It makes you feel sick. You have a teacher you dislike and another who has favourites. You're pressured by college and career decisions. You even have anxiety dreams: you are handed your exam results by the conductor on the No. 10 bus, but the paper blows away before you can read what they are. . .

This chapter shows how to make the most of your school, even if it's a jail, zoo, or pressure-cooker. It includes tips on improving your studying habits, ways to cope with teachers, and alternatives if you can't stand it a moment longer. It will help you get the best possible careers advice, choose a college or university course and explain the mysteries of the Youth Training Scheme. There is also information about making, and saving, money; being a better baby-sitter; finding odd jobs; writing a c.v.; doing well in an interview and getting employed. I want you to find a career not by chance, but by choice.

Is School Unbeatable or Unbearable?

Adults tend to romanticize their long-lost school years. Many forget how they dreaded that first school day after the summer holidays. How they steamed open the envelope containing their report. How they couldn't care less about what happens to the half-life of a radioisotope that combines to form a compound. How they prayed to be snowed in, catch flu or miss the bus.

School is no picnic. I remember that. And if I ever forget, I can always look back at my diary and re-read entries such as *'Classes warp creativity!'* or *'Someday I'll be a politician so I can express my views on education: It stinks!'*

In all fairness, school has lots of pluses, many of which I did appreciate at the time. It was great having lunch every day with Judy or Jen or my boyfriend. I loved the English discussions about poetry and novels. I miss the two or three inspiring teachers who truly cared about my intellectual growth. And I miss the *variety* of school: the way I changed teachers every hour and courses every year. Sometimes I even miss the on-top-of-things feeling I'd get when I got to the QED of a geometry problem or figured out an obscure line of poetry.

Do you realize that one-third of the world's people are illiterate? Aren't you grateful to be among the other two-thirds?

Believe it or not, learning *is* often more fun than earning. In many ways, school *is* a picnic – a picnic complete with ants.

Why Should You Learn All That Irrelevant Stuff Anyway?

While you're in school, it's hard to judge what's relevant. When I took psychology in college, I thought of it as just another class. It turned out to be one of the most useful courses I ever took, for my writing and for my social life. When I took Folklore, I thought it was great fun. It proved fairly worthless in the long run. A friend of mine joined the stage crew in senior school. Did she become an actress? No. She got interested in stage lighting design, then light in general, and now she's the most zealous (and well paid) young physicist I know.

School exposes you to so much: Shakespeare's plays, Einstein's calculations, Picasso's paintings. Sooner or later, while you're writing a program in Computer Science, conducting a fruit-fly experiment in Biology, racing around the track, singing in the choir, putting a pot in the kiln, or reading about political campaigns, you'll feel filled with energy and enthusiasm. You'll begin to find out what you like to do, what you're best at, what fields of study to pursue or what career to start aiming for. That's an exciting discovery. You'll also learn what you're not good at and not interested in, which is essential in planning your future, too.

Whether you're in your second year or your fifth, take care with your subject choices and don't neglect sport and out-of-school activities. Balance your schedule without overloading it. The more you learn, the more things you'll enjoy and the more choices you'll have. If you can't type or aren't computer literate, you're limiting your marketable skills. If you don't like reading or theatre or sculpture, you have fewer ways to enjoy yourself than someone who does. Do you know the basics of car mechanics? If you do, you're one up on the person who panics whenever his or her car sputters.

You'll never regret having that education edge. School teaches you to think, to analyse, to solve problems and to work with discipline. Not all your teachers are brilliant and/or nice, but not all your future employers will be,· either. Not every piece of homework is scintillating and important, but in the Real World there are dirty dishes to wash and boring bills to pay no matter how exhilarating your profession is. Besides, the best – and quickest – way out of a boring school is to do well there.

Your education, in and out of school, is for you – so you'll be able to lead your life instead of being led by it.

Cram Course in Study Habits

Working solely to pass an exam rather than working to learn is a shame. But marks do matter. Especially if you are college or university bound. Besides, if you're getting As and Bs, you're probably learning a lot and feeling good about yourself. And since you're in school anyway, you might as well do your best.

A few natural-born brains sail through their exams without even opening a book. Me? I got good marks by working my backside off. Some subjects came more easily to me than others, but I'm not a fast reader and I couldn't coast along in anything. At times, I couldn't believe how much homework I'd have per class per day – some sixth-form courses are harder than college ones – but I slogged through and it paid off. I'm glad I learned as much as I did in school and I'm glad I got into the college I wanted.

There are many ways you can learn more and improve your performance during the year and when exam time comes around.

---

1 **Aim high.** Try for one hundred per cent and you might get ninety. Try to scrape through and you might fail. Spend a few minutes before each class looking over your homework or reviewing the assigned chapter. If you concentrate and take notes, your classes will go by faster. Don't fall behind. And don't watch the clock and doodle, then, when called upon, have to ask, 'What page are we on?' Try to excel in at least *one* subject. Being good at one subject may inspire you to try harder in others. The cliché is true: the more you put into school, the more you get out of it. So don't get by – get ahead.

2 **Make lists.** Notebooks are lifesavers. Write down which pages you have to read for History and which problems you have to do for Geometry. Sometimes I'll even write down things like 'jog' or 'send Grandad birthday card'. It's not that I'd necessarily forget other-wise, but writing down plans frees my mind to think of other things. It also adds to my sense of accomplishment later when I cross off what I got done. (Am I making myself sound like a hopeless nerd in school? I wasn't. I swear. Ask Judy.)

3 **Revise actively for exams.** *Passive* studying means flip-ping through your notes and leafing through books. *Active* studying means taking notes on your notes, reading them aloud, reciting information to yourself, making an outline. If you own the book, highlight im-portant lines and paragraphs. Give yourself practice vocabulary quizzes or hard maths problems to figure out. Have someone test you on your foreign verb conju-gations. There are many revision aids on sale and some local radio stations may offer help with exam revision in the summer.

Think up mnemonic (memory-boosting) devices.

When I was studying for Mr Wildman's essay test on the Renaissance, I concocted the word *pranchimy* to remind me to write about Perspective, Religion, Anatomy, Nature, Classics, Humanities, Intellectualism, Materialism and Youth.

Listen when your teacher explains what the exam will cover, so you'll know precisely what to study. I used to study for exams the night before, then look over the material again right before class. The risk of counting purely on last-minute cramming is that something may come between you and your books. The guy you like may choose that day to sit next to you during your free period. Or your teacher may chat with you before class or have you hand out the exam papers when you were depending on those two minutes to commit a poem or formula to memory.

Before you begin an exam, look the paper over. *Carefully*. Find out how long it is. Read the essay questions. Pace yourself, leaving time to check your answers. If you have a lot of time for a short maths quiz, you might even do it twice, then compare your results. Approach exams like sporting events – psych yourself for victory.

4 **Write and rewrite essays and projects.** Second drafts are better than first drafts. Don't hand in a half-baked composition you scribbled off an hour before class. Don't think on paper, rambling on as you figure out what you want to say. Think first. Then write. Then do something else. Then return to your paper and revise it.

Be lively: steer clear of stilted words such as *thus* and *thereby* and bland, over-used words such as *nice* and *interesting*. Be clear and succinct: Don't write *significant increase* when you mean *more*, or *at this point in time* when you mean *now*. Be precise: Don't say *very very worried* when you mean *frantic*. Eliminate unnecessary and repeated words. Read your paper aloud – does it sound OK? Check for spelling mistakes. (I dare you to find *drownded*, *alright* or *alot* in your dictionary.) Watch your grammar – *between he and I* is wrong. Type your work if your school allows it. Learning to type is another useful skill for the future.

Can't get your exam paper started? Pretend it's an essay question in a one-hour test. Or pretend you're writing a letter to a friend. ('Dear Jen, the trouble with exams. . .')

If you want to develop better creative writing skills, read good books and quality newspapers, not just the tabloids.

5 **Cheat and plagiarize**. (Only kidding, gang.) The problem with cheating is that you're only —— —— (fill in the blanks). As your marks go up, your self-respect goes down. Yes, you may get an A, but you know you didn't really get it.

I plead guilty. I occasionally planted myself near some know-it-all in the back so I could check my multiple-choice answers against hers. Then one day I stopped. It just didn't seem worth it any more. I wanted to depend on myself.

If you cheat in French in September, you'll regret it all year because you won't have learned the basics. How can you master the *passé composé* if you don't even have the present tense of *avoir* down? Same principle in maths. Besides, you'd feel like an idiot if you and Andy were the only ones to write 23,964 when the answer was 12.

Not that cheating is uncommon. A recent statistic revealed that over half the students questioned admitted to having cheated at some point. If you're caught, some teachers will give you an automatic zero and some schools will suspend or expel you. The plagiarists who copy out of a book, or turn in papers written by former students are often caught. I knew a guy at college who was kicked out for a year for having plagiarized a paper. He'd copied it straight from an obscure tome – written by a friend of his professor's!

6 **Love your library**. Even if your desk at home is big and well lit, there are always distractions, from telephone to

television. Some people can concentrate anywhere. Not me. I like studying where it's quiet, where reference books are accessible, and desks are large enough to spread out on. Ask your librarian for any help you need with research for an important project, and how to use the indexing system so you can locate books. (Bonus: libraries even offer exotic cookbooks and manuals to help improve your chess game.)

In senior school, I often stayed behind and holed up in a classroom or the library to make a dent in my homework. That way I had fewer books to lug home and more free time at night. Decide where you are most comfortable studying.

7 **Study when you're most alert.** I remember crawling into bed one night with *Jude the Obscure* and spending about an hour a page reading it – or trying to – until about two a.m. Idiotic, because, despite the passing minutes, none of it sank in, and it is a great book! If you don't work efficiently late at night, go to bed and get up early. If it takes you forever to switch on in the morning, don't expect to study well before school. Being well prepared is crucial, but so is being well rested. Give yourself study breaks, and change subjects if you're getting drowsy. It may help to hit the books for an hour, take a fifteen-minute walk or phone break, then study for another limited amount of time. Or it may help to devise a study routine and stick to it.

You can even do some extra studying and revising at the bus stop or in free periods or whenever you get to class before the teacher. I sometimes used to study in the library for the first ten minutes of lunch period – all I missed were long queues in the canteen.

8 **Don't procrastinate.** To tell you the truth, I was going to write this section last night. But I went to a film. And d'you know what? I didn't totally enjoy the film, because I knew I should have been working.

Since you've got to do your homework anyway, you might as well get it over with. Work out your priorities, and don't wait for enough free time to complete everything in one sitting. Instead, break your work into manageable pieces, get motivated, and crank it out bit by bit. You could even set the cooker timer in your kitchen for thirty minutes and make a deal with yourself that you won't get up from your desk until the timer rings. Once you get started, it isn't so bad. I promise. The way to get into the work mood is to start working. Sometimes getting to your desk is tougher than the homework. Just begin. Often I'll write the lead paragraph before I go out. That way, when I return, my essay is started and is easier to go back to.

Work has a bad name, but hard work usually makes you feel great, especially when it's behind you. Why not reward yourself by planning something fun to do afterwards? For instance, since I know I'm going out to dinner with my friend Rochelle in two hours, I'm finding it easy to work right now.

Do you do your term projects in the last-minute panic? Or stay up working all night? Try to start papers early and do them step by step, before you become overwhelmed. It may help to set yourself a timetable. By week one, you'll have completed the research; by week two, you'll have finished the rough draft; by week three, you'll have the project polished.

Have you ever brought homework along on a holiday? I'll bet you either didn't do it and felt guilty, or did it and felt resentful. Next time try to finish it beforehand.

9 **Get help if you need it**. Most teachers are happy to explain a lesson after school and answer questions during class. You can also get help from your friends, brothers and sisters and parents. Are you way behind in maths? Don't succumb to maths anxiety that could trip you up in years to come. Of course you are *able* to learn maths – you're just not entirely willing, or as quick at it as some people. If you're having real difficulties, speak to your maths teacher. He or she will probably be

pleased and eager to help, and may even be able to arrange extra tuition for you, or recommend books that will assist you. Don't wait until two weeks before your exams – start catching up *now*, before you're in a ditch too deep to climb out of.

10 **Improve your attitude.** Don't believe for a minute that you're a terrible student. Maybe you *were* a terrible student, but as of now, you are a good student. You weren't stupid, you were a professional under-achiever. Expect more from yourself. Remember: book-worms often laugh last.

And don't swallow any lines about girls not being good at maths or about guys preferring dumb blondes. (A few insecure dumb guys may, but you'd rather date secure bright guys, right?) No law says you can't be both clever and popular.

On the other hand, if you're a perfectionist, try to loosen up a little. Your world won't cave in if you get an A− or even a B or C (it might even be good for you!). And if you do nothing but study, you run the risk of wearing yourself out.

Bright students should also be careful not to flaunt their success or wail, 'I failed that exam', when they missed only two questions. And many still need to learn to accept criticism. Most over-achievers have mastered the art of studying, but too many haven't learned the equally important art of relaxation.

Teachers: the Good, the Bad and the Ugly

Teachers, like students, come in various forms. Some are merci-less bores who constantly compare you to your brilliant older sister. Others are fascinating individuals who get so excited they tremble as they explain Newton's laws. Others are good-hearted souls who can help with family troubles and can become friends.

My history teacher belonged to the first group. He'd stare at the wall as he droned on and on. He'd show us a film about the Incas on Monday, then on Friday he'd announce he had a film about the Incas to show us. We'd watch it again. And again. And again. He knew he was absent-minded, but that just made matters worse. 'I didn't give you this test yet, did I?' he'd ask as he passed out papers. 'Yes you did! We took it yesterday!' we'd lie in unison. Most of us depended on his class to get our maths homework done.

Are you having trouble with any of your teachers? Do you have a teacher who calls you names? Ask yourself whether you are being singled out. Maybe the teacher calls everyone names, and does so affectionately. Or maybe he or she is hard on you because you've been noisy or disrespectful in class or because you've been caught cheating or passing notes. Or maybe you're called on often because you can be counted on to know the answer.

If you feel you are being treated unfairly, try to make the best of it or speak to your teacher. If you favour confrontation, do it in private, and try to keep your emotions in check. Don't ask, 'Why do you always pick on me?' Say, for instance, 'I'm trying really hard, but I feel as though you still think of me as the class clown I was last year. I've grown up since then.' If you write a letter, be sure it has no spelling errors, and sign it 'Respectfully yours', not 'Lots of love'.

Most teachers will respect you for approaching them and will make an effort to judge your words or actions in a new light. So speak up if you think you don't deserve to get a low mark or to be yelled at for some little mistake. I've even spilled tears in front of a few teachers and, although it's embarrassing, I survived.

What if your teacher is unreasonable or terrifying? What if Mr Castle insists that you regurgitate his words verbatim in exams and knocks marks off when you defend ideas of your own? Tell yourself his small-mindedness is his problem, not yours. Don't let him undermine your self-confidence. You might also consider discussing the matter with your parents. After all, if you're not learning anything because of one particular teacher's incompetence, you're being cheated.

On the other hand, some students are bothered not because they're being criticized all the time, but because they're teachers' pets. While most teachers try to hide their feelings and treat everybody equally, others are open with favouritism. If a teacher takes to you, why not feel flattered and enjoy that attention? The teacher's supportiveness may motivate you to learn even more and may boost your self-confidence. (But don't let it go to your head or make you feel you have to get an A+ every time.)

The situation can be a problem if the teacher makes such a fuss of you that the other students, feeling left out, tease you or call you a crawler. Look, if you sincerely like Mr Williams because he is sensitive and inspiring, that's wonderful. But if you are apple-polishing because you hope he'll give you a higher mark, or if you're befriending teachers while estranging your friends, who can blame your classmates for resenting you?

I came across this item in one of my old diaries: *'You know who I despise the guts of? Myra! She's pathetic. She's a brain and every teacher's pet, but I don't feel any envy _ just disgust.'* Now I can admit that I must indeed have felt envy, but if Myra had been as friendly to other pupils as she was to teachers, who knows? – she and I might have become friends.

What about crushes? I had crushes on several male teachers from the age of ten onwards, and I looked up to a few female teachers, too. It's healthy to have role models besides your parents, and it's OK to have crushes – so long as you don't make it obvious. A crush on a teacher, like one on a singer or an actor, is a fairly safe way to feel romantic. It can even put some zing into an otherwise dry class period.

When I was fourteen, I had a certified crush on my biology teacher. I could handle it fine – until I confessed to my mother, who, on Parents' Night, asked Mr Patterson if he was married. Can you imagine? When he teased me about it the next day, I nearly died. Fortunately I soon got interested in going out with biology students instead of dreaming about the instructor.

A harmless crush *can* become harmful if a teacher tries to exploit it by becoming sexually involved with a student. Don't confess your crush to your teacher (it puts him in an embarrassing position). Most teachers welcome your admiration and have no intention of letting your friendship get out of hand. But in every truckload of melons, a few turn up rotten. And, although sex with an under-sixteen is against the law, even if you're over sixteen, the teacher could lose his job. If you are ever a victim of sexual harassment – for example if a teacher says he'll give you higher marks or write you a glowing report in exchange for a sexual favour – report the incident to your parents, form teacher, or the head.

A final word about teachers. A boring teacher can take the fun out of a course on pop music. A great teacher can make any subject fascinating. I once took a course on the Spanish Subjunctive at 8:30 a.m., and would you believe Jesús Fernández made it super exciting? (On the other hand, don't start hating computers just because you hate the computer teacher.)

In school, you may not have much chance to pick your teachers, but if you do, grab the opportunity. If your school's French teachers are considered terrible but the German teachers are terrific, and you're up in the air about which to take anyway, opt for German. If you can choose one option and everybody loves Mr Simmonds, take his course – even if you don't know archaeology from a hole in the ground.

Go for the classes taught by the best teachers. You won't be sorry.

Alternatives: What To Do If You Hate School

Restless? Sick of school? Need a change? Some students, like some batteries, have to be recharged once in a while. What can you do to liven up your education?

Plenty. Travel, change schools, plan an out-of-the-ordinary summer, take a holiday or evening course at a local college, shake up your school routine.

Dropping out isn't a great idea, because you're closing yourself off from opportunities. It may seem fabulous if you can get a job waiting tables or packing boxes and earn money at sixteen. But what happens later if you want to try more interesting work, meet new people, face new challenges, or make more money? Since most good jobs require qualifications you could be left in the cold. Plus, not having those exam passes is bad for your ego. You have your whole life to be a wage earner or home maker, but only a short time to devote yourself entirely to improving your mind. There are better ideas for the student who needs a change than dropping out.

If you'd like to travel during the summer, I highly (highly!) recommend you do so. Teenagers can travel more easily than adults because they have more time, can arrange to stay with families, and can make money go further, by eating and sleeping modestly and taking advantage of youth hostels and student fares.

Several different organizations can arrange exchange visits, during which you stay with, say, a French family who have a daughter about your age. You then arrange to have her stay with you. Both of you have fun and improve your knowledge of each other's language and lifestyle. Your language teacher at school, or your local library, may be able to provide useful information. You could also try writing to the Central Bureau for Educational Visits and Exchanges *see page 279* – they have details of working holidays and voluntary work abroad. Or perhaps you have a relative or friend who knows a foreign family.

Vacation Work *see page 281* has information about summer jobs all over the world, and lots of helpful tips about working overseas. You might also consider adventure holidays such as Outward Bound courses, and working for one of the Duke of Edinburgh Award schemes. Ask teachers, and enquire at the library for details. A great way to see Britain is to join the Youth Hostels Association and go hiking or cycling. You could even combine this with another interest, such as writing or photography; try keeping a photographic journal of your travels. Write to the YHA *see page 281* if you'd like to join and use their countrywide hostels.

If your heart is set on foreign travel, go for it! Seeing another country from the inside is a great way to grow. You soak up another culture first-hand. Your history and language studies come alive. Away from family and old friends, you become more independent. And because you're exposed to another nation's values, you rethink and gain a better understanding of your own background.

When I was a student, I spent a summer with a family who lived on a farm near Cahors, France. I survived for one month with no hot water, no indoor toilet and no English. Survived! I loved it! I helped vaccinate sheep, bale hay, feed rabbits, hunt for snails after the rain, cook *coq au vin* . . . and I learned a lot of French!

Now that I'm twenty-seven, married and have professional

commitments, it would be nearly impossible for *me* to manage a summer abroad. But *you* may be able to do it.

What if you can't face another year in the same school but you don't want to do anything as drastic as dropping out or going overseas? Then you might consider changing schools. Speak to your parents about it and talk to the head of the school you want to transfer to. If the head agrees to take you, the local education authority has to be informed. Another thing to consider is the possibility of home tuition, which can be arranged in certain circumstances. It might help you to see an educational welfare officer or an educational psychologist if you are experiencing real problems.

Is it possible that, instead of changing schools, you could improve your situation in the one you're in? Is there a student council? If there is, join it and fight for changes. Ease yourself out of a gang that's grown boring. Sign up for new options, sports and out-of-school activities. (How about singing lessons, folk dancing, Dungeons and Dragons, a photography course, or voluntary work?) Do you want to discuss computers or improve your Spanish? Start a once-a-week science or language table at lunch, and let everybody know where and when it meets.

What if you're about to start working for your A-levels, your parents are moving, and you don't want to start at a new school? See if you can arrange to stay behind with relatives, or your best friend's family.

Thinking about Careers

It's too early to worry about your future career, but it's not too early to think about it. And leaving it till you get to school-leaving-age – sixteen – *is* too late! Not that you don't get a second chance, not that you can't change your mind once you've left school, but it helps if you make the right choice in the first place.

For a start, you will probably be expected to choose what subjects you want to study for GCSE when you're in the third year at secondary school. The choices you make, even at thirteen or fourteen, will influence the career you take up later. Sounds pretty scary, doesn't it? Well, it doesn't have to be – but it does mean you should think carefully, and not just carry on with music and needlework because you like the teacher, or drop chemistry because all your friends are doing so.

What *do* you want to do when you leave school? People have probably been asking you that for years already. Some girls dream of being fashion models, film stars or pop singers . . . good goals but rarely realistic. Others know from age ten that they want to be a vet, an air stewardess or a solicitor, which is fine as long as they don't close their minds to other possibilities. Most girls, though, can't read their crystal balls and may not know about all the careers they have to choose from.

If you live in an unemployment blackspot, you probably feel you'll be lucky to get any job at all.

You owe it to yourself to shop around, careers-wise. The more you know about jobs, college courses and so on, the better your chances of making the right choice. Lots of people can help you. You could start with your parents, your family and friends. What do your mum and dad do? Do they like it? Would they recommend you do the same? Your parents probably didn't have the same opportunities you have, and may be keen for you to get on and do better than they did. Or they may not understand why you even *want* a real career, instead of just a job.

There's no better way to find out about a job than by asking someone who does it. One teenager I know really liked the idea of working as a hospital pharmacist, until a friend's dad, a pharmacist, pointed out that it meant working over Bank Holidays and sometimes Christmas. People don't stop getting ill just because it's a national holiday! Ask people what they like and dislike about their jobs – it's a great way to learn.

Your school should also be able to help you with advice and information about careers. Some schools are better than others in this respect. Some offer special Work Experience classes to fourth and fifth years, so that you can sample working life at first hand. If yours doesn't, you could arrange your own. A polite letter to a local business might bring you an offer of a holiday or Saturday job. Even baby-sitting or gardening can be useful work experience. You'll learn whether you like working with small children, or in the Great Outdoors.

Don't forget the Careers section of your local library, either. This is a great place to browse and learn about jobs you may not even have thought of. Publishers Kogan Page have a series of careers books, and there are lots more. If you need help in finding what you want, ask the librarian.

The address of your nearest Careers Office will be listed in the phone book. You may have talks at school from the specially trained careers advisers, but you can still go and talk to someone yourself if you can't make up your mind.

Don't panic if you can't make a decision at this point. No one really expects you to. If you have to choose your GCSE options, it's best to study as broad a range of subjects as you can, especially if you don't know what you want to do. English and maths are 'musts' for most good jobs; science subjects, and craft, design and technology can take you a long way too.

A career isn't just a matter of getting the right exam passes though. You may spend decades in the job, and the happiest people are those who like their work. They're not just living for the weekend, because they enjoy Monday to Friday as well.

Choosing a career means asking yourself three questions:

1 *What am I good at?*
2 *What am I interested in?*
3 *What do I want out of my job?*

What Are You Good At?

Maybe you feel you're no good at anything. Other people may shine in maths, stand out on the sports field, sing mellifluously in the choir, or do terrific handiwork for the school Craft Fair; but you, you're just Miss Average. Look again. Everybody has hidden talents. Exams count, but there are lots of jobs where the right personality is every bit as important as exam certificates. Many talents aren't revealed during schooldays anyway. Debbie Moore, founder of the Pineapple Dance Centres, doesn't have an exam pass to her name, and she is now a millionaire! So don't feel there's no hope if you're not a Superbrain.

On the other hand, thinking about your favourite school subjects can give you a few clues. If you love writing and English, you could think about journalism, advertising, publishing, or public relations work. Languages could take you into travel, hotel work, translation, diplomacy or international business. A fondness for physics could lead to a career in engineering. If you're a maths whiz, you may become an accountant, air traffic controller, computer scientist, banker, bookkeeper, or – if you have an artistic flair as well – an architect.

What else are you good at? Don't just think about your marks in class, think about your skills as a person. If you are good at persuading people, maybe a sales career is for you. Lots of possibilities there, from estate agency to store demonstrator! Friends are always asking your advice about their clothes? How about a career in fashion, on the design or business side?

If you're the kind of girl everyone tells their troubles to, you might do well in a 'caring' job in the field of medicine, psychology or social work.

What Interests You?

The idea of being paid to do something that fascinates you anyway may seem too good to be true, but it's not impossible! Think about your hobbies and interests. Maybe you can build a career around one of them.

If you're crazy about fashion, pop music, horses, babies, or the latest gadgets, if you love to travel, cook or make things, it could be a starting point. Some jobs in these fields are very competitive, but even if you don't have what it takes to be a star, there are always lots of backroom jobs.

Take fashion, for instance. You may long to be a model or a top designer. And I wish you lots of luck. But for every thousand girls who share your dreams, only a few will make it. If you don't hit the jackpot, however, that doesn't mean you can't work in fashion at all. There are opportunities at all levels, from seamstress to salesgirl in a boutique, to buyer for a big store, to wardrobe consultant for a television company. *Most* fashion designers aren't big names anyway. They are responsible for the everyday clothes most of us buy – and not only dresses and separates, but shoes, bags and jewellery as well. And there are other fashion-related jobs: beauty editor for a magazine; costume designer for films; stylist for commercials. Then there are the 'organizing' jobs behind the scenes. If you don't become a model, you might still enjoy being a photographer, make-up artist or a booker in an agency which arranges models' assignments.

Similarly, you don't have to be a star to work in the pop business. Record companies employ secretaries, press officers (who give information about their stars to newspapers and magazines), Art and Research personnel (who are responsible for signing up new bands), accountants, designers, sound editors, agents to arrange gigs and tours, stylists and hairdressers to groom the stars for TV and video, journalists, photographers, cooks, chauffeurs, personal assistants and still more!

What Do You Want Out Of Your Job?

It helps to think about your priorities. What matters most to you about your job? That it's rewarding? Glamorous? Well paid? Do you want a job that involves you totally *or* that doesn't take up too much of your life? Do you want a job that has set hours and a fixed salary or one that offers more flexibility but less security? Do you want to work with people, animals, machines or all alone? Your answers will provide more clues about the career you'll be happy in.

If you like people, for instance, you may not want to go for the kind of job that leaves you on your own a lot. On the other hand, loners (writers and artists often work in solitude) won't want to work in a busy office or join the Women's Services! There are jobs for those who enjoy a settled routine (banking, business, secretarial, computer programming) and others where no two days are alike (teaching, journalism, social work, medicine, architecture). There are even jobs for those who like being out of doors and don't mind getting wet and dirty (agriculture, gardening, civil engineering, working as a kennelmaid or groom).

Think Big – But Be Realistic!

Some people say that books like this give girls today unrealistic expectations. Unemployment *is* a problem, after all. But that doesn't mean you should just give up trying. It's sadly true that in some parts of Britain, opportunities for school leavers, especially those without qualifications, are very limited. But there are still jobs about in other areas, and times may change. The answer is to make sure *you* end up with skills and qualifications that are in demand.

Aiming high means going for a job or career that interests you and that you'll find fulfilling. Being realistic means taking a long, cool look at yourself first. It's no use hoping to be a brain surgeon if you faint at the sight of blood, an opera singer if you're tone deaf, a top model if you're five-feet-nothing, or a jockey if you're six-foot-one. But remember, that doesn't mean you can't work in the worlds of medicine, music or fashion. A less high-powered job, or a backroom job, may be in store for you.

While nearly *all* worthwhile jobs require some sort of qualifications and/or training, that doesn't mean you have to be brilliantly clever, or go to university. Some practical courses may actually prove more useful in the jobs market than a highly specialized degree. (How many job ads have you seen which say Philosophers Wanted?) None the less, you should think very carefully before you decide that further education – past the age of sixteen – isn't for you. Education can make you a more interesting person as well as a more 'marketable' one.

There are schemes to help young people equip themselves with new and useful skills, like the *Youth Training Scheme*. This offers a combination of training and work experience for school leavers aged sixteen or seventeen. All sixteen- and seventeen-year-old leavers are eligible, and there are special programmes for disabled teenagers. If you leave at sixteen you'll get two years' training, paying you a tax-free allowance of £27.30 a week for the first year and £35 a week for the second. If you're seventeen, you receive a year's training, with an allowance of £27.30 for the first three months and £35 a week for the remaining nine. No, there's no guarantee of a job at the end of a YTS scheme, but you will be a lot better qualified and prepared for life in the working world.

A Word about Equal Opportunities!

You may be a committed feminist, or you may think the whole idea of Women's Liberation is just one big yawn. Either way, the fact remains that equal opportunities are there for *you*. There's no reason why guys should get all the best jobs, but they usually do. Although the Equal Pay Act was passed in 1975, women's full-time earnings are still only about three quarters of men's. Is that fair? No it's not! Part of the reason is that a lot of the bright, talented girls who *have* taken advantage of equal opportunities haven't yet worked their way to the top. Another reason is that some firms are still pretty old-fashioned in their attitudes towards women. But the saddest reason is that too many girls just don't try for really interesting, well-paid jobs. It's a shame that, with good jobs there for the taking, girls don't bother!

Maybe you just don't see yourself as a high-powered career woman. Maybe you look forward to the day when you get married, or have a family – and you want to believe that you'll be taken care of from that day forward. It's a lovely thought, but did you know that only *five per cent* of British families consist of a working father, non-working mum and children. A quarter of mums of under-fives work, and most women plan to go back once the children are at school – for money and to add another dimension to their lives. These days, most women work through most of their marriage and there is no reason to limit yourself to work that's boring and poorly paid when you could have a job you enjoy. Besides, marriage no longer guarantees security for a lifetime. One in three or four marriages ends in divorce. Single parents are among the poorest sections of society, especially single mothers – but single mums with good jobs can support their families as well as men. A wife who works is also better able, if necessary, to free herself from an abusive or unfaithful husband. Even if you have a happy, lasting marriage, your husband might become ill or lose his job. Or you may outlive him. No one wants to be a pessimist, but you'll both feel more secure if you can share the breadwinning, or if you at least know that in a crunch you can earn money.

When you're thinking about careers, don't let anyone tell you there's any such thing as a 'boy's subject' or a 'man's job'. These days many schools make it easy for girls to study science subjects and things like Craft Design and Technology, because the country desperately needs women's skills in these areas. Science and engineering are areas where there are lots of interesting, well-paid jobs with good prospects. Don't leave them to the guys, and if science intrigues you, don't let yourself be persuaded to stick to art or cookery.

Thinking about College

Going on to college can mean committing yourself to a three- or four-year university course, or spending just a year at a local polytechnic. Ask your teachers and careers advisers about which might be best for you and most helpful for the job you want to do.

Qualifications can be important, whether you head for a BSc, a City and Guilds diploma in computer technology, or a shorthand/typing certificate. That piece of paper isn't everything – your personality and attitude count too – but a degree or diploma does give your future employer some idea of what you can do, and it may give you the edge over other applicants.

Do you already feel that you've had enough of school and exams to last you a lifetime? You'll be glad to know that the atmosphere at college is quite different from school. You're treated more like an adult (and expected to behave in a more adult way – studying on your own, for instance) and career plans apart, college is a lot of fun! You'll not only learn from courses and books, but from getting to know young men and women who are interested in the things that interest you – whether that means film, marine biology, psychology, German, medicine or graphic design.

How Can You Find Out About College Courses?

Your teachers at school and the Careers Service should be able to advise you, whether or not you have a particular career in mind. If you're not absolutely certain what you want to do, read as much as you can about university and polytechnic courses first. Remember that you don't automatically have to study the subject

you do best in at GCSE or A level. There are other possibilities –
like English and Drama instead of just English; Business Studies;
Economics combined with a foreign language.

Applications for admission to university in Britain are all
handled by UCCA – the Universities Central Council on Admissions, whose address is on page 281. Each year they publish a
handbook called *How to Apply for Admission to a University*, and
your school should have a copy. Normally, you should apply at
the beginning of your Upper Sixth year. (Special rules apply if
you want to go to Oxford or Cambridge.)

Which university and which course should you choose? You
can write a postcard to the admissions office of the universities
you are interested in and ask for prospectuses, though your
school library may already have these. When you fill in your
UCCA form you are allowed five choices. Your subject teacher
will be able to advise you on the best universities for your
particular course. Read the prospectus and also consider
whether you want to be in a city or in the country, or part of a
large or smaller group of students. Find out about student ac-
commodation too, as it's sometimes a problem in cities. You may
be happier if you're able to live on campus or in special student
dormitories or hostels rather than in digs.

University isn't the only possibility, of course. It might be that
the career you're aiming for requires a different kind of training,
or a qualification from BTEC (the Business and Technician Education Council) or the City and Guilds of London Institute. City
and Guilds foundation courses are available during your fourth
and fifth year at school. Your teachers and the careers office can
provide more detailed information.

One particularly useful certificate is the CPVE (Certificate of
Pre-Vocational Education) which is for sixteen-year-olds with or
without exam passes. The course is a combination of study and
work experience, and covers areas like business administration,
technical services, production, distribution and services to
people. For more information, write to the Joint Board for Pre-
Vocational Education *see page 280*.

City and Guilds run courses in about 300 different subjects in
2,000 centres – ranging from agriculture to community care to
travel and tourism. Teachers, careers officers and local colleges
will let you know what's available, or you can obtain the City and
Guilds Handbook from the address on page 280.

The Business and Technician Education Council (BTEC) runs courses which are very much job-related. You can start a National Certificate and Diploma course at sixteen, and a Higher National Certificate and Diploma course at eighteen. Subjects include Business Studies, Computing, Engineering, Catering, Design, Agriculture and the service industries. Courses are run in colleges and at polytechnics, and may be full-time, part-time, day-release, or so-called 'sandwich' courses which involve a period of study and then a period in work. Ask for information at your local careers office or technical college, or write to BTEC (*see page 279*).

Phew! If you're beginning to get a funny feeling in the pit of your stomach and are thinking: 'But I'm still a kid. Do I really have to know all this now?' – then relax. You've got time – and this is a book for dipping into, remember? I'm trying to point you in the right direction for your future career. If you read, ask questions, analyse your own tastes and strengths and find out about careers that sound interesting, then when you *do* have to make your mind up, chances are you'll make a good choice. Your first career choice doesn't have to be your last, anyway!

For the moment, enough about your promising future. Ready to think about cash instead of careers? Let's talk about how you can have more pounds in your pocket now.

Be a Better (and Better-paid) Baby-sitter

Baby-sitting is one of the easiest and most obvious ways to make money while you're still studying, but it's not without its responsibilities. I baby-sat around the clock. I baby-sat for one family in the afternoon and another in the evening. I made enough money babysitting to go to Europe, and in Madrid, I worked as a mother's help. I baby-sat until I got baby-sitter burn-out.

During my prime baby-sitting years, age twelve to sixteen, I usually loved it. It was fun trying to answer children's questions. Four-year-old Adam, the first boy ever to take any interest in my flat figure, asked, 'Do you have big boobies?' And John said, 'We learned there is water in the air. Why isn't everything wet?' I liked letting Gary finish the sentences when I read his favourite story. I even got a kick out of the Ice-cream Crisis. Leah wanted a taste of her cousin Tim's cone. 'Give her a bite,' said I. He did – he bit her arm.

Do you like children? Are you patient? Responsible? Honest? Tireless? Diplomatic? Baby-sitting may be for you. Of course, baby-sitting is a misnomer. It's really baby-watching, baby-chasing, baby-feeding, baby-bathing, baby-changing, baby-reading, baby-bedding. Here are more pointers:

- When you say yes to a job, make sure that the parent knows how late you can stay and how much you charge. Write down the time and date of the job, the parents' name, address and phone number, and whether they'll drive you home. (If you don't know them or know of them, be cautious. Ask your parents for advice.)
- Don't ever cancel at the last minute. In a pinch, call the parent as soon as possible and offer to find a substitute – your best friend or one of the parents' regulars.
- Before you leave, let your parents know where you'll be and when you think you'll be back.
- Before the children's parents leave, get the number where they'll be as well as numbers of the police, doctor, neighbours. Ask for any special instructions about bedtime rules, pets, phone messages, what to do if the doorbell rings.
- Don't have friends over unless the parents said you could.
- Lock all doors.
- To prevent mishaps, be sensible. Pick up toys on the stairs. Don't answer the phone while you bathe the children. Don't give medicine to a sick child without permission.
- Play with the children, but be firm, too. If bedtime is at 9:00, don't let them have pillow fights and let's-pretend-the-bed-is-a-trampoline parties until all hours. Say: 'This is the last story' or 'Be quiet' in a tone that shows you mean it. Even ignoring a brief tantrum may be more

effective than screaming 'GO TO SLEEP' at the top of
your lungs. (The little darlings may be testing you to find
your breaking point, so don't be a 'sitting duck'.)
- Don't snoop or abuse phone or fridge privileges. (I especially wouldn't recommend sipping straight from the
orange-juice carton when wearing lipstick.)
- In case of emergency, dial 999 and call the police or
ambulance. In case of fire, grab the kids and run, then
dial 999 for the fire brigade and ring the children's
parents from a neighbour's house.
- Try to stay awake until the parents return. A quiet house
can be your opportunity to make money while doing
homework.

Want more jobs? Spread the word. Tell your parents, friends and
the families you sit for. Post a notice on the board at your
supermarket, library or newsagents. Or place an ad in your local
paper.

Are you being paid fairly? Find out the going rate from your
friends. When you take care of three rowdy children, you
deserve more than when you stay with a sleeping toddler. Let the
parents know ahead whether you charge extra for cooking,
washing up, additional children, or staying after midnight. Most
parents will ask you back if their kids like you and you have
common sense – even if you do charge an extra fifty pence an
hour.

Don't get cheated! I once helped out at a five-year-old's birthday party. I brought Scott a small gift and did my best to entertain his twelve wild cronies. Afterwards, the mother wrote me a
cheque (I hated cheques) for the exact amount of time at my
minimum hourly rate – no tip! I barely broke even, and boy, was
I cheesed off. I should have asked beforehand if she'd pay me
more than usual. Or I should have expressed my disappointment
then and there. Instead, here I am, over a dozen years later, still
peeved.

I know some girls who now run and advertise a baby-sitting
network. Parents call to find an available sitter. Naomi keeps
track of the schedules of ten or so girls and lines up jobs for them

constantly. Her reward? She gets a small fee for every job she places.

You may also arrange for mothers to bring their children to your home after school or on Saturday mornings while they shop. That way you and perhaps a friend can take care of a group of children together for a short time.

If you *don't* want to sit on a particular night, don't. Say, 'Thanks, Mrs Brennan, but I have something arranged. I'd love to another time.' And if *you* have baby-sitter blues, say, 'Sorry, I'm not sitting any more, but thanks for calling.' Me, I used to say, 'Aahhm, I'm not sure,' then bellow, 'Mum, can I baby-sit tonight?' while violently shaking my head and waiting for her to get me off the hook. What a wimp! You can do better.

Beyond Baby-sitting
(But Before the Big Time)

It's hard for adults to find work; it's even harder to land a job if you're not yet sixteen. Working under the age of thirteen is illegal, unless it is something special like acting or modelling (even so, the hours you work are strictly controlled and your schooling must continue while you are working). Once you're over thirteen, your position varies with local by-laws. In most cases, you can't work more than a certain number of hours at evenings and weekends. You certainly aren't allowed to work during school time. And there are some jobs you wouldn't be allowed to do because they're too dangerous (do you *really* want to drive a combine harvester?).

The kind of jobs under-sixteens are allowed to do include shelf-filling at the supermarket, being a Saturday girl in a shop or hairdresser's, delivering newspapers, clearing tables in a café, helping in a nursing home, picking fruit or vegetables, cleaning, helping in a stable. . .the list goes on. Listen for leads and keep your eyes open for 'help wanted' notices in stores and news-papers. You could even try making money by doing odd jobs for neighbours.

Are you good in the garden? A whiz at baking? Can you make dirty dishes disappear? Are you fast with a rake? Handy with repairs? A marvel at polishing silver? A pro with paint? How do you fare at washing cars? Washing dogs? Walking dogs? Running errands? Speed typing? Hemming and sewing? Dyeing Easter eggs or wrapping holiday gifts? Can you give guitar lessons? Tutor younger children in English or maths? Would your penmanship look pretty on invitations? Can you take care of a neighbour's house while the owners are on holiday – feed the cat, water plants, bring in mail, turn lights on and off – without getting scared? Are you a snappy photographer?

Yes? Then if you want work, don't just stand there. Hustle your bustle and get your rear in gear! Let your neighbours know how lucky they are. On a piece of paper, write your name, address, phone number, and special talents. Make photocopies and pop them through neighbours' letterboxes. Better still, dress neatly, knock, hand out your leaflet and explain that for a fee, you're a Jill-of-all-trades.

A 'try me' attitude is helpful, but don't insist and don't wander into houses where you don't know anybody who knows the residents.

Every week last winter, a boy rang my doorbell and asked if he could clear our icy path for a pound. Partly to encourage him and partly to have an unslippery path, I always said, 'you're on'. If he hadn't turned up, shovel in hand, I wouldn't have advertised for a shoveller. But because he takes that initiative, he makes a pound in ten minutes at many houses on our street.

Can you do the same? Or can you show up with needle and thread and promise to repair clothing or linen? How about teaming up with a friend and offering to clean someone's house or car?

Once you've got a job, work hard without constant supervision. Don't be like one of the well-meaning teenage housecleaners my working mother once hired who, every ten minutes, interrupted Mum to ask, 'Now what?' Instead, you and your employer should thoroughly go over the chores (ironing, dusting, cleaning the refrigerator) when you arrive.

It's most ideal if you can land a few regular, once-a-week jobs. It's most fun if you and a friend can work together, even though you'll have to share profits.

When I was fourteen, I told my diary, *'I wish I could get a real job and make lots of money working for a few weeks. That'd be great.'* Finding a 'real job' when you're young is not easy. But if you narrow down what you'd like to do and go after it with gusto, you *can* make 'lots of money'.

All in the Family

Families differ and pocket money differs. Many parents give their kids a certain amount each week and expect them to do a few chores each week. You may be able to make a little extra if you do a little extra.

If your parents work, and you're a good cook, maybe you can have dinner ready on certain days. If they give a party, maybe you can clean up. If the garden's looking a mess, offer to tidy it up. Would they consider paying you to baby-sit younger family members? To refresh dingy paintwork? To do the family laundry? Would they let you arrange a car-boot sale? You do most of the work and get most of the profit.

If you think you're not getting enough pocket money, you can ask for more. (Satisfaction not guaranteed.) Keep a list of where your money goes, and be reasonable and willing to compromise. Your family probably isn't charging you for room and board, so it's not fair to expect megabucks every time you're helpful. Plus, their spending money may not be astronomical. After all, they may be trying to put some aside for your future.

Many teenagers work for their parents outside the home. If your mother has a catering business, does she need a hand at weekends? Offer both of yours. If your father's a fishmonger, there may be a place (plaice?) for you behind the counter.

Working for your parents has its pay offs. You don't have to go through the job hunt runaround. You may be able to call in sick once in a while to study for an exam or go on an important date. The transport problem to and from work is simplified. You may find you have more work responsibility than a stranger would trust you with. And understanding what your mother or father does all day may bring you closer.

Drawbacks? Plenty. Parent-daughter scolding often hurts more than employer-employee criticism. And other employees might resent you or suck up to you rather than simply accepting you. My friend Laura said she felt caught in the middle when she worked for her father. 'The people I worked with felt comfortable with me and sometimes they'd slag off the boss – but the boss was my dad!'

Many disillusioned adult sons and daughters complain that, because their parents needed them, they got stuck in the family business and never developed their own skills or tested their own dreams. If you work for your parents, let them know when you feel put-upon. But also let them know if you're happy and grateful for the job.

The Great Job Hunt

Whether you are a school or college student looking for a summer job, or a school-leaver trying to find permanent work, job-hunting is a serious business – it's a job in itself. What you're doing, basically, is selling yourself and your skills to an employer. To do that, you have to convince him or her you have more to offer than the ten or twenty or a hundred other kids who have gone after that same job.

How to do that? First, find your job! And that's not always as simple as it sounds, is it? Visit your local Job Centre as often as you can. Talk to the staff there about the kind of work you'd like to do. You'll convince them you are keen to work, and when a junior vacancy does come up, they should remember you before the lazier types who drift in once a month.

Ask, ask and ask again. Ask your parents, your parents' friends, your friends' parents if they know of any jobs going. Check out the ads in the local Press – you can find them in the library and most areas now have free newspapers filled with job ads popped through the door. Look in newsagents' windows where junior and part-time vacancies may be advertised. Use your initiative, too. Write to local companies – address your letter to the Personnel Officer (telephone first to discover her or his name) and ask about vacancies. If you live in a high un-employment area, consider a move. Could you live with your gran/aunt/older sister, somewhere where job prospects are better, or maybe get a live-in job as a mother's helper? Or you could try an employment agency, especially if you can type or know shorthand. They charge the employer for their services, not you.

For summer jobs there are a couple of publications worth checking out. 'Working Holidays' is published by the Central Bureau for Educational Visits and Exchanges *see page 279* – drop them a line for details of the current price. Vacation Work International *see page 281* also publishes several directories of summer jobs in this country and abroad. If you can't get – or don't want – permanent work at the moment, a summer job earns you money and gives you work experience.

When you see a job advertisement that looks intriguing, don't delay! Read the advertisement carefully first, and follow any instructions about applying. If they say 'write with a c.v.' then do that, don't phone. How to write a letter of application and a c.v.? Read on!

Writing a C.V.

'He or she who gets hired is not necessarily the one who can do that job best, but the one who knows the most about how to get hired.' Richard Bolles wrote that in a book called *What Colour is Your Parachute?*

If you want a job, you've got to market your skills. That means you have to let the bosses out there know why they'd be lucky to have you. And that means you may have to write a curriculum vitae (c.v.).

A c.v. is a single, organized, typed page which includes your experience, education, strengths and any relevant special courses you've taken (like bookkeeping, shorthand, computer programming). From your c.v., an employer should be able at a glance to get an idea about who you are and what you've done.

When you write your c.v., sell yourself. If your marks are lousy, don't mention them. If you're a gymnastics star, say so. If you speak Japanese because your father is from Tokyo, write that down. You may have skills that you take for granted but that could knock an employer's socks off. Remember: everybody started with no experience.

Your c.v. should be neat, concise and positive. Update your

c.v. often to include any new activities, jobs or awards.

You may want to come up with more than one c.v. if you are applying for different kinds of jobs. For instance, if you want to work in the theatre, you should make a big deal of your singing and dancing parts in school plays, your two years of singing lessons, and your ushering at a local theatre. If you're simultaneously applying for a clerical position in an office and a job as a vet's assistant, highlight other skills and interests.

Maybe you think all you've done in the last few years is pass your courses and pig out on Mars bars. Think harder. There's bound to be something you can include in a c.v. No? You're sure? Then do yourself the favour of signing up for some courses, or doing some voluntary work. Not just to add zest to your c.v., but to add zest to your life!

Have a parent, teacher or professional friend of the family check your c.v., because it should be perfect before you make copies.

Send it with a neatly typed covering letter to relevant individuals. Then cross your fingers and hope the employer invites you in for an interview. If weeks pass and you don't hear from your prospective employer, you should phone him or her.

Here is a sample cover letter and c.v. that a girl seeking a position as an office junior might write.

10 Maple Way,
Notton,
Middlesex,
MY1 7DT.

July 10th, 1987

Mrs. Mary Pike,
Personnel Officer,
Zero & Co.,
31-37 Acme Avenue,
London, SW23 9FX.

Dear Mrs. Pike,

I am writing in response to your advertisement for an office junior.

This summer I left school with five GCSE passes, the details of which you will find on my enclosed c.v. I am now attending classes in shorthand and typing and hope to have a qualification shortly.

I am keen to learn all aspects of office procedure and I look forward to hearing from you soon.

Yours sincerely,

Sue Denim

Curriculum Vitae

Sue Denim
10 Maple Way,
Notton,
Middlesex,
MY1 7DT.

Birthdate: 28 June, 1971
Birthplace: London

Education
Notton Gardens Primary School
Gladstone Comprehensive

Qualifications
5 GCSE passes: English Language (B), Maths (C), Art (C),
Biology (C), French (B)

Skills
Shorthand and typing diploma course.
St John's Ambulance First Aid certificate.

Work experience
Saturday job for six months at Tesco, Notton High Street,
including helping with stock-taking. Baby-sitting.

Hobbies and interests
Walking (member of YHA), swimming, first aid, reading, drawing,
aerobics, travelling.

(P.S. Are you getting that same funny feeling in the pit of your stomach and thinking, 'But I don't need to know all this yet.' Don't worry, this book is your personal encyclopedia. It's so you know where to find out about c.v. writing – or break-ups, or sex, or college applications, or alcohol – when you *do* want to know.)

Shining In The Interview

Whether you are having a job or college interview, you want to come over as mature, intelligent, enthusiastic, polite and hard-working. Here are some tips:

- Read up on the company and prepare questions.
- Anticipate the interviewer's questions and prepare answers.
- Dress neatly and suitably. Leave your punk gear at home.
- Plan to arrive alone and early – count on a traffic jam or a railway signal failure en route.
- Introduce yourself and shake hands firmly; maintain eye contact; smile; sit up straight; use complete sentences.
- Don't gesticulate wildly, scratch, chew gum, smoke, ramble on and on, or talk about what an ogre your last boss was.
- As succinctly and positively as possible, state what you hope to offer the company, not what you hope to learn or gain from it.
- Don't be bashful about discussing hours, holidays and wages, but don't make the interviewer feel that the money is all you're interested in.
- Shake hands again and thank the interviewer for seeing you.
- Follow up with a written thank-you note.

Last week a friend had an interview at a bank. Together we staged a practice interview. She had terrific answers for, 'Why should I hire you?' 'What do you expect to be doing in ten years?' and 'Tell me about yourself.' But when I asked, 'What are your weaknesses?' she blew it. She said, 'I'm not good with numbers.' A bank doesn't want to hear that! (Later she realized she shouldn't have been applying for a bank job anyway. That was her *father's* ambition, not hers.) If an interviewer asks about *your* weaknesses, don't volunteer that you're lazy, can't get up in the mornings, or are hopelessly disorganized. A better answer would be 'I'm a perfectionist', or 'Sometimes I get so involved with a project I don't know when to quit.' Don't lie, but put your best foot forward. Talk your way into the job!

Lastly, how about sending a thank-you note, especially if the interview has gone well? The note can also be your chance to say anything important that you forgot to mention in person.

Hey, and don't be discouraged if you don't get the first, second, or even tenth job you applied for. Your interviewer skills improve with practice. And you need only one boss to say 'You're hired?'

Connections Is Not a Dirty Word

Connections can help you get a foot in the door; you still have to squeeze the rest of your body in by yourself.

Are they worth making? Absolutely. Weaving and pulling strings isn't cheating; it's a skill; it's being professional.

It won't kill you to be nice to the important businessman your parents know (who could some day offer you a job), just as you should be nice to all your parents' friends. If you don't have any family connections, make your own. Meet people who know people. Work hard and develop confidence in your abilities. Find someone you admire and let him or her know it. Get over the idea that biggies are unapproachable.

It pays to have gumption. I had never interviewed anybody, and then I interviewed the actress Joanne Woodward. She was performing at the nearby Kenyon Festival Theater in Ohio, and I told myself, 'You have nothing to lose, you have nothing to lose. . . .' as I circled my phone like a pilot above an airport. Finally I dialled and, after preliminaries, asked, 'May I interview you?' 'Yes,' she said. Just like that.

My husband Rob got a job with Broadway director Hal Prince when he was fresh out of drama school. How? On day one, Rob saw and loved Prince's *Madame Butterfly* in Chicago. On day two, he spotted Prince at Northwestern University and congratulated him. On day three, Rob sent Prince a letter and c.v. Upshot: even Big Time Successes respond to genuine admiration and may remember that sometime someone somewhere gave them a break. During the New York interview that followed, when Prince asked, 'What can I do for you?' Rob answered, 'Hire me.' Prince did. Just like that.

If the stars of your chosen profession are not on the horizon, contacts can be made from afar. And small connections can lead to bigger ones. Teachers may become heads, assistant editors may become editors-in-chief; actors may become directors; junior solicitors may become law partners; and so on.

There is such a thing as the Old Boy and Old Girl Network, and you can use it if you want to. Everyone knows somebody who knows somebody who can be of help.

It doesn't hurt to be friendly, not too modest, and willing to boost someone else's ego with a sincere compliment. I consider it cordial, not calculated, to acknowledge a favour with a thank-you note. (I thank people who can help me and people who can't.) I wish the girl I helped last week had felt the same. She wants to be a writer, so she came over and I spent two hours talking with her. Fine. But she should have followed up with a simple thank-you. It's not that I stand on ceremony. It's that if she had seemed more appreciative, she would have made a better impression, and I might have been more eager to pass her name on to editors. (When you're looking for work, your personality counts, too, not just your talent.)

In the future, you won't be the kind who forgets initial votes of confidence, will you? Stay in touch with people who've helped you. And be sure you lend a hand to people who need your help.

For now, if you want a job, don't sit back and wait to be discovered. Write a letter to someone you admire. Let your parents' friends and your friends' parents know you'd like to meet someone in certain career fields. Don't give up your dreams before giving yourself a chance. As the poet Emily Dickinson put it, 'Luck is not chance/It's toil—/Fortune's expensive smile/Is earned.'

Success with no strings attached is great. But it's OK to cultivate connections and tug strings without guilt or apology. It beats feeling beaten.

Once You're Hired, Don't Get Fired – Or Should You Quit?

No-one expects you to stay in your first job for ever and ever and (dare I say it?) you might find that being a very junior junior, in a job that doesn't seem to offer much prospect of getting on, isn't the big deal you thought it was. OK, you get a pay packet, which you didn't at school, but is it worth being bored out of your brain all day?

Ask yourself why you're bored, and be fair. There are routine moments in every job, even the most exciting. You have to start somewhere, and in nine jobs out of ten, that's at the bottom. If months have gone by and all you ever do is make tea, run up to the post office for stamps, and type the most routine correspondence, are you making progress? Were you promised a job with prospects? If you were, where are they?

Employers often complain about junior employees not giving it their best shot – don't give your boss the chance to complain about you. However boring the routine, do your job to the best of your ability. If the company is any good, you will be rewarded. If you're not, then you have gained experience to take to your next job. Be bright, willing and friendly. Ask how the photo-copying machine, the word processor, the telex works. Chances are someone will take time out to show you, you'll learn one more skill, and, most important, your keenness will be noticed.

Don't look bored, paint your nails, yawn, sigh and raise your eyes to heaven when you're asked to do something. Whether your ultimate ambition is to be a lawyer, a businesswoman, or a top secretary, this very junior position is the first step on the ladder. How fast and how far you climb is up to you! So don't stay in a dead-end job forever, but don't quit right before you would have got your lucky break.

When to Be Cheap,
When Not To

Many moons ago, my grandfather bounced me up and down on his knee and said, 'Always save your money and be cunning as a fox, and you'll always have some money in the old tobacco box.'

Money is for spending and enjoying, so you shouldn't save it all. And instead of a tobacco box, you should probably save yours in an interest-earning savings account. But Grandad's message is a good one: it pays to be thrifty. For instance:

- If every penny counts and you're going to want a box of peppermint creams at the pictures, buy it at a shop, not at the cinema where it'll be more expensive.
- Buy woolly socks and winter boots in the spring sales. In general, compare prices, look for sales, and buy items out of season. They'll always be cheaper.
- Try not to live by the adage, When the going gets tough, the tough go shopping! Don't waste money just to cheer yourself up.
- Look for interesting and affordable clothes and sundries in charity shops, Oxfam and jumble sales.
- Read magazines and borrow books from the library. (Except, of course, this book, a copy of which belongs in your permanent collection. Only kidding.)
- Swap clothes, magazines, records, and accessories with your friends and out-of-town cousins.
- Send non-urgent letters by second class post.
- Make or bake presents instead of buying them.
- When pennies count, order water in restaurants, not Coke. Don't order more than you can eat.
- Don't buy a trendy dress right after you get paid. Ask if they'll take a deposit, then go home and see if your wardrobe runneth over. If you still want the dress, then buy it. (It's a dry clean only? Add those costs into your budget.)

- Check boys' departments for bargains in T-shirts and other unisex clothes.
- Don't always go for brand names.
- When you go shopping, take a short list and a restrained friend, and leave your chequebook (if you have one) at home.
- No matter how sweet, patient, or insistent the salesperson is, never buy too-tight shoes or anything else you don't want.
- Remember that the same restaurant is usually cheaper at lunchtime than at dinner, and cinemas often have a cheap night (usually Monday).
- Don't spend lots of money on your boyfriend. Spend lots of time with him.

The other side of the coin is that you don't want to be a pennypincher. Money is the ticket to fun and freedom, but 'love of money is the root of all evil,' so

- If you and two friends go out for dinner and their meals are a little more expensive than yours, split the bill in three anyway. It can be nit-picking and mood dampening to whip out your calculator after a fun evening. If your meal cost a lot more than theirs, put that extra amount in the pot.
- Never try to travel on public transport without paying.
- If you're sending photos or a fat letter, stick on enough postage, even if it means getting the letter weighed. It's worth another stamp for the letter to get there without delay.
- Look after your clothes and shoes and keep them in good condition. You'll save in the long run. Follow washing instructions carefully and never put your red T-shirt in with your white jeans.
- If you're making a major purchase that should last many years, like a typewriter, computer, stereo, or car, it may

be worth the extra money to get the best product you can afford.

- If you're short of money and the gang is going for burgers, don't sit at home. Go with them and order just a drink or side dish.
- Tip. As a teenage girl, you can probably get away with not tipping, and, yes, you could even leave a lonely 5p under the plate, but it's decidedly not nice. And if you ever work as a waitress, you'll know that no tips is no fun. (Waitresses are underpaid because bosses expect them to make up the difference in tips.) Tip your hairdresser, too.

Don't be a tightwad or a spendthrift. Money isn't fun if it's all stashed away. But if you binge-spend or never check prices, you may have to put yourself on a budget. . .which is what comes next!

Managing Your Money

Learning to budget effectively is a skill that will stand you in good stead all your life. It needn't be boring – some people (honestly) get a buzz out of all those neat little notebooks they keep with details of just where every penny goes! You don't have to go that far. But you should be able to handle your cash – whether it comes in the form of pocket money, a student grant, Social Security or a pay cheque. If you're an older teenager living at home, don't grumble if you have to pay Mum for your keep. If you don't – if she lets you spend all your money on clothes, records and having a good time – you may be in for a rude awakening. Eventually you'll leave home, either to get married or live in a flat. So you're ahead of the game if you already know what an electricity bill looks like, or how much a giant pack of washing powder costs.

How much to give your parents? Maybe nothing. Maybe just your share of the phone bill. It depends on how much you earn, how well-off they are, how you all feel about money. Most parents don't want to make money out of their kids. On the other hand, they might not be able to afford to subsidize you. If you're an older teenager and you're adult enough to work, you're adult enough to pay your way. Consider sitting down one evening and working out how much it costs to keep you. You could get a shock! It's not just food, it's heat and light and phone bills, too. Your parents have to pay rates, repair bills on the house, fork out for petrol if you get driven around a lot. Your folks probably won't expect you to pay the full cost, especially if you're a student, or trainee, or don't have a job at all. But you should at least know what it costs to keep you – it will really make you appreciate your parents and your home.

If your money doesn't seem to go far enough, consider an evening or Saturday job – but don't turn into a workaholic. Money isn't everything and you need relaxation time, too. That's more important than being able to buy clothes in the best stores in town.

If you're a student, or unemployed, are you sure you are claiming all the grants and benefits you're entitled to? Your Local Education Authority should have a leaflet about grants, which are available for most university and college courses, but check with them. Ask at the local DHSS office for information about Social Security benefits, both for you and your family. You are entitled to these, so make sure you don't miss out.

So much for where the money comes from. Where it goes – well, have you any idea? Do you just fritter it away on nothing, and have to ask Mum or Dad for a loan before next payday? That's bad management. Work out what you need for essentials, (your keep, lunches, fares and so on), and try to divide the rest into spending-money and savings. When you're on a tight budget, don't impulse-buy – whether it's a Mars bar at lunchtime or a dress you don't really need. If you'll be tempted to spend what's in your purse leave it at home and just take what you need for the day.

Work out what you can afford, and stick to it. Sure, you are entitled to a treat now and then, like when there's a blouse in the sales that's just what you've been looking for and just your size. But that could mean you don't buy the Madonna album till next month. Learn to handle your money wisely now, when you don't have much, so that as your earnings creep up you'll find budgeting comes naturally. It's mainly a matter of common sense. If you don't spend what you haven't got, you'll be doing better than a lot of adults!

It's worthwhile thinking about savings schemes, too, even though you may not have much to save. Banks, building societies and the Post Office are all keen to attract teenage customers. They reckon that, if you open an account with them now, you'll stick with them later when you're a millionaire business-woman Most savings accounts pay interest on your money – that just means the bank pays *you* for the privilege of looking after your money. There are also all sorts of clubs for young savers, offering free gifts, magazines, sometimes discounts on records and hi-fi equipment, competitions and special offers. Sounds good? It can be, but shop around. Pick up leaflets from all the High Street banks and building societies, and see which scheme seems to offer you the most. Saving regularly is a good habit to get into, and you can start an account with as little as £1.

A Word About Unemployment. . . .

It's a drag. There's no other way to describe the hopeless, help-less feeling that you're trapped in a miserable, vicious circle of poverty because, though you've looked and looked, you can't get a job. It hardly seems worth getting up in the morning, does it? And you can't help asking yourself if it will always be like this. . . Tell yourself two things. One, *it is not your fault*. You've tried hard to find work, and so far there just isn't any. Two, *it doesn't make you a less worthwhile person*.

So keep trying. Follow up every lead, every job ad, every time someone tells you there's work going. Don't be despondent if you write fifty letters of application and none of them gets a response – it could be fifty-first time lucky!

Find out if there are special schemes for the young un-employed in your area – the Job Centre should know this. Don't forget voluntary work. Visiting an old lady or cleaning-up a local eyesore may not be what you want to do for the rest of your life, but it's all experience, and looks better on your c.v. than a great big blank.

Consider going back to school or college. Don't forget, there *are* jobs for trained, skilled people in many parts of the country. By the time you have completed a two- or three-year course, you'll be old enough to leave home, and well-qualified enough to find some sort of work so you can pay the rent on a flat of your own.

Think about starting your own business. It could be dressmaking, window-cleaning, dog-walking, dressing as a clown and entertaining at children's parties. Who knows? You may discover that you prefer being your own boss to waiting for someone else to employ you.

Money Miscellany

- Since the Equal Pay Act of 1975, it has been illegal to pay men and women differently for doing the same job. New regulations in 1984 mean that women can compare their earnings with men's in different but equally valuable jobs – which could mean pay rises for many women. It's up to us to aim for the skilled, in-demand jobs that will bring us true equality in pay and status. At present, though, the majority of women work in just three areas – education, clerical and welfare – which are generally poorly paid.
- Check out classified ads. They show what jobs are available and at what salaries.
- Every contest has a winner. But your essay or photograph won't win the prize if you don't enter.
- The T-shirt that reads 'Anyone who says "Money can't buy happiness" doesn't know where to shop' is funny, but wrong.
- The song that goes, 'All I need is the air that I breathe and to love you' is romantic, but wrong.

- If you have a rich boyfriend, examine your motives. Be sure you'd love him if he sold his sports car. (I went out briefly with a guy who always treated me to lobster – lobster! – sandwiches. I thought, 'Boy, if we got married, I could travel to Rio, Peking, Cairo, Fiji.' Then I thought,' 'I'd have to go there with him.' We broke up.)

- If you have rich parents, try not to become spoiled, feel guilty, or take material comforts for granted. Treat your friends once in a while, but don't try to buy friends. Do voluntary work. And hope that some day you can be as generous with your children.

- If your parents don't have cash to spare, try not to resent friends who are handed money when you have to work for it. You're learning the value of a pound and how to make a living. That gives you an edge. And since you know how much life costs, you're not in for such a shock in the Real World.

- Stop comparing. There will always be people better off and worse off than you.

- When you first live on your own, half your salary may go towards rent and food. (Unless you live in London, in which case half may cover just rent.)

- Don't ever be tempted to make money out of selling drugs, or any other illegal activity. You could end up in jail – or dead.

- Don't get robbed. Your bag should not be grabbable in a restaurant, disco, or public loo. Don't carry more money than you need. On trips abroad, take traveller's cheques.

- Theft is common; try not to get too attached to material objects. Remember the heirloom diamond engagement ring I told you I stopped biting my nails for? Well, I recently took it to a posh jeweller's for a slight repair. When I went to pick it up, I was told it had been a small part of a huge jewellery robbery! Yes, I was distraught. But the ring was insured, and at least I still have my nails – and my husband!

- Don't stuff loose money into your pocket; put it in your purse. If you do lose a five-pound note, think how happy the person who finds it will be. Then be more careful.

- From my teenage diary: *'I wrote down "Dad owes me £10", but I can't remember why, so he won't give it to me.'* Keep your IOUs and UOMes straight and complete with explanations.

- If you save 50p a day, you'll have £182.50 at the end of the year.

- There's usually just enough money. There's rarely more than enough.

- 'What is a cynic? A man who knows the price of everything and the value of nothing.' So wrote Oscar Wilde.

- What is success? Not a mountain of money. According to Ralph Waldo Emerson, 'To laugh often and much; to win the respect of intelligent people and the affection of children; to earn the appreciation of honest critics and endure the betrayal of false friends; to appreciate beauty; to find the best in others; to leave the world a bit better whether by a healthy child, a garden patch, or a redeemed social condition; to know even one life has breathed easier because you have lived. This is to have succeeded.'

7. Drinks, Drugs, Etc.

And I Promise Not To Lecture

Did you know that girls who smoke and are on the Pill are running a serious health risk? That if you mix barbiturates and alcohol you could die?

This chapter is about cigarettes, dope, harder drugs, alcohol and drunk driving.

You may already know a lot about this stuff. You may think you've heard it all. But I, too, knew a lot in school, and I learned tons more researching this chapter. I hadn't realized, for instance, that booze and cigarettes cause many more deaths than heroin. I hadn't even realized that a cocktail has as many calories as a bowl of ice-cream.

This chapter on the use and abuse of drugs (legal and illegal) is not alarmist propaganda, although it does contain some alarming facts. And I admit: I'm hoping you don't smoke and drink and take drugs. At least not regularly. Many of the patterns you set now will be yours for keeps. You owe it to yourself to find out what you are getting into.

Tobacco: When It's Good to Be a Quitter

Test your smoking savvy.

1 How much money does a twenty-a-day smoker spend on cigarettes each year?
   a About £50
   b About £100
   c Over £300

2 How much tar does a twenty-a-day smoker inhale each year?
   a A negligible amount.
   b About two tablespoons.
   c A full cup.

3 How long does it take for cigarettes to do a smoker any harm?
   a About three seconds.
   b About three weeks.
   c About three months.

4 How many adult smokers would like to kick the habit?
   a About 25 per cent.
   b About 50 per cent.
   c About 70 per cent.

5 How much does the average smoker smoke per day?
   a Less than ten cigarettes.
   b Ten to twenty cigarettes.
   c Over twenty cigarettes.

6 How many lung cancer victims die within five years of diagnosis?
   a About 30 per cent.
   b About 60 per cent.
   c About 90 per cent.

7 *True or False:* Smoking affects the smoker's sense of taste or smell.

8 *True or False:* If a pregnant woman smokes, her baby has an increased chance of being born small, weak or dead.

9 *True or False:* Smokers die younger than non-smokers.

10 *True or False:* If you smoke without inhaling, you don't up your risk of cancer.

11 *True or False:* Most adult smokers started as teenage smokers.

12 *True or False:* It's easy to stop smoking.

And the answers are . . .

   1 c Think about the clothes, records, tickets, and gifts you could buy with £300. If your habit costs over a pound a day, in less than three years, that's over £1,000 going up in smoke!

2 c Ugh. And tar, made up of thousands of solid chemicals, is carcinogenic (cancer-causing).

3 a One puff speeds your heartbeat, raises your blood pressure, decreases the body temperature of your hands and feet, and replaces some of the oxygen in your blood with carbon monoxide – right when your accelerated heartbeat requires more oxygen. The smoke you inhale attacks the living tissue it encounters as it travels through your body, from throat and lungs to stomach and bladder.

4 c Most adult smokers want to give up. Only thirty-eight per cent of men and thirty-three per cent of women still smoke, though men are stopping at a faster rate than women. Many got hooked before they knew how harmful tobacco was. Now that they are wising up, fewer are lighting up.

5 b The average smoker smokes about one hundred cigarettes a week.

6 c Frightening. Yet lung cancer is usually preventable. Most lung cancer victims are smokers, and most chronic lung disease is attributable to smoking. Thanks to cigarettes, almost as many women now die of lung cancer as breast cancer. In fact, it's estimated that one-third of all cancers are caused by smoking.

7 True. Not only does smoking stink, smokers have smoky-smelling clothes and bad breath (who was it who first said kissing a smoker is like licking an ashtray?), but the smoker's sense of smell and taste are impaired. Food tastes yummier and flowers smell prettier to non-smokers and ex-smokers.

8 True. If you're pregnant, you're smoking for two. Your foetus is not getting as much oxygen as it normally would and is growing more slowly and with more difficulty. Smokers have more miscarriages and pregnancy complications, and cot death is more common among babies whose mothers smoked during pregnancy. Leukaemia is also more widespread among children with mothers who smoke. Incidentally, fathers should also give up when their wife is pregnant as passive smoking is also very bad for the unborn baby.

9 True. An average smoker's life is shortened by about the number of minutes spent puffing away, which usually comes out to ten to fifteen years. At every age, there's a greater percentage of deaths among smokers than non-smokers. (No, I'm not making this up. It's based on research carried out by ASH (Action on Smoking and Health).) The good news: once a smoker stops smoking, unless irreversible damage has been done, his or her body works immediately to clean up the mess and replace ravaged cells with healthy ones. Ten years after a heavy smoker quits smoking, he or she has the same chances of living a good long life as a non-smoker.

10 False. Your chances of getting lung cancer are less than those of someone who inhales, but you've heard of mouth, lip and tongue cancer haven't you? Smokers are also more likely to get cancer of the throat, pancreas, kidney and cervix.

11 True. And seventy per cent of them have tried to stop, remember? The younger you start, and the more you smoke, the more likely you are to get cancer.

12 False. Mark Twain claimed quitting was easy and said he'd 'done it one hundred times'. Quitting isn't easy. But over thirty-three million Americans and eight million Britons have kicked the habit. Some stop instantly; others do it gradually. If you smoke, cut down on how much you smoke, don't smoke each cigarette to the very end, and inhale less deeply or less often. Filter, low-tar, or low-nicotine brands may be less harmful than regular brands, but each puff still contains such treats as formaldehyde, hydrogen cyanide, ammonia and lead. The younger you are when you start smoking and the longer you smoke, the tougher it is to give up. But if you make it through your teens without starting, you probably never will take up the habit.

Among adults, smoking is now a minority habit. Yet more than forty per cent of schoolchildren have smoked by the time they are sixteen. Why start?

To you, emphysema, chronic bronchitis, and ulcers may not seem ominous. So what if smoking accounts for a third of all cancers and doubles your chance of heart attack? Teenage smokers may not even know where the pharynx or larynx are, let alone worry about getting cancer there. But even young smokers catch colds and get winded and cough more often than non-smokers. The ads that show smoking skiers, dancers, and mountain climbers are misleading, because smoking impairs athletic ability.

Smokers on the Pill further increase their chances of strokes, heart attack, blood clots. Cigarettes and oral contraceptives don't mix.

Here's a danger you may not have considered: more than forty-two per cent of all fire deaths in Britain are caused by smoking.

If you smoke, stop kidding yourself. Stop killing yourself.

Tips on Giving Up

- Throw away your cigarettes, lighters, ashtrays. (Or if you're cutting down in preparation for giving up, lock or wrap them up so that they will be hard to get at. Or buy a cigarette brand you don't like much.)
- Think about the Government health warning on your cigarette packets. Make yourself read the warning every time you reach for a cigarette or read a cigarette ad.
- Write your own 'Why I want to stop smoking' list and read it whenever you feel like lighting up.
- If you smoke to relax, try giving up during a holiday or after exams.
- Have a friend or family member stop (or break any bad habit) with you, or bet your friend £10 you won't smoke for two weeks. Cheer each other on; don't nag.
- Think: one day at a time. The first two days are the hardest.
- Spend those first days in no-smoking places: libraries, cinemas, museums, stores.
- Tell your friends you've given up.
- Tell yourself you are stronger than your habits. Prove it.
- Stock up on sugarless gum, celery sticks, carrots, grapes, popcorn, and other low-calorie munchies. You won't gain weight when you stop unless you start eating more

than you used to. Which you won't do, right? Many ex-smokers do gain weight, but quite a few lose weight, possibly because they feel more energetic and active after quitting.

- Consider chewing nicotine gum. It's not a solution, but it will satisfy your craving without polluting your lungs.
- Take up knitting or have a coin or bead to play with when your hands want something to do.
- Change your routine. If you love an after-lunch cigarette, get right up after lunch instead of lingering at the table.
- If smoking gives you a lift, try taking walks and getting more sleep so you won't feel tired.
- Reward yourself by stashing away your cigarette money, and at the end of a week or two, treat yourself to a new pair of earrings or other little luxury. Think of what you want in terms of the cost in cigarette packets.
- Stay out of smoky bars and request the no-smoking section of planes, restaurants, and trains.
- If you slip up, don't give up. Lots of quitters succeed in unlearning and conquering the habit on the third or fourth try.
- Once you've kicked the habit, get rid of those yellow stains on your teeth and smile!

What If You Don't Smoke?

Congratulations. Unfortunately, your parents, boyfriend, mates, work colleagues, and other folks who may blow smoke in your face are doing more than making your hair and clothes reek. They're increasing your chances of an unnecessary illness. Secondhand smoke is hazardous to your health. Pneumonia, bronchitis, and lung troubles are more common among children whose parents smoke than among other kids.

Other people's smoke is particularly dangerous in closed or poorly ventilated rooms. When non-smokers sit in a smoke-filled room, the amount of carbon monoxide in their blood doubles.

My parents smoked, so when someone next to me lights up,

I've never been one to protest or flap my arms. Once a month or so, I've even said, 'May I pinch a cigarette?' But ever since I started to think about what cigarettes can do to a healthy body – have you seen any of those ghastly photos of diseased lungs? – I haven't been at all tempted to smoke. Tobacco kills about four times as many people in Britain every year as drink, drugs, murder, suicide, road/rail/plane crashes, poisoning, drowning, fire etc. put together. Makes you think doesn't it? Next time a friend says, 'Mind if I smoke?' I might even say, 'Yes, because I like you.'

If you'd like more information and help in giving up smoking, contact the Action on Smoking and Health (ASH), *see page 279*.

Marijuana – in Moderation?

OK, who out there has tried dope – cannabis or marijuana? Let's see some hands. I have. That doesn't make me cool and it doesn't make me a druggie. I mention it just so you won't think, 'What does she know?'

When you're a teenager and are working to achieve independence, why become psychologically dependent on a drug? While you're growing and developing, why risk tampering with your mental and physical health? While you're striving to forge your future, why let a chemical slow you down and dampen your ambition?

Don't forget that dope *is* illegal, although laws and punishment for possession vary. And because joints aren't government regulated, you can never be sure of what you're putting into your body. Dope is generally stronger now than it was a few years ago. Sometimes half a toke of potent hash or weed can leave you so disoriented, it's scary. Some dope is laced with unpredictable – and dangerous – extra ingredients, such as opium. Some contains the poisonous herbicide paraquat.

Remember all those cigarette findings? Well, there's more tar in a joint than in a cigarette. And dope has been linked with respiratory disease. Dope smoke is inhaled deeply and held inside for a long time – not good news if you're a lung. Joints are smoked right down to the end, where tar is most heavily concentrated. Sure, you can argue that dope users smoke much less than cigarette fiends. Yet ignoring the possible connection between 'killer weed' and cancer is naive.

Marijuana can make you gain weight, too. Oh, I know it has no calories. But when you're high and get an attack of the munchies, your willpower goes down the tubes.

Are there other not-so-nifty long-term physical effects? Does THC – tetrahydrocannabinol, the main mind-altering chemical in cannabis – damage chromosomes or the body's ability to ward off infection? Does heavy dope smoking mess up women's menstrual cycles and fertility or lessen men's sperm count and sperm concentration? Does dope impair intellectual performance? Many researchers say yes. Why expose yourself to such risks? Why be a guinea pig? After all, it took decades for scientists to discover the hazards of tobacco.

Never smoke dope if you're driving or if you're pregnant. Playing with your life is one thing; taking chances with someone else's is another.

The short-term effects you may know about. Someone who is stoned usually has red eyes, a quickened heart rate, a distorted sense of time and space, poor co-ordination, and a faulty short-term memory. He or she may become extra withdrawn or talkative or euphoric. Or hungry or sleepy or horny. While the short-term effects last only several hours, THC can remain in the body for weeks, settling especially in the brain, reproductive organs, and fatty tissues.

How would getting stoned affect *you*? It depends on the dope, your mood, and who you're with. First-time users may feel little effect. Regular users may find that marijuana magnifies moods. You're sad? You may get forlorn or paranoid. You're merry? You may get gales of giggles. Listening to music may seem more fun. The distortion of your perceptions can be a problem, however, if you make an important decision while stoned. For instance, don't imagine the romantic time you're having with a guy is based on love and respect when credit for the TLC (tender, loving care) may belong to the THC. If you've ever been the only straight one in a room full of dope-smoking acquaintances, you know that the stoned sometimes think they're being mind-bogglingly clever or so funny that it's a crime nobody brought a tape recorder. Yet their deep reasoning is usually off-target, their jokes more silly than witty. They may even seem zombie-like.

Because marijuana sometimes provides a temporary sense of well-being, it often lessens an individual's drive and reorganizes priorities. It's easier to get stoned than to tackle your history homework. Heavy dope users may find their days are a daze; entire months may dribble away with little to show for them. Some dopeheads wind up listless, unproductive, insecure, apathetic, and sapped of energy and motivation. Some smokers may be less mature than their peers because they've been avoiding certain social encounters and academic challenges while their classmates have been learning to deal with responsibility.

How do you resist peer pressure if one of the nation's thousands of regular dopeheads offers you a joint, or a piece of hash cake? Just say, 'No thanks.' Don't go into the *whys* and *wherefores*, and don't give any unwelcome holier-than-thou I-get-high-on-life sermons.

I don't think cannabis necessarily leads to harder drugs, but addicts start somewhere. Hash comes from the same *Cannabis sativa* plant that is harvested for marijuana. Because hash has more THC than dope, it is a stronger drug.

Speaking of stronger drugs. . .

Harder Drugs:
From Cocaine to Heroin

Most kids who pop pills with friends in the basement of suburban homes don't end up as thieves, prostitutes, or murderers mainlining heroin with unsterile needles. But that doesn't make pill popping any safer.

A recent survey showed that misuse of heroin increased rapidly over the last four or five years. In 1984, a fifth of new registered addicts were under twenty-one. The BBC Drugwatch survey discovered that most addicts started experimenting with drugs at school, while they were still living at home. Half of them had tried heroin, four out of five had tried speed, and the average number of different drugs tried by each individual was ten. Most were introduced to drugs by friends. Some friends! If drugs tempt you, remember:

- Never mix drugs and driving. You could kill someone, including yourself.
- Never mix drugs and alcohol. You could die.
- Never mix different drugs. One plus one can equal five.
- Never take drugs if you're pregnant, unless a doctor prescribes them. Your baby could be born addicted or with defects.
- When abused, even over-the-counter drugs can be dangerous.
- Don't use illegal drugs blatantly or in public. You could go to jail without passing go.
- Don't make big decisions (about sex or work or love or . . .) while under the influence. You could use bad judgment and regret it afterwards.
- Remember, the person selling you drugs is only interested in making money, probably to finance his or her own habit. He or she may lie about the ingredients of whatever pills or powders you are buying, or how strong they are. Heroin is often mixed with talcum powder, chalk dust, flour, or even Vim, so there's no way you can know exactly what you're buying.

Consider drug dependence. If you become physically dependent on a drug, you'll probably get ill when you try to go without it. You may suffer withdrawal symptoms like nausea, dizziness, chills, or worse. If you become psychologically dependent on a drug, you may feel nervous, bored and depressed without it.

Consider the law. First offenders in possession of a small quantity, may only be fined. *Only* . . . but is that the way you want to spend your money? Even if you get a fine, remember that you'll then have a criminal record which will do nothing to help your career or future prospects and will also restrict the countries to which you can travel for the rest of your life. And if you actually deal in drugs, you may get a *life sentence*.

Another word of warning. Never be persuaded to carry drugs or mysterious 'parcels' abroad, e.g. through frontiers or at airports. Two drug couriers were recently executed in Malaysia.

Some people are in the money because of drug dealing. Others are in jail. Others are dead. Drug dealing carries all the risks of organized crime.

If you're with someone who overdoses on illegal drugs, however, don't sit around worrying about the legal ramifications of getting help. Call an ambulance. Your friend could die while you're weighing your options.

If you haven't dabbled with illegal drugs, don't. If you have, stop. If you have been misusing drugs and want to get your life together again, drug-free, then discreet help is available. Many of the counsellors you'll be talking to are ex-drug users themselves. They don't judge; they understand and they help. Release run a helpline for people in trouble with drugs *see page 280*. Narcotics Anonymous can give you advice and help (*see page 280*), and SCODA can send you details of local treatment centres if you send them an SAE *see page 281*.

Step one to recovery is to eat well, exercise, get enough sleep and rest, and take vitamins to replenish what the drugs have depleted. Respect your body. Don't be self-destructive. Your will, not my words, will determine whether you abstain or abuse.

Types of Drugs

I don't recommend these drugs. I recommend that you know about them.

> • *Narcotics* are painkillers that induce sleep and relaxation. Doctors often use them for patients who've had accidents or surgery. Narcotics come in two types: opiates and synthetics. Opiates are made from the opium poppy; examples are opium, morphine, codeine and heroin. Synthetics, such as methadone, diamorphine, diconae and pethidine, are made in labs.
>
>   Not only are narcotics extremely addictive, but they create tolerance, so addicts need more and more to get high and to stop getting ill. Someone who injects drugs with an unsterile needle could wind up with hepatitis,

abscesses, blood poisoning, fatal heart infections, or AIDS. Someone who needs to support an £800-a-day heroin habit often resorts to crime. Overdoses can be fatal. And the life expectancy of an addict is much lower than that of a non-addict.

- *Stimulants* speed up your nervous system and make you less tired and hungry but more restless or agitated.

If you take amphetamines, or 'speed', repeatedly, upping your blood pressure and increasing your heart-beat rate, you reduce your resistance and literally wear yourself out. You may sometimes seem paranoid, manic, hyperactive, even depraved. When you come down off speed, or 'crash', you may feel irritable, lethargic, and exhausted, and your appetite returns in full force.

Someone who is crashing shouldn't take more speed but should sleep well, eat nutritiously, drink water and juices, and take vitamins. Many speed users, however, ignore their physical limits and take more speed, taxing and overloading their systems. They feel the 'rush', and may stay thin and on the go, but they may also die younger. Speed damages the liver and kidneys. Speed really does kill.

A friend confided, 'When I was at college, I used to study all night with the help of speed. Trouble is, the next few days were torture. So I got more and more behind on my work.'

Amphetamines, once widely prescribed as diet pills, are now fairly scarce. Amphetamine lookalikes are sold on the street and often contain uncontrolled amounts of the drugs in decongestants, antihistamines, and diet aids, which include a lot of caffeine. Some users have died because their blood pressure shot up too high too fast.

Caffeine? Yes, it's an addictive drug found in coffee, tea, cola drinks, chocolate, and some over-the-counter drugs. There are lots of caffeine fiends around – it's the most widely used and abused stimulant. If you down over six or so coffees or even more colas a day, you may be hooked. The drug gives you get-up-and-go, but when it wears off, you may be more tired than before. Controversy is brewing as to the health hazards of caffeine. It's wise to cut back and opt for decaffeinated coffee drinks. Why strain your system, irritate your stomach lining, disturb your sleep patterns, and invite gastrointestinal problems? When heavy coffee drinkers first cut down, they may get headaches or feel drowsy, but before long, they rediscover the natural energy within themselves. The last survey on coffee drinking (1982), found that coffee drinking is on the increase in Britain. Seventy per cent of people aged fifteen-plus drink at least one cup per day, although more and more people are tending towards the decaffeinated variety. A little coffee and cola are fine – just don't overdo it.

Some people think they are 'chocoholics'. I'd go a long way for a bar of chocolate. And if there's an open bag of chocolate digestives in the pantry, watch out. Am I hooked? No. I don't need chocolate fixes. Even *true* chocolate addicts should take heart? Chocolate bars are not illegal and won't change your consciousness so that you'd be useless in an emergency or would whisper a passionate 'I love you' to some guy you scarcely know. Still, if you over-indulge, try to cut back. Your waistline will appreciate it.

Cocaine is a stimulant now used by over ten million Americans, and an ever increasing number of Britons. Its popularity is on the rise, especially among professionals and 'yuppies'. At up to £70 a gramme (and how do you know it's pure?), cocaine costs far more than gold. Its effects last briefly. Many users experience a tremendous short-lived high, and when the drug wears off, they want to reexperience it. They take repeated doses and become psychologically addicted, even obsessed. Many neglect responsibilities and relationships and become virtual slaves to the seductive drug. In college, I knew of a guy whose values got so distorted that he robbed a friend for cocaine. And I knew a girl who continued going out with a guy long after her feelings had faded because, 'he was always good for some lines of coke'.

Coke strains the system and can cause cardiac and respiratory arrest. It can also cause nausea and insomnia and can damage nasal passages (if snorted) or veins (if injected). Some smoke the glamorized drug in a purified form called freebase, which can increase the chance of overdose and health problems. Cocaine used to be one of the ingredients in Coca-Cola until 1906, when the government stepped in.

• *Hallucinogens* are psychedelic drugs that affect the mind more than the body, altering mood and changing perception. LSD, PCP, and psilocybin mushrooms are examples.

LSD, dubbed 'acid', was popular twenty years ago and is still around. A little LSD goes a long way and can cause a whole kaleidoscopic sound and light show in your mind. A trip may begin around thirty minutes after taking a 'hit' and may last for three to twelve hours. It may seem fun, profound, truth-revealing, love-inspired, colourful. Or it may be hell, particularly if the setting is wrong or the user was depressed or fearful or if the LSD is impure or the dose too high. In a single trip the user may switch from seeming bliss to terror, insight to insanity, delusions of grandeur to feelings of insignificance. The following day users may feel sluggish, lightheaded, or downright horrible. LSD can cause nausea, but it is not addictive. Long-term side effects are still being studied. If someone you know ever panics because of a frightening trip, try to be warm, calm, and reassuring. Remind the user that the drug effects will wear off. (I for one am playing it safe – 'depriving' myself of a possible good trip and not risking a bad trip or bad side effects.)

Continued use of LSD can impair memory and leave the user strung out. In rare cases, a user may experience a flashback long after taking the drug. Flashbacks – unexpectedly going through part of the trip again – may be triggered by stress, fatigue, or use of other drugs.

So-called 'magic mushrooms', which are wild mushrooms containing the hallucinogens pscilocin or psilocybin, grow in certain parts of the UK. The effects are said to be like a mild acid trip except that they start quicker, and are often accompanied by nausea and stomach-ache. As with LSD, flashbacks can occur at a later date. Hunting for these mushrooms is dangerous: you could easily pick a similar-looking poisonous one by mistake – and die.

- *Inhalants* – glues and solvents – are chemicals that are sniffed or inhaled. They are cheap, accessible and extremely dangerous. The 'high' is neither exotic nor mystical. It's like being intoxicated with alcohol, but it takes place quickly and lasts only five to fifteen minutes. The person who sniffs a volatile solvent like glue, gasoline, cement paint, paint thinner, nail-varnish remover or typing correction fluid may feel drunk for a short while – or may OD (overdose) and become unconscious. The person who sniffs too much of an aerosol spray, hairspray, deodorant, or spray shoe polish, can coat and clog his or her lungs and suffocate. Inhalants are particularly dangerous when mixed with alcohol.

Glue-sniffing is most prevalent amongst under-age people who are too young to drink alcohol. It's not a clever thing to do because the vapours given off by the solvents are extremely toxic and can damage the liver, kidneys, nerve endings or bone marrow, and may cause sudden death.

You can tell a glue-sniffer by the chemical smell on his or her breath, traces of glue on the clothes, unusual soreness and redness around the mouth, nose or eyes, a persistent cough, slurred speech, and moody, secretive behaviour. If you suspect a friend, or even one of your brothers or sisters, is indulging in this dangerous habit, confront the person, show them this chapter, and if necessary tell an adult and get help. Call the confidential helpline for glue-sniffers on 01-733 7330, or write to the

National Campaign Against Solvent Abuse (see page 280).

People are often led into experimenting with glue by the gang they're in; in fact, nearly one in four school pupils have admitted sniffing solvents. Glue-sniffing isn't daring, it's deadly – so don't. And do your best to deter anyone else you think might be doing it.

Amyl nitrite ('poppers') and butyl nitrite (sold as air freshener or liquid incense) produce short, intense 'rushes', often repeatedly. Side effects are headaches, dizziness, nausea, dilated arteries, and lowered blood pressure.

• *Depressants* produce sleep and relieve tension. Also called downers and sedative-hypnotics, they depress the nervous system, reduce the heart rate, and s-l-o-w y-o-u d-o-w-n. Of course, while they calm you or bring on sleep, they aren't changing the problem that was keeping you awake. If you grow used to them, you become less able to relax or sleep without them.

Sleeping pills and barbiturates are psychologically and physically addictive and produce a high level of tolerance. Overdosing can be lethal. Someone who takes a downer may look and act drunk for hours. Mixing alcohol with such drugs is courting death. Addicts should not try to go off these drugs without medical supervision, because withdrawal can be accompanied by complications such as seizures, kidney failure or delirium.

Types of depressants include tranquillizers (such as Librium and Valium, the most popular prescription drug in Britain as well as in America, and sedative-hypnotic drugs like sleeping pills or barbiturates (such as Seconal, Tuinal, and Nembutal).

Let me stress again that I'm not encouraging you to seek chemical shortcuts to a fleeting, artiticial nirvana. I hope I'm providing reasons for you to say no. Drugs are dangerous. These pages offer just bare-bone facts. If you want to know more, go to the library. There's more bad news than good.

Thinking About Drinking

What don't you know about alcohol?

1 How long does it take the liver to metabolize and get rid of one pint of beer?
   a Under twenty minutes.
   b About forty minutes.
   c Over sixty minutes.

2 What percentage of the population drinks on occasion?
   a About 30 per cent.
   b About 60 per cent.
   c About 90 per cent.

3 What percentage of murders and traffic deaths in Britain involve alcohol?
   a About 15 per cent.
   b About 30 per cent.
   c About 50 per cent.

4 About how many calories are in a pint of beer?
   a 250.
   b 180.
   c 100.

5 If you've drunk too much, what's the best way to sober up?
   a Sleep it off.
   b Drink black coffee.
   c Take a cold shower.

6 If you've drunk too much and wake up with a hangover, what must you do?
   a Drink a small dose of alcohol.
   b Drink coffee with aspirin.
   c Wait it out.

7 *True or False:* How drunk you get depends solely on how much you drink.

8 *True or False:* Alcohol abuse is the number one drug problem in the UK.

9 *True or False:* Smokers who are drinkers increase their chances of getting cancer of the mouth, tongue, or throat.

10 *True or False:* Moderate drinking (one or two drinks a day) poses as many health risks as heavy drinking.

11 *True or False:* It's safe for pregnant women or mothers who are breast-feeding to drink.

12 *True or False:* No matter how much beer you drink, you can't get as drunk as you would if you were drinking the hard stuff.

13 How many synonyms for *drunk* can you come up with?

And the answers are . . .

1 c It takes the liver over an hour to metabolize one can of beer, one glass of wine, or one measure of vodka, and more than three hours for a pint. If you drink more than one glass per hour, you're on your way to getting drunk. Age, weight and sex also affect tolerance. For most girls, a little goes a long way.

2 c About 90% of the population drinks every so often. DHSS figures show that by far the highest proportion of heavy drinkers is in the 18 – 24 age group, but in another survey (by Anne Hawker of the Medical Council on Alcoholism, for her book *Adolescents and Alcohol*) 30% of girls aged fifteen reported being very drunk more than once. It's estimated that there are now some three million heavy drinkers in Britain, at least 750,000 of whom are probably seriously ill, and most of whom started misusing alcohol when they were aged 13 – 15.

3 c Fifty per cent of British murders, 80% of fire deaths, two thirds of fatal accidents to car drivers at night, and a half of those involving motorcyclists, are alcohol related. So are 40% of pedestrian traffic accidents (it's far too easy to wander out into the road after a few drinks and think you're immortal), 33% of domestic accidents, and 33%

of child abuse cases. Take away the drink factor and think of all the lives that could have been saved and the suffering avoided.

4 b Most alcoholic drinks are high in calories but not nutritious. Sweet rum drinks or creamy liqueur drinks have many more calories than do wine spritzers or light beer. A single measure of spirits has 50 calories. Plus, if you get plastered, your willpower to resist the crisps and peanuts goes down. Besides, you should never drink on an empty stomach. So, although one pint of beer may add up to only 180 calories, drinking is fattening: ever heard of a 'beer belly'? If you drink instead of eating you'll suffer from malnutrition.

5 a What do you get when you throw a drunk into an icy shower and administer coffee? A wet, wide-awake drunk. Fresh air isn't sufficiently sobering, either. Time and sleep are.

6 c There's no surefire hangover helper. If you ever do wake up with the morning-after horrors, pour lots of water and fruit juice into your dehydrated body. (It would have been better to do that, between hiccups, before you went to bed.) Alcohol depletes the body's vitamin supply, too, which is another reason for downing juice or munching something healthy, like a banana. To speed up your metabolism and help your liver get rid of the poisons you've subjected it to, take a cold shower or brisk walk or jog (unless your head throbs in protest). If you like, take aspirin or a nap. Alcohol disrupts the dreaming REM (rapid eye movement) sleep stage, so if you go to sleep drunk, you wake up less rested.

At the next party, instead of spending an evening getting drunk and blowing the following day recovering, don't drink, or sip just a little. You'll probably have more fun, and as a bonus you get to remember the good time.

By the way, although over-indulging in beer can result

in a hangover, it's more typical to feel awful after over-doing it on rum, brandy, or whisky, or after mixing different drinks. As a rule, the darker the drink, the higher its hangover potential. Some people get hung over after drinking next to nothing, whereas others drink with seeming impunity.

7 False. How drunk you become depends on how much you drink as well as how much you weigh, how much and how often you're used to drinking, how fast you drink, whether you've eaten, your body chemistry, your mood, where you are and whether you're psyched up to be drunk or sober. If a petite girl who has her period, hasn't eaten, and is not used to drinking, downs a beer at a party, it will go to her head much faster than the same drink would affect a large man sipping his daily beer over dinner. *What* you drink makes a difference, too: straight liquor is absorbed into the bloodstream and makes drinkers drunker faster than liquor diluted with mixers.

8 True. Alcohol is a drug. Parents of alcoholics who sigh and say, 'At least she's not into drugs,' are deluding themselves. Alcoholism is twenty times more prevalent than all other drug addictions combined.

9 True. Cancer, smoking, and drinking are often related.

10 False 'What is moderate drinking?' is a tricky question. Adults who drink one drink a night and do not become intoxicated are probably not problem drinkers and probably aren't risking heart, liver or digestive tract problems. Some studies suggest that for *adults*, modest drinking can actually be healthy: a drink or two relieves stress and may decrease the risk of heart attack because it inhibits cholesterol build-up. Other studies suggest that even moderate drinking increases the chances of getting rectal and lung cancer. Mixing drinks with other drugs (legal or illegal) can be out-and-out hazardous, and more than two drinks daily can be physically and psychologically dangerous. To put it plainly: too much booze pickles the brain.

11 False When a pregnant woman or nursing mother drinks, her foetus or baby also takes a swig. Women who drink heavily during pregnancy, especially during the first three months, up their odds of having babies who are abnormal, small or exhibit mental or emotional problems, because the foetus can't metabolize alcohol efficiently. Some experts say even one drink per week during pregnancy can invite trouble. Others believe once a mother is nursing, it's OK to drink an occasional beer.

12 False Alcohol is alcohol. Yes, ounce for ounce, whisky is much more potent than beer, but beer, wine, and whisky all contain alcohol. Drink a little and you get tipsy. Drink a lot and you pass out.

13 I'm not sure if I'm giving or subtracting points for this one, but if you're smashed, legless, plastered, pie-eyed, sloshed, paralytic, sozzled, soused, bombed, blotto, pissed, tight, tanked-up or three sheets to the wind . . . you drank too much.

Many people don't drink. They don't like the taste, the calories, the blurry feeling. They're taking medication or are pregnant or are in training. They have bad associations with alcohol: a car accident, a violent father, a negligent mother, a friend who got drunk and was taken advantage of. Or they just don't want to.

That's fine. That's clever.

It can be hard to resist peer pressure, but if you don't want to drink *don't*. (Though some may scoff at you for being teetotal, others will admire your strength of character.) There's no point in breaking the law and messing up your body and mind. If you're offered beer at a party say, 'no thanks'. You don't owe anybody any explanations.

If you do choose to drink, be responsible about it. Sip and

nibble rather than guzzle on an empty stomach. Know your limit and stick to it. *Never* mix driving and drinking, and *never* mix alcohol with other drugs. If you take a cold pill or antihistamine with wine, for instance, you're combining two depressants, which is dangerous. If you're taking an antibiotic and drinking, the antibiotic may be inactivated. If you're combining an illegal barbiturate with booze, you may get so mellow that you never wake up again.

Alcohol is a depressant, not a stimulant. One drink may make you feel vivacious and talkative, but that's because alcohol dulls judgment and inhibitions. It also dulls the body. Shakespeare himself elaborated on the paradox in *Macbeth* (II,iii): 'Lechery, sir, it provokes and it unprovokes: it provokes the desire, but it takes away the performance.'

Another thing: alcohol doesn't do anything for your looks. What's the point of dressing and making up to look pretty for a party, if you end the evening being horribly sick, maybe all down your best dress, then wake the next day grey-faced, lank-haired and puffy eyed? Constant heavy drinking makes you red-eyed, red-nosed, red-veined, and turns your skin yellow and puffy. Talk about being a turn-off!

A lot of alcohol slows your brain, making you slur words and lose co-ordination. Too much alcohol too fast can even result in coma or death. That's why the party-till-you-puke don't-leave-till-you-heave attitude is so stupid. There are 5,000–10,000 deaths in Britain each year from alcohol-related diseases, accidents and suicides.

Sound scary? It can be. But whereas you get hooked on opiates or tranquillizers in mere weeks, it usually takes longer to become physically addicted to alcohol. Of course, many teenagers are problem drinkers without being alcoholics. If you regularly drink to get drunk, or throw up after drinking, or end up kissing, or worse, having sex with a guy when you didn't intend to, or make a spectacle of yourself, beware! Strive to control your habit before it starts controlling you.

Alcoholism

For many people, alcohol becomes a poison, a necessity, and a nightmare.

You probably know a few alcoholics. Very few of them are winos or derelicts; most are ordinary working people. Many have, or had an alcoholic parent. No one is too young to be an alcoholic. Some alcoholics drink regularly; some go on sprees or binges. Most suffer withdrawal symptoms if deprived of the drug.

Alcoholism is a disease. Alcoholics have lost control of their drinking and drink even though the habit wreaks havoc on their health and professional, academic, financial, and/or personal lives. Alcoholism, after heart disease and cancer, is the third greatest killer in Britain and the United States. Is the alcoholic only hurting himself? No. He's often hurting his family and his co-workers, and if he drives drunk, someday he may inadvertently commit murder on the road.

Although alcoholism is a progressive illness, it is treatable. Recovery usually means swearing off liquor for good and for ever. The thousands of alcoholics who have been helped through Alcoholics Anonymous swear off booze one day at a time. Families and friends of alcoholics have also found strength and some solutions through self-help groups.

Alcoholics Anonymous (AA) got its start fifty years ago in Ohio, USA. Now groups meet in over 110 countries. At AA meetings, members are committed to staying sober and helping each other stay sober. They share personal stories about their battles with alcohol. The only requirement for AA membership is the desire to stop drinking. Meetings are free; donations are accepted.

AA is not associated with any particular religion, although there is an AA prayer:

> God grant me the serenity to accept
> the things I cannot change,
> courage to change the things I can,
> and wisdom to know the difference.

One more quick quiz. Answer the following questions *yes, no* or *sometimes*.

---

1 Is your work performance sinking because of your drinking?

2 Do you skip school or work to drink?

3 Do you lie about how much you drink?

4 Do you forget things or have blackouts (memory loss) because of drinking?

5 Do you drink to escape?

6 Do you drink in the morning?

7 Do you need a drink to feel self-confident?

8 Do you get drunk when you hadn't intended to?

9 Do you think about drinking a lot?

10 Do you think a lot about drinking?

11 Do you drink alone?

12 Do you drink instead of eating?

13 Do you drink a lot in a hurry?

14 Do you drink until you pass out?

15 Do you drink when you're angry or stressed?

16 Do you get into trouble when you drink?

17 Do you look up to friends who drink a lot?

18 Has your drinking affected your reputation and friendships?

19 Has your drinking lowered your ambition?

20 Have you tried to quit or cut down your drinking and failed?

Add up the *yeses* and the *sometimeses*. If you have more than three, take it as a warning. Try a week on the wagon. If you think alcohol is becoming a problem in your life, consider calling Alcoholics Anonymous. No one needs to know that you attended a meeting unless you tell. If there's no listing in your phone book, contact:

Alcoholics Anonymous,
P.O. Box 514,
11, Redcliffe Gardens,
London SW10 9BQ.
Tel. 01-352 9779

Another organization that can help you fight a drink problem is: ACCEPT (see page 279). ACCEPT is Britain's leading independent national charity dealing with alcohol and tranquillizer problems, and they also have a drugs helpline. It you think it would be hard to stop drinking now, think how much harder it would be to stop later. You can control an addiction, but you can never truly cure it. So don't let yourself get hooked in the first place.

Drunk Driving

If you've ever been in a car in which the driver was drunk, consider yourself lucky to be here. Of the hundreds of people who die every year because of drunk driving, many of them are teenagers. Some were drunk when they fell asleep at the wheel or said hello to a tree. Many were perfectly sober, minding their own business, singing along with the car radio, when some inebriated idiot ploughed into them. Police officers and coroners don't enjoy telling parents that their kid is dead, but they do it all the time. Road accidents are the leading cause of death in the sixteen- to twenty-five-year-old age group, and thousands are injured yearly, too. Two thirds of car drivers and half the motorcyclists killed at night are over the limit.

I knew people who died young because they mixed drinking and driving: the brother of a girl I used to baby-sit for, a guy I once worked with, a daughter of a writer friend. What a waste. It's too sad to run into the mother of a classmate at the supermarket and watch her eyes fill with tears as you mumble how sorry you were to hear about the death of her son. It's too sad to hear a middle-aged friend tell you, her voice shaking, that as much as she tries, she can't remember the sound of her daughter's laugh.

Frightening but true: on any given weekend night, many drivers who are sharing the road with you and me are not all there. Alcohol has dulled their reflexes, and if they are distracted for a second, they may crash smack into us.

Teenagers are just learning to drink and just learning to drive. When they combine the two, many are dangerous to themselves and to others.

If a policeman stops you and suspects you of driving while under the influence of alcohol, you will be asked to take a breathalyzer test. If you are found guilty of drunken driving, you may lose your licence, you will certainly have to pay high legal fees and a fire, and your insurance premium will rocket; in fact, it may be hard to get any insurance at all. But the most important reason of all for not drinking and driving is that you may kill someone, or kill yourself.

The legal limit for intoxication if you are driving is 80 mg. of alcohol per 100 ml. of blood. Before you even feel drunk, your ability to drive safely goes down. If you've had three drinks, you are probably legally intoxicated. If you drive, your chances of getting into an accident quadruple. I hope you don't try to outwit the statistics. (And if you do, I hope I don't happen to be cruising along in the next lane.)

Respect yourself and respect other drivers. If you are drunk at a party, don't drive home. Have a friend drive or call your brother or sister or parents or a taxi (always carry enough money to get home on your own.) If your boyfriend has the car and is drunk, don't risk both your lives. Refuse to let him drive. Do not worry about offending him when he is about to put your life on the line. Take his keys and have someone else do the driving. I know that's hard, but that's what friends are for. Do *not* let a drunk drive.

Some friends have a system: when they go together to a party, one member of the group stays absolutely sober. At the next party, they alternate, and another person keeps away from the booze.

I often drive. I sometimes drink. But I firmly believe: none for the road.

In 1985, two fathers whose children had been killed by drunken drivers started the Campaign against Drunken Drivers (CAD). If you want to find out more about it, write to them at the address on page 279.

By the way, even sober drivers aren't always safe drivers. A ton of moving metal can be a lethal weapon. Motorcycles are even more dangerous than cars. An eighteen-year-old motorcyclist is about seven times more likely to be killed or injured than a young car driver, and about thirty-seven more times than an adult car driver.

I still remember my boast to a blond guy I had an unrequited crush on. The car I was in won a race to a restaurant. 'We got up to ninety miles per hour,' said I, oh-so-self-impressed. 'That was stupid,' he snapped. My bubble burst, but I realized he was right (and wouldn't you know it? – his 'caring' and maturity made my crush even stronger).

Reckless driving *is* stupid. Drive carefully. Don't race through the red light at one junction just to be first at the red light on the next one. Watch out for the other drivers. Stay alert on long and short trips. Many traffic deaths occur within twenty-five miles of the driver's home. And put your seat belt on – it is illegal to travel as a driver or a front-seat passenger without it. Some cars have rear seatbelts; use them. Policeman hardly ever have to unbuckle dead people.

Enough. Let's move on to something more cheerful. How about a chapter of quizzes?

8. A Quartet of Quizzes

Getting To Know You

Are You *Too* Nice?

We all know people who would give us the shirt off their backs, and others who wouldn't give us the time of day. Which are you? After each question, circle the answer that best describes you. Then check the scoring.

1 You just baby-sat from 9:30 a.m. to 2:30 p.m. The children's mother returns, takes out her purse, and says, 'Let's see, I owe you for four hours'. You
   a point out politely that you believe she means five hours.
   b accept payment for four hours because you hate to contradict her and you want her to ask you back.
   c tell her you will not be cheated out of money you earned.
   d say, 'Hmm, 9:30 to 10:30, 11:30, 12:30, 1:30, 2:30' in a hesitant voice.

2 You don't like your date that much, but he did take you to a fancy restaurant for dinner. On the way home, he drives down a dark country road, pulls over, and turns to kiss you. You
   a talk a mile a minute each time he leans towards you.
   b push him away and demand he drive you home immediately.
   c kiss him back – you feel you sort of owe it to him.

   d tell him you enjoyed the evening, but you're not
   ready to start a romance with him.

3 You had a miserable time when you had your wisdom
   teeth out last year. Now a girl you know has to have the
   same operation. She asks you what it's like. You
   a pretend you didn't hear her and compliment her
   on her blouse.
   b say, 'You'll find out,' and walk away.
   c swear it doesn't hurt a bit.
   d say, 'Not much fun' but it's over in no time.

4 A guy invites you to the pictures and suggests a gory
   film you're sure you'd hate. You
   a say, 'Sounds great to me. I've been dying to see it.'
   b ask 'What else is on?'
   c say, 'I will if you really want to.'
   d say, 'No. I can't stand violent movies.'

5 You're cramming for tomorrow's French test when a
   long-winded friend calls. You
   a say, 'I just can't talk to you now.'
   b talk to her for nearly an hour.
   c say, 'Let's talk for five minutes, then I've got to go
   back to my studying.'
   d gasp, 'My father is calling me – I've got to go!'

6 A friend who has borrowed lunch money from you
   before but has never paid you back asks if you'll lend
   her a fiver. You
   a say no and remind her she still owes you three quid.
   b say, 'I don't have any extra money today.'
   c hand her 50p.
   d say, 'Forget it!' and grimace so she knows you can't
   believe she had the gall to ask.

7 A friend is returning a yellow sweater she borrowed –
   with a brand new chocolate stain in the front. You
   a say, 'How dare you try to give my sweater back in this
   condition!'

   b ask her if she tried hand-washing or dry-cleaning the sweater.

3   **c** say, 'Thank you' and pretend not to notice the stain.

   d hold the sweater up in such a way that she knows you see the stain and hope she volunteers an explanation.

8 You and a dozen others are on a committee to arrange the youth club's Christmas play. A meeting was scheduled for tomorrow at 4, but the chairperson suddenly wants to switch it to 3:15. She asks you to phone everyone about the change. You

   a say, 'I won't be home tonight, so I can't help you.'

   b start looking up numbers and plan an evening on the phone.

   c say, 'I'll make a few calls, but let's divide the names.'

   d declare, 'You're the one who's changing things – you make the calls!'

9 Every time you and your friend Jim get together after school, you end up helping him clean his motorbike or mow the lawn. Today he phones and invites you to keep him company while he builds a bookshelf. You

   a say, 'No. But if you're ever ready to do something away from your house that's more fun, let me know.'

   b say, 'I'll be right over.' After all, he does enjoy being with you.

   c say, 'Sorry, I'm busy right now.'

   d say something like, 'I'll help you under one condition: afterwards we go for an ice-cream and a walk.'

10 Your elderly aunt has shown you three family albums, and you're feeling restless as she opens the fourth. You

   a politely ask, 'Who is this couple, and how do you know them?'

   b say, 'I'm really tired of photographs.'   3

   c suggest you go for a stroll and save the others for later.

   d ask, 'Aren't your eyes getting tired?'

11 Five girls push in front of you in the ticket queue for a concert. You a step in front of them, shoving each one slightly so they know you're annoyed.

3 b clear your throat several times loudly and stare at them.

c stand quietly behind them – no point in causing a fuss.

d say, 'Excuse me, but the queue begins back there.'

12 The fella you have a crush on has finally asked you out, and you've ordered burgers at a crowded restaurant. Suddenly your next-door neighbour and her bratty eight-year-old son appear at your table. The mother gives you a cheery hello and asks, 'May we join you?' You

a bury your head in the menu until your neighbour, bewildered, walks off.

b say that you look forward to dropping in for a visit later, but that you and your friend have a few things you need to discuss between yourselves.

c say, 'We're having a private conversation.'

3 d hear yourself stammer, 'Of course, pull up some chairs.'

13 Even though it's her turn, an office colleague asks you to make the coffee, saying she's too busy. Here she comes now, with a sweet smile and an empty mug. You

a say, 'Make it yourself for once.'

b do it, but make a point of sighing, drumming your fingers and checking your watch while the kettle boils.   **3**

c make it as usual – it's easier than making a scene.

d explain that you're too busy and you'd feel better about making coffee if everyone took their turn, including her.

14 You've already put in plenty of overtime at the store where you're supposed to leave at 5.30 p.m., but your employer begs you to stay until late-night closing at 9. You're exhausted, you promised your parents you'd be

home for dinner, and you have some studying to do. You

a say, 'I'm busy this evening, but if you really need me, maybe I can stay.'

b apologize and refuse to work because you have other commitments.

c agree to work without complaint.

d complain that he or she forgets you have a personal life.

15 A guy you don't like at all keeps calling to ask you out. You've made umpteen excuses: baby-sitting, family plans, relatives staying, even washing your hair. But he never catches on, and he calls you again. You

a hang up as soon as you recognize his voice.

b explain as tactfully as you can that you like him, but 'only as a friend'.

c say, 'I have a lot of homework to do, but thanks for asking, and call again sometime.'

d consent to go out with him, then kick yourself for being so stupid.

Scoring

Are you too nice? Not nice enough? Find out your kindness quotient by circling the number following each letter you selected, then adding up your score.

	a		b		c		d	
1	a	1	b	3	c	4	d	2
2	a	2	b	4	c	3	d	1
3	a	2	b	4	c	3	d	1
4	a	3	b	1	c	2	d	4
5	a	4	b	3	c	1	d	2
6	a	1	b	2	c	3	d	4
7	a	4	b	1	c	3	d	2
8	a	2	b	3	c	1	d	4
9	a	4	b	3	c	2	d	1
10	a	3	b	4	c	1	d	2
11	a	4	b	2	c	3	d	1
12	a	2	b	1	c	4	d	3

13	a	4	b	2	c	3	d	1
14	a	2	b	1	c	3	d	4
15	a	4	b	1	c	2	d	3

15 to 25 Congratulations! You know what you want and you're strong enough to go after it, yet you always remember to take other people's feelings into consideration. When problems arise, you deal with them directly. Because you are courteous and confident, people respect you.

26 to 37 There are lions and there are lambs, and you fall somewhere in between. You usually manage to get yourself out of unpleasant predicaments, but instead of confronting an issue head on, you often escape through the back door, hemming and hawing and saying, 'Uh, I don't think so' or 'I can't, really.' The trouble with being wishy-washy? You find yourself with the same problem again and again. Your excuse may work once, but you have to keep thinking up new ones. Be sensitive, but start speaking your mind to eliminate the guesswork.

38 to 49 Giving, thoughtful, helpful: that's you. But being a pushover isn't much better than being pushy, so don't let your sweet generosity run wild. If you lend out your only umbrella when you're caught in a rainstorm, that's being nice to another but not nice to yourself. Many love you for your soft heart, yet others try to take advantage of you. Some sweet-talk you into doing them favours, then, instead of showing appreciation, may treat you like a doormat. When you're too concerned with pleasing others, you forget to please yourself. So give, give, give – but don't give yourself away. After all, *you* count most of all. Develop your self-esteem by asking yourself what you want and learning to express it diplomatically.

50 to 64 Watch out! You're fearless and firm and you usually get your way, but your brusqueness may be scaring off friends. It's possible to be forceful without being rude and to make your wishes clear without hurting or alienating others. Brush up on your manners, and imagine how the other person will feel before you say or do something you may regret later. Being assertive is one thing. Being aggressive is another.

How Well Do You Know Your Best Friend?

Let's say you know your best friend adores *Dynasty*, dogs and doughnuts . . . but do you know her future plans? Or her favourite kind of party?

Do this quiz with your best friend at your side. Read each question together; then, on separate pieces of paper, write the number of the question and the letter of the answer that best describes your friend. She should choose the answer that best describes herself. When you've completed all fifteen questions, find out your score and see how much you really know (or don't know!) about her. Then do the quiz again and find out how much she really knows about you!

1 If she could specify only one quality in a computer-matched blind date, she would ask that her date be
   a intellectual.
   b handsome.
   c sensitive.
   d athletic.

2 If a guy wanted to win her over, he'd do best by giving her
   a a framed photograph of the two of them.
   b fresh bread that he baked himself.
   c a pile of 10p pieces for the Space Invader machine.
   d a bouquet of wild flowers.

3 She'll admit she sometimes envies you because

a you get along with your parents.
b you're so popular with guys.
c you're so good at sports.
d you're so clever.

4 Provided she meets the right guy, she thinks a good age to get married is
a 21 or younger.
b 22 to 26.
c 27 or older.
d never.

5 If she won the Pools, she'd probably
a buy a completely new wardrobe.
b travel around the world.
c contribute most of the money to a worthy cause.
d save most of the money for her future.

6 The best way to snap her out of a bad mood would be to
a take a walk and talk.
b accompany her to a movie.
c put on her favourite album full blast and dance crazily together.
d go out and splurge on everything from ice-cream to make-up.

7 On the subject of Women's Lib, she
a supports it completely.
b thinks it's done more harm than good.
c thinks it has pros and cons.
d knows little about it.

8 Her second favourite subject at school is, or was,
a maths.
b foreign languages.
c social studies.
d English.

9 Which of the following situations would upset her most?
a if she received a bad school report.

b if a girl flirted with her boyfriend.
c if she saw a friend shoplifting.
d a political crisis in the news.

10 If someone offered her a joint, she'd probably
a ask, 'What's that?'
b say, 'Great!'
c say, 'No thanks.'
d steer clear of that person from then on.

11 Her immediate plans include
a getting a job.
b taking time off to work or travel, then going to college.
c taking a secretarial or business course.
d going to university.

12 If she could magically change one part of her body, it would be her
a legs.
b bosom.
c hair.
d nose.

13 She would most enjoy spending an afternoon
a sunbathing at the seaside.
b hiking in the mountains.
c shopping in the city.
d playing or watching some kind of sport.

14 At a disco, she's most likely to wear
a the absolute latest fashion gear.
b a frilly dress, high heels, and flowers in her hair.
c faded jeans, a T-shirt and some zany accessories.
d Laura Ashley-style skirt and blouse.

15 Her favourite kind of party is
a an all-girls gossip session.
b a big open house with old friends and new faces.
c a small gathering with her very best friends, male and female.
d a fancy dress party.

Scoring

How well did you guess each other's responses? Compare your answers and add up the number of answers that match.

11 to 15 You know each other very well and you share the gift of true friendship. Your conversations are open and trusting, whether you're discussing parties, pastimes, or politics. You're both lucky. But remember, friendship is like an old house – the shelter is warm and the memories happy, but the roof may spring an occasional leak. Take care of your treasured bond and try not to let a new boyfriend, a summer apart, or any other circumstance ever weaken it.

6 to 10 You know a lot about each other, and you know you enjoy being together. Maybe the reason you can't predict every twist and turn of your best friend's personality is that her opinions change often, or that she's more comfortable keeping certain thoughts private. Perhaps, with time, you'll explore new topics of conversation and learn even more about each other. Meanwhile, your friendship is important to you both, and only you two know if it feels wonderful as it is or if it needs a bit more talking, more listening, more caring.

0 to 5 Why so few answers in common? Is your friend that mysterious? That private? That shy? Or could it be that you've been doing all the talking? Maybe there's a reason she isn't opening up to you. Did she ever tell you a secret only to find out that you'd spread it about? Or perhaps you never think aloud with her, so she hesitates to be the first to expose her innermost thoughts. Begin to share your thoughts and insights, and learn to ask about and listen to hers. You'll both win in the long run.

Are You and He a Good Match?

Are you and your boyfriend really right for each other? Are you like two peas in a pod or like apples and oranges – and which makes for a more compatible couple?

Like the friendship quiz, you two take this in tandem. Unlike that quiz, you each answer for yourselves. You and your boyfriend should each number a separate piece of paper from 1 to 22. Read the questions together, then write down the letter of your answer. When you finish, add up the answers you have in common and check the scoring.

---

1 Your bedroom is
   a stylish, immaculate – right out of a glossy magazine.
   b neat but 'lived in'.
   c somewhat eccentric – there may be a huge mobile hanging from the ceiling or a hand-painted mural on the wall.
   d buried under layers of books, clothes, and records.

2 If you've planned to meet a friend at 3 p.m., you arrive
   a ten minutes early.
   b at 3 p.m. exactly.
   c ten minutes late.
   d who knows? There is no pattern to your punctuality.

3 Which best describes your attitude towards animals?
   a You're a cat person: happiness is a kitten purring in your arms.
   b You're a dog person: nothing beats walking with a tail-wagging canine.
   c You adore horses, budgies, tortoises – any creature with fur, feathers, or fins.

d Animals? Yuk! They bite and leave hairs everywhere, they're noisy and messy, and some even make you sneeze.

4 On Saturday evening, you're paid £20 for your Saturday job. Next week, you'll probably
a spend £25.
b buy one big item that costs around £15.
c save £10 and spend the rest on little things.
d put it all in the bank.

5 As far as astrology goes . . .
a when you learn someone's birthdate, you feel you know a lot about that person's character. You read your horoscope every day, and if it says 'Avoid travel', you stay at home.
b you think sun signs have some effect on personalities, and you often read your daily horoscope.
c you'll admit some Virgos are perfectionists, but when you read your horoscope, it's just for kicks.
d you think zodiac signs and horoscopes are nonsense.

6 When it comes to clothes,
a you like being in style and you update your wardrobe regularly.
b you favour the classic and conservative (the Sloane Ranger look, for instance).
c you take it to the limit with wild colours and eccentric styles.
d you've never gone out naked, but you hardly notice what you wear.

7 Your feeling about sports is that you
a would love to be the most valuable player on the team.
b would like to at least make the team.
c enjoy going to watch games and matches.
d couldn't care less about sports of any kind.

8 In school, you especially enjoy, or enjoyed,

    a maths and science
    b English, foreign languages, and history.
    c art and music.
    d lunch period and the final bell.

9 It's your usual bedtime, but tonight you still have lots of work to do for school or college. You
    a go to bed; sleep is important, too.
    b stay up another forty-five minutes finishing your work, however carelessly.
    c continue working conscientiously until you're satisfied with your efforts.
    d set the alarm for 6 a.m.

10 Your ideal holiday is
    a skiing down snowy mountain trails.
    b going to a city you've never seen and exploring its restaurants, museums, shops, parks and tourist attractions.
    c having a fun time at the seaside.
    d staying at home and catching up on reading, seeing friends, and everything you don't usually have time for.

11 If you spent a week on a warm beach, you'd
    a enjoy lolling around with no decisions to make except which flavour ice-cream to order.
    b use a lot of effort and oil to achieve the perfect tan.
    c spend the whole time swimming and practising water sports.
    d complain about sand, heat, sunburn, and boredom.

12 You've won a free go-anywhere holiday, so you're packing your bags for
    a China.
    b Kenya.
    c France.
    d the USA.

13 Of the following meals, your favourite is
    a a cheeseburger and chips.

b roast beef and Yorkshire pudding.
c spaghetti bolognaise.
d a nice, crisp salad with lots of healthy ingredients.

14 You find swearing in public
a normal for guys and girls.
b OK for blokes but not for girls.
c somewhat offensive.
d totally vulgar and off-putting.

15 Cigarette smoking is
a OK every once in a while, but you'd hate to be hooked.
b enjoyable – you don't feel guilty about smoking.
c not for you, but it doesn't bother you when others smoke.
d unattractive, unhealthy, and impolite.

16 Regular exercise? Yes, you
a jog daily, rain or shine.
b do sit-ups, push-ups, or aerobic stretches every so often.
c take part in a sport regularly, you belong to the local tennis team or sports centre.
d make many round trips to the sweetshop.

17 Which do you go to most often?
a classical concerts.
b rock concerts.
c the theatre.
d football matches.

18 When you are eighteen, you
a plan to vote in local and national elections and campaign for a political party.
b think you may vote at general election time, if you can decide whom to vote for.
c think politics has nothing to do with you and you won't bother to vote.
d think politicians are all con-merchants, and if you get as far as a polling booth, you plan to spoil your ballot

paper or vote for Screaming Lord Sutch!

19 If you found a £20 note on the floor of a shop, you would
   a pocket it and feel giddy.
   b pocket it and feel guilty.
   c quietly ask, 'Did anyone lose some money?'
   d hand it over to a salesperson.

20 Your ideal home is a
   a modern flat in the heart of a bustling city.
   b rose-covered cottage in the country.
   c house in the suburbs with a double garage and a nice garden.
   d a converted lighthouse on an isolated headland.

21 You think divorce is so common nowadays because
   a marriage itself is too limiting. It's unrealistic to expect two people to stay married for decades and decades.
   b people get married too soon and for the wrong reasons.
   c married couples don't try hard enough to get along.
   d women's and men's roles are changing too fast today – no one knows what he or she wants.

22 Children? Ideally you'd like to have
   a none.
   b one or two.
   c three.
   d four or more.

Scoring

How many times did your answers match? Add up and see what your score means.

16 to 22 A toast to two of a kind! You and your special guy are well suited. You have similar values, tastes, opinions, and habits, and you are truly compatible in all aspects of your lives. Enjoy yourselves, you perfect pair, but be careful not to lose your individuality. In the long run, you could be bored going out with your double. Continue to grow separately and together, discussing insights, feelings, and projects. Being a good match is a good start; the future is up to you.

8 to 15 You two have your differences, but many of your priorities, character traits, and viewpoints are similar. You and your boyfriend probably complement each other well and have a dynamic, exciting relationship, with plenty to talk about all the time. If you can learn to discuss politics, religion, and which film to see without causing hard feelings, you're all set. Compromise and tolerance are the necessary glues to keep you both smiling for a long time.

0 to 7 You've just proved the old adage: Opposites attract. Lots of liberals and conservatives, spenders and savers, cat people and dog people, talkers and listeners do make happy couples. If you can each allow for some give or take, you may find you get along as well as the couples who seem like identical twins. But your bond *is* more challenging. Little quirks can drive you crazy, like his being late when you're always early. And big issues must be reckoned with: If you want a Ph.D. and he wants to drop out and go on the road with a punk band you probably aren't a heaven-made match. For now, have fun, learn from each other, and enjoy finding out why your characters, values, and tastes are often different.

Are You the Jealous Type?

Nobody is immune to jealousy. But while the green-eyed monster makes some feel blue and makes some see red, others rarely suffer the aches of envy. Test yourself honestly in the following situations. Then check the scoring to learn how you can understand and tame the monster.

1 Your boyfriend is working part-time in a bar and you're sure the pretty barmaid has a crush on him. You

   a don't worry – the pub's much too busy for any hanky-panky.

   b quiz your boyfriend lightheartedly on everything the two of them say and do every evening.

   c are very uncomfortable with the situation but don't say anything.

2 You're upset, so you call an old friend who's recently moved away. You catch her in top spirits: her premium bond's just come up, she has a new boyfriend and she's landed a summer job on a cruise ship. You

   a listen, mumble 'That's great', swallow the lump in your throat and tell her your saga.

   b are delighted for her, say 'Congratulations,' and ask for all the details, not mentioning your own woes.

   c say that your mum suddenly needs to use the phone, and cut the conversation short.

3 Your sister never wears jewellery or make-up and is oblivious to fashion and diet. Yet she always looks stunning! You

   a wish she'd wake up, just occasionally, with a few pimples on her nose and forehead.

   b often remind yourself that while she's particularly pretty, you're especially bright, funny, or artistic.

   c are proud to have such a beautiful sister.

4 Your boyfriend still speaks wistfully of his former girl-friend, who moved away last year. You

   a hope that if she ever comes to town, he doesn't find out.

   b insist that if he expects a future with you, he must get over his past with her.

   c think she sounds nice and are curious to meet her.

5 You and a friend are working on a joint project for the school or college magazine. In front of the class, the teacher lavished your partner with compliments and

didn't even acknowledge your contribution. You

a don't mind; the vital thing is that both your names will be in the magazine.

b write your colleague a note saying you resent her not reminding the teacher of your share of the work.

c plan to find the teacher later and say something subtle, like, 'I'm glad you liked our project. We both enjoyed writing it.'

6 Your boyfriend loves cycling. So much, in fact, that when he's not at work or in school, at sports practice, or studying, he's cycling into the wild blue yonder. You

a tell him you won't play second fiddle to his bicycle any more: if things don't change, you want out.

b don't mind: he's happy, you admire his athletic prowess, and better your rival be a bicycle than another girl – even if you hardly see him.

c accept his cycling enthusiasm but say that you want to see him at least twice a week on legs, rather than wheels.

7 You've just seen a film together. You're raving about the special effects. Your date is raving about the teenage actress. You

a agree that she's a talented beauty and bring up other films in which you've admired her.

b point out that the male lead was sensitive and charming, then change the subject.

c say that while she's not unattractive, you've never been impressed by her acting.

8 According to your mother, your brother can do no wrong. She recites the list of his accomplishments. You

a ignore her, feeling hurt.

b are glad to see her so proud.

c listen, nod, and hint that you're nothing to sneeze at yourself.

9 The guy you've secretly had your eye on for months just asked your best friend to the disco. You

   a cry and decide you hate them both.   *3*
   b feel hurt but since nobody really betrayed you, you try not to let it drag you down.
   c tell yourself it's no big deal. There are other guys out there and nothing could ever come between you and your friend.

10 You live in an ordinary semi. You visit a friend's house for the first time. House? It's a mansion, complete with everything from food processor to word processor. Her room has an en-suite shower, and there's even a swimming pool – into which you both dive. You
   a say with a sigh, 'This is the life,' and enjoy yourself thoroughly.
   b are so overwhelmed by the contrast between your two homes that your stomach is knotted and you can scarcely keep afloat.
   c drift merrily but think with a passing pang, 'I wish our home were like this.'

11 You and a guy you've just met have been flirting at a party. Suddenly the pretty new girl in town asks him to dance. He accepts with a big smile. You
   a glare at her and ask a good-looking guy to dance.
   b smile at them and go and talk with another friend.
   c study the record collection and consider cutting in if they dance the next number together.

12 You and a friend start work together. After three months, she is offered a pay rise and you are not. You
   a realize that she works harder than you, and so deserves the bonus.   *2*
   b congratulate her, but are privately sure she only got it because the boss likes flirtatious blondes.
   c refuse to speak to her.

22

Scoring

1	a 1	b 2	c 3	7	a 1	b 2	c 3
2	a 2	b 1	c 3	8	a 3	b 1	c 2
3	a 3	b 2	c 1	9	a 3	b 2	c 1
4	a 2	b 3	c 1	10	a 1	b 3	c 2
5	a 1	b 3	c 2	11	a 3	b 1	c 2
6	a 3	b 1	c 2	12	a 1	b 2	c 3

12 to 19 You are unselfish and unpossessive, and these qualities save you from many needless heartaches. But before you stick a gold star on your forehead, be sure you are being truly honest with yourself about your feelings, not just repressing emotions. Could your nonchalance be a mere façade? Don't be afraid to open up and deal with any anger and fears inside you.

20 to 27 Hurray! You are in touch with your full range of feelings, jealousy included. Sure you'd be happy if your neighbour won the Pools, but you'd be even happier if you won. You are mature enough to recognize your occasional envy as natural and legitimate, and wise enough to control it rather than letting it control you. When you are jealous, ask yourself why and explore it. For example, maybe you think your boyfriend is tempted to roam because *you're* restless and you're projecting your feelings on to him. Or maybe you're feeling insecure because things in and out of home aren't going well. If you think your jealousy is well founded, let it serve as a warning that you two need to re-examine your relationship.

28 to 36 Nobody will ever steal your friends without a fight: you're the jealous type. You are also a devoted girlfriend, and you like commitment in return. Fine. But if debilitating jealousy often gets the better of you, it's time to defuse it. Talk your jealousy out with someone you trust. And work on staying busy, building on your good points, and bolstering your self-esteem. The better you feel about yourself, the less vulnerable you'll be to jealousy.

Goodbye

You have a lot to look forward to and you have hurdles ahead. Sometimes I envy you. Sometimes I worry for you. Mostly I hope you go after and get what you want. Getting there is half the fun, but if you're ever in a bind, remember that there is always some person or organization who can help you out. And you may just find that life gets easier once you get the hang of it.

Good luck! Take care of yourself. Give it your best shot!

Love,

Carol Weston

Addresses

ACCEPT
200 Seagrave Road
London
SW6 1RQ
Tel: 01 381 3155/2112
ACCEPT Drugs Helpline:
Tel: 01 727 9447

**Action on Smoking and
Health (ASH)**
5-11 Mortimer Street
London
W1N 7RH
Tel: 01 637 9843

Al-Anon
Alateen Tel: 01 403 0888

Alcoholics Anonymous
P O Box 514
11 Redcliffe Gardens
London
SW10 9BQ
Tel: 01 352 9779

Anorexic Aid
The Priory Centre
11 Priory Road
High Wycombe
Bucks
Tel: 0494 21431

Basingstoke Clinic
54-56 Newmarket Square
Basingstoke
Hampshire
Tel: 0256 28128

BBC Childline
24 hour helpline
Tel: 0800 1111

**British Agencies for
Adoption and Fostering
(BAAF)**
11 Southwark Street
London SE1 1RQ
Tel: 01 407 8800

**British Pregnancy
Advisory Service (BPAS)**
Austy Manor
Wooton Wawen
Solihull
West Midlands
Tel: 05642 3225

Brook Advisory Centres
Tel: 01 708 1234/1390
Phone for details of your
nearest centre.

**Business and Technician
Education Council (BTEC)**
Central House
Upper Woburn
Place WC 1H
Tel: 01 388 3288
Berkshire House
High Holborn WC 1V
Tel: 01 379 7088

**Campaign Against
Drunken Drivers (CAD)**
c/o Graham Buxton
Ringsmere Orchard
Pershore Hill
Little Comberton
Nr. Pershore
Worcs
WR10 3HF
Tel: 0386 74426

**Central Bureau for
Educational Visits and
Exchanges**
Seymour Mews House
Seymour Mews
London
W1H 9PE

**City and Guilds of London
Institute**
(Sales Section)
76 Portland Place
London
W1N 4AA

Herpes Association
41 North Road
London
N7 9PD
Helpline telephone
number: 01 609 9061

Incest Crisis
Speak to
Shirley on 01 890 4732
Richard on 01 422 5100
Ann on 01 302 0570

**Joint Board for
Pre-Vocational Education**
46 Britannia Street
London
WC1X 9RG

**London Friend Women's
Line**
01 354 1846 (Thursdays,
7.30 p.m. to 10.00 p.m.)

**Mothers' Union 'Message
Home' Service**
Birmingham 021 426 3396
Bristol 0272 504717
Liverpool 051 709 7598
London 01 799 7662
Leeds 0532 454544
Portsmouth 0705 733899
Scotland 0968 76161

Narcotics Anonymous
P O Box 246
c/o 47 Milman Street
London SW10
Tel: 01 351 6794

**National Association of
Youth Counselling and
Advisory Services**
17-25 Albion Street
Leicester

**National Campaign
Against Solvent Abuse**
Box 513
245a Coldharbour Lane
London SW9 8RR

**National Children's Home
Family Network**
North of England
Tel: 061 236 2033
South of England
Tel: 0582 422751
Wales 0222 29461/2 or
0792 297798
Scotland – dial the
Operator and ask for
Family Network

**National Women's
Aid Federation**
During Office Hours:
Tel: 01 837 9316

**National Deaf Children's
Society**
45 Hereford Road
London W2 5AH

NORCAP
49 Russell Hill Road
Purley
Surrey CR2 2XB

**Physically Handicapped
and Able-Bodied (PHAB)**
Tavistock House
North Tavistock Square
London WC1H 9HX

**The PMT Advisory
Service**
P O Box 268
Hove
East Sussex
BN3 1RW

Registrar General
CA Section
Titchfield
Fareham
Hampshire

Release
During office hours: 01 837 5602
24-hour helpline:
01 603 8654

Royal National Institute for the Blind
224 Great Portland Street
London W1N 6AA

The Spastics Society
12 Park Crescent
London W1
Tel: 01 636 5020

Standing Conference on Drug Abuse (SCODA)
1-4 Hatton Place
Hatton Garden
London
EC1N 8ND
Tel: 01 430 2341/2

Sister Marion
Advisory Service
Smith & Nephew
Consumer Products Ltd
Alum Rock Road
Birmingham B8 3DZ

Stepfamily
Ross Street Community Centre
Ross Street
Cambridge
CB1 3BS
Telephone Helpline:
0223 215370

Universities Central Council on Admissions (UCCA)
P O Box 28
Cheltenham
Glos. GL50 1HY

Vacation Work
9 Park End Street
Oxford

Weight Watchers
11 Fairacres
Dedworth Road
Windsor
Berkshire
Tel: 07535 56751

Women's National Cancer Control Campaign (WNCC)
1 South Audley Street
London W1Y 5DQ

Youth Hostels Association (YHA)
Trevelyan House
St Stephen's Hill
St Albans
Hertfordshire
AL1 2DY
Tel: 0727 55215

Index